Essence of the Throne
Book Two
Dakota Monroe

Copy editing and proofreading: K. Morton Editing Services, L.L.C.

Cover: Drakana at GraphicSoulArt

Internal illustrations: Dakota Monroe, V_solnyshko, whett_paint, and efa_finearts

First Edition 2025

Contents

Content Warning

This book is a dark fantasy romance, with topics that some may find disturbing or triggering.

For the full list of warnings, please visit dakotamonroe.com/con tentwarnings

AURORIA

MENEAU OCEAN

FROSTWELL

GRENPORT

ELYSARAN

EBONWOOD

VEXAIL

VERDANTIA FOREST

CINDARA DESER

THE EPHEMERAL
REALM

THE
AETHER
REALM

WHISTERRA

Essence Weaving Magic System

Essence is the fabric of magic, woven from the very energy that underlies all existence. Weavers are individuals born with the innate ability to tap into this essence and shape it. They connect to one of three main affinities:

Living, which communicates with life and growth.
Elemental, which commands the raw forces of nature.
Ethereal, which guides mystical and psychic energies.

Within each affinity are finer strands - specific abilities that a weaver specializes in. For instance, under the Ethereal Affinity, one might find the the umbral strand, which allows for the manipulation of shadows and concealment. The skill of weaving is as diverse as the weavers themselves.

How much essence can a weaver have?

Single Essence Weaving: Most weavers specialize in one affinity and usually have one primary strand within, instead of the ability to weave all of them. **Example:** elemental weavers can have a focus of fire but not be able to weave water magic. Or living weavers can heal, but are not able to grow plants. Some are able to do multiple, and this is the part that's heavily influenced by training and environment.

Multi-Essence Weaving: Some weavers have more than one affinity. These individuals are often considered prodigies and can be powerful, but also more susceptible to the risks of imbalance and political tension.

Universal Essence Weaving: It is nearly unheard of for a weaver to specialize in all affinities and strands. Any who are found to weave all types of essence will be executed on site for the danger they are thought to bring.

Shadows of the Crown Recap

You want to know where we left off in Shadows of the Crown? Fine. Here's the short version: once upon a time, I was just another shadow in the kingdom, a ghost slipping through the dark alleys of Valoria. My name? Ariella Mistaire. Some called me the Silver Wraith; others didn't live long enough to call me anything at all. My job was simple—kill who they told me to kill, vanish before anyone noticed. I didn't ask questions, and no one dared to ask me any.

And then the King decided to make my life his next game. He dragged me—a fucking assassin, mind you—into his twisted competition, pitting me against every blade-wielding, power-hungry fool in the Eldorian Kingdom. All for what? The promise of glory, a few coins, and some shiny position at his court? Please. I had no interest in any of that. No, I wanted the king dead, and this was the perfect opportunity to get inside castle grounds.

But then there was Caspian. Prince of Valoria, heir to the throne, and a royal pain in my ass. I swear the Angel made him just to piss me off. At first, he was just another piece to my plan. Killing the king would be fun and all, but murdering his heir?

Sweet revenge. But somewhere between his brave tongue and maddeningly stubborn presence, he burrowed himself under my skin. And that made him dangerous in a way I hadn't anticipated.

The competition wasn't just about killing, though. Oh no, that would've been too easy. Angel-forbid anything in my fucking life be easy. After being shredded by a griffin, secrets bubbled to the surface—secrets about the Accord, the Aether, and me. Turns out, my parents' deaths weren't just a hinderance to my life...and now I need to figure out what twenty-year-old journal entries mean when they say the balance has weakened.

By the end of it all, I'd survived betrayals, the death of my best friend, unraveled truths I wish I hadn't, and made a choice with the prince I'm still not sure I won't regret. And even after every-thing, the king still lives, and I am riddled with more problems than I ever wanted. So, what now? Where the fuck do I go from here? Well, let's just say the chaos has only begun.

So, if you're expecting a happy ending, don't hold your breath. This is my story, and I'm not done fighting yet.

Essence Weaving Strands

Living Affinity

- **Flora strand:** the essence of plant life, growth, and natural fibers
- **Fauna strand:** the essence of animal bonding and communication
- **Vital strand:** the essence of healing and life force

Elemental Affinity

- **Pyro strand:** the essence of fire, heat, and combustion
- **Aqua strand:** the essence of water, ice, and vapor
- **Terra strand:** the essence of earth and metal
- **Aero strand:** the essence of air and close atmosphere
- **Kinetic strand:** the essence of physical objects

Ethereal Affinity

- **Luminal strand:** the essence of light and illumination
- **Umbral strand:** the essence of shadows, darkness, and concealment
- **Spectral strand:** the essence of souls and spirits
- **Temporal strand:** the essence of time and memory
- **Psionic strand:** the essence of mind and consciousness

To those who are angry and hurting: know that your voice, your strength, and your rage will always find a safe space here, and will always be a part of my books. We will continue to stand tall against a world that tries its best to make us small.

Prologue

Raine

My head throbs as consciousness creeps back, each pulse more painful than the last. Through the fog, I try to remember what happened—where I am. The last clear memory I have is from bed... I woke to someone covering my nose and mouth with a pungent cloth. But that's it. How long has it been? Is this the third trial?

Cold metal presses against my bare back, sending ripples of discomfort through my muscles. When I attempt to move, leather straps bite into my wrists and ankles. Something covers my mouth, strapped tightly around my head.

Panic surges through me as my eyes snap open. Harsh light assaults my vision, forcing me to squint against its intensity. Dark shapes move at the edges of my sight, but I can't turn my head enough to track them.

This is without a doubt not the third trial.

"—strongest from the trials. His essence readings were off the charts." The voice is familiar, though I can't place it through the fogginess filling my head. "If this one doesn't work..."

My heart hammers against my ribs as I yank at the restraints. The leather holds firm, only succeeding in rubbing my skin raw.

I try to call out, but the strap around my face muffles my voice to meaningless sounds.

More figures move around me, their features blurred by the tears gathering in my eyes. Not one of them even bothers to look at me as I struggle.

Healer equipment lines the stone walls, though it's obvious this is no standard healing room. The tools laid out on nearby tables look more like instruments of torture than healing. Needles, blades, and strange vials are arranged with unnerving precision, and my heart races faster with each item I see. My nose scrunches at the reek of chemicals in the air—sharp and sour, like burnt flesh and rotting food.

"Begin the prep work." This voice I recognize in an instant—King Thalion. "I want to start as soon as possible. I need to leave for the arena soon."

Footsteps approach, and a face finally comes into focus. The man peers down at me with austere detachment, his eyes black voids behind wire-rimmed glasses. He prods at my chest with gloved fingers, mapping out something only he can see.

"Remarkable muscle density," he mutters, more to himself than anyone else. "The physical conditioning from Valoria's guild provides an ideal foundation. It's too bad we do not have access to the other two."

I move my lips to demand answers, to ask what's happening, but only muffled grunts escape. The man pays no attention to my attempts at communication, continuing his examination as if I'm nothing more than an interesting specimen.

My eyes dart around the room, desperate for anything familiar. Through the gaps between people, I spot another figure propped against the far wall. They're slumped forward, held up by thick chains, with some kind of metallic device protruding from their chest. Even from here, I can see the dried blood caked around the entry point.

By the Angel.

Terror claws up my throat as one man wheels over a cart carrying an identical device. The metal is dull and twisted, with sharp prongs extending from its base. They can't possibly mean to...

"Hold him still," the man with glasses orders. "This part is always unpleasant."

Hands press down on my shoulders and legs, though I'm already restrained. A woman approaches with a thin blade, perfectly crafted for precision cutting. She doesn't meet my eyes as she positions it over my sternum.

"Remember," the king's voice cuts through my rising panic, "we need the connection point to be perfect this time. The last three failed because the device wasn't properly seated."

Last three? What happened to them? I thrash against the hands holding me down, but it's useless. The blade touches my skin, and pain explodes through my chest as the woman begins to cut.

I scream behind the gag, my body arching off the chair as much as the restraints and hands allow. The woman works in a proficient manner, slicing through layers of muscle and tissue with practiced ease. Blood runs down my sides, pooling beneath me on the cold metal table.

Through the haze of agony, I hear the distinctive crack of bone. They're breaking through my sternum. The sound drones through my head, mixing with my muffled screams until I can't tell which is which anymore.

"Device," the woman commands, holding out her bloody hand.

The twisted metal contraption is passed over, and I watch in horror as she positions it over the gaping wound in my chest. The prongs align with the broken edges of my sternum, and then she begins to push.

If I thought the cutting was painful, it is *nothing* compared to this. The device burrows into me, the prongs spreading out to anchor themselves in my flesh. My vision whites out repeatedly as wave after wave of agony crashes through me. I'm dimly aware that I'm still screaming, though my throat feels shredded.

"Good," the woman says with a bright smile after what feels like hours. "The connection is solid. Begin essence transfer preparations."

I lie hopeless, wheezing, tears streaming down my face as my body trembles with aftershocks of pain. The device in my chest pulses with my heartbeat, each throb sending fresh spikes of agony through me.

The king moves into view, looking down at me with an expression that might be pity. "You should be honored, Raine," he declares, though his words sound distant through the ringing in my ears. "Your sacrifice will help create something magnificent."

Sacrifice? The word bounces around my head as the group bustles around me, connecting things to the device. What are they planning to do?

I send out desperate prayers to the Angel, begging for help, for salvation, for *anything*. But no divine intervention comes. Just more pain as they finish their preparations.

My head lolls as they finalize adjustments to the tubes connected to my chest. Through blurry vision, I watch light flow through clear piping toward me. My eyes widen past anything natural, the sight sending fresh waves of terror coursing through my body.

"Begin essence transfer." The king's voice sounds eager, almost giddy with anticipation.

The light reaches the device embedded in my chest, and immediately I know something is wrong. So devastating and wrong. Heat spreads from the entry point, but it's not natural warmth—it's like molten metal being poured into my veins.

I try to scream, but my voice is gone. Whether from the previous screaming or something else, I don't know. All I can do is watch, helpless, as more of the bizzare, thick substance pumps into me.

The heat intensifies, transforming into something that feels alive. It writhes under my skin like thousands of snakes trying to burrow deeper into my flesh. My muscles spasm violently as foreign things flood my system.

"Remarkable," someone says. "His body isn't immediately rejecting the essence."

Essence. They're giving me essence from the chained body.

They sound pleased, but I'm unable to focus on their words. The invading power is *wrong.* It doesn't belong in me. My own essence rises up to fight against it, creating a war inside my body that threatens to tear me apart.

Colors start bleeding into my vision—colors that shouldn't exist. They swirl and pulse with each erratic beat of my heart, creating patterns that hurt to look at. I squeeze my eyes shut, but the colors are there too, more vibrant against the darkness.

"Heart rate increasing," an emotionless voice announces. "Blood pressure rising at a steady pace."

The wriggling under my skin becomes more aggressive. It feels like the foreign essence is desperate to consume me from the inside out, replacing everything that makes me, *me* with something else. Something twisted and wrong.

My back arches off the table as a particularly violent surge rips through me. A scream not my own escapes my throat. The restraints creak but hold firm as my body contorts. Every muscle feels like it's being shredded and reformed, over and over again.

"Fascinating," the man with glasses murmurs. "The integration is progressing much faster than previous subjects."

Integration. The word bounces around my head as another wave of agony crashes through me. They're trying to force someone else's essence into me. To make it part of me. But essence isn't meant to be transferred like this—it's tied to our souls, our very being.

The pressure in my head increases until I'm certain my skull will crack. My thoughts scatter like leaves in a storm, replaced by fragments of memories that aren't mine. I see flashes of places I've never been, people I've never met, all tinted with those impossible colors that shouldn't exist.

"Sir," a worried voice cuts through the chaos in my mind. "His temperature is reaching critical levels."

"Continue the transfer," the king commands. "We're too close to stop now."

The foreign memories come faster, slamming into me with a brute force. I watch a young boy train with wooden swords, his movements graceful despite his age. But it's not me—I never trained as a child. The guild found me much later.

Another flash: the same boy, older now, sneaking through castle corridors. The thrill of avoiding guards mingles with my own terror until I can't detect which emotions belong to me anymore.

My heart pounds so hard I fear it will burst. Each beat circulates pulses of wrong essence through my system, trying to overwrite what's already there. My own essence fights back, desperate to save me, but it's losing. I can feel it being consumed, replaced by this corruption they're pumping into me.

"His body is rejecting it," someone far away shouts. "We need to—"

"Continue!" the king roars.

The pressure in my skull reaches unbearable levels. It feels like my brain is trying to expand beyond its confines. Blood trickles from my nose, then my ears. The taste of copper fills my mouth as my teeth clench hard enough to bite through my tongue.

Please, I beg silently. *Angel, if you can hear me, make it stop. Please make it stop.*

But no help comes. Just more pain as the essence war rages inside me. The foreign memories overwhelm my own. Who am I? Raine, or the boy from the castle? The one whose essence races through me? Both? Neither?

My vision fractures, splitting into prismatic patterns that make me nauseous beyond comprehension. The impossible colors expand in time with my lungs, each flash bringing fresh waves of misery. The pressure in my head builds and builds until I'm certain something has to give.

"Sir, his vital signs are critical. We need to stop or—"

"No!" The king's face appears above me, his eyes wild with desperation. "This one has to work. He's the strongest body from the assassin pool we've found. Keep going!"

More essence floods into me, but my body has no more room for it. It feels like my skin is splitting open from the inside, unable to contain the war being waged beneath it. The foreign memories come so fast now that I can't process them. I can't process anything. They blur together into a nightmare cascade of sounds and colors and feelings that aren't mine. Maybe they are.

The pressure in my head reaches a crescendo. Blood pours from every orifice as my body fails to contain the corrupted essence they're pumping into me. I try one last time to pray to the Angel, but I can't form coherent thoughts any longer.

Through the haze of agony and aberrant memories, I watch the king's expression shift from desperate hope to bitter disappointment. He turns away with a disgusted sound, already walking toward the door.

"Another failure," he spits. "Dispose of it like the others."

The king's advisor hurries after him, his voice soothing. "We're learning more with each attempt, Your Majesty. Raine was our strongest subject yet—his survival time was nearly double the others. We're getting closer."

Their voices fade as they leave, abandoning me to my fate. The pressure in my head is impossible now. Something has to give. My skull feels like it's being crushed and expanded in a simultaneous rhythm.

With my last moments of clarity, I realize I'm going to die. Not in glorious combat like I always imagined, but strapped to a table as a failed experiment—a mere statistic. Will anyone even know what happened to me? Or will I just become another disappearance, explained as one more mysterious death during the trials?

The final surge of essence hits me like a large wave. My back arches one last time as the pressure reaches its peak. Through eyes that no longer feel like my own, I watch those unyielding colors explode outward.

Then everything goes dark.

"Clean this up," someone says distantly. "And someone fetch the staff—there's brain matter on the ceiling again."

Chapter One

Ariella

Shadows consume me as I slip behind a bookcase and pinch my nose from the onslaught of dust that invades my senses, lest I sneeze and give away my presence. I reach into my core, locating my psionic strand to send out a pulse through the too quiet library. This strand from the ethereal affinity allows me to slip into the head of others to hear their thoughts, give my own, control their bodies, or even influence them a certain way. But weaved in this manner, it touches the mind of any living presence, offering me a count of how many others are in the vicinity. The relief I feel when my essence confirms there's only one other being is short-lived as my target turns to walk in my direction.

I crouch, scrunching my left eye closed to better see through the infinitesimal space between two books that haven't felt the warm touch of another since the Angel walked this realm. The loud hammering of my heart threatens my concealment, and it takes great effort to keep my breathing slow and shallow.

My target shelves the small book he was holding, his lip quirking at whatever he finds amusing on its thin spine. His hand lifts to trace his fingers across a few of the other books with reverence before he decides to return to his desk empty-handed.

I stand, only to freeze mid-step when my boot scuffs against the tile that makes up the majority of the castle floor. The resulting sound is small. Barely audible. But that is no excuse for my thoughtless behavior. This last week I spent at the guild—not only to search for answers, but to get a break from this damned castle—has coated me in a level of comfort I cannot afford to give in to. The competition may be over, but that was never the threat to begin with. I almost laugh; the embarrassing manner in which my plan to kill the king played out grates on my nerves every single day. My jaw clenches—images of unwanted sympathy flit through my head. Marek watching me with a sharp, calculated focus, more so than he ever has. Jaxon's inability to look me in the eye. Even Isolde was in visible pain as she bit her tongue to keep from making stupid, mediocre remarks to me.

Fuck all of them.

Isaiah is gone, and there is nothing I can do to bring him back. Feeling sorry for me is the worst way to uphold his memory. Not that they understand that.

And even then, thoughts of reaching out to him haunt my every lonely moment. I haven't attempted to call on my spectral strand in two decades, but that hasn't ceased the bone-deep need inside me that begs to try. It would be easy—in theory—reaching out to the Aether in search of the one soul I seek. But would Isaiah be the one that answers?

I'm unsure if my hesitation is a result of my nervousness at seeing Isaiah in such a manner, or that I wouldn't be able to call to him at all. Regularly engaging my forbidden essence has been impossible my entire life...and as much as it pains me to admit, I'm not certain I could weave most strands with confidence. I'm comfortable with my kinetic strand as I use it often, but I've spent more time with a blade than I have with the rest of my essence combined.

Well, aside from my umbral strand.

I've found a comfortability with the shadows, as they have with me. A mutually beneficial understanding.

Rustling papers snap me from the adverse thoughts I fell into. I focus my trained senses on the other side of the shelf, shuffling forward when nothing seems amiss. My feet carry me without a sound to the back of the room, darkness steadying my breathing the more it covers me. This shouldn't be difficult. I've played this game a thousand times, not having lost once. I curse the unsettling feeling in my stomach and press my back against the end of the bookshelf. Peering over my right shoulder, I tense as my teeth grip my bottom lip at the sight of my target.

Foolish idiot—he hasn't a clue that I'm here. Has he learned nothing?

My body straightens once more, and I stretch my neck in each direction. Some may call it stalling—I call it being prepared.

I am stalling, though.

I will berate myself for hesitating later; right now, I must concentrate. Not allowing any more wayward thoughts to seep through the cracks that have appeared in my mind uninvited, I step my left foot over my right and spin to stalk down the aisle that will lead to my target.

My jaw drops on a breathless gasp as a blade slides into my abdomen with a questionable force the moment I turn. If this were anyone else, their heads would already be on the ground. But the purpose of my current mission is entirely different—not to harm, but to teach. My eyes drag up the wrinkled, black shirt, pausing for a moment at the expanse of skin showing through the half that remains unbuttoned.

The prince's face is a mirror to mine; though instead of meeting my gaze, his horror-stricken irises are fixated on the hand that still grips the blade he just impaled me with.

"By the Angel," Caspian whispers through a cracked voice. I tense as his hand begins to tremble, causing the tip of his blade to cut me further. "Ariella...I—I didn't know it was you..." My hand snaps out to grab his wrist, forcing him to still so that I may focus on something other than the pain. "I mean, of course I knew it was you, I just didn't think—oh, fuck, I'm so—"

"Prince," I bark, effectively shutting him up, and his eyes slide to meet mine. For a moment, I forget about my potentially fatal wound as I look at him for the first time since returning to the castle.

His dark hair is disheveled and clunky, as if he hasn't washed it in the time I've been gone, while also running his hands through it a hundred times a day. Dark purple shadows line the spaces under his eyes, and his lids look as if they're struggling to remain open, even in their alarmed state. His mouth—tense and dry—is surrounded by ashen skin. I've the sudden urge to pinch his cheeks and ensure blood still runs through his veins.

He looks...bad. Worse than I've been feeling. What the fuck happened?

I grunt and clench my teeth when I release his wrist without thought to feel the temperature of his face.

Right. He stabbed me.

My eyes find the wound and roll hard. "Why must blood always be spilled on my freshly cleaned clothes? Have you any idea how long it took me to rid these leathers of Desmond's blood?" Until this last week, I'd never spoken to Desmond at the guild before. He must be just a year or so younger than me, but Isaiah was the one person I was ever willing to give my attention to.

Unfortunate really, because Desmond is a decent fighter and made a good opponent these last few days. I'm not sure he reciprocates the feelings as it was his blood soaking the ground each time we sparred, but I do not care, nor am I surprised. No one faces me and turns away with a pleased smile on their face.

I refuse to acknowledge the one exception to that standing in front of me.

The prince didn't seem to hear my question, as he just stares at me as if he's seeing a spirit. I don't have time for this. I sigh, grasping his wrist once more and rip it back before I allow myself to think twice about the decision. My breathing stalls and the prince begins to speak frantically, but I do not notice either as I tug on my vital strand and coax the essence to the oozing cut. I cover the area with a hand to dim the light beneath my skin; it's dark enough in here that anyone would notice the healing essence before realizing there is not a healer present.

The skin stitches together and a breathy sigh escapes my mouth as the worst of the pain dissipates, along with my already lacking energy. My head tilts. I must not have noticed, but I've been unusually fatigued since arriving at the guild. There is no reason I should feel this tired; I'm aware of all that has happened in these last weeks, but trauma and exhaustion are two things I refuse to let coexist together.

So I ignore the dull heaviness in my muscles, and shake off the thoughts as I focus on Caspian. "You look like shit," I mutter, crossing my arms to remove his attention from my wound, but he only rolls his eyes and scoffs.

"Yeah, so do you." He spins to trudge back to his table without another word, or even the smile that never seems to leave his face around me. There must be something wrong. I stride forward, stopping when I reach the chair opposite the prince, yanking it in a rough manner. His forehead creases while his eyes scrunch closed, and he takes a few deep breaths before focusing on his work once more.

Interesting.

"Has Gavriel finally decided to stop worshiping you, or is your crappy mood related to your father?" It's a genuine question. I wouldn't be surprised if it was both the guard and king upsetting Caspian; their single talent is pissing everyone else off.

The prince's exhausted eyes drag up my chest to my waiting glare. "And who's to say it isn't your presence souring my *mood?*" I swallow at the sting of his words, but my face gives away nothing but amusement as I raise a brow and allow my lips to curve.

But something about the question doesn't settle right within me. What if he's being truthful? Has this week apart allowed him to see that I am the monster everyone believes me to be? Perhaps he no longer wants anything to do with me. I wouldn't blame him...though that doesn't mean I will allow it to happen.

Angel save him from me, because I am no hero. I will be his undoing and gladly introduce my blade to any who thinks they can stop me.

I do not wish to fight right now, though. I'm too tired to keep this unfeeling facade going. "Okay. Let me know when you've grown tired of being a dick." I shift to march from the library like a fucking child, pausing when the prince speaks again.

"Wait—" he says in a frantic tone, reaching a hand across the table as if to stop me, though he makes no real effort to do so. "I'm sorry, you're right, I'm being a dick. It's not you, I...I just haven't been feeling like myself the last few days."

I shrug and cross my arms, frowning at the still-wet blood that seeps through my sleeve. "Don't apologize. It's not as if I've ever treated you," I pause, pursing my lips before continuing, "or anyone really, with kindness before."

Instead of moving back to the chair across from him, I pull at the one to his right, spinning it backward and straddling its base. His truth snags my interest. I will find whoever has made him feel this way. I am his guard, after all—so of course I must ask, "You said you're not feeling like yourself. What happened?" His hand drags through his hair, tugging at the ends before dropping to his lap.

"I don't know. I just feel so empty and tired. And yet I can't sleep, or focus, and it's just—*fuck*. I don't know."

His feelings are familiar, though I press in a different direction. "What are you working on?" I take notice of the books and stacks of paper chaotically organized across the table. Trade agreements with Meridian and Lumarna sit off to the side, along with what looks to be residential plans and a budget for the upcoming bi-annual Frostwell competition. One *lucky* citizen will reign champion and be afforded the opportunity to serve as a royal sentry.

I'd offer up my position, but no one would find themselves worthy of protecting the man in front of me. Not even Gavriel is suitable, regardless that he's been Caspian's guard for years. I chuckle before yawning behind my hand—I truly look forward to the day I can end his miserable existence. I do not care for the laws prohibiting murder—I'm a fucking assassin, why would I?—so the one thing stopping me is *him*.

They're *friends*. Or so the prince claims.

"I have been sitting in on my father's council and shadowing his activities, looking for...*things*." I've also been in search of these *things*. Answers to my father's journal, my mother's letter. Everything I'm tired of thinking about. Something heavy settles in my gut—the prince is more likely to find what we need, but his current state tells me his efforts have been just as fruitless. "I haven't gathered anything I believe will help" —*of course*— "but there are some interesting things I've picked up on. I don't know, maybe they'll be a start and this will just take much longer than we anticipated."

"He wasn't thrilled when I told him you'd were my new guard, by the way—not that you'd know, considering you ran off for a week. He's probably off brooding somewhere, cursing my name for defying his orders again to remove you from the castle."

I nod as my finger taps against my other arm. I rest my chin on their crossing, ignoring the way Caspian drinks in my presence. I may have missed his lack of subtlety. It's refreshing—not suppressing everything I am and endlessly wondering what those around me are also hiding.

My world is exhausting.

Wholly opposite of the prince's; and yet here we sit, exchanging secrets and both looking as if the Angel itself is draining our inner essence.

"And what are these *interesting things* you mentioned?" I press when he doesn't continue, choosing instead to watch me. I'm sure he's looking for a reaction about his father's displeasure at my presence in the castle, but he will not get a response.

He breaks his perusal to scan the empty library. "Not here," he breathes, shaking his head. I know we're alone in this massive space. The closest person to us is three hallways down, in a paralleled staff corridor.

Until another presence enters the barrier of my psionic strand that I've kept engaged, and my lip curls.

"Well, allow me to escort you to your room." The prince perks up at my offer; those eyes make it difficult to hide my smile, but

I manage. "Where you will sleep *alone*. It's clear you're exhausted and will be nothing of use without rest."

He grins, clasping his hands behind his head to stretch over the back of the chair. The movement tugs at the hem of his shirt, exposing a sliver of his abdomen. His smile widens as he takes my mere curiosity as encouragement and somehow stretches even further. I have the flitting urge to push him back and leave for another week.

I cringe at the thought.

"Actually, I'm feeling a bit better. Less achy and tired...likely your doing," he drawls with a confident energy that doesn't quite meet his eyes. I raise a brow and offer my best disbelieving look, to which he laughs loud enough for the presence—just outside now—to hear. Perhaps he does seem lighter, though it's near impossible to tell with how dark it is in here. "Don't believe me, but it's true."

I do not bother responding as I pull back on my psionic strand and wait for the library doors to burst open with the force of an unbearable brute.

I look over my shoulder just as Gavriel throws the doors open, looking just as angry as I'd anticipated. "What the fuck did you do, wraith?"

My lips threaten to smirk, and a familiar giddiness swirls through my stomach. I swipe my blade from its sheathe and twirl it through my fingers as I face the dramatic male stalking toward me.

"I'm sure I don't know what you mean," I purr, stopping him in his advance when I take a step. And another. "If you've interrupted your prince's working just to threaten me, get on with it."

His jaw clenches, and I can practically see the effort it takes him to not swing one of his white-knuckled fists at me. I haven't felt this light in days. "I know it was you—none of the other sentries would dare."

"Dare what, Gav?" Caspian asks, stepping next to me. His arm grazes mine, and my eyes nearly roll—

What the fuck is wrong with me? I need to get a hold of myself. "Yeah, Gav, what *are* you referring to? Has yet another woman found your bed lacking and took her frustrations out on you?" He's seething essence, warming the space around us with his pyro strand.

Intentional or not, his control over the affinity is impressive. Though I'd offer myself as griffin meat before ever considering uttering such words aloud.

"You're lucky that fucker," he spits, shoving a finger into the prince's chest, "has forbidden me to lay a hand on you. I'll relish the day he tires of your blackened heart, so that I may cut it out with that blade you seem so fond of." A wide grin spreads across my face.

Not one heartbeat later am I in front of the brute holding said blade against his cock while the one from my left thigh grazes the sharp line of his jaw. "Oh, don't tease me, Gav. Perhaps the prince will allow you to spar with me." I pull my hands back and step around Gavriel, kicking the backs of his legs and forcing him to his knees. Both of my blades cross against the taut skin of his throat before he has a chance to process what just happened. "Be a good boy and ask him nicely." Heat prickles the back of my neck, and not the kind I feel when I'm about to take a life.

I swallow around the tightness in my throat before my eyes focus on the figure standing just ahead. Where I expect Caspian to be glaring at the blades threatening his other guard's life, he instead watches me.

No, not me—my eyes.

There is some heat within the depths of his, but his stare is so focused that it feels as if he's searching for something inside my head. My skin prickles while my mind begs me to look away from his intensity. It's far too knowing and intimate.

I don't, though. I remain so still that only the beat of my heart could give away my discomfort. I want so badly to shift on my feet, or even for Gavriel to speak, just to give me an excuse to break Caspian's stare. But it's as if I am stuck in a trance—like I could give every bit of my essence in attempting to move, only to remain unsuccessful until the prince finds what he's seeking.

He *finally* severs the hold, allowing air to fill my burning lungs.

"—and go find a fucking room. I do not want to watch this." Gavriel's voice startles me, and he hisses as I nick his throat. At least I wasn't caught unaware. The blood seeping from his skin only serves my purpose.

I want to respond and tell him every detail of what I'll do to his prince if I go find a room, but I cannot summon the words.

The man himself rubs a hand over his face as he scoffs. "As long as you don't kill each other, I do not care." He turns to drop back into his seat and rubs the sides of his head.

Ah, yes. He's referring to the sparring Gavriel was supposed to ask about.

All previous conversation since arriving at the castle is pushed to the back of my mind. I release the brute and sheathe my blades while I saunter back to the table, reaching to gather the mess of materials. My arms are ungraceful as they shovel the books and paper together, making a less than appealing pile of everything.

"What are you doing?"

I'd think it was obvious, so I don't respond. I lift the materials and spin to stalk from the library.

It's dark in here; the lamps fixed to various places along the walls barely illuminate the space. I suspect that is the purpose of the three-story windows that span the back wall, but it is dreary and stormy outside the castle, the clouds dark enough to mask most light from the sun.

I don't mind it, though, creepy as it is. Ornate, gold-filled shelves seem to stretch endlessly through the space, each one overfilled with books that wait for their time to be read. I can barely make out four stories as each side of the library rises further than I thought the castle could accommodate. There are no stairs in sight, located in the back, where the space is conveniently covered by limitless shadows.

Despite the eeriness, there's something comforting about this place. The way each shelf seems to embrace me, offering me safety amongst the ancient wisdom. The heavy scent of aged literature that is an intrinsic part of the atmosphere and reminds me of a certain prince.

It takes me a few moments as I consider my comfortability in this space before I realize why it feels so natural to be here—it reminds me of home.

I do not possess the capacity to think further about it, and I quickly shove at the thoughts before they hold hostage my mind. They're too much.

I pause my steps when a slight tremor radiates through my feet. I curse before dropping everything in my hands and spinning to reach Caspian before the shaking intensifies. It's relieving to find him just behind me. The panic in his eyes as he reaches for me stings, but I do not have time to acknowledge his feelings. I snatch the front of his shirt and yank him into me as the vibrations in the ground become so loud I can no longer hear my own thoughts. I chuckle when Caspian bends me so that his body covers my head.

He can be sweet sometimes.

I don't resist him, needing to concentrate on my essence. I reach with my inner awareness to the surrounding environment and tug on my aero strand, but lose control when the prince and I fall to our knees from the violent quaking. I try once more with a frantic urgency that is never useful in these situations, successfully crushing the air above us together until it forms an impenetrable barrier. I'd feel far more comfortable weaving my umbral strand for this, but I will not risk Gavriel seeing that essence.

My arms tighten around the prince's stiff body. I release a thin breath when the first objects reach us, thudding against my barrier before sliding to crash into the ground. Caspian winces at the sounds, lifting his head before his chest bounces under mine.

"You're incredible," he says with enough force that I can make out his words. If he's expecting a response, he will be disappointed. I'm too focused on maintaining my essence to have attention for much else.

I have practiced with most of my strands for years, but never to such a degree. My shadows are the only essence I have held for long periods of time and used to ward against things. My aero strand? Never had I considered needing to use it in such a manner, so I find my body trembling after just a few minutes.

"It's okay, I've got you," Caspian whispers in my ear, likely thinking I'm shaking from fear.

Maybe I am.

I've never struggled with my essence like this before. It's pathetic.

The prince's hold does not waver as the ground sways in various directions, feeling as thought it's throwing us from one side of the library to the other. Too many objects continue to slam into my barrier—a vexation of the highest degree.

If this lasts much longer, my grip on my aero strand may falter...but I would first drain the entirety of my essence, emptying my body of its life source, before allowing this *weakening Accord* to claim Caspian's life.

Because that's all this is. It must be. This is the second time the ground has shaken this week, but if I consider all the strange weather over the last few months...it is too coincidental to be anything but the Accord. I've yet to discern just what it means and how it is affected by a sort of balance, though I have no doubt that this incessant fucking quaking is connected.

It feels as if I've aged years by the time the ground levels out and the tremors slow to nothing once more. "Fuck's sake, *finally*," I mumble as I push from Caspian and stand on wobbling legs.

The library looks just as dreadful as I'd expected. Books cover the floor as far as I can see, along with chairs and tables that are far from their normal resting places. A few taller plants lay strewn across the ground, their soil smeared over open pages and previously clean tile. I look over my shoulder at a loud pattering to find one of the windows cracked, with a large piece missing. Chilled rain and wind welcome themselves into the space, ruining decades-old texts and wooden furniture.

My eyes scan the prince before focusing on an object under the broken window. I walk toward it, ignoring Gavriel when he scoffs from my lack of awareness of what I am stepping on.

I'm aware—I just don't fucking care.

He scoots from under a table as I walk by, mumbling something to himself about how I'm the worst kind of human. It's too easy to ignore his taunts, especially when a large wooden object is laying propped against a shelf—none of which seem to have fallen. They must be fused to the tile in some manner.

My steps halt me just beside the aged wood, twice my height if I'm seeing correctly. There's a salty air surrounding it, and the grooves along it seem almost mushy. Disgusting.

This is certainly what came through the window, as shards of glass surround the immediate area. Against every rational instinct I have, I press against the wood, testing its weight.

Curious.

Something I couldn't lift without aid had managed to fly several stories up at such a rate that it smashed through a window...when the ground was shaking. I cannot make sense of the logic, but I'm far too tired to think about it any longer. I used more essence than I'll ever admit holding that barrier up. I need to train my stamina.

After I sleep.

My chin remains high as I walk back through the library, grabbing the prince's hand and pulling him from whatever he and Gavriel were discussing.

"Excuse you, I was talking with my guard." He sounds just as frustrated as I am.

"Is that so?" He exhales, the noise loud. "Because, as I recall, I'm your guard."

"I'm not in the mood for this, Ariella," he mutters as he pulls his hand from mine, though he continues to walk next to me.

I don't answer, instead leading us down the unaffected hallways aside from a few dropped portraits. How satisfying it is that each of them is torn, ridding the castle of some of the king's ego.

We make it to our rooms, and before Caspian can speak I nod to his and walk into mine, shutting the door loud enough that he thankfully doesn't come knocking. I shed my bloody clothes and drop to the bed, scrunching my eyes closed. It feels like the first time in weeks that I can allow myself to relax.

Though that's a false hope.

This quake was far more violent than the first, filling me with a sense of urgency I didn't feel before.

I thought I'd have more time to figure this out. But it's clear I need to increase my efforts and accelerate my timeline. This is no longer just about some nonsense words I discovered in my father's journal—there's so much more at risk than I realized.

Chapter Two
Ariella

When did my skin become so sallow?

I pinch my cheeks and frown at the lack of color that appears. I haven't looked into a mirror for weeks, but if I'd known just how sickly I look...

I swipe damp hair from my face, curling it behind my ears before studying my features some more. On a normal day, the silver covering my head compliments the tone of my skin, though I am a fair bit more pale than usual and the colors are not sitting well together.

I shouldn't care so much. I've never worried over my appearance before.

Foolish thoughts. I shake my head and walk into the ostentatious room I've been assigned as a *royal guard*. As much as I love the color of blood, the use of it here makes my stomach turn.

I'll have to see about redecorating. I'm sure Thalion would have something to say about ruining such decor, but there's nothing left for him to take from me. He wouldn't dare harm his heir, his single son, so I'm antsy to get under his skin in any way possible.

Until I kill him for good. Then I'll actually be under his skin, only to toss it aside and watch as it rots enough for the maggots to feast.

Caspian was foolishly not against my declaration of murdering his father, as if his loyalty to his family means nothing in the wake of my presence. The man is truly in love with me—it's disturbing. We've known one another for mere months, though that is not even the worst part of his obsession.

It was the day we met in the training room that I saw his infatuation settle around his being. I'd convinced myself that his pursuit was some personal endeavor he sought to achieve, the thought of which never bothered me much before. I'm sure that is all he wished for at first. He's the prince—it isn't difficult to conclude how he'd brag for fucking *the* Silver Wraith and lived to shout the achievement from rooftops.

But nothing with him is ever so simple.

He ruined every plan I'd devised. I should have torn his heart out just for standing in my way too many times.

That would have been simple. Much easier than the storm of emotion constantly surging through me that I continue to fight with everything I am.

But my life has never been so easy.

The Angel despises me—something I couldn't care less about, but will punish all the same.

I slide on my usual leathers—black, as I refuse to don the hideous outfit every sentry is made to wear—and turn from my closet, pausing.

The gilded egg I took from my encounter with the griffin sits on the table next to my bed. I've yet to decide what to do with it because fuck if I'll toss it out for the king to find and fuck if I'll return it to the creature that almost tore every organ from my body.

She may have spared me, but even I am not foolish enough to test fate again.

Sucking in a deep, grating breath, I tug on my umbral strand and unwind the wards from my door. It's satisfying, barely needing to flick my fingers to weave my ethereal affinity. The other affinities require more effort, their essence originating from the surrounding realm instead of inside me.

My fingers jerk in the slightest movements, grasping at the different tendrils of shadows and weaving them from their meticulously arranged, intertwined patterns. I could save time while creating my wards by throwing a tangled mess of essence into the door and frame, but it would take ages to undo. Over the years, I've settled on a routine, using the same pattern each time, and am now so familiar with it that it takes mere seconds to ward a door. It's not like there's anyone else who possesses the umbral strand that would figure out my technique, so how I do it doesn't necessarily affect anyone but me.

My steps slow as I approach Caspian's room, and I smile—genuine, for once.

"I don't know how many times we must have this conversation, Cas. She needed to go before, but after seeing her in the library?

I'm not fucking playing this run-around game with you and her anymore."

I lean against the wall, my leathers doing nothing to keep the cold of the stone out. A finger taps on the blade sheathed at my hip as I chuckle when there's a deep sigh following Gavriel's hissed declaration.

"I do not wish to continue having this conversation, but it seems it's something *my friend* will not leave alone."

"How do you not see it? The girl has gone crazy! Her eyes were somehow even more emotionless earlier than they normally are. I'm worried for your safety if you do not rid of her." Strange—I felt far too *full* of emotions when I'd returned to the castle.

He's just pissed that I ruined his sleeping arrangements. At least he's angry enough that he won't question just how I imbued his mattress with as much water as it would hold.

"I'm done talking about this with you, Gavriel. Bring it up again and we'll have a problem," the prince snaps, earning himself a growl from his brute of a friend.

I twist to my right and throw Caspian's door open with my usual dramatic grace. "Aw, please don't stop, Gav; I wanted to hear just how crazy I've become."

The stalky guard faces me with a sneer that would make any weaker man piss themselves.

But I am no man.

"This is a private conversation, wraith." My lips curve before I drop into a cushioned chair and wave a hand.

"Surely you're aware half of Valoria could hear you barking at your prince," I drawl, disinterested. Though my eyes snap up when Gavriel adjusts himself to be a barrier between Caspian and me—a rather unattractive one. "Don't stress yourself too much, Gav. I won't bite him." My tongue runs along my lower lip as I meet the prince's amused gaze. "Unless he asks, that is." He swipes a hand along his chin, a slight twitch appearing at the corner of his mouth.

Gavriel's face contorts. "You're proving my point, wraith."

I roll my eyes, crossing one leg over the other. "Oh please, as if you haven't thought about it yourself. Perhaps you're just jealous?"

The guard's hand flies to the hilt of his sword, but Caspian steps forward, placing a firm hand on his friend's shoulder. "That's enough, both of you," he says, his voice carrying the weight of his command.

I cannot help but smirk at the way Gavriel's posture stiffens, his ingrained obedience to the prince overriding his hatred for me.

It's almost endearing.

Caspian turns to me, his moonlit eyes softening. "Ariella, what brings you here?"

I shrug, feigning indifference. "I was bored." I unsheathe my blade and rest my cheek on the point, needing some way to ground myself for the conversation to come. "And we need to discuss the Accord." My eyes narrow on Gavriel's face, and my suspicions are confirmed when he shows little reaction to my words.

Caspian indeed informed him of our little secret.

The prince sighs as he drops to his bed and leans back on his hands. "That we do. Gavriel," he says, catching the guard's attention. "You have training soon, so please inform us of what you've discovered." He gestures a hand out as if in offering, but Gavriel's lip just curls.

He doesn't respond for a moment, seeming to contemplate something before deciding to ask. "You wish for her to hear?" Caspian nods once, leaving no room for argument.

The brute crosses his arms and faces the prince, widening his stance while he pointedly ignores my presence. Foolish fucking man.

"I was able to find a way into the tunnels without the other sentries suspecting, but I didn't uncover much. There were," he stretches his neck to each side as he pauses, "*sounds.*"

"Sounds?" I ask, my interest piqued despite my distaste for the messenger. "What kind of sounds?"

Gavriel's jaw clenches, but he answers, still refusing to look at me. "Inhuman. Like...like something crawling—*scratching*—against the stone."

A chill runs down my spine, but I mask the unease with a smirk. "Scared of a few rats, Gav?"

He whirls on me, eyes blazing. "These were no rats, wraith. Whatever's down there is not right."

Caspian leans forward, resting both elbows on his knees. "Could you see anything?"

The guard shakes his head. "No. It was too dark, and fuck if I was going to use a light. But I could feel them. Their presence." He shudders.

Curious. My gut is telling me that his story is relevant to our current search, but how?

There's something I am missing—something important. If I could just figure out what it is, I know that this will all make sense.

As much as I despise his presence, perhaps Gavriel could be useful. We need to know what the king is doing in the tunnels, and I will—with great enthusiasm—volunteer the brute to go in deeper. If one of us needs to be sacrificed for answers, it will be him.

I lean back in my chair, twirling my blade absently as I consider our next steps. Caspian stands, pacing the room with a thoughtful expression. "We need to explore further. If there's something in those tunnels that could pose a threat to us or the city—even the Accord—finding it is a top priority."

"Or aid it," I interject, earning a sharp look from both men. I shrug. "What? We don't know what these *creatures* are. They could be useful."

The prince shakes his head. "We can't risk it. I won't allow you down there, not without more information."

I scoff as I rise from my seat, sheathing my blade. "Then, by all means, *Your Highness*, let's get more information."

The library is still a disaster from yesterday's quake. Shards of glass litter the floor, glinting in the sunlight that now streams unobstructed through the shattered window. Books are strewn everywhere, their pages stuck open from their fall.

It seems the staff has cleaned up a bit, as the large piece of wood is no longer here.

I walk my way through the debris, my eyes scanning the shelves that remain intact. "We should start with the historical texts," I mutter, more to myself than to Caspian.

Thank the Angel Gavriel did not insist on following the prince around like an obedient puppy, though I could tell the idiot wanted to. How in the Aether Caspian ever saw any redeeming qualities in the man is far beyond my comprehension abilities.

He nods, already moving toward a far corner of the room where the dustiest books rest. "I'll check the older records. Maybe there's something about the tunnels in the original castle blueprints."

We work in silence for a while, the only sounds the rustling of pages and the occasional curse when one of us steps on a shard of glass. The quiet is almost peaceful, but there's an undercurrent of tension that I can't quite shake.

I run my fingers along the spines of the ancient texts, dust collecting on my fingertips as I search for anything remotely useful.

My mind races as I try to piece together the fragments of information I've gathered. The balance seems to be at the heart of everything. But how does it connect to the Accord? The Aether? To the strange creatures in the tunnels? To my parents' cryptic warnings?

I pull out a promising-looking volume and flip through its yellowed pages, my eyes scanning for any mention of the Aether or the Accord. A few passages catch my attention, speaking of a delicate balance between realms, of cosmic forces that have been relied upon for centuries.

My eyes widen as I read an intriguing passage:

"The balance, the mystical force which binds both realms, flows through the veins of our land like lifeblood. It is the source of peace, the harmony of essence itself. But beware, for as the Accord gives, so too can it take away. Should the balance be disturbed, the very fabric of reality may unravel."

I frown, my mind racing. This sounds eerily similar to what my father's journal hinted at. The balance shifting, the Accord weakening...could it all be connected to the Aether?

I flip through more pages, searching for any further mention of the Accord. My frustration grows as I find nothing concrete, just vague allusions to ancient rituals and binding agreements. It's as if the true nature of the Accord has been deliberately obscured—hidden from something that's deemed a threat.

Or someone.

I force the useless book shut, dust puffing into the air. My eyes sting, though whether from the particles or dissatisfaction, I'm unsure. Tossing the text back on its shelf, I reach for another when a warm breath tickles my ear.

"Find anything interesting?"

I whirl, my hand darting to the blade at my hip. Caspian stands there, an infuriating smirk on his face. How did he manage to sneak up on me? My senses are slipping in his presence. Unacceptable.

"Nothing substantial," I mutter, annoyed at both his stealth and my lack of progress. "You?"

His smirk widens as he holds up a weathering, leather-bound book. "Actually, I might have something. Look at this."

He flips the book open to a marked page and points to a faded illustration. It shows a network of tunnels beneath what appears to be the entirety of Valoria, some branches stretching into the Elysaran Mountains. The calm I was beginning to feel melts away as a heavy weight settles in my gut.

"Fuck me—they're not just under the castle." I sigh and lean back against a shelf, crossing my arms. "There is no possible way we could search through every one of those tunnels within the next century." I barely finish my words before the prince shakes his head.

"That's not necessary," he answers, running his fingers along the book he holds. "Whatever my father is doing is big. I know you've felt the essence emanating from him and how wrong it is.

He wouldn't risk something so important outside the castle walls. There are too many variables—too many people he would need to rely on to keep his secret. Here, he and Varrick can monitor things without seeming suspicious. I'm certain whatever we need to find is under the castle."

I nod, considering his words. "You're right." His brows shoot up at the words. I may not normally speak with such kindness, but perhaps I'll indulge him once in a while just to see this playful curiosity in his eyes some more. "It makes sense to focus on the castle tunnels. But even that's a significant area to cover. We'll need a plan." I lean in closer, studying the illustration. The drawing is worn, but it's easy enough to surmise the different landmarks illustrated along the pages. The castle, the guild, the lesser district. There is no mistaking the areas in which these tunnels run.

But why? Why are they there?

Though I wouldn't speak the words aloud, I trust Caspian's word about the king. But I do not trust Thalion, and fuck if I'll dismiss this entire map just because the prince believes his father doesn't make use of it.

Caspian's eyes meet mine, a determined glint in them. "We'll start with the areas closest to where Gavriel heard those sounds. Work our way out from there."

"And what about your guard dog, prince?" I ask, raising an eyebrow. "Will he be joining us on this little expedition? Now that you've informed him of everything we wanted to keep hidden, that is."

The prince sighs, running a hand through his hair. A puff of air sweeps over my skin as he closes the book and steps toward me. I may be angry with him, but it's a relief to not see the dark circles under his eyes any longer. "Gavriel is loyal."

"To you," I point out, tilting my head as I press a finger to the center of his chest and push. He remains still—close enough that the heat of his body warms the chill in mine. "Not to me. Not to what we need to do."

"He'll do as I say, angel," Caspian assures me, his voice firm enough that I know he will welcome no more talk of his guard.

Too bad I do not answer to him.

"And how far does that loyalty reach, hm?" His eyes drop and track the movement of my fingers walking up his chest. I hold back a smile when his muscles tense under my touch. "Gavriel is loyal to his kingdom. The man loves his rules. How can you be certain he won't turn on you the moment you reveal your treasonous thoughts against the king?"

My hand drifts over his throat and catches his chin, jerking it enough for his gaze to meet mine once more.

I need to move away from him—the hunger and tension emanating from him are pure torture to my traitorous body.

But I don't move. Not even when he steps closer, dropping his book on the shelf as his arms raise to each side of my head. He leans closer, and I use every bit of control I've learned over the years to stabilize my breathing. I cannot stop the flip of my stomach, and I wince as my shoulder jerks, instinctively wanting to cover the violent storm in my abdomen.

Caspian's lips rise as he searches my face. "How do I know *you* won't turn on me the moment I help you find answers?"

I narrow my eyes, a smirk playing at my lips. Smart man, finally thinking with his head instead of his dick. "You don't."

His breath hitches, and for a moment, I think he might kiss me. Part of me—a part I desperately try to ignore—wants him to. The memory of his full lips pressing against mine, fighting for dominance as we both take what we want...

But instead he leans in, his lips brushing against my ear as he whispers, "That's what makes this so exciting, isn't it?"

A shiver runs down my spine, and I hate myself for it. I loathe how my body responds to him—how my heart races when he's this close. It's a weakness I cannot afford.

But one I'm increasingly convinced is worth the cost.

"Exciting isn't the word I'd use," I mutter, pushing against his chest. He doesn't budge, instead pressing the lightest of kisses just under my ear. "Dangerous, perhaps. Foolish, undeniably."

Caspian chuckles, the sound low and rich and enough that a breath of raw need gets stuck in my throat. "Since when has danger ever stopped the illustrious Silver Wraith?"

Since you became more important to me than anything else.

I jump at my internal admission—something I've refused to acknowledge. I shouldn't be thinking so openly. It's messy and will cause more issues than I can deal with right now. It is all just repressed lust, anyway; nothing so important it requires more than a few mere heartbeats of my attention.

But the prince's lips slide over my cheek, brushing faintly against mine, and suddenly I cannot remember why this isn't a good idea. His hands lower to grab my waist, and I am but a willing hostage as their grip locks and prevents my retreat.

This position, these feelings, are dangerous. But Caspian is right...when have I *ever* avoided it, instead of falling head first into its waiting embrace?

I open my mouth to retort, but something prickles at the edge of my senses. A presence, watching. Observing. My instincts scream danger.

In an instant, I clamp my hand over Caspian's mouth and spin us around, pressing him against the bookshelf. His eyes widen, but I silence any protest with a sharp look.

My body is flush against his, every muscle taut as I scan our surroundings. The library appears empty, but the feeling persists. Someone—or something—is here.

I lean in close, a whisper barely leaving my lips. "We're not alone."

Caspian's body tenses, understanding flooding his eyes. He gives a slight nod, his hand moving with a careful slowness to his sides as he considers his options.

He has none, but I let him think, anyway. He is my charge to keep safe, not the other way around.

I maintain my hand over his mouth, using the position to shield him from the darkened opening at the end of the shelves. I tug on my psionic strand and send the essence away. It gets no more than a few feet before a wave of wrongness touches it, and I recoil so hard that the strand slips loose, the essence slamming back into me.

I have never felt something so utterly revolting. Whatever that thing is, it's not natural, and for the first time since meeting the griffin, a trickle of fear settles under my skin. But not fear for myself. No, this thing is something evil—hostile. Its energy is indescribably death, and it will kill the prince and me without hesitation.

But it will not get so far. No one touches him but me.

I step away from Caspian with caution, my movements slow and deliberate. Every sense is on high alert as I inch toward the darkness at the end of the aisle. The wrongness I felt earlier intensifies with each step as a haze of decay and corruption threatens to overwhelm me.

My mind races as I attempt to make sense of whatever the fuck this is. Is it connected to the sounds Gavriel heard in the tunnels? To the Accord? To my parents' warnings? There are too many questions and not enough answers.

And I'm beginning to get fucking irritated about it.

The wrongness I felt when my essence touched it reminds me of the corruption I've encountered before in the throne room, but this...this is different. More potent. More needy.

A memory flashes through my mind—my mother's face, twisted with fear as she whispered to my father about the balance being disturbed. How they had thought I was sleeping, but I had already been listening for minutes after sinking to the floor from their frightening conversation. Chaos. The word that had repeated in my head for days after hearing them speak. Disappointing that I had not connected this memory before now.

But was this what she meant? Perhaps this is the consequence of the balance or Accord being endangered.

There is a shift in the air, and in one fluid motion, I spin and fling my blade down the aisle, right in between the eyes of—

"What the fuck is that?" Caspian's words echo the stall in my thoughts.

I walk forward slowly as the creature's distorted form twists and writhes in pain, its limbs elongated and its skin a sickly yellow. It shudders before falling still, allowing me to study its strange form.

It may be dark in this part of the library, but I am unfortunately able to make out what I'm seeing. The creature is a strange amalgamation of human and...something I do not understand. There are mismatched limbs jutting at odd angles and bright red veins pulsing underneath its near-translucent skin. Its eyes are wild and unseeing, glowing with the same frenzied energy I felt minutes ago.

I crouch next to it, covering my nose as the scent of burnt flesh and blood fills the air. I can only describe the revolting smell as living rot—something that's not quite dead, but should be.

Even through each uncanny difference, it's obvious this being was human at one point. Everything about it defies explanation. Whatever it is, I can't shake the sense that its purpose wasn't to harm Caspian.

Caspian steps closer, stopping next to me as I look up at the horror settling on his features. "Is this...was this a person?" My only response is a nod.

My head whirls at his sharp intake of breath. I turn to see him clutching his arm as a dark stain spreads across his sleeve.

"You're hurt." Without thinking, I jump to my feet and grab the lower part of his arm. My forehead creases as I inspect the wound. A clean slice, matching the small blade Caspian holds in his hand. Not one of mine, nor his, so the creature must have thrown it before I cut off its life.

I'm unsure of how to proceed. The wound is deep enough that it needs attention, that much is obvious. And I should be able to heal him with my living affinity...but I've never used my vital strand to heal anyone other than myself. I'd be nothing but an embarrassment to the Angel's will if I attempted to heal him.

Pathetic fucking excuse, but I swipe the thought away and make a decision.

"We need—" I pause with my mouth open when I catch the prince's eye. He's staring at me with a fondness I do not deserve. I sigh, because of course I let him see my worry. Clearing my throat, I release his arm and step back. "We need to get you to Elowen."

The slightest hint of pain flashes through his gaze before his face hardens, and he nods to the creature. "Let's burn the body—we'll find nothing we haven't already gathered, and we cannot leave it here for my father to find. The more he believes us ignorant of him, the better."

I raise a brow at the hardness of his tone, but do not stop to question his command. Reaching for my pyro strand, I coax the neglected essence out, demanding it to destroy the body and leave no trace before spinning to stalk from the library.

I do not bother to check if Caspian is following—there's never been a need to. I realize, with a chilling certainty, that he will always be right behind me with unwavering loyalty. The thought is more relieving than it should be.

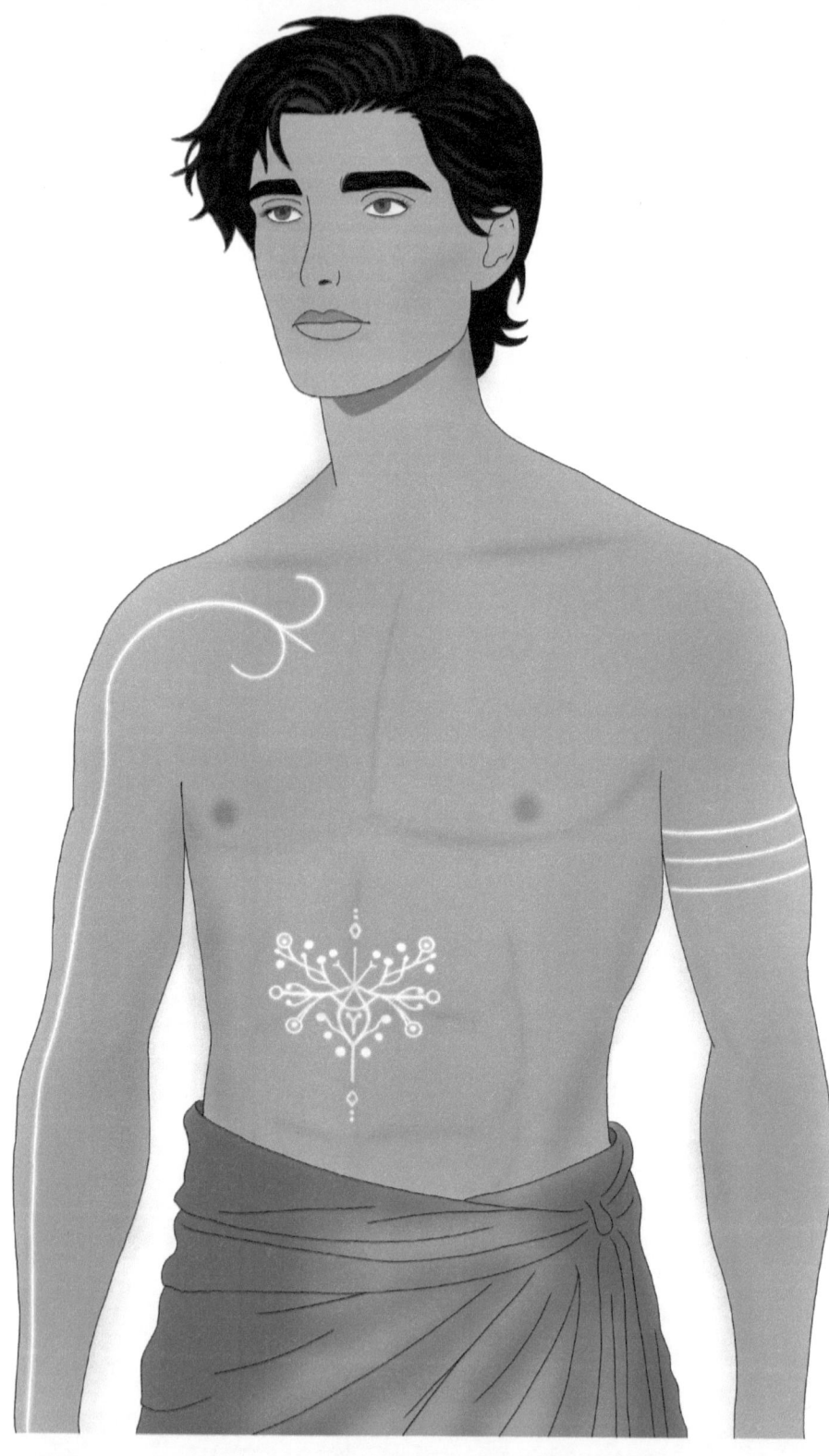

Chapter Three
Caspian

I follow Ariella through the winding corridors, my arm throbbing with each step. The wound isn't as deep as she believes, but it stings like a bitch. I can't shake the image of that...*thing* we found in the library. What was it? What has my father done?

Ariella moves with purpose, her steps quick and sure. I notice the tension in her shoulders, the way her finger taps against her blade—a nervous habit, I've surmised. She's on high alert, scanning every shadow we pass.

The little wraith *cares* for me. The thought lightens my souring mood.

"You don't have to worry so much," I tease, trying to get *something* from her. I'm fucking tired of her ignoring her feelings and pushing me away as a result. "I am not going to keel over from a minor cut."

She doesn't turn, but I watch as her shoulders stiffen further. "Don't be ridiculous. I'm not worried about you."

I can't help but smile. Even now, she maintains her prickly facade. But I saw the concern in her eyes...fleeting, but very much there.

We round another corner, and I find myself studying the graceful curve of her neck, the way her silver hair catches the dim light. She's beautiful, dangerously so, and I'm drawn to her like a moth to a flame. I know I should be more cautious, more guarded, but I cannot help the way my heart races when she's near. Nor can I lessen the intensity of emotion under my skin, begging me to stay near her and keep her safe from anyone that would dare harm her.

I would do anything for her—*anything*.

That haunting discovery is a war I've been fighting since the moment I first saw her; the Silver Wraith, or loyalty to my kingdom? Somewhere deep inside, I have known the answer from that day in the training room, but it's something I still refuse to acknowledge. It's far more difficult to accept the truth than it is to shove it to the back of my mind.

My eyes close for a moment as I picture the confident assassin that challenged the prince of Eldoria without a second thought. Fuck, she was beyond anything I could find words for.

As we near the healer's wing, my thoughts drift to the tunnels, to the creature we encountered. What other horrors has my father unleashed? The wrongness I felt oozing from that thing...a deep shiver seizes my body. I've always known my father to be a harsh ruler, but this? This is something else entirely.

I clench my fist, wincing as the movement pulls at my wound. How long has this been going on?

I've been blind. Ignorant of the darkness festering at the heart of my kingdom. How many other atrocities has my father committed in the name of power? How many more of those things are hidden away in the tunnels beneath our feet? What in the Aether is he even doing to them?

I've always known politics was a dangerous game, especially for our family. But this goes beyond political maneuvering or whatever the fuck my father is doing with his essence.

This is a perversion of nature itself.

And yet, a small part of me whispers that perhaps there's a reason. Maybe my father believes he's doing what's necessary to protect the kingdom. To keep us strong in the face of external threats...

But even as I form the thought, I know it's a lie. There is no justification for what we saw in the library. No greater good that could come from twisting a human being into such an atrocity. We need answers, and this has put a whole new strain of urgency on my shoulders.

Getting my father to let me in his inner circle will be difficult, though I'm certain I've made progress already.

I've made a conscious effort to engage more with the ruling side of politics. Attending council meetings, offering opinions on trade agreements, showing interest in the day-to-day operations of the kingdom. It's tedious work, but I can see my father's approval growing with each passing day.

Varrick has appeared suspicious of my sudden interest, but the man has never been anything but a snake and I'll not allow him to sabotage my efforts.

The king has even started inviting me to private dinners, just the two of us. We discuss matters of state, and sometimes, when the wine flows freely, he hints at greater plans for Eldoria's future. But he's still guarded, still keeping his deepest secrets hidden inside his sick fucking head.

It's a far cry from my childhood, when I was content to spend my days training with the royal guard or exploring the castle grounds. Back then, the weight of the crown felt distant, abstract. Now it looms over me, a constant reminder of the responsibilities that await.

We reach the healer's wing, and I lead Ariella to Elowen's workspace, knocking lightly on the door. The healer greets us with a warm smile that quickly turns to concern when she spots the blood on my sleeve.

"Caspian! What happened?" She rushes over, her sage green eyes almost too wide.

I wave off her concern with my good hand. "It's nothing serious, El. Just a minor mishap during training."

Ariella snorts softly beside me, and I catch her eye. She raises an eyebrow, questioning my lie. I give an imperceptible shrug. No need to worry Elowen with the truth—most of it, anyway.

"Well, let's take a look, shall we?" Elowen says, already guiding me to a nearby cot. "Shirt off, please."

I comply, wincing as I pull the fabric over my head. It sticks to my wound, the blood already drying, and I watch as the threads lift the already scarring skin off with a painful ease.

Tossing the shirt aside, I study the familiar space.

The room is lit by flickering candles, casting shadows on the numerous shelves filled with jars and bottles of various herbs and ingredients. A small table in the center holds a mortar and pestle, where Elowen spends much time mixing and grinding her medicines.

Having grown up together, I often found myself in this wing while she trained for the day she would claim the position as the royal healer. I'd question why in the Aether the healers would need to know anything about preparing healing concoctions when they could just weave their vital strand.

And each time she would tell me: *all essence has limits.*

I'll never question it again—not even as a joke—after she saved Ariella's life when she was poisoned with hallow. Without the saida, my conniving little assassin would have died.

Essence may have its limits, but I do not. My debt to Elowen will never be paid for what she did that night.

Clearing my throat, I lean back on my good arm and continue perusing. On the wall across from me hangs a tapestry depicting a lush forest, likely a way to comfort the injured that find themselves in this room.

Or perhaps it is just something nice to look at—not everything has a hidden meaning.

"Okay," Elowen sighs, drying her hands with a clean towel before walking over to me. "This is going to—"

"Be cold, I know," I deadpan, feigning outrage at her subtle jab in my ribs. She narrows her eyes before focusing on my arm once more.

"Perhaps I should just sew the skin together without any pain relief. See how funny you find *that*." I chuckle and shake my head. Despite her words, Elowen's hands are gentle as she cleans the blood from my arm and inspects what needs healing.

My eyes slide over to Ariella, who leans against the door while she glares at the woman next to me. She twirls a blade through her fingers, not seeming to pay any attention to the action.

What a captivating fucking specimen she is.

I run a hand over my mouth to hide a smile when my angel's eye twitches, as if she's fighting every instinct in her body to not slice Elowen's throat right here.

The healer's spine stiffens as she pauses her work and peers over her shoulder. She hums, repressing a smile and returning to my wound.

"It's okay, El; she's just jealous." I study Ariella as she processes my words before running her tongue too slowly over her bottom lip.

"Is that so?" she challenges, pushing from the door and dropping her head back. "That would imply there's something to be jealous of." She pins me with a wicked look, her eyes saying more than her mouth ever will.

I fucking love this game.

She continues before I can reply. "I think your friend is wise enough to not touch what doesn't belong to her. Isn't that right, Elowen?" Ariella stops next to the shelves, her brows furrowing as she runs her fingers over the wilted plants at the top.

"Ariella," I berate, remaining calm. Her brows snap up, the surprise of my tone evident in her unmasked reaction. "Fuck with anyone else, I do not care, but you will refrain with Elowen. She is off-limits to you." Her jaw and fists clench, the white of her knuckles increasing with each second. I level her with an admonishing look, warning her to test me on this; I almost think she will before she exhales and mutters under her breath—something I'm sure is not her listing every way she would kill me if she could.

Elowen smiles as if this is amusing, and she has not just been threatened by the realm's deadliest assassin. "That is correct, Ariella. You've nothing to fret over with me—the Angel would sooner fall from the sky before I ever approached Caspian in such a manner."

Ariella's eyes narrow as she continues to study the shriveled plants. "These herbs...are you not caring for them?"

Elowen glances up from my arm, her brow furrowing. "No, I am. Well, *trying to*—I've been having trouble keeping them alive lately. It's odd."

"Odd how?" Ariella presses, her fingers ghosting over the dried leaves.

Elowen sighs, applying a salve to my now closed wound before answering. Strange, I didn't even feel her heal it. "It's like they do not want to be alive. Of course, I've tried using my flora strand, but I'm so desperate I've resorted to mundane methods like watering them and providing sunlight. Nothing is working, and I can't explain why." She tosses my shirt at me before joining Ariella by the shelves and crossing her arms. "It's affecting my ability to provide proper treatments, so if you have any ideas, I'm all ears."

I watch as Ariella's posture stiffens, her eyes darting to meet mine. There's a silent communication between us—this isn't a coincidence. I nod at the unasked question in her gaze, trusting her to decide how much to divulge.

She faces the healer, the intensity in her gaze enough to make most men fall to their knees weeping. And I'll gladly be one of them if that's how she wishes to be worshiped.

Ariella's voice is low, measured as she asks, "How long has this been happening?"

Elowen scowls, considering. "It started gradually, maybe...three months ago? But it has gotten worse in the past few weeks."

"And it's not just these plants?" Ariella presses. "You're having trouble with all your herbs?"

The healer nods. "Yes, even the hardiest ones are struggling. It's like..." She pauses, searching for the right words. "It's like the essence itself feels different. Wrong, somehow. I don't know how to explain it, but I can just feel it."

I watch the exchange intently, trying to follow Ariella's line of questioning. Where is she going with this? This is information we already know.

"Have you noticed anything else unusual?" Ariella continues. "Any changes in your essence, specifically?"

Elowen hesitates, her eyes darting between Ariella and me. "Well, now that you mention it, my vital strand has felt strained for some days. Like it takes more effort to access and control. I assumed it was just stress from all the extra work."

Ariella nods, her eyes distant as if piecing together a puzzle. "And have you noticed any changes in the patients you treat? Anything out of the ordinary?"

The healer's brow furrows deeper. "Come to think of it, wounds have been taking longer to heal, even with my assistance. And there's been an uptick in strange ailments—things I've never seen before."

I can't help but interject, "What kind of strange ailments?"

The healer shakes her head and bites the inside of her cheek. "It's hard to describe. Fevers that won't break, inexplicable pain, hallucinations. Probably just a sickness floating around the city."

Ariella taps a finger against her thigh, her eyes distant. I can practically see the wheels turning in her mind, connecting dots that I'm still struggling to see. I want to traverse every corner of her head and learn how she thinks—discover every little thing that makes her tick.

But that will have to wait as she nods at Elowen before stalking from the room, disregarding all formalities. Not that anyone in this room expected her to partake in such trivial matters. I mumble a thank you to my friend and move to follow Ariella, but the healer's voice gives me pause.

"Caspian." I peer over my shoulder and catch her hardened gaze. She's nervous. "Whatever you two are planning...please be careful. I don't know what's happening, but the flora whisper things sometimes and the coming change is unmistakable." She shifts on her feet, seeming torn before skipping forward and pulling me into a tight hug. My arms instinctively wrap around her small body—a comfort I've needed after this last week. She buries her face in my shoulder and mumbles, "Just be careful. You are an impulsive idiot, and I'll not have word of your death because of it." She pulls back, gripping the sides of my arms. Her eyes flick over my shoulder so quickly I almost miss the awe that glimmers in their depths. "Stay with Ariella, Cas. She's going to need you—but as stubborn as she is, do not leave her side until this is over. The realms' survival depends on it."

Elowen has always had impeccable intuition, though I've found those that possess the flora strand usually do. I somehow believe her claims that the flora whisper, which is strange as I've not felt such a connection to the land myself. Perhaps it is different for the strands in the elemental affinity.

I open my mouth to ask what she means, but someone clears their throat behind me and I jolt, spinning to find a composed assassin waiting against the wall. She's too calm...it's eerie. I give Elowen what I hope is a friendly smile before walking from the room and passing a still-waiting Ariella. Her steps are silent as she follows, but I do not need to look to know that she's there. Her essence is like a beacon to mine—the longer I'm around her, the more aware I am of her presence.

Sometimes I'm certain I could locate her with a mere thought, but that's a foolish hope. Such essence doesn't exist.

I flex my fingers, the familiar tingle of my elemental affinity waits so patiently under my skin. The dual affinities—kinetic and aqua—have always come naturally to me, though the water and force often partake in a dance of power as they attempt to be my primary source of essence. It has been just those two my entire life, yet lately, I've felt...something else. A hint of darkness at the edges of my consciousness, elusive and intangible.

I shake off the thought. Now isn't the time to dwell on strange sensations—especially considering how terrible I've felt recently. We have more pressing matters to attend to.

"Have you fucked her?" I'm so taken aback by the question that I pause in the center of the hallway. Ariella must have been close to my back as she immediately spins around my left side and walks backward, continuing our journey.

A soft vulnerability settles in her eyes, both of them studying me while awaiting an answer. If this woman has any insecurities, they certainly are not about me, so I break our stare and continue walking.

"Come again?" I ask, though I'm confident my ears heard her correctly.

"Have. You. Fucked. Her." Ah, she's wondering if there's more than platonic history between Elowen and me.

"Who, exactly, are you referring to?" The tapping against her thigh stops as her palm clenches around the hilt of her blade. It is too easy to provoke her. As entertaining as it is, part of me wonders if her reactions indicate her lack of experience.

Not with men, much to my absolute dismay, but with feeling anything other than anger.

From what I know of Ariella's past, I suspect she's never truly had the chance to experience these softer emotions. Lust, sure—her preternatural beauty would ensure no shortage of admirers, even if the color of her hair gives them an immediate lock on her identity. But love? Genuine affection? Those are foreign to her, as if she's never allowed herself to be vulnerable enough to feel them. She made that very clear the two times we've been intimate.

And I want to be the one to show her what she's missed

I want to break down those walls she's built, to see the woman beneath the mask. To be the safe harbor where she can let her guard down, even if just for a moment.

But I know pushing too hard will only make her retreat further—I need to continue unraveling her slowly. So I play along with her game. For now.

"Ah, you mean Elowen," I say, feigning realization. "No, I have not *fucked her*, angel." It's difficult to hold in my laugh, but I manage.

"Don't *angel* me. You looked quite cozy together." I watch as she blatantly avoids my gaze, and I cannot help but chuckle this time.

That pisses her off, if the grinding of her teeth indicates anything. Stubborn fucking woman.

"Even if I wanted to, *angel*," I tease, turning right down the hallway that houses our rooms, "she wouldn't ever agree. But lucky for you, you seem to be the only thing I can ever think about."

She scoffs hard and runs that fucking tongue across her lip. Angel, what I wouldn't give if she'd just allow me another bite. "And why wouldn't she agree? Does she know of some secret of yours I'm not yet privy to?"

"You truly are the most obstinate woman I've ever met," I mutter under my breath before doubling my stride and pivoting to a halt just in front of her. She rolls her eyes dramatically, moving as though she's about to step around me. I catch her shoulders as I close the distance between us and shove her face into my chest. She stiffens at the forced hug, but doesn't move to push me away.

Actually, she remains completely still.

I rest my cheek on her head and savor the feel of her silky hair as I run my fingers through it idly. "I haven't fucked Elowen because she prefers the company of women." Did her muscles relax a bit, or is that just wishful thinking? "I have indeed fucked other women—" I grunt as she half-heartedly attempts to leave my arms. I hold tighter. I need her to hear this—because as much as it frustrates me that all my other declarations have gone un-believed, I will continue to reassure her of my truth even after she begins to trust it. I'll tell her every day, if that's what she needs. "But they are in the past. You are my future, Ariella, and I don't fucking care how much you fight or deny it. You're mine. Every other woman in both realms is but a drop in the ocean compared to you."

She pokes at me again, and this time I release her. It's so difficult not to smile when I look into her eyes. The feeling is beyond euphoric and so *right* that my body lights up at the simple action.

"Why are you telling me all this?"

"Because you continue to push me away and fight every single feeling you have telling you to do otherwise. Crazy or not, you're it for me and I will not allow you to forget it." I lean forward and press a light kiss to her nose before turning toward my room. "Now, care to share what brilliant deduction you made back there?"

She remains silent for a moment, her eyes fixed ahead as I close the door to my room. Just as I'm about to prompt her again, she speaks. "The Palmluvela."

I blink, caught off guard. "The what now?"

"The Palmluvela," she repeats, her tone impatient. "They reside in the Verdantia Forest, not far from Ebonwood, I believe."

I've never heard of them, and I feel clueless as I wait for her to continue. But she doesn't. "Why are they of importance?"

She sucks on her teeth before dropping into a chair. She looks exhausted. "Their people are made of the strongest living affinities. They specialize in flora and fauna. Marek sent a student there once to train, though I haven't seen them since. Said the child was some sort of prodigy with how potent their living essence was." Something unsettling festers in my abdomen. "Whatever—that's not important. All I know is they consider themselves *one with the realms,* and I think they could help us."

"Okay," I breathe, dragging the word out.

I sit with the idea for a moment, mulling over the implications. A community of powerful living affinities, hidden away in the Verdantia Forest...

It could be exactly what we need. But something doesn't sit right.

"How did Marek know about them?" I question, unable to keep the suspicion from my voice. "And why haven't I ever heard of them?"

Ariella's eyes close as she shrugs and leans her head against the back of the cushioned chair. "He has his sources. And they're not exactly common knowledge—they prefer to keep to themselves."

I nod to myself, shifting on my feet. "And you think they could help us understand what's happening with the essence and balance?"

"It's possible," she says, her fingers drumming against the arm of the chair. "At the very least, they might have knowledge we lack. Their connection to the realms is...unique, I'm told."

I pace the room, considering our options. If she believes this is our best chance at answers, I will not doubt her. But it means I will need to leave the castle for a time—something I'm not very comfortable with. I could lose all the influence I've gained with the king, but I also will not have her venturing through the Verdantia Forest alone. Especially to a place neither of us knows much about.

A chill runs down my spine as I recall the tales I've heard of the forest. It's said to be a place of ancient magic, where the veil between realms grows thin. Where time flows differently, and hasty travelers find themselves lost for years, emerging unchanged while the world has moved on without them.

Those may be mere stories, but there's a reason people do not wander through those woods. The stories must have been created from somewhere.

"It won't be an easy journey," I say, voicing my concerns.

She nods, meeting my eyes once more. "I don't expect anything my parents' writing discussed to be easy." She's right. There was never a thought in my mind that whatever we were searching for would be as simple as scouring a few texts.

"What's your plan, then? How do we find them?"

Her gaze hardens as if she wishes to fight whatever she found offensive in my words, but she holds back. "I don't need Marek to know anything yet, so I'll need to pay a visit to an old *friend.*"

The way she said friend makes me think this will be far more than a pleasant visit across the city.

Chapter Four

Ariella

M y eyes roll as Caspian insists on accompanying me. His overprotective nature is both irritating and oddly endearing, though I'd never confess the latter.

We approach the modest house on the outskirts of Valoria, its weathered exterior a categorical contrast to the castle I've been made to live in. My stomach twists as memories of my last visit here surface. The man's anguished cries...I'd almost felt bad for him.

Almost.

I push the thoughts aside—this is necessary. Caspian's voice breaks through my reverie, muffled and distorted by the mask I've ordered him to wear. There would be an uprising if the kingdom's people knew their prince was accompanying the Silver Wraith on her missions. "Are you sure about this?"

I nod once. "He's our best lead to finding them." Other than my mentor, but I've already decided he won't know about this.

"And you're certain he'll help us?"

A humorless smile tugs at my lips. "Oh, your sweet, royal-forged naivety. He has no choice, prince."

The moon casts a ghostly light through the dusty windows, illuminating the worn-down furniture and faded wallpaper. Seems our friend has let himself go. I walk straight to the front door, not bothering to hide from wandering eyes—the people of Eldoria know better than to act against me. Anyone watching will just lock their doors and send a prayer to the Angel that I do not visit them next.

The darkness of the house envelopes us, barely illuminated by the slivers of moonlight that peek through the windows. My nose scrunches as the smell of damp wood and musty old furniture hangs in the air, mingling with the faint scent of smoke, as if someone had lit a candle recently—an unpleasant one.

The only sounds are our muted footsteps and the occasional swish of fabric as we navigate our way deeper into the house. I can feel Caspian's presence behind me, his breaths coming out slightly ragged with the adrenaline I'm sure is coursing through his body.

He's never done something this dark in nature before. I hold back a laugh—this is the least dark thing I've done in a while. My world, it's intimidating. But he demanded to join, so he will learn very what it truly means to be friends with me. This is everything political meetings are not, and civil, amicable outcomes do not exist here.

I pause in the family room, this one seeming the most lived-in. There is a chair on the opposite side that faces the entry hallway, which is perfect for my needs. Alexander should be home soon, if my memories recall correctly. He works as a tailor, catering to the royal family and their guard, which keeps him out a majority of the day.

I drop into the chair, nodding behind me to where I want Caspian to stand. "Should you need reminding, you are not to speak or reveal your identity."

He scoffs and settles in the area I'd indicated. "Yes, *my queen.*" I bark out a laugh, unable to stop myself. His tone is light and playful. I enjoy this side of him—too bad we have business to attend to.

A refreshing giddiness settles inside me as a door opens down the hall, clicking shut after a moment. I lean back and cross my legs, switching the blade to my right hand as I continue to twirl it through my fingers. Caspian may think I'm *being funny*, but if he so much as utters a word out of turn, I will slice his dick right off.

This isn't a pathetic little meeting at the castle, nor is it a soiree with Eldorian nobles from other cities. This is my job—one I take very seriously.

It would be a pity, though—the prince losing his cock. It is quite nice.

I blow out a frustrated sigh. But in my world, threats are indeed binding, and I *always* follow through with mine.

My eyes flick up as a lamp at the front of the room illuminates and our target sucks in a sharp breath. "Hello, Alexander," I purr, exuding a confidence that was trained into me. The target moves the smallest step back, but I do not miss it. "Ah, ah. I don't recall granting you permission to run. Try not to piss yourself just yet—we have matters to discuss."

"You," he breathes, stumbling back another step.

I stand in one fluid motion. My body is so in-sync with its ingrained focus that not even my fingers falter in twirling the blade as I move through the room, never taking my eyes from Alexander. I stop directly in front of him, smirking. My blade slides across the base of his neck, catching the beads of sweat that have accumulated there in the last minute. "Me." A confirmation he does not need, but one I am too happy to give.

"Silver Wraith," he grits out, his tone subdued. His gaze swings to Caspian as the prince adjusts his position behind me and my lip curls, slapping the blade against his already reddened cheek, the tip just barely nicking skin.

"Do not look at him. You answer to me tonight." I step back and cross my feet, pivoting to the wall of photos Alexander keeps of him and his wife. "Actually, I'm in no mood for generosity. Unlucky for you. So if you so much as acknowledge his presence again, you and I will have some extra fun. He doesn't exist to you—do you understand?" My head whips to the side, and I raise a brow, pressing for an answer.

"Yes, wraith." The target breathes in deep, wiping a hand down the front of his cashmere jacket. He's nervous. Good, he should be. "As..." He clears his throat, and I simply wait for him to find the confidence to continue with what I'm sure is meant to be an enlightening sentiment. "As honored as I am that you have graced me with your...presence, I do not believe we have any more business with each other."

His gaze betrays him as the lines of his face crease imperceptibly when he looks at the photo I'm standing in front of. Him and his wife, drawn standing on a beach as they watch each other with smiles that promise forever.

A promise they had no right making.

"I decide when we have business, Alexander," I snap. "Tell me how to find the Palmluvela."

His face pales further, quite the juxtaposition to the dark panels that make up his walls. "I-I don't know what you're talking about."

I advance on him, my patience wearing thin. "Don't play dumb. We both know your thievery against them is the reason your wife is dead."

Out of the corner of my eye, I see Caspian stiffen at my blunt words. I ignore him, focusing on the trembling man before me.

"Please," Alexander whimpers. "I can't...They'll kill me if I reveal their location."

I lean in close, my voice a deadly whisper. "And what do you think I'll do if you don't?"

The internal struggle that plays out across his face is satisfying. The fear of them versus the immediate threat I pose. I've seen this dance before, and I know how it ends.

"You don't understand," he pleads, a touch louder than me. "What I took from them...it's not just some trinket. It's powerful, dangerous. If they find out I've led others to them—"

"I'm not interested in your excuses," I cut him off, pressing the sharp edge of my blade against his throat. "Location. Now."

He swallows hard, and his throat bobs, jerking my hand. "There's...you don't find them, they find you." My last nerve was desecrated with his non-answer. He must see the finality of my gaze because he barks out his next words as if he desperately needs to say them before I can move. "I'm not messing with you! The exact location of their community is unknown, but travel west through the forest, keeping south of Ebonwood. If your intentions are pure, they will find you."

"Fuck, Alexander, you truly do not care for your life, do you? Will I meet the Angel there, too? The Aether?"

Alexander whips his head side to side. "It's true! The forest is—it's alive. It *protects* them."

I step back, considering his words. It sounds like nonsense, but I've heard stranger things about the Verdantia Forest. And if he's lying...well, I know where to find him. Even if he runs, he will meet his end with my blade. If he remains alive long enough to do so, that is.

"For your sake," I say, voice low and menacing, "you better hope my intentions are *pure* enough for them."

He deflates, though whether in relief or utter defeat, I'm unsure. "I swear on my life, it's the truth."

"Your life isn't worth much these days, is it?" I remark, turning away from him. "Come," I say to Caspian, not bothering to look back as I head for the door.

Alexander reaches for his bottle of cider, though before he can chug the heady liquid, the prince is there snatching it from his hand. "Don't," Caspian mutters, setting the bottle back on the wearing mantle. My teeth grind from the effort it takes to not castrate him right here, and I am quite impressed with my level of control.

The moment we are outside and in an alley, however, that minute amount of control snaps. I whirl on the prince and grab his throat, shoving back against the brick wall. I rip the mask from his face, tossing the stupid thing aside.

"What part of 'do not speak' did you not understand?" I hiss, my face a mere inch from his. His scent is a distraction I do not need, but I allow myself to indulge for a few moments.

Caspian's eyes widen, though he doesn't struggle against my grip. "You think I didn't see you drop something in his cider, Ariella? The man didn't deserve to die when he gave you the answers you sought after." He's not wrong. I did slip phecin into the cider when we'd arrived, though I hardly think it warrants such a reaction. The man could have tossed the alcohol before consuming it—unlikely, but possible. The colorless, odorless poison would have had him dead within the hour after bleeding out internally.

Relatively painless. I deem that a mercy, considering what I'd wanted to do to him instead.

"Fuck's sake, Caspian. Must you be so *noble*?" I squeeze his throat harder, relishing the way I hold his life in my hand. "That was not your decision to make." The ire in his eyes prickles the hair along my neck; I've not seen him look so angry before.

I'm unsure of whether I'm amused or annoyed.

"My apologies, Silver Wraith, I wasn't aware you were above everyone else and your word was final." I chuckle, the sound low and malicious. I am certainly annoyed.

"I *am* above all of them—that's part of the depravity you claim to love so much about me. I do not fucking care whether he deserved to die or not, but it was *my* decision." My throat tightens at the hurt in his eyes, though I continue. "You need to understand something, prince. I have been telling you the truth of myself since the day we met, and yet you've continued to insist that you want every part of me, killer and all. This," I gesture between us, "is precisely why I haven't believed you. I knew that your opinions would change the very first peek you got into this part of my life."

"Well here I am, Caspian. Take a good fucking look, because I change for no one. So you'd better decide if your declarations are true, or if your feelings are just as every other man who becomes infatuated with me because fucking someone with my reputation will win them bragging rights amongst others." He grunts as I shove into him, pushing from my spot and stalking back toward the castle, my fists clenched at my sides. The cool night air does little to soothe the fire raging inside me.

Fuck him. Fuck his nobility and his misplaced sense of morality. I've been perfectly clear about who and what I am from the start. If he can't handle it, that's something he needs to deal with—alone.

And yet...

A small voice in the back of my mind whispers doubts I've been trying to ignore. What if he's right to be appalled? I am the monster everyone believes me to be. I am the subject of stories told in the night and the fear that crests when they take one look at my hair.

I shake my head, trying to banish the thoughts. I cannot afford to second-guess myself now. Not when there's so much at stake. Stupid that I've allowed the prince—*a man*, of all things—to make me question myself.

But the hurt lingers, an unwelcome ache in my chest. For just a moment, I'd allowed myself to hope that maybe, just maybe, someone could accept all of me. The bad and the worse, the dark and the shadows.

How foolish of me.

I'm the Silver Wraith—a product of this regency's making. I do not need acceptance or understanding. I need no one.

Then why is it so painful?

I quicken my pace, desperate to put distance between myself and these unwanted emotions. The mission comes first—finding the Palmluvela, getting answers. Everything else is a distraction.

At least that's what I'll tell myself.

Chapter Five

Ariella

I suck in a deep breath, the calm of the night settling in my lungs. I may have overreacted, but there are times when I want to rip Caspian's head clean from his body. I wouldn't—*couldn't*—so my possibly exaggerated reactions are the next best thing.

This part of Valoria smells of warm bread, mixed with the sharp tang of smoke from chimneys and the faint hint of herbs from open windows. The city is shrouded in darkness, with only a few flickering lamps lighting the streets, and my shadows beg to come out and play. It's dark enough to hide them, but I'm in no mood. I need to release some essence soon, however. Each ripple under my skin drives me mad, and I do not wish to deal with the buildup any longer.

Something wraps around my arm, and I have my blade against the prince's wrist before my next heartbeat.

"Do that again and you'll find yourself sympathizing with the pain your cousin was in on the night of the ball." He chuckles, calming the tension between our bodies.

"Bastard deserved much worse than that." True. His gaze softens as he maps every bit of my face, as if he didn't see it just a few minutes ago. "I fear my words came out wrong before...I didn't intend to upset you."

I blink. "And what did you intend?"

He shrugs, gesturing forward to continue our trek back to his home. "Honestly, I just wanted to give the guy a break and didn't think it would matter to you either way." More laughter leaves him as he turns his head toward me, his eyes lighting up with something I do not care to discern. "I swear to the Angel I thought he was about to piss himself when he saw you—it was magnificent." I offer a nod in response.

We're quiet for a few moments, and the tautness of my posture lessens. Caspian breaks the silence once more. "Will you forgive me, angel? I may question you sometimes, but I have nothing but good intentions with you. I wouldn't ever do anything to harm you." He nods to a woman dusting around her window, and her mouth drops when she realizes who the prince is walking with.

Instead of answering, I drop the subject because I wasn't angry with him to begin with. I'm angry with myself—always myself. And for the first time, my stomach churns knowing I'd just treated Caspian how I do everyone else.

"Are you hungry?" I blurt before biting my cheek so hard the taste of blood slides over my tongue. It is suddenly too hot out here; I need a cold shower.

When he doesn't answer, I look over to find the prince smiling boyishly at me. Aether, does he know how to make me uncomfortable. Not such an unwelcome sensation, though.

"Did you just ask me on a date, Ariella Mistaire?"

My face heats as I move to refute his accusation. "What? I only asked if you were hungry, because I'm starving and there's a place close by that makes the best tarts."

"Sounds like a date to me," he declares, grinning so wide I'm certain his lips will split in half.

I shove him to the left, toward Pyro's Bite. I could come just imagining the taste of their food. Ronan, the owner, weaves the pyro strand and uses his essence to cook. He claims that he does nothing special, just makes sure customers get a warm meal, but the man is an Angel in his own right. I've no idea what he does with his recipes, but there's nowhere else like it in Valoria.

We approach the hidden little restaurant; the entrance nestled in a small, creepy alley—I love it. I reach for the handle, but Caspian's voice halts my steps.

"Are you sure this is safe?"

I throw my head back, laughing loudly. Still chuckling when I catch my breath, I find the prince watching me with a look I've only ever seen from my parents, Marek, and Isaiah. Three of whom are now dead.

"Nothing in this part of the city is safe, prince. Lucky for you, you're being escorted by the one person in this realm that no one in there would dare fuck with." I pause, considering my words. "Actually, I'd bet you're the safest person here because of that. Let's go."

I grab the handle and yank at the door, cursing under my breath when the hinges squeak and stick. The door itself isn't heavy, just covered in years worth of what I assume is alcohol, piss, and probably cum. It sticks to itself and I pull hard, my elbow grazing Caspian's stomach when it gives. I remind myself to reprimand Ronan again for not yet fixing it before stepping into the space.

A small smile tugs at my lips as I breathe in the familiar air of sweat, meat, and my favorite tarts.

Ronan had stopped making them at one point, claiming they cost him more than they're worth; but one look from me and they were suddenly a permanent item on the menu. Sometimes being me has its perks.

A waitress squeals when we step into the dining area, nearly tripping with a tray full of food in her hands. I catch her wrist, steadying the tremble before letting go. Her mouth opens and closes twice before I save her from any more embarrassment.

"Tell Ronan I'm here," I remark before grabbing Caspian's hand and stepping around groups of people to claim an empty table at the corner of the room. The waitress is not one I've seen before, but I'm not attempting to hide my hair, so she'll know what to tell the owner.

I nod at the outer chair for the prince to take while I sit in the one opposite, providing me a clear view of the entire room. Every single person is staring at me as if they cannot believe I'm real—it's pathetic. I meet each pair of eyes glaring my way until they drop and continue with whatever the fuck these people talk about.

Interesting that no one looks twice at Caspian. I wonder if it's my presence, or that they do not know what the prince looks like.

I settle into my seat, scanning the room once more before turning my attention back to Caspian. He's looking around with wide eyes, taking in the raucous atmosphere and extensive mix of patrons.

"Not quite what you're used to in the castle, is it?" I smirk.

He shakes his head, a small smile playing at his lips. "Definitely not. But I like it. It's...real. Everything in my life is always so painted over; fake smiles and money hide the reality of it all."

Before I can respond, a booming voice cuts through the chatter. "Well, well, well! If it isn't my least favorite customer!" I level Ronan with a glare that would make most weep, but he just laughs and waves it away.

The man saunters over to our table, his footsteps resonate through the room like the confident beat of a drum, announcing his arrival to any that care to listen. His broad frame fills my vision as he nears us. He towers over Caspian, his muscular arms and chest straining against a tight shirt. Dark stubble lines his jaw, giving him an air of virility. As he reaches the table, Ronan's hand slaps against the aging wood, displaying his calloused skin.

He's a few years ahead of my age, but there's always been a sense of ripened wisdom about him. If I wasn't sure of his age, I'd be convinced he was far older.

"Your least favorite customer?" I quip, my tone void of any warmth.

He snorts and crosses his thick arms. "You scare off most of my customers when you visit. Of course you're my least favorite. Ah, at least I can finally rid of my stock of tarts, though, so I suppose you're not the worst this time." Ronan is one of the very few people that have never treated me differently because of my hair or my reputation. He insults me far more than I would allow anyone else, but he knows I won't kill him.

I'd miss his cooking too much.

"Is that right?" I challenge, leaning back in my chair. "Who is it this time, then? I've not met my kill quota for the day yet, so I'll take care of them."

He bursts out laughing while Caspian folds his hands on the table, grinning as he looks between Ronan and me. "Truthfully, Benny has been troublesome in your absence—I wouldn't mind a break from him." I mutter something about Benny being gone by the end of the night, not paying much attention as I watch the prince relax in this new environment. Ronan narrows his eyes, scratching his chin for a moment before saying, "I can never tell if you're being serious or not."

That catches my attention. My eyes snap to the dark irises of his as my forehead creases. "When have I never been serious? I said I'll take care of him, and I will. But first, I'm starving, so we'll have my usual."

The man nods before knocking his knuckles against the table and stating he'll be right back. He pauses mid-turn, looking back at me with obvious concern. "Just so we're clear, I do not want you to kill Benny. It was a joke."

I raise a brow. "And yet I'm not laughing."

I examine Ronan's face as he processes my words. His bright expression falters for just a moment before he forces out a chuckle. "Right, well...I'll go put in your order then." He hurries away, glancing back over his shoulder once before disappearing into the kitchen.

Caspian leans forward, his voice low. "You're not actually going to kill this Benny person, are you?"

I meet his gaze steadily, forcing a smile down. "Why wouldn't I? Ronan said he's been causing trouble."

"But he just said it was a joke," Caspian protests, his brow furrowing.

I shrug, picking up a knife from the table and twirling it between my fingers. "Joke or not, if someone's causing problems for Ronan, they're causing problems for me. And I don't like problems."

The prince opens his mouth, likely to argue further, but I cut him off. "Relax, Caspian. I'm not going to murder some random drunk. Not tonight, anyway." I smirk at the relief that washes over his face. "Besides, we have more important matters to discuss."

He nods, leaning in closer. His aura engulfs me, the rest of the room falling away at his proximity. "Do you really think we'll be able to find them?" *We.* As if I'd permit him to join me.

"I have to," I mutter, my eyes scanning his face. He is far too pretty, and the bastard knows it, smirking at my examination. "I'm unsure of how else we'll get the answers needed otherwise."

I lean back as Ronan returns, setting down plates piled high with steaming food. The aroma of spices and roasted meat fills the air, making my mouth water.

Ronan looks the prince over, raising a brow before addressing me. "Enjoy," he says with a wink before retreating.

Caspian eyes the spread with wonder. "This looks incredible. What is all of this?"

I gesture to each dish as I name them. "Roasted boar with blackberry sauce, herb-crusted potatoes and, of course, the tarts." I pick up one of the flaky pastries, savoring the burst of sweet fruit as I take a bite. My satisfied moan draws the attention of those closest to us—I let them stare. Including Caspian, who bites his lip, looking pained.

"You'd do well to stop making such noises before I disregard my dinner and indulge in the taste of you instead." Heat sparks low in my abdomen, and I nearly squirm in my seat at the promise in the prince's eyes. Fuck, I may continue making those sounds just to see if he follows through.

"Perhaps I'd love to be ravaged by the Prince of Eldoria in the middle of a lesser district tavern." I'm surprised at the breathiness of my voice, though Caspian doesn't comment on it as his lips quirk and he bends forward. A moment later, I jolt from a featherlight touch on my inner thigh. Our table is thin enough that his fingers can trail just to the base of my center.

He continues to tease me, drawing circles around the area, creating an uncomfortable ache in my core. He knows exactly what he's doing to me.

"*Would* you like that, Ariella?" The hunger in his voice is too much—I cannot do this with him. "Because I'll drop to my knees right now. Throw your leg over my shoulder while I hold the other open, and give the entire building a view of what they all dream about, but will never have." Fucking Aether, *his words*. He is so impassioned...something I'm beginning to appreciate. "I'll drink your sweet fucking cum until you're the only thing my body will accept as sustenance. Angel, I'll stay between these exquisite thighs for as long as you'll let me. Just say the word and I'm there, in front of all these people, status be damned."

I am speechless. What do I say to such a confession when I want so badly for him to do everything he just said, but don't want to give in?

I'm too stubborn for my own good.

"That is...intense." What a pathetic response.

He shrugs, pinching the sensitive skin of my inner thigh. "I don't care. I know what I want, and I'll not hide what's mine." I hum, nodding as I lift my glass of water and gulp it down.

"Eat," I whisper, unable to get the word out without needing to clear my throat.

I finish my tart and the prince follows suit, his eyes widening at the taste. "Angel above, these are amazing."

I nod, swallowing. "Of course they are. Now, about the..."

We discuss our plans in hushed tones as we eat, debating the best approach to finding the Palmluvela and what questions to ask once we do—well, once *I* do, but I don't correct him just yet. The food and conversation flow easily, and I find myself relaxing despite the urgency of our mission.

As the night wears on, the crowd in the tavern thins. Ronan stops by every so often to refill our drinks and chat, his earlier wariness seemingly forgotten. He ignores Caspian's title, treating him as he always has me: as just another customer.

As the last patrons stumble out, Caspian leans back with a contented sigh. "Thank you for bringing me here. I've never experienced anything quite like it."

I shrug but can't quite hide my pleased smile. It's impossible to describe the satisfaction inside me at being the one to show the prince of life outside the castle. Why does it feel so good, and why do I want to have more nights just like this?

Shaking my head and ignoring the tightness in my throat, I hand Ronan a few coppers for our meal and grab some tarts to-go. Caspian and I walk the short distance back to the castle in a comfortable silence, alone in our thoughts but surrounded by the company of one other.

He nods to those we pass in the dimly lit halls as we approach our rooms. I consider slitting his throat for asking me to give up one of my tarts, but surprisingly, that thought is just a fleeting thing before I give in.

I reluctantly allow myself a moment to think about how I'm going to miss this when I walk away—this easy, mundane company.

Just a moment before I empty my mind of the feelings and suppress the tingling under my skin. I mutter a goodnight to Caspian before tugging at my umbral strand and undoing the wards along my door.

It's a pity that good things never last.

Chapter Six

Ariella

I turn when Caspian calls for me, halting mid weave. His head tilts as he scrutinizes every inch of my body before his expression settles on something warily. "You weave wards, yeah?" He doesn't wait for an answer before continuing. I'm unsure if he realizes the distance he's closing between us as he idly steps forward. "So you possess the umbral strand..."

He speaks as if this is news to the both of us.

"I do not need a history lesson, prince. What is your point?"

"You use the absence of light—the shadows—to create them, do you not? Show me."

I blink. "Show you what, exactly?" The click of his shoes stops, and his hands slide into the pockets of his pants. He watches me, not with his usual cocky smirk, but with warm eyes and a small tilt of his lips. As if I am something to be cherished instead of a product whose only value is to kill.

"Your shadows. Will you show me?"

"I—" I pause, unsure of how to answer that. See my shadows? I suppose sharing essence is not...uncommon; but aside from my parents, Caspian is the only person who knows I possess all three affinities. And even then, he has no idea that includes every single strand, as well.

But to show him my umbral strand?

I've never presented my forbidden essence to *anyone*. A brief ache in my chest points out the blatant lie. That circumstance was different from this one—I was dying from the griffin's attack, not willingly giving him access to my most sacred secrets. I shift, crossing my arms as I look at anything but the prince.

The questionably rational, defensive part of me is desperate to lash out and deny everything he just said.

But there's a fragile sliver of hope in my soul. A part of me that was lost the moment the life drained from my father's body and soaked into the stone I now walk on. One that the prince—against my entire will—has exposed and nurtured until it was just bright enough for me to notice.

The part of me I ache to feed after having repressed every fucking bit of it for twenty years.

I want to show him my shadows—show him all the essence I possess. The *thought* of just sharing that secret with someone, with him, is already relieving in a way I didn't know I could feel. An ache forms behind my eyes as the steel walls just under my skin retract a little more—an instinctual response to such feelings.

How could I even think about sharing this with him?

Especially after the years Marek spent training me to be the best and most secretive; he's never truly known about my essence, but he's far more intelligent than even I give him credit for. He *knows*. And after my mother and father begged me to keep such things hidden, dying for what I can only assume is the very thing Caspian is asking to see.

Fucking Angel, the air surrounding me has become significantly heavier.

I haven't warred with such...*feelings* in so long that I'm unsure of what to do. I'm frozen, stuck in a loop of right and wrong.

But is it truly so wrong? To crave for just *one* Angel-damned person to carry some of the weight that's been clinging to my shoulders for years? And is it wrong if I want it to be him?

No, it's not.

At least that's what I tell myself before allowing the brittle 'okay' slip through my lips.

I lead him into his room and remove my boots before crawling to the middle of his bed and sitting with my legs crossed. I nod my chin in front of me, directing him to mimic my position.

This goes against everything I've ever known. And yet...

Fuck it.

"Give me your hands," I whisper, holding my palms out in silent invitation. Unlike mine, there is no hesitation in his movements as he wraps his fingers around my wrist. His skin is warm. Soft. The skin of someone who lived their childhood in royal privilege.

It's exactly what I need to calm my raging thoughts and center my focus.

With one last look between his inquisitive eyes, I close mine and tug—

I barely touch my umbral strand before releasing it, wincing as I sink further into myself again.

I need to do this. No, I want to do this. And fuck if I'll allow my past to dictate any choice I make.

No one tells me what to do. Not even myself, apparently.

After a few deep breaths, the heaviness in my chest lifts as my mind falls into the calm I thrive in during assignments. The kind of calm that pushes me forward and is confident instead of hesitant in all decisions.

I reach for my umbral strand once more and coax the shadows out from beneath my skin, relaxing at their cool touch. The hitch of the prince's breath is the only encouragement I need to pull them out fully. I can't quite grasp how I feel as I open my eyes and take in his shocked expression in front of me. He watches the tendrils of my essence slide over my arms and around my torso, as if they are greeting me with the lightest of hugs.

I know they are not sentient, but there is certainly more to them than being just the absence of light that I bend to my will. They feel almost...*full.*

I absorb every small detail of Caspian's reaction as the shadows drift to his hands and caress his arms. He seems to be in pure disbelief, laughing softly and watching as the essence studies him. My brows furrow. I didn't expect him to be scared, but I also did not expect him to be so happy and open to forbidden essence touching him.

It is against his father's laws, after all.

Laws that he's been raised to one day uphold.

The shadows seem to have a chosen path, swirling around him playfully. The feel of the prince's body is distracting as they mold to each ridge of muscle. I've always appreciated this little quirk about the shadows—they are almost an extension of me; as if I had extra limbs that I used to feel the realm around me. I send a tendril to capture his throat, tightening until I feel his pulse as a phantom of touch under my fingers. It's beating almost as fast as mine.

But that's not all I sense—no, there's something...more? If the shadows had the capability to feel, I'd describe their current state as fondness. Their aura seeps with an air of familiarity, as if they recognize the human they're exploring.

"This is incredible," Caspian whispers to himself. His movements lock me in a trance as he pulls a hand back to run his fingers along the different tendrils circling him.

And what a sight it is to see.

Image of Ariella showing Caspian her shadows.

I clear my throat when heat builds deep inside my abdomen. I'm utterly fascinated by the view before me. I hadn't considered how it would affect me to watch my essence slide across the prince's body. To *feel* every detail they do—places that my own hands have yet to explore.

Caspian grins as he continues to dote on the shadows, and if I did not know any better, I'd suspect they were blushing at his attention. The areas he focuses on darken under his scrutiny, but they do not express any negative sentiments, so I leave them to explore.

I sweep a finger upward, coaxing a tendril to spread through his hair. I've always preferred my ethereal affinity to the others. The strands in those affinities weave essence from land and objects outside of my body, whereas those in the ethereal affinity weave from the essence that resides *inside* me; I'm unsure of where, though the humming—what I believe is my essence—feels to be as close to my soul as it could be.

That was a long and difficult lesson that I struggled with in the guild. Even as a child, I knew the importance of not exposing my ethereal affinity. So when the time came to train the essence listed on official documents, I took much longer than the other children to grasp that the strands I used did not weave from the essence inside of me. They came to life through the essence offered by the realm. Learning to weave entirely out of my body, relying on my surroundings, was disconcerting. Frustrating.

And sitting here with the prince, watching him marvel over the essence as if it hasn't been the single most threatening thing about my existence, it feels almost the same. Frustrating, strange, overwhelming. Fuck, if someone told me before the competition that I'd be sharing such intimacies with the heir of Eldoria, I'd have slit their throat just for uttering such nonsense.

An unfamiliar sensation ripples through me.

"Ariella, I ca—" His sentence cuts off abruptly as I do something I've refused to for years.

Something I'm making a problem for the future, more rational side of me.

But right now? I need to do this.

I tug on my psionic strand and melt the essence into Caspian's head the moment I catch his eye.

Don't speak, I instruct his body, fascinated with the way his mouth continues to form words, but no sound leaves his lips. It's almost amusing—the degree in which his eyes widen in my direction.

Ideas swirl through my head and...*Oh.* I never considered just how fun my essence could be.

My lip quirks in time with his rising heart rate. I've long wondered if others could feel my essence claiming their bodies as my own, though it seems not if Caspian's reaction is to be believed. He's looking at me as if he's worried I will experience whatever ailment has overtaken him. His hands snap to his throat, and I don't like that. I don't like that at all.

I desire to command his body and bend it to my will until he submits to me in the way he was born to do. His mind, his body, his soul—they're mine. Created by the Angel itself to complement every jagged edge of my existence. He was made to worship every part of me, and I am deeply satisfied when I remember that he already does. His essence calls to me, calls *for* me, in the way it was meant to, Aether be damned.

I need to feel him. The writhing presence growing under my skin will not wait much longer. It demands we complete what has only been half-forged.

It takes not even a mere thought before my shadows wrap around his torso and drag his body back against the headboard. His immediate panic wars with the heat clouding his gaze as he watches me like I am the most fascinating creature he will ever see.

I am.

Shh, I call to his mind with the link I've created. *Your panic is misplaced, Cas.* I lean forward on my hands, crawling over his stiffening legs onto his lap. I sit straddling his thighs, close enough that our chests press together. I sigh at the relief inside me that's been building from the distance between us. *You know who I am, Aetarys...I would never hurt you,* I whisper into his mind.

I lift a hand to trace my fingers down his cheeks before pinching his chin, forcing him to hold my stare. "Only the fools who *would* hurt you."

You may speak, I drawl, amused when his mouth opens to do just that.

But I do not want his words. No, I want to taste the sounds I'm going to wring from his body.

I close the minuscule distance between our lips, melting into him when he moans just how I imagined. His hands slide over my hips and, though I crave his touch, my shadows encircle his wrists and flatten the full length of his arms to the headboard. I smile into our kiss when he tugs against his restraints, thoroughly enjoying the hardness growing under me. My hands run through his soft strands of hair and pull his head back. I chuckle when I find his wide pupils, puffy, wet lips, and heated cheeks.

Image of Ariella's shadows holding Caspian.

His brows scrunch. "Ariella," he barely utters my name, just as breathless as me. I'm pleased with how much I affect him. "Your hair." My gaze slides down to my breasts, already knowing what I will find but humoring him, regardless. Silver covers my chest, the strands emitting the faintest glow between the dark clothing we both are still wearing.

I need to fix the latter.

But I pause my focus on the buttons of his shirt when he manages to pull a wrist from one of my restraints. *Yes*—I need him here with me. His fingers trail through my hair, the cause of his confusion, moments before I see what I've been waiting for: the suppressed half of his nature awakening in his eyes.

"There you are," I purr, my core fluttering over the responsive twitch of his straining cock. I cannot contain the need for connection much longer. "Caspian." The name snaps him from his daze, and my hunger for him grows feral the moment those irises meet mine. "Your eyes," I whisper, basking in the glowing rings of silver before diving for his mouth once more.

I invade his lips with my tongue roughly. My body is prepared to bury itself inside him and finish what we started mere weeks ago.

We've waited too long already. It's not natural and pulverizes our bodies and minds each day we delay.

My fingers tug his head back until his neck is exposed to me. I lick from his lips to his ear before dragging my tongue down the crease of his throat until I reach the crevice that connects to his shoulder. My center clenches at the guttural moan that leaves him when I touch the sensitive spot, the sound radiating through my very soul and forcing me on. I gently lick the spot and smile into his reddened skin when he arches his head back even further.

Every nerve in my body ignites when I graze my teeth over his skin as they beg me to continue. I listen. My jaw clamps down on his neck, the taut skin aiding my need to break through it.

But I don't.

My teeth are not quite sharp enough in this body to force through without immense pressure, and it takes me a few moments to realize I'm whining from the build-up of *something* I feel inside me. I need to release it. I must give it to Caspian, but I do not wish to harm him.

Before I can pull away, one of his hands connects with the back of my head, pushing me further into him. "Do it," he mutters so quietly I almost miss the words over our heavy breathing. My stomach flutters—I could *live* in the desire seeping through his voice.

Any hesitations I had about hurting my prince melt away at his command, so there is no more time to waste. I bite. Hard. It takes more effort than I'd hoped, but Caspian's hold on me is so tight that I know I couldn't stop even if I wanted to. The give of his skin is the catalyst for the deep, animalistic groans that fill the room.

I would not be able to confirm who is making what sound; I'm far too gone in the hot liquid that coats my tongue. In claiming him. My entire body shudders, and I almost come at the taste of his blood. My prince—so in harmony with every part of me—clutches my hips hard enough to bruise before grinding me down over his cock. But it's not enough.

None of this is enough.

I pull my mouth back to capture his eyes. "I need you to fuck me." My demand is a whisper over his lips, and I move to reach for the buttons of his pants only to wrap my hand around the length of his bare dick.

"What?" I mutter to myself before snapping my eyes downward.

How the fuck are we both naked? My head wars with itself, both sides fighting for dominance.

"It doesn't matter, sit up," the prince orders, forcing all questions to the back of my mind. I lift myself, allowing him to rub the head of his cock through my arousal before pausing at my entrance. His eyes hold mine as something playful and wicked flashes through their depths. "Now sit the fuck down." I shiver from the possessiveness dripping off him.

Before I can comply, he snatches my waist and shoves me down until he's buried to the hilt. My head drops back from the immense, overwhelming pleasure that radiates throughout my body. I have *never* felt like this before.

I eagerly follow his lead and slide him in and out of my core at the tempo he sets with his hands, his fingers trembling against my skin, though he holds tight. Honestly, I'm not sure I could pry his grip from me right now—he's holding me as if his life will end the moment he lets go.

My eyes slide to the minute space between our gleaming chests, slick with sweat and something a little more delicious.

His blood, I remind myself.

Caspian glares at my breasts with an intense hunger, bending forward to catch a drop of crimson that must have escaped my mouth.

Pity—I wanted all of it for myself.

But that disappointment lasts for only a moment before the prince's tongue slides up my breast to the crevice of my throat. A pounding need overcomes me, and I know that what he's about to do will be more pleasurable than anything in this life. His thrusts increase, faltering slightly. It feels as though he cannot control his body—as though he has succumbed to the force of this moment, lost amongst the infinite amount of places our bodies connect.

"*Yes.* Fuck, my prince, *please,*" I beg, the sound ardent and desperate, and tilt my head back in complete submission. I have been waiting for this very moment for *so long.* Too long. And now it will finally be complete.

His teeth drag over my skin, and hair rises along my arms. The anticipation may ruin me. Bless the Angel, he does not make me wait long. His jaw opens and prepares to bite down; to take what we need to—

My eyes fly open as a piece of reality breaks through the haze. "Stop!" I shove at his chest, darting off his lap and crawling backward with my hands until I feel like I can breathe again. He makes no move for me, even as my shadows sink into his skin, releasing him—it appears we are both just as confused.

His wide, horror-stricken eyes meet mine for a heartbeat before they home in on my mouth.

Where his blood dries.

The blood I sucked from his neck.

Against every bit of my pleading stomach, I look down at his neck to find the small, round wounds I caused still oozing. The fucking wounds I *ached* to cause—the same ones Caspian *begged* me to cause.

I'm going to be sick.

I slap a hand over my mouth just in time to hold in the gagging. I fumble with the blankets on the prince's bed, nearly shredding them into non-existence, and start running to his bathroom. The rate at which my abdomen is spinning...

I'm almost there, one hand still stuck to my lips while the other holds my breasts, lest I pull a fucking muscle running without support. I could heal it in a moment, but I'd rather not have something else to think about right now. The door to Caspian's bedroom swings open, and Gavriel practically falls through the doorway, followed by another sentry.

I will never speak about how this is the first time in my life I have felt self-conscious of my naked body.

Gavriel's jaw drops while the prince says words I cannot focus on. "What is going on? We've been trying to break down the door since I heard glass shattering! Whe—" The guard pauses his rant as he looks between Caspian and me, his face the picture of incredulity. "Did you fucking *bite* him?"

I gag once more, turning toward the bathroom just as something wraps around my shoulders. A blanket, I think—a small kindness that I do not deserve. I barely reach the toilet before retching violently. Red liquid splatters against the porcelain, the sight of it causing me to heave even harder.

"What did she do to you, Caspian?" Gavriel's shout is so loud I'm certain half the castle—no, half of Valoria—can hear him. "I'll fucking kill her." There's a loud crash following the guard's declaration, though I don't look to see what has happened. My stomach is giving me a break, and I will rest my forehead against the cool tile on the floor until I die. There's nothing left for me to do in this life if this is how I'll feel.

Fuck, I sound like a whining child. But...have I ever been sick before?

My mind runs through years of memories, a needed distraction from the soul-consuming nausea that hasn't been relieved by throwing up every organ in my body. I shift slightly—no, I have never once gotten sick. Especially not to the taste or sight of blood.

"You will not touch her, Gavriel. Take Benson to the pit with you." Caspian's calm, assured voice settles me a little. But not enough that I'm confident I could sit up without another round of my face in the toilet. "If you *ever* speak against her like that again, the pit will seem like a fucking blessing compared to what I will do to you. Leave." Gavriel mutters several things too quiet for me to hear before barking at Benson to get out of the door. The slam of it startles me, but I keep my face pressed into the tile.

How have I never appreciated the therapeutic effects of it before? It feels *so nice.*

It only occurs to me how ridiculous I must look curled up on the floor of Caspian's bathroom when his footsteps get louder. "Ari," he murmurs, his voice much softer than it was just moments ago. "Are you okay?" I peek through my lashes and find him crouching next to me with nothing but concern on his face. I can tell he wants to touch me, to comfort me in the affectionate way he's so accustomed to, but doesn't. Instead, he locks his fingers together and waits for something.

Oh, right, he spoke to me.

"I'm fine," I croak, rolling to my back to look at him better. "Just nauseous, but it's going away." I take a deep breath, wincing. I need to clean my mouth—I taste disgusting.

Actually, if I'm being truthful with myself, the taste in my mouth is pure bliss. Something I could get addicted to.

It's the realization that is disgusting. How in the Aether could I ever think the taste of *blood* is...

I cannot even finish that thought.

"Can you heal it?"

I'm shaking my head before he's even finished speaking. "No, there's nothing to heal other than my own revulsion of drinking—" I groan, squeezing my eyes shut. I must stop thinking about it before I begin retching once again.

"My blood," the prince breathes into the tepid air. I look over at him as he leans against the wall and slides to the floor. "What the fuck was that, Ariella? Why did you do it? And why did I *want* you to?" He grimaces, his face contorting to a wince when he runs his fingers along the bite I made.

"Do you think I know what just happened? As if I gallivant around ripping people's necks open with my teeth?" He stiffens in my peripheral, sighing before relaxing once more.

"Well maybe I'm wrong, but you sounded like you knew exactly what you were doing. And then I suddenly was there, but not?" He says it like a question, one I have no answer for. I sit up and stand in one motion, reaching for the sink to rinse my mouth out. I don't answer him, instead walking back into the bedroom in search of my clothes.

A memory flashes through my head of how confused I felt when we were clothed one second and naked the next. I have no recollection of removing anything.

I need to leave.

I need space to *think*.

My jaw drops, my stomach sinking further at the sight of his room. I pause, too aware of when Caspian halts mere inches behind me. "By the Angel," he breathes, echoing the horror I feel in myself.

How did this happen?

Pieces of wood that were once the prince's desk cover the floor. The blankets I struggled to leave just minutes ago are black, as if they'd been burnt through. My head spins as I look down and note the smeared soot across my thighs.

Each lamp attached to the walls is shattered, leaving behind only the mounts that can no longer do anything but darken my confusion. The tapestry above Caspian's bed is unrecognizable—shredded to pieces, with only a few threads left hanging. I grimace at the state of his bed, the frame severely damaged and unable to hold the mattress any longer.

Now sit the fuck down.

It isn't something I wish to acknowledge, but the memory of a faint cracking follows his words. Did we do this?

Stupid fucking question—who else would have?

I'm certainly in full control of my essence, having held him against the wall while we fucked, which makes everything I'm seeing even more unclear.

Something heavy settles at the front of my mind. I try, but fail, to grasp it. I cannot tell what it is, but it feels important. Like the reason all of this happened.

I back away from the devastation, heart racing, mind swirling like a tempest. The walls feel too thick, closing in around me, and I need to escape. "I can't," I whisper, the words barely escaping my lips as I turn and push through the door. The hallway outside is too quiet, shadows waiting in every corner, mocking me with their stillness.

Footsteps echo behind me—Caspian is following, his persistent presence a weight on my shoulders. "Ariella," he calls, but I don't stop. The need to find comfort in his arms is primal, clawing at me like a thing alive and hungry; and I will not allow myself to indulge again.

I storm toward my room, fingers brushing against the cool metal handle of my door as if it could provide solace.

"Ariella!" His voice sharpens into a commanding tone that feels foreign in this moment. "You can't just leave without talking about this!"

I spin to face him, fury igniting under my skin like fire. "You think talking will change what just happened? That we can dissect our mess like some kind of twisted science experiment?" My voice rises above the plangent emptiness of the hall. "We destroyed your room! We—" Fuck, my eyes are burning. I swallow past the lump in my throat before finally meeting Caspian's eyes and taking several breaths. "Can we talk in the morning?" I shouldn't need his permission, but I want it, anyway.

The emotion in his gaze is heavy enough to weaken my resolve, but he moves before I can say anything else. Stepping forward, he grabs the back of my head and pulls me into his chest. I draw his scent into my lungs and let the simplicity of this moment calm me. He presses a kiss to the top of my head before stepping back to offer me a warm smile.

Suddenly all my eyes can think about is falling into bed—

"Your bed...it's ruined."

He chuckles, shaking his head. "Don't worry about it. If you hadn't noticed, there are hundreds of bedrooms here—I'll be fine. Get some rest, angel." He swipes his thumb down my lips before spinning back toward the destruction of his room.

Chapter Seven

Ariella

I fasten the last buckle on my travel bag, the sound sharp in the otherwise silent room. My fingers hesitate over my father's journal, lying half-hidden beneath a pile of maps on my desk. Its worn cover is rough against my fingertips, the edges frayed from years of handling, from the nights I clutch it too tightly. I should bring it...perhaps whatever I find in the forest will give me the context I need to understand some of the entries.

My gaze shifts to the window. The darkness outside is still thick, untouched by the exposing sun. I've risen early, but not just because of my restless thoughts. It's because I have no intention of letting Caspian follow me into the Verdantia Forest. He's been adamant about joining me, but the risk of this journey is one he doesn't need to take. The stubborn bastard won't understand, but I couldn't fucking care less. He doesn't need to understand. And after yesterday, I'm not inclined to give him my attention so that we may talk about what happened.

How would I even discuss such a thing? It's difficult to talk through something you barely remember. Pieces of it flow through my mind, but they're scrambled and confusing.

I swing my pack over my shoulder, the weight molding to my back. My steps are soft against the tile as I move toward the door, careful not to disturb the eerie silence of the castle. I need to visit the guild before heading to the forest, but I can't think about why, not yet. There's a heaviness inside me that feels like a promise I have yet to fulfill.

I reach for the door handle, my fingers cracking it open not an inch before a voice cuts through my sanity.

"You really thought you'd get away that easily?"

I freeze, my heart lodging itself somewhere between annoyance and reserved amusement. Caspian leans against the opposite wall, a smug smirk curling his lips, his arms folded casually across his chest, clad in fitted black leather. The material molds to his frame, emphasizing his muscular build and tapering down to a narrow waist. His pants, also dark leather, sit low on his hips and hug the same thighs I was all too happy to grind against just hours ago. Despite the unfamiliarity of the leathers, as he normally wears more formal clothing, he manages to look both lethal and impossibly attractive. The outfit only amplifies the danger in his gaze as he watches me with a knowing smirk.

"Nice try, angel," he continues, the nickname rolling off his tongue in that infuriatingly familiar way. I like it far too much. "But I knew you'd venture to sneak out without me."

I force my face into an expression of boredom, even as an unwelcome giddiness pricks under my skin. "Go back to bed, Caspian. You do not need to be involved in this."

"Actually, I do," he states, pushing off the wall and closing the distance between us. "We've been over this—I go where you go."

"Not this time." My voice is sharp, colder than I intend. "This isn't your mystery to solve." But fuck do I want it to be right now.

"Isn't it?" He steps closer, his proximity making it harder to think clearly. "I will not waste time arguing with you, Ariella. You're not going into that damn forest alone—not a fucking chance."

I draw my blade, the metal flashing in the dim light as I press it against his stomach, just above the scar I gave him. His smirk doesn't falter; if anything, it deepens.

"This is not up for debate," I growl, keeping my grip steady. "You're staying here, Caspian."

"Do it," he purrs, and the heat of his breath slides down my abdomen. "But don't you dare miss this time, angel, because that is the only way you will go alone."

I hate how his words send a shiver into my spine. How they claw at my carefully constructed walls. I press the blade a fraction harder, cursing my mind as his eyes darken. There's no fear there, only a glimmer of excited amusement—a dangerous kind of determination that mirrors my own.

"Fuck's sake, prince," I mutter, dropping the blade to my side and pressing my finger into the sharp metal. "Fine. But if you get yourself hurt—"

"I won't," he interrupts, the smile returning, softer this time. "I've got you to keep me alive, remember?" Fucking tease.

I roll my eyes but don't argue. This battle is already lost, and we both know it. I pivot toward my door, my heart still hammering, and weave enough wards to keep out even the Angel. Overkill, but whatever. We navigate the empty halls of the castle before running into a sentry that follows us from the entrance, insisting that he was ordered to join our small party. I offer him a glare that he impressively doesn't cower from and allow Caspian to take care of his father's foolish meddling.

I adjust the straps of my bag, fingers moving with practiced efficiency as I attempt to suppress the frustration simmering under my skin. The sky above is still dark, the pre-dawn light peeking through the heavy mist that clings to Valoria like a damp, unwelcome cloak. It's cold, but the chill doesn't touch me—my mind is far too tangled to feel the temperature. I glance across the courtyard at Caspian, chuckling at the heated exchange he and the guard are having. His brow is furrowed, and his voice is low but forceful, carrying just enough urgency to lend credibility to his excuse.

"Medicinal herbs," he mutters in explanation, as if anyone is supposed to believe that's the real reason we're venturing into the Verdantia Forest. But he has a way with words, and the guard seems to buy it, nodding reluctantly before stepping aside.

The king must have insisted on another sentry accompanying us when Caspian informed him that he would be gone for a few days. Why? I'm unsure of what Thalion said when they spoke, but thankfully, the prince seems to have more sway over most of the royal guards than his father does.

I tilt my head, watching as Caspian approaches with that same confident stride he always carries. The leather satchel slung over his shoulder looks heavy, its contents a mix of rations, herbs, and whatever else he deemed necessary for this excursion.

"Ready?" he asks, his voice a bit too casual for the situation. I can't decide if it's because he's trying to convince me he's ready or if it's some self-soothing mantra he's using to prepare for our journey.

I nod, peering over my shoulder at the guard who stands rigid, watching us. We don't linger. I pull my cloak tighter, breathing easier at the comforting weight of my hidden blades within its folds. Caspian walks beside me as we move toward the northern gate, past the fountain, our footsteps echoing off the cobblestones.

The guild stands like an omen at the center of the city, its stone facade both inviting and memory-inducing. I hesitate at the threshold, the familiar creak of the heavy oak door scraping against my nerves. This place once felt like home—a sanctuary filled with promises of revenge, training, and the thrill of sparring with—

I pause to suppress the increasing demands of my lungs.

Now, every corner is shrouded with the pieces of Isaiah's skin I watched float in the reddened water, as if the walls themselves are stained with his blood. I step up to the door slowly, each one a betrayal of the girl I used to be. Determined, loyal, ready to protect the two people in the world left that meant something to me.

What a fucking joke I am.

The heavy wooden door creaks open at my touch, releasing a faint hint of spices and smoke that wraps around me with such familiarity that I falter. Memories flood my mind—flashes of training, blood-stained leathers, and hundreds of injuries I had to let heal naturally.

"Are you waiting outside?" I blurt, stretching my fingers out over my thighs.

"No—but I would have you show me around. I've never been in one of the kingdom's guilds before."

I chuckle and wrench the door open fully—the same one I kicked off its hinges just a few weeks ago.

Fuck. *Everything* reminds me of him.

"I'm sure the students will be delighted to see their prince." Not entirely a lie, though I won't pretend I don't anticipate the backlash I'll receive for bringing him here.

We step into the main area, and I thank the Angel that it's empty. Traveling early does have its perks. I lock hands behind my back and pivot to my left, watching as Caspian takes in the space. From a simple look, the guild appears as just a home for the children who do not have one. But with just a little focus, the other purpose of the guild hides in plain sight.

Schedules hang on the wall, one for those who are only students and one for those like me, who have far more blood lust than mere textbooks can satiate. Our schedule is more rigorous than the normal students—we are expected to remain at the same education level while succeeding in combat lessons.

It has always felt like two separate worlds venturing to coexist together. The regular students kept their questions to themselves and paid no mind to the bloodied clothes and skin my side would often return to the guild with. And for that, none of them ever met my blade.

Well, it was mainly at Marek's request after I threatened Eli a few times and he ran to my mentor crying like the pathetic idiot he is.

"This..." Caspian pauses, his tone hesitant. "This is not what I was expecting."

I blink. Of course he wasn't—I know the stories that are told.

"Ahh, you thought that you'd walk right into a dungeon, where there was so little light that you couldn't see the ground in front of you, but enough light that you'd see layers of bloodstains on the wall from years of us keeping and torturing prisoners."

His brows scrunch together as he chews on his lip and hums to himself.

"Fucking Aether, you did think that," I groan, walking through the main room toward the labyrinth that travels through the rest of the building. "Don't worry, my innocent prince, the dungeon is downstairs. What a waste of space it would be to have it here—and quite inconvenient, as we're right next to the street."

"I cannot tell if you're being truthful or sarcastic."

I whirl on him, not needing to feign my outrage. "Why would I lie about that? I need somewhere that will hide the screams of those I'm seeking answers from—the main floor is not sound-proof and there would be fucking riots if people *heard* the torture." I must be in a mood this morning as I continue, my voice sounding as disgusted as I feel. "They may know what this place is, Caspian, but they are not privy to what happens inside its walls. They're able to sit comfortable in their willful ignorance because they've never been forced to witness the truth of what they already know. Until they see it with their own eyes, it doesn't exist to them and they have no moral obligation to do anything about it."

I suck in a deep breath before nodding behind me. "Back to our tour."

I point to the various rooms as we walk, keeping my pace slow so he can take in the details as if there is anything but plain walls and basic decor. Caspian's gaze lingers on the weapons mounted along the walls of the training room—swords, different sized blades, and spears, each one worn from use.

The prince speaks to me, but my ability to hear is muddled by the heavy weight on my chest when I stare at the mat in the center of the room. When I was here the last week, I refused to spar Desmond in this room. I certainly would not divulge that coming in here would break me just as much as where I'm about to go, so I would make excuses: *I need fresh air, we can spar outside. It's too cramped in there, the common area would suit our needs better.*

But seeing it now—it hurts.

I must get weaker by the day. I have not allowed any of the recent events to cloud my thoughts or goals up until the last few days. It's as if the block I spent years building is crumbling, falling apart one grain at a time, letting in fragments of things I would kill to never think about again.

And here? There are far too many memories clinging to each of the walls. The weapons. The fucking mat. My fingers twitch with the urge to grab a weapon, to relive the motions that are instinctive at this point.

As a child, this room was my entire world. This was the place where I'd learn everything I needed to get justice for my father. This is where I would look into the eyes of each person that I fought and imagine they were the king's. My rage built this into what it is today as I spent more time in here than I did elsewhere. Years of marks and chips line every surface of the room, where they will remain long after I have left the realm.

This was what kept my mind from falling apart—it may have been fractured, but everything that happened in here was the glue holding those pieces together, offering me a purpose in this life.

This is where Isaiah and I had our happiest memories.

And I never want to see it again.

I spin to stalk back through the door with the prince on my heels, barking out places we pass but allowing him no time to discern all the minute pieces of the past that created who I am now. Before I realize, I'm standing in front of a bedroom.

Not mine. The one next to it.

"You will wait here." My instruction to the prince is barely audible, but harsh enough that he doesn't question as I push open the door to my best friend's room and step inside. There's a faint click as the door closes, leaving me alone in the space I forbid *anyone* from entering—including Marek.

I wasn't planning to ever see the walls of Isaiah's room again, but he had always kept our *hunting gear*—as we'd call it—and I need the supplies for my trip through the forest.

Our trip, I remind myself. Stubborn fool of a prince.

My chest tightens, but I force myself forward. This is not a time to be weak. Not now, not here.

The room feels colder than I remember, and I shiver as bumps raise along my arms. I take a slow, deliberate step forward, my eyes skimming over the familiar chaos Isaiah never bothered to tidy. Books are scattered across the floor, some still open to pages marked with smudges of ink—likely from nights we spent scrawling notes when Marek insisted we complete our assigned schoolwork.

My gaze drifts to the corner of the room, where a faded towel hangs over the back of an old wooden chair. It's streaked a dull, muddy brown, the color uneven as if someone had tried to wash out a stubborn stain but gave up halfway. I chuckle—he was always so messy.

I move past the bed and step toward the far wall, where a chest rests beneath a faded tapestry that's filled with a crimson forest under a starry sky, the trees seeming to flow impossibly together. Bending to open the chest, the wood creaks before revealing the contents within.

Just what I needed.

I pull out a weathered tent, compact but reliable, with iron stakes that could use refreshing. After stuffing the tent and two water packs into my bag, my fingers reach for the cloak folded at the bottom. Its ratty fabric is enough to disorient me as Isaiah's scent drifts into the air, stronger than the rest of the room. My eyes burn, and I bite my inner cheek until my teeth jerk from the tear of the sensitive skin.

My mind has been far too unfocused, but with every breath I take in this moment, the desperate rage that consumed me when I found Isaiah's body builds once more. Thalion has taken *everyone* from me that he can—not his son, of course, lest he lose his heir and give the throne to a woman when his daughter reaches the proper age.

I have a king to kill, family to avenge, and answers to find.

With that reminder, I set the cloak back in the chest and stalk toward the door, ready to find the Palmluvela and get this fucking trip over with.

The king has a date with my blade, so I best not keep him waiting much longer.

Chapter Eight

Ariella

My feet pause at Isaiah's door when a feminine voice filters through, and I press my ear against the wood to make out the words.

"I just can't believe *the prince* is here! Would you like a tour? I could show you our classrooms, training room, where the other bedrooms are..." Isolde. That bitch. She emphasizes the last two words in what I'm sure she believes to be a sultry voice.

I have the sudden urge to rush out of the room and drive my blade into her pathetic ass until she's bleeding out at Caspian's feet.

But I wait, curious of what the prince will respond with.

"That is kind of you, but I must decline—" He halts mid sentence, silently requesting her name.

"Oh! Angel, I'm over here babbling and didn't even have the manners to introduce myself. My name is Isolde."

"Then, I must decline, Isolde. I've already been given a tour." I chew on my bottom lip, quite pleased with the royal mask he's donned for this interaction.

"Oh, okay." She sounds disappointed—good. "Why are you out here, anyway? This room is no longer occupied since the student died. A waste, really, but that's all Ariella leaves in her path: blood and death. Honestly, I have no idea how he was her friend for so many years. I've always said he was coerced into keeping her company since she's never had anyone else. Oh, sorry, you would know her as the Silver Wraith. Stay away if you ever see her. She will just ruin your life. She deserved what happened to Isaia—"

I throw the door open so hard it cracks, and before she can even blink, my hand is around her throat, pulling her back just to slam her body against the wall. There's a satisfying snap of bone, where I'm sure I fractured her skull. She attempts to scream, but my fingers trap the air in her lungs.

It's difficult to keep the smirk from my face when sweet blood begins dripping from her nose and right ear. Her head must be bleeding as well, but her unwashed, frizzy hair will soak that up first.

My next words are laced with so much venom it shocks even me. "I should kill you just for daring to speak Isaiah's name." Her eyes flick to Caspian, a desperate plea shining through them. "The prince won't save you. Actually, look in his direction again and I will rip your throat out with my teeth and fuck him in your blood. I don't fucking care about Marek's rules—your right to stay alive is no longer anyone's decision but mine. Do. You. Understand?"

A tear falls from her eye, creating a path through the blood that coats half of her face. Her lips are turning blue, but I wait until she attempts to nod before releasing her. She doubles over before coughing hard, spitting pooled up blood and saliva on the floor.

I spin to grab Caspian's hand—Isolde will find a healer herself; and if she doesn't, I'll be disappointed for missing her final breaths. The prince stares at the sputtering mess on the floor with his brows raised, not noticing my outstretched hand. I cannot discern how he feels about my little performance, but he'll get over it. This is the consequence of him entertaining other women.

My hand snatches his and tugs him down the hall. I release my grip once we're walking down the stairs toward the common area.

"I don't know what you've done to me, angel. I shouldn't be painfully hard from your threatening aura...and yet here I am."

A laugh slips out before I can stop it—the things he says are so strange. I peer over my shoulder, my eyes making a show of examining his dick. "Stay hard. We have places to be."

"One of these days I'm going to bend you over the nearest surface and fuck you until you lose your Angel-damned attitude." I freeze and swallow past the heat in my throat.

The man isn't afraid to say anything that flits through his mind. It's so refreshing.

My heels cross and spin me to face the prince, who's a few steps up, leaving me nearly eye-level with the obvious bulge in his pants. Maybe I should let him do just what he promised...

"Is that so?" I breathe, not confident in my ability to speak normally.

He drops the remaining steps between us, pinching the hem of my top and running those icy fingers along the base of my abdomen. Something tingles down the back of my neck. "I really love the fire inside of you. The way you fight everything I say even when your soul is *begging* you to give into me and your feelings." He hums when his free hand rubs a thumb over my breast, and I know he's feeling the hardened evidence of my reaction to his words. "You mask your desire so beautifully, but your body makes you a liar, Ariella. You want me as I crave you, and it's just a matter of time before you let go of whatever is holding you back."

I blink. I haven't the faintest idea of how to respond, because he's right. I can admit to the deepest parts of myself that I want him so badly it turns my stomach, but will I confess such asininity out loud? Never.

He smiles, the happiness glimmering in his eyes enough to keep me here under his charm-addled will. "It's okay—I'll get you to acknowledge it, eventually."

"Not likely, prince."

It is curious...my entire life I've struggled to maintain eye contact with anyone, even my parents. When I seek to intimidate or engage in conversation, I find myself focusing on the space around others' eyes. But Caspian? I could stare into the silver depths of his for years and never once feel uncomfortable or intensely nauseous.

Such an anomaly must be studied.

What is it about him that challenges everything I'd thought I knew about myself? Why does he affect me *so much*? The bastard is borderline obsessed and just as possessive as I feel.

Unwanted scrutiny floods my mind, my feet shifting under the prince's gaze, and I can't help but think back to how things used to be. I've always thrived in routines—sharp, predictable, and un-yielding. They were my armor, allowing me to maintain control and focus on my goals without distraction. I preferred solitude, finding comfort in the silence that others often found unbearable. It was easier to exist that way...moving through life with singular purpose, unbothered by the noise of others' needs and emotions. Even Isaiah never disrupted my ways, instead melding himself into my life, complementing all that I was.

But Caspian? He's disrupted everything. His relentless pursuit of me has shaken the foundation I've spent years solidifying. His presence pulls at me, constantly contesting my resolve and throwing off my plans. I hate how unsettled I feel now—he's upended the very structure I've lived comfortably on for years.

And yet, instead of losing myself to the uncertainty of my life changing, he calms that part of me. His insistence has kept me grounded, providing me the level mind I've desperately needed.

He's both my villain and my redemption.

My destruction and its savior.

The assassin, destroyed by the same prince she once drove her blade into.

A finger taps on each of my thighs as I open my mouth to respond. "Ariella?" Marek's voice pierces the tension, and I drop back into the reality I keep finding myself distracted from.

Caspian hesitates to lower his hands before I turn to descend the remaining stairs, where my mentor waits with a look that says, *what the fuck is the prince doing here?*

"He's with me," I confirm to no one in particular. We reach the main floor, and Marek steps back two paces, crossing his arms. His eyes narrow as they dart between Caspian and me, inspecting every detail.

He nods to my guest before speaking once more. "Why are you here? And why is it you've brought the prince?" he questions me as if Caspian isn't right here, but if the prince is bothered by the blatant dismissal, he doesn't show it.

It is clear Marek is pissed at me walking Eldorian royalty into the guild, but I do not answer to him anymore. I haven't for years—my conformity has been but a choice. One he does not dictate.

I shrug. "I needed something from Isaiah's room." He watches me for a minute, seeming to debate whether pressing me on the topic is worth it. He knows I will not hurt him, but he also knows better than to provoke me.

Whispers filter through the air—an audience of whom I do not wish to have right now. Marek hears them as well, nodding his head back. "My office." I motion for Caspian to walk ahead of me, not trusting any of these bitches to not pull a stunt like Isolde's.

Money and power corrupt even the best of us, so I've no doubt some of the students are already salivating at the thought of exploiting the prince's status.

We step inside my mentor's unaltered office, and I click the door closed before dropping into one of the two plush chairs across from Marek's. He leans forward, resting his elbows on the desk.

"Okay, what's going on?"

"I'm not sure what you mean. I told you last week about what I was seeking." I chose to not disclose the full truth until I have more information to give, so he still only knows the basics. I pin Caspian with a look that tells him to keep his damn mouth shut. Marek does not need to be privy to everything we're looking for until we ourselves know what it is. He'll just worry and insist on including himself—unacceptable, as I'd be forced to watch over two people, which would remove my focus from the task at hand.

Marek sighs, the lines around his eyes crinkling as he chuckles. "You don't have to be so difficult, Ariella. More-so than usual, I might add." He points a finger at me before speaking once more. "What are you doing with the prince? Is he forcing you into anything?"

Caspian huffs a breath. "I'm right here—what if I *was* forcing her? Why ask that in front of me, then?" Marek and I burst out laughing, and the prince looks as shocked as ever.

"Respectfully, Your Highness," Marek starts, amusement laced in each word, "you wouldn't make it out of your seat before she had your head on the floor."

Caspian hums appreciatively, nodding. "That is true," he mumbles to himself while Marek seems to solidify something.

"Are you two...*together?*"

Oh, do I love making him uncomfortable. "If by together you mean am I fucking him? Then, yes, we're together." My mentor winces hard, pinching his forehead and growling low.

"Dammit, Ariella, why? You may not be my daughter by blood, but I am just as any other parent—*please* do not speak of your intimate relations around me."

"Then don't ask." I could feel guilty for saying what I did, but now he'll not ask any further questions, and I'll not have to lie.

"Fine," he mutters. "Do you need anything before you go?"

I shake my head. "No, we've got what we need. And judging by the sounds out there," I gesture to his door, where the sounds of Valoria awaken, "we're well past the time we needed to leave at."

My legs push me to stand as I grab my pack and throw it back over my shoulder. Marek gives Caspian a charged look—it hurts.

I am certainly not the embodiment of a girl who brings her crush to meet her parents, but this is as close as I will ever get to experiencing that.

I stretch my neck, shaking my hands off. This is just another one of those firsts I knew twenty years ago I'd never have—thanks to my companion's father.

We exchange our goodbyes and walk through the common area, where at least a dozen students tense as their jaws drop when they notice Caspian.

I let them look. It's the only time they'll be in such a presence, anyway, and I can be benevolent sometimes.

I halt at the door Caspian just walked through when something grabs my arm. Marek steps around, blocking my view of the others. "You sure you're okay? You know you can tell me, or ask me, for anything."

My lips rise at his concern, and I nod. "I know. I'll see you soon."

We share a silent understanding before I follow the prince down to the street. We turn west and begin our trek to find the Palmluvela.

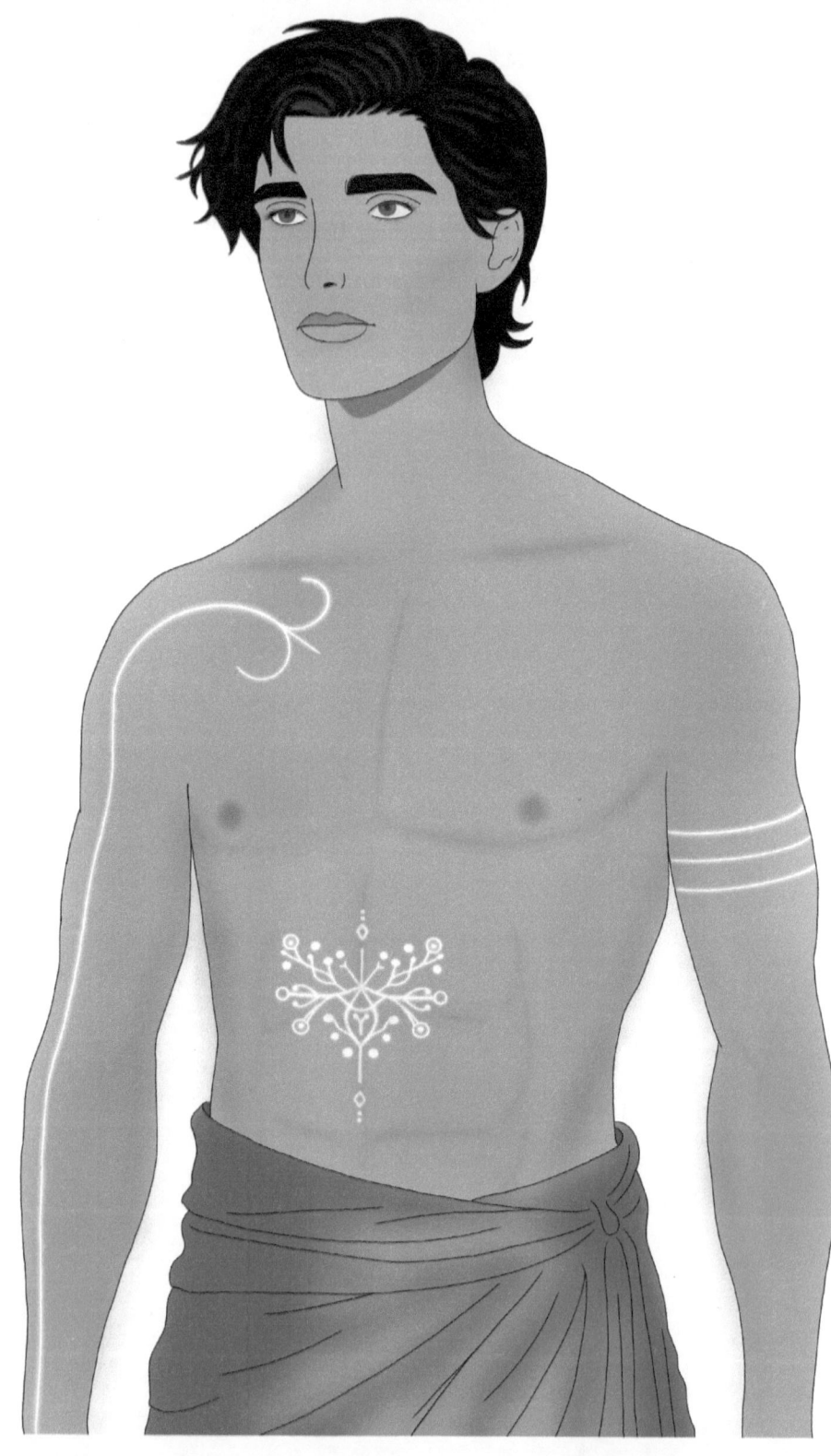

Chapter Nine
Caspian

Too many hours pass in a blur of silence, the kind that's taut with barely contained tension. Ariella strides ahead, her steps relentless and purposeful, as if she's prepared to keep walking through the remainder of the night. She hasn't spoken a word since we left the guild this morning, and I suspect it's her attempt to avoid processing what just happened. I can't blame her—if I had nearly killed someone in a fit of rage after walking through my dead friend's room when the night before I'd bitten into someone's throat...

But I'm fucking tired. I'm not used to being dragged through a darkened forest for hours on end without rest; and as much as she'll deny it, neither is my wraith. I'm worried her body is going to give out on her if she doesn't at least eat something soon. I've tried to give her food, yet she ignores me and keeps pressing forward, fueled by whatever flood is churning inside her.

"Ariella," I try again, my voice low and calm. "We need to stop."

She doesn't slow down. If anything, she quickens her pace, her shoulders tightening as if my words are just one more annoyance she's determined to outrun.

Fucking Aether, I have never met such a frustrating woman.

I catch up to her, stepping in front of her path. The moon is bright enough that I can make out most of her features. "Angel, you need to rest."

Her eyes flash with a cold stubbornness, and I groan as that means I'm about to lose this argument. "No," she snaps, her voice raw and edged with fatigue. "We keep going."

I sigh, clenching my pack and resisting the urge to rub my temples. "This isn't a race. We need to keep our strength up if we're going to reach the Palmluvela in one piece." These last hours I've voiced my concerns of her, but perhaps bringing myself into the conversation will get through to her.

She glares at me as a spark of defiance flicks through her gaze. "I'm not weak."

"I know you're not." I keep my voice gentle, though I'm starting to lose my patience. Truthfully, I'm well past that threshold, but I don't wish to fight. "But you're human. And so am I, in case you forgot."

Her jaw works, and my stomach coils as she tenses again. For a moment, I think she's going to push past me and keep walking, but then something in her expression shifts—a trace of uncertainty, quickly masked. It's enough to make me soften my approach.

"Ariella," I say, stepping closer. "You can't run from this. Whatever is going on in that brilliant head of yours...it's going to catch up to you, eventually."

Her eyes drop to the ground, and she exhales, a sharp sound that's more frustration than surrender. But it's a start.

"I'm not running," she mutters, though her voice lacks the usual conviction. "I just need to keep moving."

"I know," I reply, reaching out to grasp her arm. Her muscles are rigid beneath my fingers, but she doesn't pull away. "But you'll burn out if you don't rest. I'm here, Ariella. You don't have to do this alone—not anymore."

She meets my gaze, her eyes searching mine for something—trust, maybe, or the assurance that I won't abandon her. It's a vulnerability she rarely shows, and my heart squeezes with the weight of protectiveness and something dangerously close to loving affection. That's new, though not unwelcome.

"Fine," she relents, her voice no more than a whisper. "We'll stop."

I nod, trying to hide the relief that floods through me.

We find a small clearing off our self-designated path, hidden enough to avoid any unlikely prying eyes but open enough to keep watch. I gather wood from the abundance of it scattered on the forest floor and set up in the small area we found between trees. Ariella settles on a patch of grass, weaving fire into existence with the twist of her fingers. Her movements are slower now, the exhaustion catching up to her. She's stubborn as fuck, but even she has limits.

I sit across from her and we both eat from our packs in silence. Moss and vines cover most trunks of the large trees, giving the forest an almost mystical feel. As if time itself refuses to abide by the rules of the realm. My eyes close of their own will, and I breathe in lungfuls of the fresh, crisp air. I suspect the atmosphere here is quite humid during the warmer days, which would have made this trip wildly uncomfortable.

Aside from the sounds of flame, the forest is quiet around us. I hear no birds or insects, or even larger animals—I thought the Amyst Wolves lived on these lands...

A loud crackle of the fire sounds between us, and I open my eyes to study Ariella in the flickering light. Her face is drawn, shadows accentuating the angles of her cheekbones. She looks as fierce as ever, but there's a weariness in her posture that I'd be damned to ignore.

"Tell me something," I say, breaking the silence. "What do you think Gavriel's reaction was when I told him he couldn't join us?"

Ariella's lips twitch, the closest thing to a smile I've seen from her all night. "I'd bet my blade that the brute dropped to his knees and kissed each of your feet while begging you to let him come."

I chuckle, rolling my shoulders. "I won't pretend to understand why you two hate each other so much, but I'll admit it's entertaining. You are wrong, though. I told him I needed someone to keep an eye on my father and Varrick, and he insisted on arguing with me until he gave in—not unlike you, actually." I know I'm pressing her buttons, but I can't help it.

"What did I tell you would happen the next time you compared me to him?"

My head tilts as I grin. "You going to cut my dick off, angel? Because I don't think you will."

"Hm—I seem to recall that the last time you underestimated me, my blade appeared in your abdomen."

"You are a stubborn fucking woman," I mutter, adjusting to lean against the cool bark of a tree. "Are you always so difficult to work with? Or am I just special?"

Her gaze softens in the slightest, the tension easing from her shoulders. "I don't *work* with anyone else. This is strange, however." She gestures between our bodies. "I'm not familiar with being alone with someone who is not trying to stab me in the back."

"I am not your enemy, Ariella," I assert, though I know it's a lesson that's been hard for her to learn. One she still hasn't fully grasped. "Some of us actually want to see you succeed and be happy."

Her eyes narrow, accusing. "And what's in it for you, Caspian?"

I pause, considering the question. There's the obvious answer—uniting against our common enemy, ending the horrors my father has unleashed, and learning just what her parents' writing referred to—but there's also something deeper, something she's not ready to hear.

"Let's just say I have a vested interest in keeping you alive," I reply, maintaining my light tone. "Besides, you're far too beautiful to lose so soon."

She snorts, shaking her head. "You're impossible."

"Impossibly handsome and charming, yes," I lilt with a grin.

My wraith turns away, the hint of a smile playing at her lips. It's something, at least.

We travel for two more days, and I again struggle to stop her long enough to do any self-care. How she's kept herself alive this long is a mystery I'll never solve, though she did mention she has never traveled anywhere before. This is the farthest journey she's been on, and perhaps that's why she's continuously tapping her thigh and sounding so frustrated.

This is new to her. She's uncomfortable. This cunning, beautiful, brilliant woman doesn't like change.

I hum to myself and set aside that information.

We've fallen into an easy routine; Ariella prepares the tent while I gather wood and fill our water packs. After she weaved away the wards at her door and I confirmed she possesses all three infinities, it had never occurred to me that she had access to more strands than I'd already knew of. How many is that now? Flora, vital, aero, aqua, pyro, kinetic, and umbral. After our unexpected tryst, when she demonstrated her shadows, I suspect she is also able to weave the psionic strand.

I've no fucking clue what happened that day, but I *know* she was talking in my head. The things she'd said didn't sound like her, but they felt so right.

Then she bit me.

I wanted to bite her back. *Needed* to.

And I loved every bizarre second of it.

I shiver as sticks drop from my arms onto the bed of sand I've designated as the fire pit. My hand mindlessly reaches for the two dots on my neck and rubs the almost healed skin. Neither Ariella nor I have spoken about what happened after that day, though my mind has been churning from holding the questions back. I can tell the topic is discomforting to her, but we cannot lurk around the unspoken conversation forever.

Releasing a breath, I step back as Ariella starts the fire and reach into my pack for salted meat and a honey cake I think she will like. I will force it down her throat if she refuses to eat...she's consumed nothing but water since yesterday. And as I watch her rearrange her bedding for a moment, the tension in her shoulders betrays just how well she's faring.

I wordlessly set the food next to her and grab her water pack, calling my essence to reach into the realm and allow me to use my aqua strand. Once her pack is filled, I drop next to the fire and lean on my side, resting high enough on my elbow that I can eat without choking.

We sit by the small fire in comfortable silence. I trace every detail of her face as the radiance of the flames flicker across her features. She's beautiful in this light—fierce and angelic, with the kind of allure that's more dangerous than inviting. I've never been one to indulge in such thoughts about women, but she makes it difficult not to. I was not lying when I'd explained why I call her angel—I'm still not fully convinced she isn't *the* Angel. She's unpredictable, volatile, and yet, I've never seen anything so beautiful...and my soul wants nothing more than to protect her, regardless that she'll never need it. Well, physical protection, that is. Her heart? I'll keep it safe until she's ready to care for it on her own. And even then, I'll be here, prepared to hold on to it when she cannot.

That realization is harrowing.

I've never felt this way before. I chuckle to myself, because of course I fall for the one woman who insists on fighting me at every turn.

"You've been quiet," I say, breaking the silence.

Her eyes find mine momentarily as she shrugs, tearing a piece of dried meat with more aggression than necessary. "I have nothing to say."

"Bullshit," I retort, earning a glare. Something warm builds inside me at having her full attention. Seemingly negative attention—but I do not care. "You're thinking a thousand things right now. I wish you'd share one of them."

Her eyes narrow. "You really want to know what I'm thinking?"

"Yes."

She leans forward on her hands, her voice low and rough. "I'm thinking that trusting you is a risk I can't afford, but I'm doing it anyway." I am...not sure what to say to that. It's the most honest thing she's ever said to me, and it feels like a step forward, even if it's a small one.

Her laugh is hostile, something breaking in her gaze. "I'm thinking that I don't know what I'm fucking doing anymore, Caspian. I mean, *what* are we doing? How did I go from wanting to kill you and the king to traveling through this ridiculous forest because of some nonsense things my parents wrote twenty years ago?" Her admitting she wanted me dead doesn't bother me as much as it should. But I throw those thoughts out, focused on the shine in her eyes. "For so long, I knew what I needed to do, and I spent every single day training for it. Everything was planned so meticulously. And now *fucking nothing*," she's just shy of screaming at this point, "is the same, and I feel like I'm going insane, which is just fucking pathetic! How did someone like me, who clearly cannot handle a little fluctuation of plans, end up with the reputation I have? I'm nothing but a fool with a title."

She looks up at me, and my hand clenches the closest thing to keep me from going to her. She doesn't need to be coddled, but she needs to learn that what she's feeling is okay.

I hadn't realized just how much this would affect her—she's suppressed everything but anger for so long that her body has adopted a permanent survival mode. Difficult is not the word to describe what it's like watching her reach a breaking point.

It means something that she's allowed herself to be so honest and vulnerable with me, however. I want to be her safe space, but I will not be her savior.

She falls to her back and presses the heels of her palms against both eyes. I let the silence stretch for a moment, allowing the weight of her words to settle between us. "You're not pathetic," I say after a pause, my tone firm but soft. "You're human. You're allowed to feel lost—to struggle with the unknown."

She scoffs, dropping her arms and turning her face toward the fire, but I catch the way her jaw tightens, as if she's trying to hold on to her anger. "Easy for a prince to say." Fair. And true.

I keep my voice even, refusing to let her retreat into the self-loathing I feel her sinking into. That's not who she is. "Ariella, you've built yourself up for years on rage and certainty. It's no wonder everything feels wrong right now. But you're no fool, and you're not weak for feeling this way. Adjusting to change is not the same as failing."

"Then why does it all feel the same?" Her response is instant, as if she's clutching at my every word.

"Because it's new." My gaze follows hers as she studies the trees and gleaming sky above us. The view seems to have a calming effect on her.

"How do I get it to go away." It's not a question, not really. More of a resigned acceptance.

"Angel, look at me." Not a heartbeat later, Ariella rolls to her stomach, resting on her hands as those inquisitive eyes find mine. Will my heart skip every time she looks at me for the rest of our lives? "Living doesn't mean erasing the pain so that you never have to deal with it; it means finding a way to keep moving despite all the scars and unhealed parts of us."

She regards me for a moment, something akin to appreciation falling over her features. "What if I don't accept that?"

I shrug. "You can either live alongside the darkest parts of you, or you can let them destroy that fire inside until you're nothing but a shell." I lean forward, a challenge in my gaze. "But that doesn't sound like the Ariella I know."

"You *don't* know me," she whispers, uncertainty lacing her tone, and I snort.

"Don't I? I know how you tap your fingers against your thigh when you're nervous or overwhelmed. The way you tilt your head just a little when you're deep in thought, like you're weighing every option once or twice before making a decision. How you hide your hair beneath the hood of your cloak when you don't wish to be perceived, because it must be fucking exhausting to have every person in the realm know your identity. I know that you twirl a blade through your fingers when you're trying to hold yourself back. You mindlessly touch the little scar on your wrist whenever Isaiah's name is brought up.

"You're always the first to notice the smallest details—things that any other person would have taken days to discover. I know that you never eat food out of order, only eating one thing at a time until you're finished—and that's how I also know you thrive on control. You have to know what's going on at all times and where you stand in every situation. I've seen how you run your fingers through your hair when you're frustrated, but you never pull. How you hold back a wince each time I step close to you, because the need to defend yourself from touch is so instinctual that you can't help it.

"I know who you are, Ariella. But whether you're ready to accept the truth that you're a human—and not a tool whose only purpose is to kill—is something you will need to figure out on your own."

Ariella's eyes widen at my words, but she quickly covers it with a glare. "You pay too much attention," she mutters, her voice a blend of annoyance and something softer.

I grin as I rise from the ground. "You're hard to ignore."

She huffs, but there's no real bite to it. My stomach flutters when her lips twitch, a smile threatening to break through the heavy silence. "I suppose I should be flattered."

"Suppose you should," I tease, throwing her a sidelong glance. "Besides, someone has to keep an eye on you. You're liable to stab yourself out of sheer frustration."

She shakes her head, but a small laugh escapes her. "If I did, I'd make sure to miss anything vital."

"Good to know you have some sense of self-preservation," I say, my tone light, even as the tension of our conversation hangs in the air.

I think I hear her say *for now* under her breath, but she clears her throat and pushes to her feet. "It's late. We should try to rest." She glances toward the tent, hesitating. "You know...you don't have to sleep outside every night." This is surprising—I've wanted to as it gives her space to herself, but I'm not going to pretend the offer doesn't make me feel giddy.

I raise a brow. "What's this? An invitation to share a tent with *the* Silver Wraith?"

Her expression is deadpan. "Hardly. But don't think I'm going to cuddle you or anything." She emphasizes the last word, and I feign panic.

"But how will we stay warm, then?"

She tosses her head back to laugh, and it's the sweetest sound. There's no response, but she doesn't protest when I move toward the tent. We settle down, the space awkwardly small but heated enough.

Or perhaps that's just the inferno under my skin.

We both have to lie on our sides, lest our shoulders press together. Not that I'd mind...

Just as I'm adjusting my blanket, Ariella's voice cuts through the darkness. "If you snore, I'll kick you."

I chuckle, turning my head toward her. "I seem to remember *you* are the one who snores, not me—or is that only after a griffin attacks you?"

"Shut up," she mutters, and the smile in her voice brings out one of my own.

For a moment, the weight of everything lifts, replaced by the unfamiliar bliss of sharing a laugh with someone who's seen you at your worst.

The silence that follows isn't uncomfortable; it's a tentative peace, always fragile but always real. I close my eyes, enjoying as the faint sultriness of her scent fills the small space, and listen to the soft sound of her breathing.

Tomorrow may be just as hard as today, but for now, this is enough.

Chapter Ten
Ariella

The forest's damp chill seeps into my bones, every step a reminder that this journey is dragging on far longer than it should. My patience, already wearing thin, feels more like a raw nerve.

This was supposed to be simple: find the Palmluvela, secure their help, and leave. But nothing about this journey has gone as planned—something I should expect by now, it seems. Days have passed, and they remain as elusive as ever. I catch myself glancing through the mist, half-expecting to see an imperceptible movement among the trees. But the only persistent presence is the one I need a break from. I did not realize how difficult it is to spend every second of your life next to someone.

And it's not even Caspian getting under my skin, it's *me*. I keep repeating what he said over and over, unwilling, and the damned thoughts will not rest. I need a break from me and my fucking head.

Caspian's boots crunch on fallen leaves behind me, the sound grating on my nerves like nails on glass. His steps are steady, casual, as if he's taking a stroll through a garden instead of an overrated forest. The bastard has impeccable self-regulating capabilities. Every little noise he makes—his sighs, the clearing of his throat—feels like a deliberate attempt to irritate me. I doubt he's foolish enough to play such games, though.

"Are you always this restless?" he asks, breaking the silence with the same ease he's shattered a dozen others.

I ignore him, pretending to focus on the path ahead. Silence used to be my ally—a weapon I welcomed with open arms and sharpened over years of training. But around Caspian, it feels like surrender.

"You could try talking to me about that storm raging inside your head, you know. It might make the time pass faster...or at least quiet the noise a bit." His voice is light, but I can hear the taunting edge in it. And still, I ignore him. "Ouch. And here I thought you enjoyed my company, angel." He almost sounds hurt—which I also neglect to acknowledge because something deep inside me snaps.

"I don't know what the fuck you want, Caspian!" I shout, clenching my fists to keep from ripping his tongue out. I whirl to face his tired eyes; not the same tired as when I found him in the library, but more like bone-exhaustion. I can relate. "You may call me *your guard* to those who wander the castle, but you are *not* my keeper. I do not owe you my time, and I especially do not owe you any part of my body, including my mouth." I realize my mistake the moment I speak it.

The prince smirks, humming to himself. "Shame, I do love that mouth of yours." My eyes hold his as he approaches, refusing to stray even when his head tilts and he peruses my lips with the same hunger I feel in myself. It should be impossible to want to fuck him and kill him at the same time.

How does he manage to burrow under my skin so effortlessly? If anyone else dared speak to me in the manner he does, their bodies would no longer have heads. My jaw clenches. His playful banter rivals even Isaiah's, though the latter knew when to stop his advances.

There were so many times growing up that Isaiah would taunt me, watching just how far he could push me before I lunged for his throat. It may have angered me at first, but I grew to enjoy the back and forth. I never did tell him as much, though. Truthfully, I allowed him to see how upset it made me, as he would eventually relent and offer me one free hit of my choosing.

I usually chose his dick. I would rear my body back and send my leg forward as hard as I could, knocking him several feet away. He may have been my best friend, but he was a pompous ass and he knew it. Maybe he didn't deserve the exhilarated force I put into those kicks, but he shouldn't have kept offering.

It was years later before I realized just what Isaiah's intentions were with the relentless antagonizing. I'd been on an assignment—taking out someone who thought he'd been successful in stealing from his employer—when the realization struck. The man shouted vulgar names at me, *as they do*, and instead of my blade already being inches deep into his throat, I stood un-moving and watched him squirm when he didn't get a reaction from me.

Patience, Ari.

Two words I'd heard from Isaiah almost every day for years, and until that moment, I didn't notice how he ceased repeating them months prior. It may have been foolish for him to test me so often, but his methods were effective. I gained a deeper respect for my friend that day—just before I sliced the throat of my target.

But that was Isaiah. The prince does not seem to hold the same intentions as he pinches my chin and forces my dazed eyes back to his. His smirk grows with whatever he sees on my face, and I'm certain he's about to increase his taunts.

"Do you have a death wish?" I spit, venom prevalent in my tone. He opens his mouth to speak, but my fingers close the distance between us to scrunch his lips together. "I am in no mood for your petty games, Caspian. Go annoy the trees if you are that bored; or, better idea, shut the fuck up." His dark lashes lower over increasingly playful irises, and my eyes roll as I shove his head back and spin to stalk away.

I squeal—*squeal*—when a hand wraps around my throat and yanks me back into a distractingly hard chest. My fingers itch to reach for the prince's grip, though I force them to still. He's not squeezing enough to cut off my air, but just enough that my lips part to compensate.

If I'm honest with myself for just a moment, I am intrigued. His hold is not malicious, nor does the bulge against my backside indicate he means harm...no, his grip is carnal. Possessive.

"I don't think so, angel," he breathes as soft lips graze my left ear. His free hand slides around my waist, flattening against my abdomen before fusing my back to his chest. My body's reaction is immediate, threatening to melt under his rapt attention.

Fuck, the things this man does to me shouldn't be possible.

"You want to try that again? Or should I just punish you right now for being so fucking frustrating the last few days?"

I shift, chuckling at his words. "Punish me? As if I'd ever let you do such a thing." I would, but the cocky bastard behind me does not need to know that.

I bite my top lip—hard—when he presses the lightest kiss just under my ear. I cannot hold myself still much longer, and if he continues...

"Somehow I don't think you *letting* me would be the problem," he remarks. His hand squeezes harder, a barely perceptible movement.

"And what is that supposed to mean?"

My eyes roll when he smiles against my neck. "You may still act as though I do not affect you, lying effortlessly through your teeth and solidifying that blank mask on your face. But your body cannot deceive, angel. I feel the effort it takes for you to swallow each time I kiss you here." He provides an example, and I am no longer aware of anything outside the scorching places our bodies connect. "I feel how your pulse increases the more I touch you. How you're trying so hard to breathe normally, but fail to suppress the rapid rise and fall of your chest. A cute effort, really, but pointless." The hand on my stomach drags so fucking slowly up and up until it reaches my chin, pulling my head to the side so that my eyes meet his. "I bet you're already dripping for me. Shall we find out?"

I shiver as his fingers trail down between my breasts, over my abdomen before hooking just under my shirt to reach the top of my pants. I tense as one finger inches under the hem, and he drags it languidly across the slick skin, remaining under the fabric but never venturing lower. As if he isn't at all affected by this, while the loud beating of my heart rivals the sounds of the forest.

Caspian's lips press against my ear as he removes one finger from his grip on my throat to caress the delicate space above my airway—a reminder of the power he holds. So much more than the physical piece of me under his hands.

He knows it, though I will never admit it.

But the cocky fucking bastard chuckles as if I expressed every thought out loud and presses on my lower abdomen until the ridiculously hard length of him is the only thing I can feel.

"You don't need to be embarrassed, Ari," he placates in a teasing manner as the flat of his hand drifts toward my center. "I know you can feel that I want you just as badly. More, if we're being truthful."

"You've no Angel-damned idea what you're talking about. The day I want you is the day I decide to never pick up a blade again." His hand pauses its exploration, and I almost regret letting the lies slip from between my lips.

Almost.

"You don't, huh?" His hold on my throat tightens. "I suppose I will just stop touching you, then. My apologies, angel." The fingers on my abdomen trail back up, and *fuck me*. I know I shouldn't give in or fall for his ridiculous taunting—but I do. His smile grows wide when I move to grip his wrist, stopping it from abandoning its original path.

No one—*no one*—has ever made me feel the way he does. I want to fight it. Push against his every advance until he's sick of pining for me.

I want to shove him so far away from me that there's no chance he could burrow inside my heart and break me from the isolation I've thrived in for so many years.

But I know that would be a fool's mission. He's already carved a place for himself, and fuck if I don't want to give him so much more.

And yet, how can I? It would ruin everything that I have worked for. To let him in fully—to let myself change—would be to lose focus of what we're here to do. Right? It would be impractical to feel so deeply for him.

It would mean I've failed.

I do not need feelings for this, though. I can allow him to pleasure me in the ways we both so desperately want without crossing that hazy line I drew between our hearts.

So I give in.

My head falls to his shoulder, and he curses under his breath as he feels my body sink into his—submitting to him. It's as if he cannot hold back any longer, shoving his hand the remaining distance to my slick heat. We both groan at the same time.

"Fuck, you're so wet." I do not have a moment to respond before he slips from my pants and uses his grip on my throat to twist and shove me back into a tree. A small sound of surprise escapes me, and he smirks before reaching under my clothing once more, circling the arousal that has been infuriating me since we left the castle.

His lips run down my jaw as he releases my throat and continues on, kissing the exposed skin. He pauses at the same spot his teeth almost sank into the last time, and a small whimper falls from my lips.

"Don't worry," he says as his mouth finds mine for a brief moment. "I'll take care of you." I gasp when he pushes three fingers into me. The burn from his stretching is utterly exquisite, and I'm so on edge that my shaking hands snap to his wrist.

"It's too much...*oh, shit,*" I groan into his mouth when his fingers curl and press against something delicious. He grabs my leg and pulls it over his hip, giving him far more access to my sensitive flesh.

"It's okay, angel, you can take it," he mumbles against my lips before kissing me so passionately my head spins.

I can't think. The world blurs, caught in this suffocating haze of lust and desperation. He drives me fucking mad, each thrust of his fingers igniting boundless sensation that claws at the edges of my sanity. The tree's rough bark digs into my back, grounding me while he devours every gasp and moan spilling from my lips like secrets shared in the quiet of the night.

"Caspian..." His name is a prayer, a curse—my plea for release, and my call for restraint. I want to push him away and pull him impossibly closer. Shove him to the farthest corners of my mind where no one has ever dared to tread, but he won't allow it. He radiates warmth, and I find myself caught in this cruel paradox. His touch should be unbearable, yet here in the midst of this forest, it feels like salvation.

"Fuck, Ariella, you're gripping me so good," he breathes against my mouth, the tension building far higher than I can comprehend. I mean to say *I'm so close*, but the words don't make it past a fleeting thought as he presses his palm against my clit and I shatter. "That's it. Take your pleasure, angel." I think my hand rips some of his hair out as I grip his head—though if it bothers him, he does everything but show it.

The waves of pleasure last for so long my vision blurs. Caspian continues to undulate his fingers even when I plead that it's too sensitive, insistent on wringing out every bit of this orgasm he can.

I'm pissed that he's so good at this.

But I'm also pleased that no one other than me will experience him in this way again.

His nose grazes mine as his hand slips from between us. The prince holds up his fingers, drowned in my arousal, up where we both can see, spreading them wide before his ravenous eyes hold me hostage. "I could *live* off the little noises you make right before you come, and the sweet fucking taste of your pleasure on my tongue."

My jaw slackens as his index finger dips into his mouth. He leisurely pulls it out, sucking me from his skin and not once breaking our stare. I've never been so fucking turned on in my life.

I'm also particularly happy I decided to wash in a small lake earlier, despite that I just about met the Angel from freezing to death.

Something feral glimmers in his eyes. "Open," he demands, his tone stern. *Fuck me*, I cannot handle this side of him...because I'd obey his every command. Just as I do now, spreading my lips until a satisfied hum sounds from his chest. He shoves the next two fingers into my mouth and presses down on the back of my tongue, forcing me to hold in a gag. "Now clean up your mess."

Chapter Eleven

Ariella

I choke on his fingers, desperation mingling with the sharp thrill of surrender. The taste of myself floods my senses, overwhelming and intoxicating. My instincts urge me to rebel, to claw my way back to the world of blades and blood—the world I'm familiar with—rather than suffocate in this mess of desire and inevitability. But beneath that instinct lies a hidden hunger I can't deny—not from him, not from the warmth that seeps through my skin.

I swirl my tongue around his fingers and pull away just enough to gasp for air, eyes burning with defiance I don't feel. He smirks. Cocky bastard. "You think you own me now? Just because you made me—"

"Made you?" he interrupts, his voice low and dangerous. "Ariella, we both know I could never make you do anything you didn't want. But that's the thing...you're mine, and you fucking love that truth more than you hate it."

His confidence cuts deeper than any wound ever inflicted on me, and it sends a shiver down my spine—something I will think about later.

Caspian presses a light kiss against my cheek before lifting my shirt off and moving to remove the rest of my clothes. I let him. I study the purposeful movements, completely stunned and fascinated.

His feet step back as calculating eyes peruse my naked flesh. He tugs his shirt up and tosses it to the side, wasting no time as he moves to grab my thighs and lift until I'm wrapped around him. He walks a path I cannot see, and for once, I do not feel the desperate need to know where I'm going. His mouth finds my breast and I gasp, arching up in offering. I chew on my lip and drop my head back, lost in every sensation the prince is wrenching from my body.

There is something so relieving about surrendering to my baser desires. Not caring about anything other than the man worshiping me and the euphoria we bring each other.

I jolt as my back is shoved against another tree, this one full of bark so rough I'm certain there is blood seeping down my heated skin. Caspian releases my breast with a pop and straightens, a wicked smile plastered across his face.

"Figured you needed some pain with your pleasure this time," he drawls, reaching between us to undo the buttons on his pants.

"And what are you implying, exactly?"

He chuckles, pulling his cock free. "That your attitude the last few days has rivaled that of a griffin, and I need a little help to fuck it out of you." The smooth head of his dick slides over my center, provoking a groan from me. "You are a work of art, angel." I've not a moment to respond before he sheathes himself inside me with one rough thrust.

The realm fractures at the edges as he fills me, a jolt of raw energy surging through my veins. I cling to him, nails biting into his shoulder as the sensation tears a sound from my throat that teases the line between pleasure and pain—exactly as he'd promised. Each thrust ignites a wildfire within, spreading heat into every corner of my very essence. My body wants to arch against him, to match his movements with my own, yet every motion feels like an act of defiance.

"Caspian..." His name lingers on my lips, clinging to the atmosphere like the mist surrounding us, thick and intimate. I'm lost in him—lost in this strange realm where we exist away from the declarations of chaos and the political games of the king.

The prince groans in response, the sound deep and primal as he begins to move with purpose, his hips digging into mine with relentless force. The bark presses as deep as his cock—a concept I didn't realize I'd love so much. His pace is unforgiving, and I'm certain my body is a heartbeat away from splitting in half.

And yet, I've never felt so alive.

"Tell me you want this," he hisses, his breath hot against my ear, a challenge disguised as a question. I can feel the weight of his words cram into the space between us, igniting every nerve in my body and burning the space behind my eyes.

I know full well that he's not referring to the sex. And still, I can't find the will to deny it.

"I want this." The confirmation escapes me before I even think to swallow it back. My own voice betrays me, honeyed and eager, as it balances on the edge of surrender. I'm at war with myself, every thrust erasing the ragged lines I'd drawn in my mind, drawn between us—the assassin who once claimed power by stabbing the same man who now reduces her to a mere vessel for pleasure.

Caspian smirks—Angel damn him—and increases his rhythm, driving deeper, impossibly harder. Each slide of his cock into my heat is a declaration. He knows just what he's doing to me. "You're doing so well, Ari," he murmurs, and my insides twist with both anger and desire at those words.

His hands grip my hips tighter, pulling me in at a new angle. I curse with a loud moan, disappearing to everything but the feel of how high he takes my body. The pain of the wounds on my back is nothing compared to the feeling of him sliding in and out of me.

My lips search for his and our kiss is nothing less than messy and perfect. I pull back just enough to speak. "Caspian, fuck, I'm so close, I can't—" The broken words seem to renew the fire in him as he holds me still and continues pounding into me at that same exquisite angle and speed.

I'm going to slit his fucking throat for being so good with his fingers and cock.

But I'm not a complete monster, so only after I make him watch as life leaves the eyes of the women he decided to fuck before me. He at least deserves to witness all the fun.

His base grinds against my clit twice more before stars line my vision. I've no idea what I'm saying—or screaming, if the rawness in my throat is any indication—but I do not care.

Caspian bites my shoulder as his hips slow and warmth coats my walls, causing me to clench around him again. I lean my head back against the tree while my hand explores the thick strands of the prince's hair—far too soft after having traveled for days.

We remain wrapped around each other for several minutes after, Caspian leaning me forward to caress the relaxed muscles of my back. How is it possible for someone to be so demanding and rough, yet so attentive and caring at the same time? The prince is a walking paradox.

He pulls back, the intensity still simmering in the air between us. I breathe hard, panting as the forest beyond begins to shift back to reality. The tree's rough bark fades from my awareness once more, replaced by a warm glow that surrounds us both.

"Angel knows how I've craved you," he breathes against my skin, voice hoarse and thick with satisfaction. But that satisfaction feels like sand shifting beneath my feet—fuck, I always do this. "You're a tempest wrapped in silver hair..."

"And who gets caught in the storms, prince?" I whisper, sudden defiance sparking within me. "Men that drown."

His smirk falters for just an instant, and I hate myself. I don't know how to fucking do this—how to be the woman he needs, when I cannot even satiate my own. But my words hurt even me, the sour heat in my chest overwhelming. I open my mouth to apologize—something I would have died before doing for anyone else—but he shakes his head and places a brief kiss on my lips.

"Small steps, angel. You'll stop second guessing yourself, eventually." Another kiss before he slides out of me, and I wince as my feet touch the ground. He tenses, but I wave away the concern.

"I'm fine, I'll just heal—" My eyes widen when they finally notice our surroundings. There are no words to describe the glowing wings that have seemed to fill the entire forest.

"By the Angel..." he breathes, reaching out to touch the remnants of light from one of the floating sets of wings. "It's the Khyla."

My head snaps in his direction. "You know what they are?" I pull on my clothes as the prince studies the things. Uncertain whether they pose a danger or not, I remain next to him in case my presence is needed.

"I'm not sure, I think so? I mean, I've heard stories, but they were just that."

I hum. "In your stories, did these *things* harm people?" He chuckles, pivoting to face me.

"No, the Khyla are supposedly little creatures that originate from the Aether. It's said their purpose is to discover the intentions of those who enter their territory, as they're tasked with protecting something or someone." My face scrunches, and I'm certain I'm giving Caspian a look full of disbelief. He smiles. "Listen, I'm just repeating the stories."

"Why would they care about our intentions?" One of the moth-like things flutters past my face.

He shrugs, slipping behind me to run his hands down my arms before lacing his fingers through mine. "Think of them as scouts, of sorts. If they believe we have bad intentions here, they're said to have the ability to influence those intentions, leading us from this area and the forest. If they are what I think, we must be very close to finding the Palmluvela. I'm not certain what else they would be protecting out here."

Caspian lifts my hand, holding it out for one of the Khyla to land on. I'm not fearful of insects or small creatures, but there's something so *other* about these. There is no awareness in my chest that screams danger—no, these things, *moths*, only seem curious.

The one on my finger takes flight, and I reflexively step from Caspian's arms toward the others. The forest glows with a soft, golden light from the thousands of Khyla fluttering around. They are like tiny lanterns as their wings emanate the light and cast shadows on the surroundings. The trees themselves seem to be illuminated from within, their leaves rustling in the moths' wake. Interesting, though, that the normally silent forest hums in time with the languid movement of the Khyla.

Another floats toward me, my palm lifting to hold it. Its weight is imperceptible as it lands and fans its glowing wings, settling into my hand. I pull my arm closer to inspect the creature—words I never thought I'd utter. Something thrilling prickles under my skin at their presence, however.

The Khyla wanders to the tip of my finger, closing the distance between its little body and my curious eyes. My expression is a mirror of Caspian's when I showed him my umbral strand.

"Do you see it?" I murmur, entranced. The Khyla flits its wings, as if acknowledging my question, and I can't help the small smile that blooms on my lips—an unguarded moment I immediately wish to snuff out. But I'm too focused on the translucence of the moth, appearing to be made of the glow itself. Their bodies are physical, but not. Neither here nor anywhere else. They just are.

It's strange...I'd be convinced this was a mere dream if I didn't know in my gut that these are as Caspian said. Though I don't have the sense that they're measuring our intentions. It feels more like a greeting. As they close in around Caspian and me, their fluttering begins to sound like whispers.

The prince drifts closer, his breath warm against my neck. "They seem drawn to you," he remarks, eyes tracing the delicate contours of my face. "It's almost as if they..." My eyes slide to his and pause for a moment. The warmth of the Khyla's glow sinks across the expanse of his skin, contrasting the cool silver of his irises. It's beautiful.

"As if they, what?" I study his features, unconstrained, allowing myself a moment to appreciate him while we're safe within the Khyla.

He shakes his head. "Truthfully, I don't know. Their glow just seems familiar." I nod and drop my head to his chest when the moth lifts from my finger. I do not cuddle or engage in such intimate behaviors, but there's a thickness in my soul pushing me into his arms. I go willingly, needing a few seconds of *him* before I force myself to pull back.

He looks at me with such adoration that it stings—probably the fucking moths making us feel far more deeply than normal. "They don't seem to hate us. Perhaps they'll tell the Palmluvela we're not here to kill anyone and we'll finally get answers." He snorts at my words, looking as exhausted as I feel.

My mind drifts from awareness as I sink into the realization that, for the first time in my life, in this moment, I feel unequivocally safe and content.

Image of Ariella and Caspian surrounded by the Khyla.

Chapter Twelve

Ariella

A sharp sting radiates over my hip, painful enough that it wakes me. I groan and roll to my back, barely slipping back into unconsciousness before another sting forces my hand. I shove at Caspian before murmuring, "Prince, I told you I don't fucking cuddle. Stay over there." He doesn't respond, nor does the pattern of his breathing change.

That may have been enough to satisfy me and allow sleep to take me once more, but something fresh and pungent settles in the damp air. A mere heartbeat later, I have my blade against the throat of whoever the fuck thought it was a good idea to step into our tent.

Unlucky for them.

My eyes are quick to focus, marking the two people who are crouched over me and Caspian. The one I assume was poking me drags his blade over my hip until it's pressed deeply into my abdomen. I glance between the two and note the elongated blade the second holds over my sleeping prince.

If I slit this one's throat, the other will get to Caspian before I can. If it were only me in here, they'd already be dead. But with him? That is not a risk I am willing to take.

The three of us remain quiet as we study each other. If they invaded our tent to hurt us, they could have done so when we were sleeping instead of waking me. They must want something.

But that is not a conversation I will have with Caspian's life at risk, so I hold the knowing eyes in front of me and nod toward the entrance of the tent. He nods, barely perceptible in the lack of light. He pointedly looks at my arm that holds the blade, but I shake my head and tip it at the other person.

We watch each other, both of us trying to determine if the other will hold their word when weapons are drawn back. The man makes a decision and nods at his friend, who withdraws his blade and scuttles out of the tent without question.

My heart pounds as the remaining figure eyes the blade in my hand. I can sense Caspian's tension behind me, the way he instinctively shifts, though he still remains unaware of our predicament. "Now," I whisper, voice low and dangerous, "your turn."

The intruder's lips twitch into a smirk that serves to fuel my anger. "You're just as they say," he concedes, but there's a sly glimmer in his eyes. Who? "Careful with that edge out here, love."

"Do they teach you to mock your captors where you come from?" I counter, pressing the blade just hard enough to draw a bead of crimson from his throat. It slides down and mixes with the sweat pooling on his skin. "You're still here because I'm generous. But that generosity has limits."

His eyes flicker, momentarily darkening as the bite of my blade registers. But the smirk remains, twisted as if he finds humor in the unpredictability of the moment.

"Generosity, is it?" he muses, voice low enough not to wake Caspian, but taunting enough to push my patience. "We've heard much of your...benevolence."

"Then you know not to test it further," I reply, my voice a taut threat.

The man's gaze darts past me, settling on Caspian. "If I were here for the Prince of Eldoria, he'd be gone by now," he says with a strange mix of resignation and conviction. "But we do not want him."

His words prickle under my skin. I shove him back and follow as he removes himself from the tent. I stand at guard, protecting what's mine, surveying the area to find at least two dozen men. "Then who sent you?"

"We are not sent, silver one," he answers, a hint of offense coloring his tone. "The forest heard you coming long before you arrived. They are not pleased, yet they are curious and eager to meet you."

My eyes narrow. "They?"

"The Seer," he clarifies, his expression softening for the first time. "They wish to speak with you both. But understand this: our people do not welcome outsiders lightly. Your people have already disturbed the balance of the realms. However, the Seer believes you will restore what has been stolen, so you and the prince are permitted to enter our home."

I study his face for signs of deceit but find none. The Palmluvela are rumored to be nearly mythical, with a connection to the land that borders on sacred—I'm certain that is who I'm dealing with right now. And they don't waste time with empty threats. But I can't let down my guard, not even for a moment. I'd be forced to use much of my essence to kill them all if they attack, but I'm prepared for just that.

"And if I say no?" I press, my grip steady on the blade. Caspian and I began this journey to find them, to gather answers. But they do not need to be privy to just how desperate I've been for this moment.

"You won't," he states as if it's that simple. "The forest has its ways of guiding even the most stubborn souls."

The unsettling calm in his voice leaves a sour taste in my mouth. "What the fuck does that even mean?" The blade twirls through my fingers.

He smiles, the movement a little eerie. "It means that the forest does not ask twice. But you already know that, don't you?" he adds, his voice full of peculiar certainty.

I shake my head as my eyes roam the group forming a half-moon around me and the tent. Their skin isn't painted—it's marked, almost like the veins of leaves, pulsing with deep greens and browns that seem to shift with the light just as the forest around us. Not tattoos. Something more...alive.

Their clothes are practical but strange, woven from fibers that shimmer faintly like dew on grass at dawn. No bright colors or bold patterns; just soft, natural hues that let them blend seamlessly into their surroundings. It's clever. Calculated. Every movement is silent, each step deliberate, like the forest itself gave them permission to exist here.

But it's their eyes that stand out—sharp, vivid, knowing. There's a weight in the way they look at me, a kind of judgment that doesn't need words, and I cannot decide if I should consider it a threat.

"Where is your leader?" They stare. It's difficult to hold in the product of my irritation. "Surely you weren't sent to find *me* without a leader?"

A low rustling comes from the tent behind me. I tense, prepared to defend Caspian as he stumbles out and rubs sleep from his eyes.

"Was it really necessary to have this party without me?" he mumbles, blinking at the scene like he's just walked into a casual conversation. I'd laugh if I wasn't so on edge.

I risk stepping back to his side, finding an alert prince waiting. "Stay next to me." The words barely leave my mouth, but he hears them all the same.

He nods and glances around at the gathering of the Palmluvela, his expression shifting to something malignant. "And here I thought the morning couldn't get any better," he quips, offering a lazy grin to the nearest person.

If I could strangle him...

"Your prince is bold," the man I've been speaking with observes, a hint of amusement in his tone.

"Foolish," I correct, shifting in front of Caspian without hesitation. "And under my protection."

Before Caspian can retort, a figure emerges from the shadows—a tall, imposing man with sharply lined features and a solemn presence. His skin is painted in swirling patterns of green and gold, streaks that shift through his black hair and blend into the surrounding forest as if he is a living part of it. He moves gracefully, but his silence is fucking commanding. This is who I asked for.

"This is Rael," the man who led me out of the tent announces. "Our leader. He will speak with you."

But Rael does not speak. Instead, he begins moving his hands in a fluid, deliberate series of gestures. His eyes, sharp and discerning, stay fixed on mine as he does so.

Another man steps forward to translate. "Rael greets you as the Silver One—the Serathis—and the Prince of Eldoria. He apologizes for the intrusion, but says it was necessary to ensure your intentions. You have entered sacred ground...words can lie, but the flora cannot be deceived."

Rael's gaze is intense, but I don't waver. "We're here for answers," I remark, keeping my voice steady. "To understand what's happening to the realms." Curiously, the translator does not relay the message, Rael seeming to have either heard me or read my lips, though it's much too dark for the latter.

The leader's response is quick, his hands a blur of graceful motions. "The answers you seek come with a price," the translator says. "The forest does not give without taking something in return. You must be prepared to face what is required."

My jaw tightens at the cryptic answer. "What price?" I demand.

Rael's hands move again, slower this time, as if choosing each word with care. "The price is not just the past, but the present. You will be tested, not just by the essence but by the choices you make from this point forward. Only then will you earn the full truth."

"Fuck's sake, this is ridiculous," I murmur to myself. A chill settles in the air, mingling with the damp grass beneath us. "Fine," I say louder, straightening my stance. "But know this: if I sense *any* deceit, you won't have time to regret it."

Rael's lips twitch into a faint smile—one that holds no malice, only acknowledgment. He raises a hand, motioning for us to follow. The others step aside, parting like everyone does when I amble in their direction.

"Walk ahead of me," I instruct Caspian, handing him his pack and thanking the fucking Angel he doesn't challenge me this time.

He chuckles, peering over his shoulder. "I love your domineering side."

I roll my eyes, already regretting bringing him into this mess. "Just try not to die before we get some answers."

He grins, but the humor doesn't reach his eyes. "I'll do my best."

With Rael leading the way, we venture deeper into the forest, my unease growing as it feels like a living presence that is watching and calculating our every move. My senses remain sharp, every step intentional. I don't trust this place—or its people—but I trust the urgency that's driven us here. Whatever answers lie ahead, we're too far gone to turn back now.

The walk is long, with Rael leading us deeper into the forest's belly. It's not silent—far from it. The rustle of leaves overhead, the occasional creak of old wood, and the faraway creatures fill the air. But there's a strange rhythm to it all...like the forest itself is breathing, keeping pace with us.

Every so often, Rael's hand flicks in a quick gesture, answered by soft murmurs from those who follow in our wake. I listen, trying to pick up pieces of the language, but it's nothing like the common tongue.

Caspian's footsteps are steady beside me. I glance at him occasionally, searching for any hint of unease, but he holds himself like he was born for this kind of uncertainty. I suppose he was. I'd be impressed with his mask if I wasn't too busy trying to keep us both alive.

The ground shifts beneath us, becoming softer, almost spongy. It's the first hint that we're approaching something new. Then the forest parts, revealing the city hidden above us.

The homes are invisible at first glance, built into the thick canopy. They're not crude huts, but complex structures made of thick wood, branches braided into walls that twist upward like massive vines. Their placement is precise, interconnected by bridges of twisted roots and translucent vines that reflect light like the Khyla. It's a stunning sight—nothing like the stone walls, musty smells, and hard angles of Valoria.

But it's the gardens that strike me. Even from here, I can smell the heady mixture of unfamiliar herbs and flowers. There are clusters of vivid plants, their colors shifting as the breeze separates the leaves, allowing the sun to enter. Fruits hang heavy from some branches, their shapes irregular and foreign. Strange blue ferns curl along the ground, releasing a sweet, loamy scent as we pass.

Each step feels like walking through a living maze—one that's trying to make sense of me as much as I'm trying to make sense of it. At least that is what it feels like with the dozens of eyes that peek from in between the gardens and buildings.

"Beautiful, isn't it?" Caspian whispers, his voice a low murmur beside me.

I give a sharp nod. "Distracting," I correct.

He just shakes his head with a faint smile, but he knows I'm as awed as he is. We're not meant to see this world; that much is clear. It's a sanctuary for the Palmluvela—and suddenly I understand the secrecy and strange moths.

Rael guides us through a series of narrow paths, weaving around gardens filled with iridescent flowers that shift between shades of purple and blue. Finally, he stops in front of a hollowed-out trunk, wider than five men standing side by side, and motions us inside.

The space within is dim, lit only by small fire-filled lamps spread throughout. I wonder if they worry of burning down their city...

Rael moves to a low table in the center, gesturing for us to sit. His movements are precise, and there's a solemnity to his eyes that was not there before, as if the silence here allows him to shed the guise of ritual and authority.

He begins to sign, his hands moving slowly. Deliberately.

It doesn't appear so different from weavers who need more exaggerated gestures to access their essence; only he's weaving words, not commanding strands.

"He welcomes you to our community," the translator says, stepping forward. "He says the time has come to speak of the Accord."

My eyes narrow. "Right to it, I see—I appreciate the lack of facade." I lean forward and rest my elbows on the table. "What do you know of the Accord? And why tell me?"

Rael's response is swift, his hands a blur of emotion and urgency. "The Accord, as our ancestors have described for centuries, is the binding entity between the Aether realm and ours. It balances the essence between both realms, so that no one place—or person—has too little or too much.

"We know that it is weakening," the translator continues. "The balance has shifted too far, and the essence that sustains the realms is being drained faster than it can be replenished. The Accord was meant to maintain harmony, and we believe someone—or something—has been taking too much, leaving everything else unbalanced."

My chest tightens. "Who would dare to do that?" I already know the answer, but I keep my stare blank.

Rael's eyes meet mine, steady and certain. "That is not for us to know," the translator says. "We hear whispers from the flora—they speak of a time when the Accord could have been repaired, but now...it is too late. The damage is irrevocable."

"What does that mean?" I press, trying to keep my voice steady. "If the Accord can't be fixed, then what?"

Rael's hands slow, each gesture heavy with the same kind of resignation I feel in my soul. "It means a new Accord must be forged," the translator says, his voice carrying a note of finality. "This one is beyond repair. The balance has been shattered, and we've already seen the effects through the unnatural weather phenomena."

I can feel the weight of Rael's gaze as I chew on my lip and cross my arms, the unspoken question hanging between us. "Why tell us this? Why invite us here and throw this information at us without any hesitation?"

The leader smiles, his dark eyes flitting between Caspian and me with a strange warmth. He appears to consider something before lifting his hands, speaking. The translator attempts to hide a smile before meeting my cold stare. "As we've said, the flora whisper to us. We knew who you were before you had even decided to find us. *Thava Serathis éna, aneth éri Aetarys. Thava utela lira esthara.* You will be given any help we can offer for your role in forging a new Accord."

I scoff, so fucking ready to rip my hair out. "Of course you have more languages. What does that mean?"

The translator speaks himself, offering a gentle smile. "You will know when time decides."

Groaning, I give up trying to understand. "And how do we create a new Accord?" I ask, my voice low.

Rael shakes his head slowly, his hands making a small, helpless motion. "We do not know," the translator admits. "Our knowledge comes from the land, who know of the Accord's purpose, but refuse to share its creation. Rael believes the Seer can help you." He pauses, watching the leader's movements. "He says that it is imperative you destroy that which has shifted the balance. A new Accord will be a wasted effort if the evil is not removed first."

"Obviously," I mutter.

I lean back, feeling the frustration churn low in my gut. "So, let me get this straight," I drawl, forcing the words through gritted teeth. "You're telling me I have to *forge* a new Accord without knowing how, and also deal with an unknown threat that's powerful enough to destroy the realms' balance, and subsequently the Accord that has remained perfectly intact for centuries. Sounds perfectly achievable."

Rael's expression remains unchanged, but there's a frustrated glimmer in his eyes. The translator's voice is steady as he relays Rael's next words. "The task ahead is not easy, but you are the Silver One. The Accord chose you as its guardian for a reason."

My gaze shifts to Caspian, who's been unnervingly quiet throughout the conversation. His eyes are sharp, focused—taking it all in with that calculating look I've come to know too well. It's the look he gets when he's weighing the odds, trying to decide if we can survive what comes next.

"Save the *chosen* shit. What really makes you so certain we're capable of this?" I ask, not bothering to hide the edge in my voice.

Rael's response is immediate, his hands moving with fervor. Is it possible that I recognize some of his gestures already? The sign for flora has become obvious, his fingers pressing together before stretching open. The translator hesitates to speak, but one look from Rael and he sighs. "The flora have spoken. They say the

Serathis éna éri Aetarys are bound by more than fate—you will both succeed in this."

A laugh escapes me, bitter and raw. "Fate? You think fate is going to help us stop whatever the fuck is ruining the realms? And why isn't the Aether realm helping if this is so important? Where is the damn Angel?"

Caspian finally speaks, his voice low and measured. "Ariella, maybe we should listen."

I whip around, heat coating my chest. "And what, Caspian? Just accept that we're pawns in some ancient game that must be played by the rules, but somehow no one knows what the rules even are? That we're supposed to fix a broken Accord we didn't even break?" This is far more than I expected to find here—it's overwhelming and frustrating.

He doesn't flinch, his gaze steady. "We came here for answers, and we're getting them. Maybe not the ones we wanted, but it's more than we had before." His tone softens, his hand sliding over my thigh and squeezing. "Clearly, we made the right choice coming here."

The weight of his words presses down on me, and the air in my lungs thickens. I hate that he's right. I hate even more that I feel it, deep in my bones—the pull of something I never asked for, something I can't refuse. My mother referred to it in her letter, but that was so vague it could have meant anything. Why this?

A deep sigh flows through me as a finger taps against the prince's hand. "Where do we find this Seer?"

Rael nods. "The Seer will find you when they are ready," the translator explains. "For now, we will have housing prepared and food made for you."

Caspian smiles. "Thank you."

I exhale through pursed lips, the reality of everything settling over me like a suffocating cloak. "Great," I mutter. "How many Seers are there?" The thought of too many makes me nauseous.

Rael's gaze doesn't waver, but he studies me for a moment before signing. "There is one Seer. Their visions do not assume a gender, and neither do they."

I nod, relieved. "Okay. I'm done with this conversation."

Rael motions for us to rise and step back outside; the soft, shifting light of the city seems colder.

Everything feels colder.

"Well," Caspian says, breaking the silence as we begin to follow Rael's lead once more, "at least we've got a direction now."

"An ill-defined direction doesn't mean much," I retort, my voice hard.

He chuckles. "True. But it's a start." My fingers do not resist when his slip through and hold on to me tightly. It's a needed comfort—something else Caspian just knows how to interpret perfectly.

I don't respond, my mind too tangled with thoughts of the Seer, the Accord, the balance, and I've no doubt Thalion is behind shifting the latter. But beneath it all, a small, stubborn part of me believes we can do this. We have to. Because if not us, then who?

We move back through the winding paths of the city, my senses still alert as my mind struggles to process everything Rael has laid before us. I wanted answers, but this is absurd.

The people of the Palmluvela are more visible now—no longer hiding in the gardens. They seem curious, almost bold, as we pass. Some whisper to one another, while others offer hesitant smiles.

But it's the look in their eyes that strikes me most. It's not fear or suspicion. They're not angry at my and Caspian's presence. No, they almost look to be regarding us with grateful fondness. Reverence, even. I catch a few murmurs that sound much like those I hear in Valoria. I focus ahead, doing what I'm best at and ignoring everything around me.

"They seem to like you," Caspian murmurs beside me, his voice quiet.

I grit my teeth, unwilling to be comforted by the misplaced faith of strangers, and shrug.

He lets out a small, amused huff. "I mean, I can relate. I had the same reaction the first time I saw you, too."

I shoot him a sidelong glare. "If you think you'll gain my favor with nice words, just know it's the opposite."

He grins, and for a moment, the weight of our future feels a fraction lighter.

We continue deeper into the heart of the city, the scent of cooking fires and unfamiliar spices filling the air. There's a tanginess to it, and I have the urge to run over and ask what it is. My stomach growls in response—another reminder of the long days without proper food.

Rael stops before a large tree with a spiral staircase carved into its trunk. He gestures for us to ascend. The translator lingers at the base, watching us carefully. "This will be your housing during your stay," he explains. "It has been prepared for you and is separate from all others."

I can't help but snort. "Is that to keep your people from me, or me from them?"

The translator raises an eyebrow at me, but Rael just smirks and dips his head before turning back and leaving.

I ignore Caspian's amused expression and start climbing the stairs. Each step creaks under my weight, but the wood holds firm. The air grows cooler as we ascend, the thick canopy blocking out the remaining daylight.

When we reach the top, I pause, taking in the small living quarters. It's surprisingly homey, though simple, with furniture carved directly from the living wood. A bed made of woven vines is set against one wall, and a low table sits in the center of the room, surrounded by cushions. There are shelves along the walls filled with potted plants—some familiar, some strange, all glowing faintly. A common occurrence here.

"Cozy," Caspian comments, moving past me to inspect the room. "And look—there's even wine."

I glance over, spotting the bottles stacked in a corner. "If it's not poison," I mutter.

"Always the pessimist." He uncorks one of the bottles and sniffs it. "Smells decent enough." He chuckles at my incredulous stare and swallows some, humming to himself. He mutters something about how it's the best thing he's ever tasted and offers me the bottle.

My head shakes, too tired to argue. "I'm not interested in drinking around strange people who probably just want to make us comfortable so they can kill us."

Almost as if summoned, a soft knock sounds at the door, followed by the entry of a woman carrying a large tray of steaming dishes. She's young, with the same markings on her skin, but there's a warmth in her eyes that makes me pause.

"Essara," she murmurs, offering a small bow. Her eyes catch the confusion in mine before she stammers, "I-I'm sorry. I didn't realize you wouldn't be familiar. It means welcome in the common tongue. This is for you." She presents the tray, setting it lightly on the table.

Caspian stands and offers her a gracious nod. "Thank you."

The woman grins, but lingers for a moment, her gaze flicking between us. "The Seer is not far," she adds, hesitant. "When they are ready, you will be called."

I nod once. "Understood."

She retreats quickly, leaving us alone. Caspian settles next to the table, grabbing my waist and yanking me down next to him. I don't resist, my body too fucking tired to care. The prince lifts the lid from the tray, revealing an array of unfamiliar foods—steamed vegetables, roasted meat that smell faintly of the same spices I can't identify, and a collection of roots and herbs that are foreign to my senses.

"At least it's not the dry meat and bread we've had for the past few days," he says, settling into one of the cushions.

I sit next to him and lean my head against his shoulder, barely able to keep my eyes open. I should not be this tired—something feels wrong.

I force my body to move and pick at the food with more caution than hunger. "Do you think this Seer will be able to help?"

He chews thoughtfully before answering, adjusting until his hand grips the back of my neck and begins massaging. I moan into his hold. "I think they'll have more answers we don't. Whether those answers are what we need...I'm not sure."

"Always the diplomat," I mutter, but there's no real heat behind the words.

We eat in silence for a while, the food surprisingly good despite my wariness. The spices have a kick to them, a slow burn that lingers on the tongue. It's oddly satisfying.

When we're done, Caspian leans back, pulling me with him. "Ariella," he says, breaking the stillness. "Are you okay? You seem down."

I stare at the shifting light outside, my voice low and raw. "I'm just tired."

He's quiet for a moment, and then his hand reaches across my abdomen, brushing the line of exposed skin below my shirt. He lifts me effortlessly, and I laugh as I lean into him. "Well, we cannot have a tired assassin when the Seer calls for us." His tone is light and comforting. It's not just his words or his gentle actions.

It's everything I can't explain—but something inside me shifts toward him.

"Rest," he says after a moment, pressing a kiss to my head. I'm placed on soft blankets, warmth covering me as he lies next to me, cocooning my body with his.

I nod, the exhaustion too much to fight. I don't trust the Palmluvela, don't trust their cryptic words or utter willingness to share exactly what I need. But for now, there's nothing more I can do. And for the first time in days, the thought of sleep doesn't seem like a luxury—it feels like a necessity.

My head rests against the thud of Caspian's heart, something I didn't think I'd find calming. I don't speak, and neither does he. There's nothing left to say.

As my eyes drift shut, I can almost hear whispers, faint and distant. It's a promise, a threat, a question that I can't yet answer—things that they want me to know but are hesitant to share.

But one thing has become shockingly clear these last weeks: whatever lies ahead, Caspian and I are in it together. Stubborn bastard he is, but at least this is something real and tangible I can hold on to.

Chapter Thirteen

Ariella

*T*he wind screams, a vicious howl that drowns all sound except the pounding of my heart. The ground is unstable beneath my feet—more like a series of shifting illusions than solid terrain. I swear I can see the streets of Whisterra peeking through the sky. I keep running anyway, not having any other choice, stumbling but driven forward by sheer will. Black tendrils of void-like essence snap at my heels, eager to consume anything in their path. I clutch the artifacts against my chest, their energy pulsing through my hands. They're impatient, ready to forge the Accord that will hopefully save the realms by binding them together. It's the theory of a seer, but we've no time to think of any other options—or what will happen if this Accord doesn't work. So I hold on to the artifacts as if my life depends on it...because it does. Their touch burns cold, sending spikes of pain up my arms, but I can't release them. Not now. We're almost there.

"Hurry, Aris!" Caelum shouts, his voice barely audible over the deafening chaos.

I risk a glance at him, catching the briefest glimpse of his determined face, streaked with sweat and dirt. His hair, once a rich, vibrant hue, is now tangled by the violent gusts of raw essence whipping wildly around him. Even in this chaos, there's a fire in his eyes—a mixture of faith and desperation.

"We're running out of time!" he adds, his voice strained. His arm snaps out, shoving me to the side just as a piece of the ground breaks away and falls into the sky.

My chest constricts—not just from the air that feels like thick sludge, or the fact that I've been running like this for hours, but from the weight of what I haven't told him. He deserves to know, a voice whispers in my mind, but I shove the thought aside. There is only the Accord now. Only the fragments of reality I must bind...before it costs us everything.

The air is suffocating, each breath more a struggle than the last. I gasp, my throat raw, the taste of metallic essence coating my tongue. Pressure from the other realm bears down on me, making my limbs feel heavy and foreign. For a moment, I falter as the atmosphere itself tries to crush my resolve. The twisting strands of essence, pulling our realms together, seem to grow more frantic and demanding by the second. Their pull is both physical and mental—a gaping void threatening to devour everything.

"It's too much!" I yell, my voice cracking as I try to fight the dread rising, churning every organ inside me. "Everything's breaking apart faster than we expected! We're not going to make it, Caelum!"

He grabs my hand as we sprint, fingers warm and firm against my cold, trembling skin. "Whatever happens, I'm here with you," he replies, silver eyes locked on mine.

There's a beat—a silent promise exchanged between us. I nod, even as a lump forms in my throat, and we continue to press forward. The world around us is a riot of clashing colors—brilliant whites colliding with demanding blues, pinks, and purples, like dawn and dusk locked in battle. The wind cuts at my face, leaving stinging welts, burns forming from the relentless assault of the elements. More essence strands whip past, each one shrieking like a wraith.

As we approach the steep incline, the ground beneath us trembles violently again. I squeal, almost slipping, but Caelum's arm hooks around my waist, steadying me, though not stopping our momentum. For a fleeting moment, I lean into him, seeking reassurance in his touch.

"Stay with me," he breathes, so close I can feel the heat of his words against my ear. It's not a command, but a plea.

I want to respond, to reassure him, but the truth lodges in my throat. "Just a little further," I manage to say, voice thick with a fear I cannot hide.

We crest the incline, and I cry out as the crystal finally looms ahead—its massive form a stark contrast to the chaos. It glows with a steady, eerie light, a beacon of stability in a realm collapsing around us. I can feel its pull, like a magnet drawing my essence toward it.

"It's here," I yell, grasping the artifacts tighter. I want to feel relieved, but I know better. "This is it."

Caelum releases my arm, moving beside me to shield my body from a burst of wild essence that lashes out, black and jagged.

He blocks it effortlessly, his strength unwavering. Our essence is volatile and unpredictable, yet he somehow manages to weave enough to cover us. "What now?"

I fumble, placing the artifacts—a heartstone, my mother's favored hand mirror, and the jewelry box that's served generations of my family—down before the crystal. My hands shake as I start the ritual, the strands of essence fighting against me. Each one feels like a barbed wire, slicing through my concentration. The process is excruciating, but I cannot afford to falter.

"Eris'ena ēthra ulthira, sey'enya varan'dai élum. Arisēth velūra, éna na'yris." Become one with the binding essence, take form within the eternal vow. Seal your power, accept the sacrifice.

I push the first artifact into the crystal as it opens itself to the binding, and a relieved breath fills my lungs. The first part of the Accord is done, just three more to go. Caelum watches me intently as I grab the mirror next. "What's happening?" *he asks, voice barely audible over the winds.*

My stomach twists. I don't look at him as I answer before repeating the words to bind the second artifact. "It's...complicated," *I reply, my voice tight and urgent.* "I have to bind them using part of my essence."

He doesn't move, but I sense a shift in his aura—a silent acknowledgment of the stakes. "And what do you need from me?"

My heart feels like it's breaking. "Just stay close," *I say after the crystal accepts the next artifact.* "Stay with me, no matter what. If this doesn't work, I love you."

I want to say more, but force myself to focus, to channel the energy through the last artifact. The crystal hums, responding to the ritual, its surface glowing brighter. It feels like I'm tearing reality apart to piece it back together again. Everything sharpens—the colors, the sounds, the pressure against my skin. The air vibrates with tension, almost like the realm itself is holding its breath.

And then, a sound—a horrible, wet crunch.

I whip around, eyes wide as the ritual's words die on my tongue. Caelum stands there, his expression shifting from confusion to pain. The jagged shard of dark essence juts out from his chest, black ichor dripping down its edge. His breath catches, a choked gasp escaping him. His eyes lock onto mine—they express so much without any words. Admiration, love, regret, acceptance.

"No!" I scream, the word tearing from my throat.

I reach for him, everything around me blurring into a nightmarish swirl as I drop the jewelry box. He tries to speak, but blood bubbles at his lips. His knees buckle, and he collapses, his gaze still fixed on me, full of nothing but happiness through our shared bond.

"I'm sorry!" I cry, lunging forward, but I'm too late. The vision fractures like shattered glass.

The darkness splinters as I jolt awake, heart still pounding from that final, brutal image. It must have been some kind of vision, because that was no dream. My breath is ragged, each inhale clawing its way into my chest. My fingers clutch the rough blanket beneath me, needing to grip reality itself.

What in the fucking Aether was that?

Caelum. His bloodied form still lingers in my mind, the haunting image too vivid to shake. Who was that? I force a brittle exhale as I try to ground myself in the present.

My surroundings come into focus slower than I'm comfortable with—the dim glow of embers in the fire pit, the fresh scent of the growing herbs lingering in the cool air. I'm in the room Rael provided. The fabric is soft but foreign, and for a moment, I feel unsteady, unsure of where the vision ends and reality begins.

I've never felt so terrified as I did moments ago.

I turn my head, finding a pair of dark eyes already fixed on me. Rael sits in front of the bed, his expression one of eerie calm, as if he's been waiting for this moment. His long, dark hair flows over the shoulders of his black robe, severe against the gold marking his skin. But it's his eyes that keep catching me. They seem to shift—what was a deep brown not a moment ago is now golden and inquisitive.

My attention darts to Caspian as he stirs, his muscles tense, having placed himself at the edge of the bed between Rael and me.

"Rael," I rasp, my voice weaker than I'd like, as if I haven't consumed water in days. "You knew. Did the Seer warn you of this? Is that why you were so eager to escort us to this room?"

Rael's head tilts, his gaze steady as his translator steps forward, speaking his leader's words with practiced ease. "Yes, the Seer informed me of the vision you were to have shortly after arriving." The translator's voice is low but assured. There's no surprise, only curiosity and expectation.

I swallow hard, my throat painfully dry. "Why didn't you tell me." It's not a question; more an accusation. My chest tightens as I fight the urge to lash out, to demand answers I can't even form into words yet.

Rael nods once, still watching me with an unwavering gaze as the translator continues. "Not a choice of mine, Serathis. the Seer believed your ignorance was necessary."

The weight of those words settles over me, and I loathe their suffocating presence. Who does he think he is? "I felt *everything*," I growl, the words leaving my mouth before I can stop them.

Rael's eyes soften, but there's no comfort to find in his gaze. The translator speaks again. "It is not over, Serathis. The vision was necessary for you to understand the gravity of what has yet to be revealed." Rael stands, his robe brushing the floor as he pivots toward the door, not looking back. The translator repeats his next word without pause, "Come."

I push from the bed and snatch a water pack, eyes rolling as I down the contents too quickly, coughing. Caspian gestures for me to follow, and we walk down from the room, almost losing Rael as he disappears around a structure. We catch up, and I shake out my hands, feeling jittery and on edge.

The prince leans in, keeping his voice low. "Are you okay? I tried to wake you when he showed up, but he was adamant that I not interrupt whatever you were experiencing."

I nod, though whether it's to his question or statement, I'm unsure. I bite the inside of my cheek as we pass through the city once more. The sun has begun setting, meaning I was asleep for at least a few hours.

It felt like days inside that dream—no, vision.

The temple isn't what I expect. Instead of descending underground, we climb higher into the ancient trees. Their massive trunks twist together, forming natural pathways that spiral upward. The bark beneath my fingers thrums with energy—essence woven so deeply into the living wood that it feels like touching a raw nerve. It seems different to me now, after the vision. More alive.

Rael guides us through the winding path, his movements fluid and precise. At the entrance to what appears to be a tunnel formed by intertwined branches, he signals for his people to remain behind, aside from the translator. Caspian and I follow.

He holds up a hand, asking us to wait while he fetches the Seer. But before he can leave, a chuckle of air bursts from his chest as a figure emerges from the shadows.

My breath catches. The being before us is striking—tall and otherworldly, with features too perfect to be human. Their white hair cascades like liquid moonlight, but it's their eyes that hold me. Where eyes should be, there are empty sockets that somehow still seem to see everything.

"Not of this world, indeed," they say, responding to my unspoken thought.

My hand twitches toward my blade, but before I can reach it, they're beside me, fingers brushing my arm. "That won't be necessary, Ariella." Their touch lingers for a moment before they draw something from within their robes—a blade unlike any I've seen before. The hilt gleams a soft gold, as though it emits its own light, with intricate patterns etched deep into the metal, winding toward a rounded edge. A deep-purple stone sits at the center, seeming to absorb every bit of light and energy grazing its surface. The blade itself is black—an interesting change from the silver metal I'm accustomed to—and I now wish for all of my blades to be made in the same manner. It's beautiful. The Seer offers it to me with both hands, reverence in their motion. The silver coating their fingernails is a curious choice.

"You will need this. Keep it with you and ensure it does not reach the wrong hands."

I hesitate, my hand hovering over the blade. It hums faintly, its energy alive and curious. "What purpose will it serve?"

The Seer tilts their head, the empty sockets of their gaze unreadable. "Even I cannot see all paths clearly. Take it."

The weight of the blade in my palm feels heavier than it should, as if it carries more than its physical mass. Something twists inside me, that incessant need to ask more questions until I know everything. But I hold back, nodding as the blade slips into my sheath.

Rael's hands move in explanation. "This is Eris, a Seer who left the Aether. They removed their own eyes to see more clearly after a vision led them here."

"Ah, yes, but they were nothing but a distraction. They kept me from truly seeing what needed to be perceived. I've lived this moment hundreds of times," Eris says, their voice like wind through crystal. "I've waited so long, knowing you would come, but not when. What happened to your parents changed everything—the entire fate of the Accord."

My throat tightens. "What do you mean?"

"The Accord is broken," they say, each word heavy with meaning. "The artifacts that maintained it were stolen, weakening its ties to the Ephemeral realm, leaving it open for abuse. And abused, someone has. They are actively destabilizing it. The Accord lives by using recycled essence to hold the realms together, but it's failing. Your mother, and others from the Aether, sacrificed themselves over the years to buy time when the Accord found itself lacking essence from that realm—time you shouldn't have needed if your father hadn't died. He was fated to guide you through this when you were of age."

The blood drains from my face. "How much time do we have?"

"Barely any. You must stop whatever is weakening the balance; then follow the necessary steps to forge a new Accord, using what you were shown in the vision of the first Accord. There won't be time otherwise."

Questions flood my mind, but Eris raises a hand. "I cannot tell you more. Those answers would destroy the only path that leads to restoration."

"Then at least tell me what happens if we're too late," I demand. "If the Accord dies?"

Eris's expression darkens before they utter something I did not wish to hear again. "Chaos."

Chapter Fourteen

Ariella

I pull over the soft fabric of the new top with confident hands, adjusting it as best I can—it is surprisingly small and will expose my breasts if I'm not careful. The material clings to my skin in a way that's more intimate than comforting, the cool silk emphasizing just how exposed I am.

The low neckline and the high slits of the skirt weren't what I expected, and I almost laugh at the irony. *An assassin's body draped in seduction.* I don't know whether to feel empowered or objectified.

Caspian had lingered in the doorway before leaving, his gaze caught on the revealing outfit before I told him it was fine to go ahead. I needed space, and he seemed to understand without my having to say, though there was a glimmer of something in his eyes—concern, perhaps, or maybe something darker as I had just described the vision to him. How the realm felt up and down, twisted into exactly as I imagine chaos to be. The artifacts that felt so important in that body—Aris' body. Significant enough that I considered my life theirs and the Accord's.

I shake off the thought and turn to the mirror, studying my reflection.

The vision lingers, refusing to be pushed aside. Every detail of it—*the twisted strands of essence, Caelum's bloodied expression, the monstrous shard that ended him*—is etched into my mind like a scar. I feel raw, as if the very air around me could slice open wounds that haven't healed. The words from the ritual still echo through my head, a relentless nuisance that scratches at the back of my skull.

Eris'ena ēthra ulthira, sey'enya varan'dai élum. Arisēth velūra, éna na'yris.

I lean forward, bracing myself against the small table beside me, my body tired. I feel caught between realms—tethered here in the physical but haunted by the Aether. The vision was unlike anything I've ever experienced before. Even possessing the entire ethereal affinity, having visions is not guaranteed and even more rare than the essence itself. This one was *too real*. I felt the heat, the pain, the crushing despair.

And Caelum's eyes—*Angel, his eyes*. So familiar I'm not sure I'll ever look at Caspian the same way again.

My hands clench into fists, nails digging into the wood, creating damage I'd care about if I was a better person. Every truth Eris gave is a weight I'm not ready to carry. I keep trying to tell myself it was just a vision, only words that the Seer says are important, that none of it was real. But deep down, I know better. I doubt the Angel offers empty warnings. Actually, I'm surprised it would offer me anything at all.

I release a slow, unsteady breath and move to the bed. The ornate blade they gave me sits on the edge, a token of honor for tonight's gathering. I grab it, appreciating its familiar heft. A weapon is at least something I understand. The rest—the vision, the Seer's cryptic words, and whatever this *party in our honor* is supposed to mean—feels like one massive manipulation. A farce to waste my fucking time.

Who are these people? And why do they know so much?

I can't shake the feeling that I'm being pulled into a game I don't fully understand. Something else I need to adapt to, lest both realms collapse at my inability to get it together.

I take one last look in the mirror, straightening my spine. The soft silk flows down my form, its hue shifting with the light. I may be exposed, but it feels right. Like armor now—at least to those who might underestimate me. I can still wield a blade, nude or not.

I harden my gaze as I turn toward the door, swallowing thickly from the strange weight of the night ahead that's pressing down on me. I might not know what's coming, but at least I'll face it head-on.

Walking through the city is a different experience at night. There are no lights to guide, but the flowers placed in each garden emit a soft glow, providing just enough for me to navigate. I slow my feet in between gardens, breathing in the sweet air. It's peaceful—especially as the Palmluvela are at the edge of their city, where the gathering is being held.

How grating it is that my first urge in experiencing something like this is to wonder what Caspian would think. How it would feel to experience it with him.

Fuck's sake, I'm far too attached.

And he's right...I can fight these emotions all I want, but we both know the genuine truth.

My feet speed up, leaving behind those pathetic thoughts. I just wish to get this party over with, then leave in the morning. We have much to do, and according to the Seer, such little time that I'm nervous to waste even the smallest amount doing anything but what's needed of us.

Light flickers ahead, becoming brighter as I walk, and the sounds of music and chatter increase. I stride down the path I assume leads to the party through these trees, my breath catching at the hundreds of luminescent flowers lining it. This city is beautiful.

Through the thick of the trees, I finally spot the fire, but pause as I'm about to leave the safety of the shadows when I hear a familiar chuckle.

"What's it like to be the prince? I mean, you must have people fawning over you all the time." If I thought I was annoyed before, the heat spreading through my veins tells me my mood is about to become much worse.

I peek around the trunk of a tree to see two women dressed much like me, standing in front of Caspian with pathetic stars in their eyes.

Angel save them, because I will not be responsible for my actions after the day I've had.

"Ah, sometimes, I suppose. I've learned to ignore it, so I do not notice it much any longer," Caspian answers, his voice sounding too light for my liking.

Actually, knowing that he's nearly naked with just fabric wrapped around his waist and still standing near them...

Breathe, Ariella.

There are a lot of people that live here. Surely they wouldn't notice if two went missing?

I press my back against the textured bark, memories of the other night surfacing like an unwanted storm. Perhaps instead of tearing their hearts out, I'll just make the women watch him fuck me against this tree. That seems a reasonable compromise.

"Are you betrothed?" one of the dead women walking asks, the smile in her tone evident.

The prince's response is immediate. "Not in my father's eyes."

She hums, and I peer around the trunk again, weaving my umbral strand to cover me from any flickering light. The women give each other a loaded look and fuck if I don't know exactly what they're about to offer. I want to march over there and assert my claim over the prince, but I stop myself before my body moves.

I'm interested to hear what Caspian has to say.

"So you have no loyalty to any woman, then?" the second one questions.

The prince chuckles, clasping both hands behind his back as his head tilts. "I know you're both aware of who I arrived with. I am loyal to her." I think I've ceased breathing. Did I hear that correctly?

"The Silver One?" Both women laugh as the first reaches out to trace a finger down Caspian's abdomen. My fingers dig into the tree so hard I feel the give of their skin just before hot liquid coats the tips. "We didn't get the impression you two were together—she seemed to ignore your presence whenever we saw you both..." As if that would have stopped them. "I wouldn't think that's a way for any woman to treat her lover. Especially the Prince of Eldoria, of all people!"

His lips purse. "Is that what you saw? I seem to remember her attention quite differently."

The second woman, a mere inch taller than the first, leans forward with a sort of urgency. "We didn't mean to offend you, Your Highness." I'll be surprised if my teeth do not crack from the way my jaw clenches. "The opposite, actually. We thought you might enjoy some company, as you're only here for the night." She gestures between her and her friend.

It takes every bit of self-control I possess to remain unmoving.

Caspian clicks his tongue as his gaze roams both of their bodies. "The two of you being that company, I assume?" They nod and their smiles widen when he steps closer. I wasn't planning on answering for three deaths tonight, but what has to be done will be done if he moves even a hair closer.

"Listen carefully," he continues, his voice dropping to a seductive tenor. The first woman reaches back out to trace his taut muscles, and he seems to not notice as he smiles. "I do not appreciate you trying to make me a fool. You two are very aware of who Ariella is to me, so the fact that you thought your collective worth was even in the same realm as her is insulting."

My jaw drops, and suddenly I'm feeling hot for an entirely different reason. Fuck. I want to walk over there and drop to my knees before him.

I've never pleasured a man with my mouth, but I'm practically salivating to show Caspian just what those words did to me.

I will later...but for now, I have egos to ruin.

Stepping from the shadows, all three heads snap my way as I look between the women. They're pretty. I'm certain they acquire much attention, especially together, and that makes this so much sweeter. They both watch me with palpable hatred, but my focus shifts to the prince, who's eyeing me like a predator.

I say nothing as I stalk up to their group, grab the back of Caspian's neck, and pull his lips to mine. His hands find my waist not a moment later, the touch tingling as he slides them back to mold us together. His tongue meets mine, and I moan against his mouth, arching further into his hold. I pull at him harder, as if he could get any closer, and he bites my lip, drawing blood when I rub against his erection.

The taste of copper hangs sweetly on my tongue as the warmth of his body envelops me, drowning out the venomous stares from our audience.

I'm dizzy from the unconditional passion and reverence in his kiss. I could lose myself here, in this moment that speaks louder than any words we've shared, but I'm painfully aware of the eyes lingering on us. I can sense their fury coiling in the air, and it is sweet.

I pull away just enough to meet Caspian's eyes—hungry and alert—as our heavy breaths share the non-existent space between us. He flashes a warm smile, dragging a finger down the length of my spine. My heart catches, and I shiver.

"Angel, I'll publicly reject every woman in the realm, one at a time, if this is the response it will garner." I'm so enraptured that I almost forget about the scheming women—almost.

Looking to my left, I raise a brow at the women. "Are you waiting for him to humiliate you again, or were you hoping to see exactly how I *treat my lover*?" I mock their earlier words, continuing when the first opens her mouth. "Leave before I change my mind to skin you both alive and feed your rotting flesh to the griffins."

Their expressions shift, mouths agape, as if the promise in my words renders them mute. The taller one fumbles, stepping back, shock painting her face a ghastly white. The other blinks, disbelief flickering before she's dragged away and they disappear into the crowd of people.

Caspian faces me, his smirk growing wider, as if I've just unveiled a new layer of myself for him to admire. "My fierce assassin," he teases with a giddy lightness, his voice a sultry whisper that makes my blood sing. "Dare I say you've grown? Months ago, you would have had their heads for even looking at what's yours."

I roll my eyes but can't help the smile tugging at my lips. He's not wrong—admittedly, I've gone soft. It's shameful.

A shame I'll deal with tomorrow...right now, the prince is all I wish to focus on.

"I'll admit that was quite attractive." My voice is no louder than a breath, but Caspian's eyes shine like I've given him the realm.

He shrugs. "Perhaps I've grown, as well. It's time I stop living blissfully unaware in my ignorance and begin focusing on what's important."

"And rejecting two beautiful women that were offering themselves at the same time was important?"

"No, Ariella," he murmurs against my mouth, and my stomach feels like it will explode from the fluttering. "What's important is you."

I lean back, attempting to push some distance between us, but Caspian only squeezes me harder, refusing to separate our bodies. His words linger in the air for a moment, so simple yet undeniably significant.

But, who am I if I do not challenge everything good in my life? I force a laugh, a soft sound tinged with disbelief. "Me? That's a fucking joke, prince. There are at least a hundred other things you could consider important—like your kingdom, your duties—"

He cuts me off, his lips brushing against my ear as he whispers with a seductive fierceness, "None of that matters without you. I've lived foolishly, thinking being a prince only meant wearing the crown and entertaining the nobility." His breath sends shivers cascading down the back of my neck, igniting a fire that simmers in my veins. "I know differently now, but all of it is obsolete in comparison."

"And what would you say to the people of Eldoria that wonder why their prince prioritizes the subject of their worst nightmares over them?"

He smirks as his fingers weave through the hair along my back. "I'd say they just haven't met you yet."

I grin—the movement genuine—and drag my hand over the smooth expanse of muscle along his abdomen, erasing whatever disease those women shared when they touched him without permission. "You are too good at being charming...it's not natural."

He flexes under my hand—something I am beginning to very much enjoy.

"Well, let's not keep our hosts waiting, angel. We are the guests of honor, after all." He pulls back, sliding his fingers between mine before leading us into the crowd.

They part as we approach, their eyes following our movements with an intensity that makes my skin crawl. The clearing opens to reveal tables laden with food and drink, surrounding a massive fire that reaches toward the stars. Flowers bloom everywhere, their ethereal glow casting strange shadows across faces turned our way.

Rael stands from his seat at the head table, arms spread wide before he gestures. "Our honored guests arrive." The man to his right speaks, his voice carrying across the gathering, and to my shock, every single person drops to one knee.

I grip Caspian's hand tighter. "What the fuck?"

"Please," Rael's companion translates as the leader gestures to two ornate chairs beside him. "Join me."

We make our way through the kneeling crowd, and I fight the urge to draw my dagger. This feels wrong. Like we're walking into something bigger than ourselves.

"You seem unsettled," the man says for Rael as we take our seats. He waves his hand and the crowd rises, returning to their festivities.

"Why wouldn't I be? Your people just bowed to us like we're—"

"Royalty?" His eyes sparkle with hidden meaning. "Perhaps it is because the Prince of Eldoria *is* royalty. Or perhaps there are things about yourselves you've yet to discover."

Caspian leans forward. "What exactly are you insinuating?"

Rael smiles and raises his glass. "To fate," he gestures, then turns to address another guest before we can question him further.

The night progresses in a blur of strange customs and cryptic conversations. Every time I try to press Rael for answers, he deflects with practiced ease. By the time the moon reaches its peak, exhaustion weighs heavy on my bones.

"We should rest," Caspian whispers against my ear, and a deep shiver overtakes my insides. "We have a long journey ahead."

I nod, grateful for the excuse to escape the suffocating attention. As we rise to leave, Rael catches my arm.

"Remember what I said about the price you must pay," the translator murmurs at his leader's unspoken words. "The path ahead will be difficult."

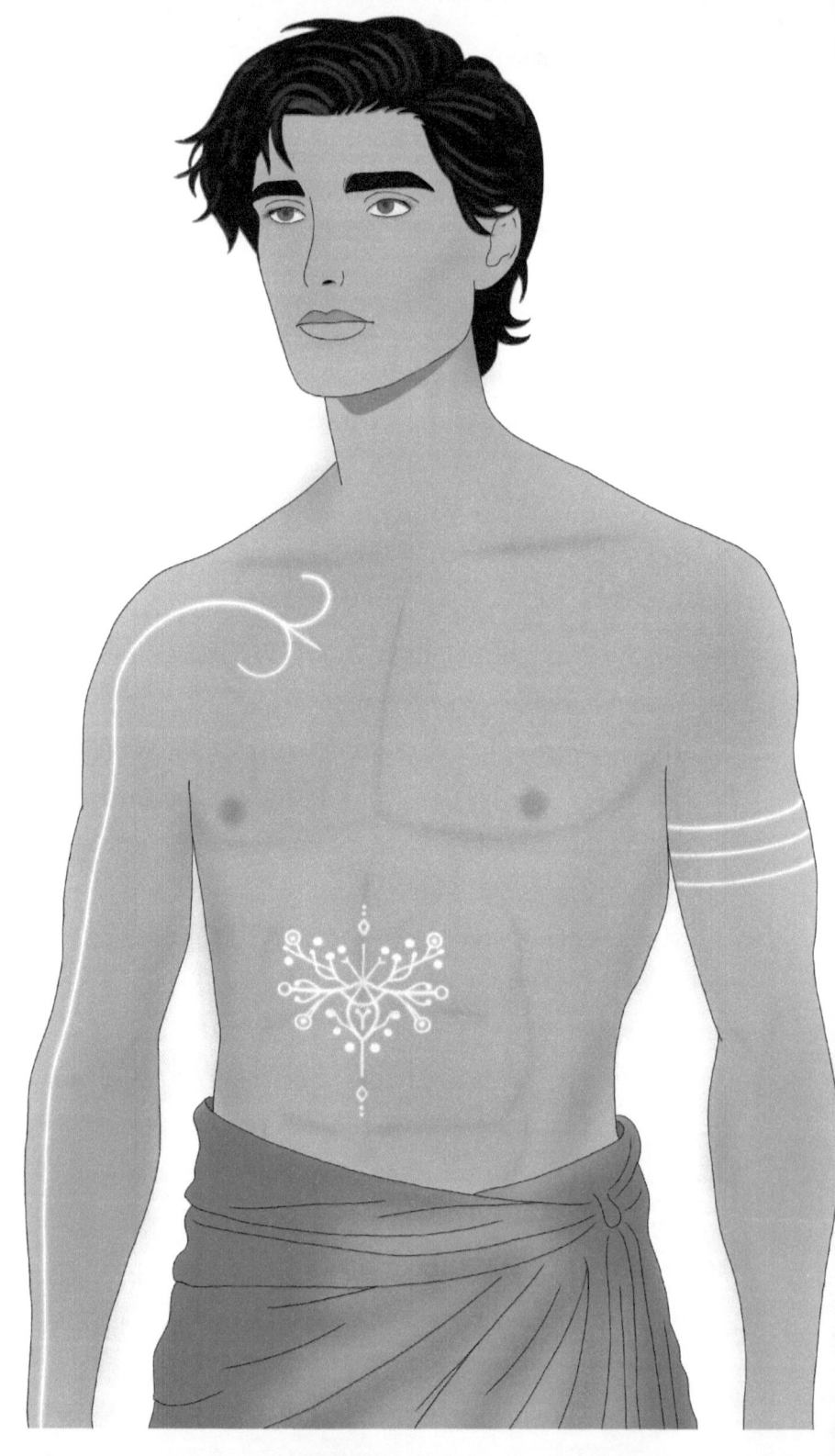

Chapter Fifteen

Caspian

I stare at the city walls of Valoria rising before us, my heart heavy with the weight of decisions yet unmade. The morning sun casts long shadows across the path, and I can't shake the feeling that everything's about to change.

"You're brooding again." Ariella's voice cuts through my thoughts. "Your face gets all scrunched up when you do that."

I turn to her, drinking in the sight of her silver hair glinting in the sunlight. The past few days since leaving the Palmluvela have been...different. Quieter. More intimate in ways I never expected.

"Just thinking about my father." The words taste bitter on my tongue. "About what choosing you over him means." Shit—I should not have said that aloud.

She stops walking, her green eyes narrowing. "I never asked you to choose."

"No, but we both know it's coming." I run a hand through my hair, frustration building in my chest. "He's my father, Ariella. The king. Everything I am, everything I was raised to be, ties back to him. But when I look at what he's done—to you, to others, that person in the library..."

"Then don't choose." Her voice is soft, but firm. "Walk away. Let me handle him."

"And watch you die from his decisions?" The mere thought sends ice through my veins. "I'd rather burn his entire kingdom down."

Something flashes in her eyes—surprise, maybe even fear. Not of me, but of what my words mean. What I'm willing to sacrifice.

"Caspian." She steps closer, close enough that I can count the freckles dusting her nose. "You don't mean that."

"I do." The truth of it is daunting. "Angel help me, I do. These past days with you...I've seen more humanity in one assassin than in all my father's years of rule."

She opens her mouth to respond, seeming defensive, but movement at the castle gates catches our attention. A crowd has gathered, their faces twisted with an anger I've never seen before.

Something is very wrong in Valoria.

The crowd's shouts grow louder as we near the gates. I shift closer to Ariella, though she's undoubtedly more capable of handling any threat than I am. Her fingers brush against mine—a warning or reassurance, I'm not quite sure.

"Death to the king! Death to the royals!" Someone screams from within the mass of people. My jaw clenches as the cry is taken up by others, the sound echoing off Valoria's walls.

"Well," Ariella mutters, "seems like your decision might be easier than you thought."

I shoot her a look, but there's no humor in her eyes. Just that calculated intensity she gets when she's analyzing a situation. Her hand rests on one of her blades—not drawing it, but ready.

"What happened while we were gone? It hasn't even been two weeks?" I ask no one in particular, scanning the faces before us. These aren't the usual inciters or drunk idiots. I spot merchants, craftsmen, even a few nobles among them.

A rock sails through the air, striking one of the guards. He stumbles back, blood trickling from his forehead. Before his companion can react, more stones follow.

"We need to get inside," I say, grabbing Ariella's arm. She doesn't resist as I pull us toward a side entrance I used to sneak out of as a child. The guard stationed there recognizes me immediately, his eyes widening at the sight of the wraith by my side.

"Your Highness! Thank the Angel—your father has been demanding your return."

"What's happening?" I question, but he just shakes his head.

"It's not my place to say, but things have changed since you left. The king, he's..." The man swallows hard. "You should see for yourself."

I feel Ariella tense beside me. Whatever is waiting inside those walls, I know one thing with absolute certainty: neither of us will face it alone. Not anymore.

I step through the side entrance, the familiar musty scent of the castle's stone walls affecting me differently now. Each one seems to hold secrets I was too naïve to see before.

"Your father's in the throne room," the guard offers, his eyes darting between Ariella and me.

I nod, though my feet refuse to move. The wraith beside me radiates a deadly calm that makes even the guard take an unconscious step back. Her wary eyes scan our surroundings with predatory focus.

A commotion from the main hall draws our attention. The shouts from outside have penetrated the castle walls, their anger seeping through stone like poison.

"I should go to him," I say, though every instinct screams otherwise.

"And what if I told you no?" Her lips quirk up in the slightest.

"You know I would, anyway."

"Yes." The single word carries more weight than it should.

We move through the corridors, passing staff who flatten themselves against walls to avoid us. Their fear isn't wholly directed at the notorious Silver Wraith for once—their eyes are fixed on me.

"They truly love reminding themselves of what I am," Ariella states, winking at a woman who just dropped her basket at the sight of us.

I can't help but smile, despite everything. "As do I. But unlike them, I love your temper and murderous nature, angel."

Her eyes narrow at the endearment, but there's something else there, too. Something that makes my heart race faster than any blade of hers at my throat ever could.

The throne room doors loom before us, and I take a steadying breath, stretching my neck before nodding to the stationed sentry. Something in my gut tells me that whatever is waiting for us beyond this barrier is worse than I've anticipated.

The heavy doors creak open to reveal my father on his throne. The familiar crimson and gold of the room feels stifling now, the tapestries hanging limply in the still air. He sits straight-backed, his untarnished crown glinting in the afternoon light streaming through the tall windows. The emptiness of the vast chamber makes his presence even more imposing.

Ariella's steady breathing beside me is comforting. The soft sound of her boots on the polished floor echoes as we approach the dais. Her presence radiates an impassive calm that somehow steadies my buzzing thoughts.

"So, you've returned." My father's voice carries that same authoritative tone I've heard my entire life, but it's different now. Harder. "And with the wraith, I see."

The muscles in my jaw clench. The way he says 'wraith' makes my skin crawl—like she's beneath him, beneath notice. I feel rather than see Ariella's amused reaction. She's probably fighting back one of those cutting remarks she loves to make.

I wouldn't mind hearing one right now. Maybe it would mask the sound of my racing heart.

"What's happening outside?" I ask, ignoring his obvious disapproval. "Why are the people calling for your death?"

He waves a hand dismissively. "Mere peasants who don't understand the necessities of rule. They'll be dealt with."

The casual cruelty in his voice stuns me. How had I never noticed it before? Or had I simply chosen not to see it? The weight of the sword at my hip doubles, and I'm acutely aware of every guard's position in the room. I itch to examine each one, to see if I would consider them loyal to my father, or if they would be loyal to me, but I do not dare break the king's stare.

"Necessities of rule?" Ariella's voice drips with venom. "Is that what you called it when you murdered my father, too?"

The temperature in the room seems to drop several degrees. My father's eyes narrow as he looks directly at her for the first time since arriving, and I resist the urge to step between them. The tension crackles like lightning before a storm.

It's strange, hearing her speak the words aloud. We all know the truth—fucking Aether, the entire kingdom knows the truth, but it's never spoken.

I keep my breathing steady as I watch the scene unfold, refusing to show any reaction to Ariella's words. My father's face darkens, his fingers tightening on the armrests of his throne.

"You dare speak to me of murder?" His voice fills the chamber. "You, the lowest of the kingdom's scum, who has taken countless lives?"

"At least I'm honest about what I am." Ariella's tone is calm, deadly. "I don't hide behind a crown and pretend my kills are for the good of the realm. Nor do I hire *scum* to do my killing for me."

I shift my weight, aware of the guards' hands moving to their weapons. It's hard to breathe around all this tension. Every instinct screams at me to intervene, to prevent what's coming, but I know better. This moment has been brewing for years.

"You know nothing of ruling," my father spits. "Of the choices a king must make."

"I know enough." Ariella takes a step forward, and several guards flinch. The air around her seems to disappear, silencing her advance. "I know you whipped an innocent man to death in front of his daughter—in front of the entire Angel-damned city. I know you murdered Isaiah because I dared to speak to your son."

I show no reaction, though my organs flip at a rapid pace. I'd suspected, of course, but hearing it confirmed is entirely different.

"Watch yourself, wraith." My father rises from his throne, his voice carrying that dangerous edge I remember from childhood. "You may have my son fooled with your charms, but I see you for what you are."

A laugh escapes Ariella's lips—the sound sharp and cruel. "And what am I, *Your Majesty?*"

"A whore of a mistake I should have corrected years ago." He gestures to the guards. "Take her down below."

I move without thinking, positioning myself between Ariella and the advancing guards. "Stop."

The single word echoes through the oversized room. My father's eyes widen—whether from surprise or rage, I no longer care.

"Step aside, Caspian."

"No." The word tastes foreign on my tongue. I've never outwardly defied him before. But as I stand here, finding strength in

Ariella's presence behind me, I know I've made my choice. The glimmer of disappointment in his eyes confirms he knows it, too.

I won't watch him take anyone else.

I sense Ariella shift behind me, her breath ghosting across my neck. "Move, Caspian."

"No." I keep my eyes locked on my father, refusing to back down. "I won't let him hurt you."

"You foolish, noble prince." Her words carry an edge of frustration. "This isn't your fight."

"It became my fight the moment I laid eyes on you." The confession slips out before I can stop it, echoing through the throne room. I hear her sharp intake of breath, feel the way she struggles to even her breathing.

My father's face contorts with rage. "You dare choose this murderer over your own blood? Over your duty to the crown?"

"I choose what's right." My voice is steadier than I feel. "Something you seem to have forgotten how to do, father."

The guards hesitate, clearly torn between their king's orders and my intervention. I can discern the uncertainty in their eyes—they've watched me grow up, trained with me, shared meals and jokes. Now I'm asking them to pick a side.

"This is treason," my father snarls, descending the dais steps. "You would throw away everything? Your birthright, your future—for *her*?" I'm offended he knows nothing of me.

Ariella's fingers brush against my back in a silent warning. Or perhaps a comfort. The touch sends warmth through my chest, solidifying my resolve.

"I would throw away far more." The words taste like truth on my tongue. "But this isn't about her right now. This is about what you've done. To her father, to Isaiah, to countless others. The people outside aren't calling for your death because of one wraith—they're calling for it because you've forgotten what it means to be a true king. What have you done, father?"

My words hang in the air as memories flood through me. The pieces I'd ignored for so long finally clicking into place. Reports of missing children from the outer districts. The way certain noble families disappeared, only to have their estates seized by the crown. The increasing number of public executions, each one justified with vaguer charges of treason. The paperwork regarding the outer housing population—

"You've been taking them." My voice sounds hollow even to my own ears. I thought it an unlikely assumption, but the look in his eyes confirms my reasoning. "The children from the lower districts."

Behind me, Ariella tenses. The kind of stillness that precedes violence.

"You know nothing," my father spits, but there's something in his eyes—a flicker of...pride? The sight makes me sick.

"I know enough. The reports crossing my desk, the ones you insisted I handle personally...they weren't just routine paperwork, were they? You wanted me to see them. To understand what ruling really means." The words taste like ash in my mouth. "Those families weren't being relocated to other cities. The children weren't being sent to *special schools*."

A cruel smile twists his lips. "Finally showing some wisdom, my son? Yes. Sacrifices must be made to maintain order. Their essence—their power—it strengthens the crown. Strengthens the kingdom." He rolls his shoulders, stretching his palms. "How do you think we've maintained our rule for so long? The Blackwood line has always understood what others refuse to see—power requires sacrifice."

I think of all those missing children that have gone unnoticed. Of families torn apart. Of Ariella's father, who likely discovered the truth and paid for it with his life. Of Isaiah, who simply got too close to someone the king couldn't control.

"You're a monster." The words slip out, though I do not care enough to regret them.

His face hardens. "I am a *king*. And you are still my son, despite your...current confusion." His eyes flick to Ariella. "Though perhaps it's time I reminded you of what that truly means."

The silence that follows is deafening. My heartbeat pounds in my chest, and the weight of every eye in the room presses down on me. The king's face is blank, but his eyes burn with an intensity that would have made me flinch just days ago.

He nods, clasping his hands before speaking once more. "If you do not make the correct choice, then you are no son of mine." He turns to the guards, his voice cold as ice. "Leave them. You have a week, Caspian. A week to make the decision on your own before her head decorates the front gates." He nods toward Ariella, not looking at her but grimacing all the same.

I draw my sword, the sound of steel against leather echoing off the stone walls. Behind me, there's the familiar whisper of Ariella's lethal chuckle. "Do it, Your Majesty."

He shifts his attention to her as he snarls his next words, "You have no idea the pain I could put you through, wraith."

I clench my jaw as Ariella steps around me, her predatory grace making even my father's guards shift uncomfortably.

"Oh, but I do know pain, *Your Majesty*." Her voice drips with mockery. She takes another step forward, and I fight the urge to grab her arm. "Tell me, Thalion, did you enjoy watching the life drain from his eyes? My father? Did it make you feel powerful to execute an innocent man?"

My father's face contorts with rage. "Erendor was a traitor who deserved far worse than what he got."

"He discovered your secrets, did he not?" Ariella's laugh is sharp and cruel. "Found out what you were doing... That's why you had to silence him."

"Careful, wraith." My father's voice carries a dangerous, desperate edge. "You're treading dangerous ground."

"What will you do?" She spreads her arms wide, a cruel smile spreading across her face. "Kill me like you killed him? Like you killed Isaiah? Go ahead—I've been itching for a good fight."

The air crackles with tension as they stare each other down. I sense the essence building around Ariella, though she keeps it carefully contained. One wrong move and this whole room could erupt in violence.

"Enough." I grab Ariella's arm, surprised when she doesn't move to break my grip. "We're leaving."

"Listen to him," my father sneers. "Run away while you still can. But remember my warning, son—one week."

Ariella's muscles coil under my hand, and I know she's about to do something we'll all regret. Before she can move, I drag her toward the door, ignoring her attempts to break free.

"Get your fucking hands off me," she hisses as we exit the throne room.

"Not until we're far enough away that you won't go back in there and get yourself killed." I continue pulling her down the corridor, my heart pounding. "I know you want revenge, but not like this. Not when he's expecting it."

She could break free if she wanted to. We both know that. But she allows me to lead her away from my father and his sentries, though her entire body vibrates with barely contained rage.

I don't stop until we're several hallways away, releasing her arm and hating as she immediately puts distance between us.

I watch as Ariella paces the empty hallway, several fingers tapping the blade on her thigh. The afternoon light streams through tall windows, casting her silver hair in a beautiful glow. Any other time, I'd be mesmerized by the sight. Right now, I'm too focused on keeping her from storming back to kill my father.

"You should have let me end him," she snarls, her green eyes flashing threats.

"And what? Let you die in the process?" I run a hand through my hair, fighting back my own anger. "Ariella—*he was waiting for you to attack.* He *wanted* you to give him an excuse."

She pauses her pacing to glare at me. "I don't need your protection."

"Angel's sake, I know that." I step closer, pleased when she doesn't back away. "But this isn't about protection. This is about being smart. You heard what he admitted in there—about the children and what he's planning to do to the people outside. We need proof before we can move against him."

Her lips curl into a cruel smile. "I don't need proof of anything to put a blade through his heart."

"No, but the kingdom does." I close the distance between us, desperately wanting to touch her but knowing better with the way she watches me. "If we kill him without exposing what he's done, nothing changes. Varrick will rally the noble families to enthrone a puppet king and continue everything he's doing."

She freezes, that eerie calm washing over her features that makes her look more wraith than human. I'd read about wraiths once, though have refrained from doing so again. The creatures are terrifying—much like the woman in front of me. Whoever gave Ariella her title knew her too well. "Then I'll kill all of them."

The words tumble through my stomach. Not from fear—never from fear with her—but from the raw truth in them. She will be my father's death, one way or another. I chuckle. She'll likely be my death, too. The thought should horrify me. Instead, I find myself fighting back a smile.

"Give me time," I plead. "One week. Let's gather evidence and build support among the royal guards. Then we can make him pay for everything he's done."

Her eyes search mine, looking for any trace of deception. I steady my emotions and hold her gaze, letting her see the truth of my words. Finally, she gives a sharp nod.

"One week," she agrees, though her tone suggests it's against her better judgment. "But I do not dabble in patience, so if he makes one move against me or anyone else, I won't wait."

I lean against the stone wall, enjoying its cool surface as my mind races. My fingers absently trace the pommel of my sword, finding comfort in its familiar weight.

Everything I thought I knew about my family, about ruling, has been shattered. The memories assault me—all those reports crossing my desk, the disappearances I'd written off as routine matters. How many children had I unknowingly condemned by signing those papers? The thought makes bile rise in my throat.

My father's words repeat in my head: *Power requires sacrifice.* Is that what being king means? Sacrificing innocents to maintain control? If so, I want no part of it. The crown suddenly feels like a noose around my neck, threatening to strangle everything good and right from my soul.

But then there's Ariella. She paces before me like a caged beast, all lethal grace and simmering fury. My breath catches. Even in her rage—or perhaps because of it—she's the most beautiful thing I've ever seen.

She represents everything I was taught to hate, to fear. An assassin, a wraith, someone who kills without mercy. Yet watching her, I see the truth my father missed. Her kills may not always be justified or right, but she's never shied away from the truth. She's been irritatingly clear about who she is since the day I met her.

In her own way, she's more noble than any of the preening lords and ladies who fill my father's court. Far more than my father himself.

I know I should let her go, should focus on gathering evidence against my father so that she can take the day before we resume our attempt to stop his shifting of the balance. But the sight of her prowling the hallway sets my blood on fire. Without thinking, I reach out and grab her arm, needing to touch her, to ground myself in something real.

She whirls on me. "Touch me again without permission, and you'll die before your father does."

I can't help the smile that spreads across my face. "Then kill me, I don't care. But I'm going to fuck you first."

She sputters, her resistance loosening, and I use the hesitation to drag her toward my room. I'm tempted to take her back and claim her in front of the king, but I selfishly want the week he's given me. We both know I will not bow to his demands, so I'll play his game for now.

Chapter Sixteen

Ariella

T he heat is unbearable today. Sweat drips down my neck as I circle Caspian on the training grounds, my muscles tensing with each calculated step. His silver eyes follow my movements, a predatory gleam flickering through them when I shift my stance. The prince has improved significantly since we began training together—though I'd never tell him that. He has an immense ego as it is.

"You're favoring your left side," he taunts, that insufferable smirk spreading across his face.

I narrow my eyes. "And you're talking too much."

He chuckles, the sound firing an unwanted wave of heat through my core. His chest rises with heavy breaths, sweat glistening along his skin in a way that shouldn't be so fucking distracting.

I nearly miss his smile when he grabs the bottom of his shirt and pulls it over his head, tossing it aside with expert nonchalance. My jaw clenches—he knows exactly what he's doing.

"Getting warm, angel?"

Two can play at this game. I maintain eye contact as I strip my top off, leaving me in just my shorts and training bra. His pupils dilate, hands flexing at his sides. Good.

"Fucking Aether," Gavriel mutters from where he leans against the stone wall. "Can you two not make everything sexual?"

I flip him off without looking his way, focusing on Caspian's approaching form. "Jealous, brute?"

The guard scoffs but says nothing else. The tension between us has worsened since Caspian and I returned. Not that I give a fuck what he thinks of me.

"Focus," Caspian demands, throwing a punch that I easily dodge. His bare chest brushes against my arm, and I bite back a groan at the contact.

This is going to be a long fucking day.

My blade meets his forearm as I spin past, just missing the kick he aims at my leg. He's getting better at reading my movements—though his form is still shit. His shoulders tense when I shift my stance, preparing for another attack.

"Your balance is off." The words slip from my mouth, and I curse under my breath. Fuck's sake, I'm not here to teach him.

"What?" He straightens, dropping his guard. Foolish.

I sweep his legs out from under him, watching as he lands hard on his back with a grunt. "Never let your opponent distract you." I press my boot to his chest, raising a brow when his hand wraps around my ankle. "Even if they're trying to help your pathetic stance."

His eyes darken as he yanks my foot, attempting to throw me down next to him. I allow myself to fall, using the momentum to roll and spring back up.

"My stance is not pathetic." He pushes to his feet, running a hand through his sweat-dampened hair.

"Then prove it." I circle him, noting how his weight shifts too far forward. "Stop compensating for your height by leaning into your strikes. Ground yourself properly and you won't need to."

He adjusts his footing, a determined look crossing his features. When he advances this time, his movements are more controlled. His fist grazes my jaw as I dodge—closer than he's gotten before. Something flutters in my stomach.

"Better." I catch his wrist and twist, a little surprised when he breaks my hold using a technique I showed him in the forest last week during our downtime. "Though your center is still vulnerable."

"Stop analyzing me and fight," he growls, throwing another punch that I dodge.

"I can do both." I smirk when frustration flashes in his eyes. "What's wrong, prince? Don't like being told what to do? Don't like that I refuse to grovel at your feet and tell you, you're the best at everything?" I glance at his guard, winking when I find him already glaring in my direction.

He's so fucking lucky Caspian won't allow me to kill him. I'd have some fun before taking his sorry life.

A smile forms at the thought, and the prince's answering grin sends heat coursing through me. "Thinking about violence again, angel?"

Gavriel makes a gagging sound. "I'm leaving before this gets worse."

"Good," Caspian and I say in unison, neither of us looking away from the other.

The moment Gavriel's footsteps fade, Caspian lunges. I spin away from his grasp, but he anticipates the movement and catches my arm. His chest presses against my back as he attempts to pin me, his breath fanning over my neck.

"Tired, darling?" His low voice sends shivers to places I do not wish to acknowledge at the moment.

I drive my elbow back, connecting with his ribs. He grunts but doesn't release his hold. "You wish."

Using his weight against him, I flip us both to the ground. We roll through the dirt, each fighting for dominance. His knee slides between my thighs when he pins me, and I bare my teeth at his triumphant expression.

"I win," he purrs, leaning closer until his lips brush my ear. "What's my prize?"

I buck my hips, throwing him off balance enough to reverse our positions. "You haven't won shit." I press my forearm to his throat, not hard enough to cut off his air, but enough to make a point. His hands slide up my thighs to grip my waist.

"No?" His thumbs trace circles on my heated skin. "Because from where I'm sitting, this feels like winning."

"You're not sitting," I remind him, applying more pressure to his throat. "You're lying in the dirt where you belong."

He laughs, the sound vibrating through my body, shaking my arm. "Only because you put me here." His fingers dig into my hips. "Tell me, Ariella...do you enjoy having me under you like this?"

"Shut up." Childish response, but I feel so weak being this close to him. It fucks with my head.

"Give me a better use for my mouth, and I will."

I lean down until our faces are inches apart. "Is that what you want? For me to shut that pretty mouth of yours?" I shouldn't feed his taunts, but it's impossible to not match his playfulness.

His pupils dilate further, eclipsing the silver. "I want a lot of things from you."

The raw honesty in his voice tightens my chest. This isn't part of our usual game. There's a heaviness to his gaze, something that makes me want to run.

Instead, I press my lips to his.

He responds immediately, one hand sliding up my back while the other tangles in my hair. The kiss is rough and desperate, filled with all the tension we've been dancing around for weeks that doesn't seem to let up, no matter how many times we fuck. Waves of deliciously nauseating pleasure funnel through my abdomen, making my limbs wither under his attention.

His tongue slides against mine as a hand grips my waist, pulling me impossibly closer. The heat of his skin burns through my remaining clothes, making me wish we were somewhere more private. My fingers trace down his chest, memorizing every dip and curve.

Suddenly, he breaks the kiss and flips us over, pinning my hands above my head. His eyes are dark with desire as he smirks down at me.

"Now who's in the dirt?"

My lips purse. "Not for long." I buck my hips and twist, but his grip is strong. He's learned too fucking well.

Or perhaps I do not care to get him off me as much as I want to believe.

"Frustrated, are we?" The man clearly wishes to die.

I manage to free one hand and slam it into his side. He grunts but maintains his position above me. We grapple, trading blows and holds until we're both covered in sweat and dirt.

"For fuck's sake, I leave for five minutes..." Gavriel's annoyed voice cuts through our struggle.

I shove Caspian off me and spring to my feet, wiping dirt from my face. "Miss me already, brute?"

His response is a burst of essence that catches the side of my shorts, burning through the fabric. I glance down at the smoking hole now exposing my upper thigh, a giddiness tingling under my skin.

"These were my favorite pair, you jealous prick." I brush off the charred remains. "Though I suppose I should thank you—they were getting a bit restricting."

"Shut your fucking mouth for once," he snarls, advancing toward me with his fists raised.

My answering smile is wicked. Finally, some real fun.

A drop of rain hits my cheek as Gavriel charges at me, his pyro essence blazing through the air. I duck under his attack, my feet sliding in the quickly dampening dirt.

"Come on, Gav. Is that all you've got?" I taunt, dancing away from another burst of flames. The rain intensifies, steam rising where his essence meets the water.

His dark eyes radiate a cold hatred. "You think you're so fucking special." He throws a punch that I barely dodge. "Walking around like you own the place, like you deserve him."

I laugh, the sound harsh against the pounding rain. Caspian stands off to the side, arms crossed, with a concerned look etched in his features. I shake my head at him—he understands that this fight between me and Gavriel has been simmering for a while. "Jealousy doesn't suit you, Gav." My fist connects with his jaw, and he stumbles back.

Lightning flashes overhead as we circle each other. His usual controlled demeanor cracks, rage seeping through every movement. Good. I want him unhinged.

"You'll get him killed," he spits, launching forward with a combination of strikes I wasn't expecting. One catches my ribs, forcing the air from my lungs. Fuck, he's strong. "Everything you touch turns to shit."

My shadows writhe under my skin, begging to be released. But I can't—not here where anyone could see. Instead, I drive my knee into his stomach and flip over his shoulder, using his momentum against him.

He recovers after a moment, spinning to grab my ankle. I twist free but slip over the mud, giving him an opening to slam me into the ground. Rain pelts my face as I roll away from his boot.

"You know *nothing* about me," I growl, sweeping his legs. He falls hard but rushes to kick up, catching my chin. The metallic taste of blood fills my mouth.

"I know enough." He wipes rain from his eyes. "You're poison. And when he finally sees that—"

My blade appears at his throat before he can finish. His essence flares, but I press harder. "Careful. You're not the only one who cares about him."

The admission surprises us both. His eyes widen the slightest before hardening again. We stay locked in that position, rain washing away the blood on my lip as a storm crashes above us.

Thunder cracks again, and I use the sound to mask my movements as I sweep Gavriel's legs once more. He catches himself before hitting the ground, flames erupting from his hands as he charges at me. I dance away from his attacks, my muscles burning with each dodge.

"You think you're protecting him?" I taunt, blocking a particularly vicious strike. "You're suffocating him with your pathetic devotion."

His eyes flash with a dangerous threat—I thrive in it. "And what would you know about devotion? You've no family. Your only so-called friend is dead. You kill for money, for fun." He spits blood onto the muddy ground. "You're nothing but a murderer playing at being worthy of a prince."

The words sting more than they should. I slam my elbow into his face, satisfaction coursing through me when his nose crunches under the impact. "At least I don't hide behind duty to excuse my feelings."

That hits home. His essence flares, wild and erratic, the rain sizzling as it hits the flames surrounding him. "You fucking bitch—"

"What's wrong, Gav?" I circle him, noting how his control slips further with each word. "Angry that he chose me? That he's probably sick of your *protective* facade?"

He roars, charging at me with reckless abandon. I sidestep his attack, but he anticipates the movement and catches my arm. The heat of his essence burns through my skin before I can break free. I wince but manage to keep in the pained sound wanting to escape.

"I've watched over him for years," he snarls, throwing another punch that I duck around. "Protected him from people like you."

I laugh, the sound dark. "People like me? You mean people who actually challenge him? Who see him as more than just the precious prince who needs constant coddling?"

"You'll destroy him!" His fist connects with my jaw, sending me stumbling back. "Everything you touch turns to rot, and I won't let that happen to him."

Blood drips down my chin as I straighten. "Hate me all you fucking want—I don't care. But you're right about one thing." I wipe my mouth with the back of my hand. "I do destroy things. Care for a demonstration?"

My shadows pulse under my skin, begging to be released. Just a taste. Just enough to show this arrogant prick exactly what I'm capable of.

But Caspian's worried eyes catch mine, and he jolts forward, stepping between his guard and me before I can release anything.

Raised hands push against both my chest and the guard's. "Enough." His voice carries the weight of command, but there's an edge of concern to it.

"Move," I growl, my shadows still writhing beneath my skin. The rain continues to pour, plastering his lush hair to his forehead.

"No." His silver eyes lock with mine. "You're done."

Gavriel scoffs behind him. "Of course you'd defend her."

"I'm not defending anyone," Caspian snaps, turning to face his guard. "But this pointless fighting needs to stop. We have bigger problems to deal with."

He's right. The strange behavior of the realm, the increased security at the castle, whatever the fuck the king is doing—all of it is far worse than Gavriel's jealousy.

"Fine." A finger taps against the blade on my hip as I ignore the burn of essence on my arm where Gavriel's flames touched me. "But keep your *dog* on a tighter leash next time."

Gavriel lunges forward, but Caspian blocks his path. "Both of you, *stop*." He runs a hand through his wet hair, frustration evident in every movement. "You're acting like damn children. We need to focus on my father and the Accord. We need to help the people of the kingdom."

"They tried to kill you," I remind him, the memory of those people attacking him still fresh in my mind. Their words echo in my head...*death to the king, death to the royals.*

"I know." His shoulders tense. "And their reactions are valid. I fear my father is only going to get worse now that he's confessed to me. So this petty fighting is on hold for now."

The castle looms behind us, its new fortifications making it look more like a prison than a palace. The Frostwell guards stationed along the walls watch us with cold eyes, their presence a stark reminder that things have changed in the week we've been away.

"Whatever. I'm tired." I push through both men and start walking toward the castle, not waiting to see if Caspian follows. The rain begins to ease, but the chill remains in my bones.

I storm through the castle doors, water dripping from my clothes and creating puddles on the pristine floor. The staff will hate me even more for this mess, but I couldn't care less right now.

"Ariella, wait!" Caspian calls from behind me. I ignore him, too focused on getting to my room and away from his insufferable friend.

I nearly collide with someone as I round a corner. The queen stands before me, her perfect posture and immaculate appearance making me feel even more disheveled. Her eyes rake over my mud-covered form with poorly concealed disgust as the lights above illuminate graying strands of hair around her face.

"I don't believe I've had the pleasure of meeting my son's new guard," she says, her voice dripping with false sweetness.

"I'm not your son's anything," I snap, just as Caspian catches up to us.

"Ignore her, mother. She enjoys being dramatic," he says, placing a hand on my lower back. I resist the urge to stab him.

The queen's eyes narrow as she takes in our appearance—both of us soaked, close to naked and covered in dirt, my shorts partially burned away from Gavriel's essence. "You certainly don't look like one of our sentries. Why are you not wearing the proper attire?"

I smirk, unable to resist. "Well, according to your husband, I'm just Caspian's whore. Though, like everything else he thinks of me, he has that wrong too."

"How's that?" she asks, her perfectly shaped eyebrow arching.

"Because Caspian is my whore."

The prince groans beside me while the queen and I glare at each other. I've never liked her—there's something calculating behind those eyes, something venomous beneath her pristine exterior. She always looks unhappy, like there's a constant bitter taste in her mouth.

Her gaze drifts to my hair, and there's a barely perceptible shift in her expression as it darkens. "You look so much like your mother," she muses. "In fact, the first time I saw you at the trials, I thought you were Valyria."

My fingers twitch toward my blade. The way she says my mother's name, like they were close...it sets my teeth on edge.

Seraphina's smile never wavers. "I only worry for my son's reputation. A prince consorting with...well." She gestures vaguely at my appearance. "I'm sure you understand my concerns."

"Mother," Caspian warns, his hand pressing firmer against my back.

"Oh, darling, I'm simply being honest. The kingdom talks, you know." She steps closer, her pressed dress rustling. "And they're saying such awful things about you both."

I bare my teeth in what could pass for a smile. "Good. Give them something real to talk about."

"Angel..." Caspian sighs.

The queen's eyes glitter with false concern. "You see? This is exactly what worries me. Such...aggression. Such disrespect for our traditions, our ways." She reaches out as if to touch my face, but I jerk back. "Your mother would be so disappointed to see what you've become."

My shadows writhe beneath my skin. I've yet to use them to choke the life from someone, but I'm happy to start now. "Do not speak of her."

"Why not? We were quite close, you know. Before she..." She trails off, sighing. "Well. Before everything went wrong."

"Nothing went wrong," I spit. "She was murdered."

"Is that what you believe?" She tilts her head, studying me like I'm some curious creature, before her gaze shifts into something akin to worry. "How fascinating. Though I suppose it's easier to blame others than face the truth."

"And what truth would that be, Your Majesty?" My voice is deadly quiet.

She pats Caspian's cheek. "My dear boy, you really should find better company. Someone more suitable for your position." Her eyes slide back to me. "Someone who isn't quite so broken."

Caspian and Seraphina have a tense, aggressive exchange, though I hear none of it. I shrivel into myself, her words replaying at an impossible speed in my head.

I've nothing to respond with because she's absolutely right. My instincts tell me to grab my blade and ensure she can never speak again, but my body no longer answers to me.

She ripped open the one insecurity I've refused to acknowledge, and suddenly my chest feels heavy. Dense.

My fingers grip the stone wall as I force myself to breathe through the queen's words. She knows nothing of my mother, of what happened that day. But her implications dig under my skin like poisoned blades.

I was only six when my mother took her life. Too young to understand why she'd leave me, but old enough to remember finding her body. The image is seared into my mind—her pale form sprawled across our floor, crimson pooling beneath her like some macabre painting.

Some nights I still wake tasting her blood in the air.

Marek says trauma shapes us, molds us into who we need to become.

But Marek...after he found me, he saw something in me worth saving. He took me to the guild, taught me to channel my rage into something deadly. *"Pain either breaks you or forges you stronger,"* he'd say during our training. *"Choose, Ariella"*

Always the wise man.

I chose to become the blade that would eventually sever the king's head from his shoulders. Every kill, every drop of blood I've spilled has been practice for that moment. Twenty years of honing myself into the perfect weapon, and I've not once allowed a single insecurity to plague my thoughts.

Yet here I stand, trembling before the queen's words like that helpless child again. Because she's right—I am broken. The little girl who lost everything never truly healed. She just learned to wear her scars like armor, and that is not something I've ever questioned. I have reveled in the fragmented pieces. Allowed them to burrow under my skin until they became a necessary part of me.

My past didn't ruin me—it patched up the splinters my parents caused and made me whole.

But now, with Caspian...he makes me want things I can't have. Makes me question if vengeance is all I'm meant for.

And that terrifies me more than any blade ever could, because it's all I've known.

"I would like to speak with my son," she announces in my direction. "Alone." My eyes flit between the mother-son duo, a heartbeat passing before I stalk down the hall to shower this day off. I'm so fucking sick of letting the royal family slither their way into my head. It's pathetic.

Once the king is dead, I will leave this tainted castle and figure out what artifacts are needed for the new Accord—with my luck, they'll not be the same as in the vision. No longer will I have to deal with the likes of the queen, or Gavriel, thank the fucking Angel. Just a few days until such freedoms are mine. I've waited twenty years for this; I can wait a little longer.

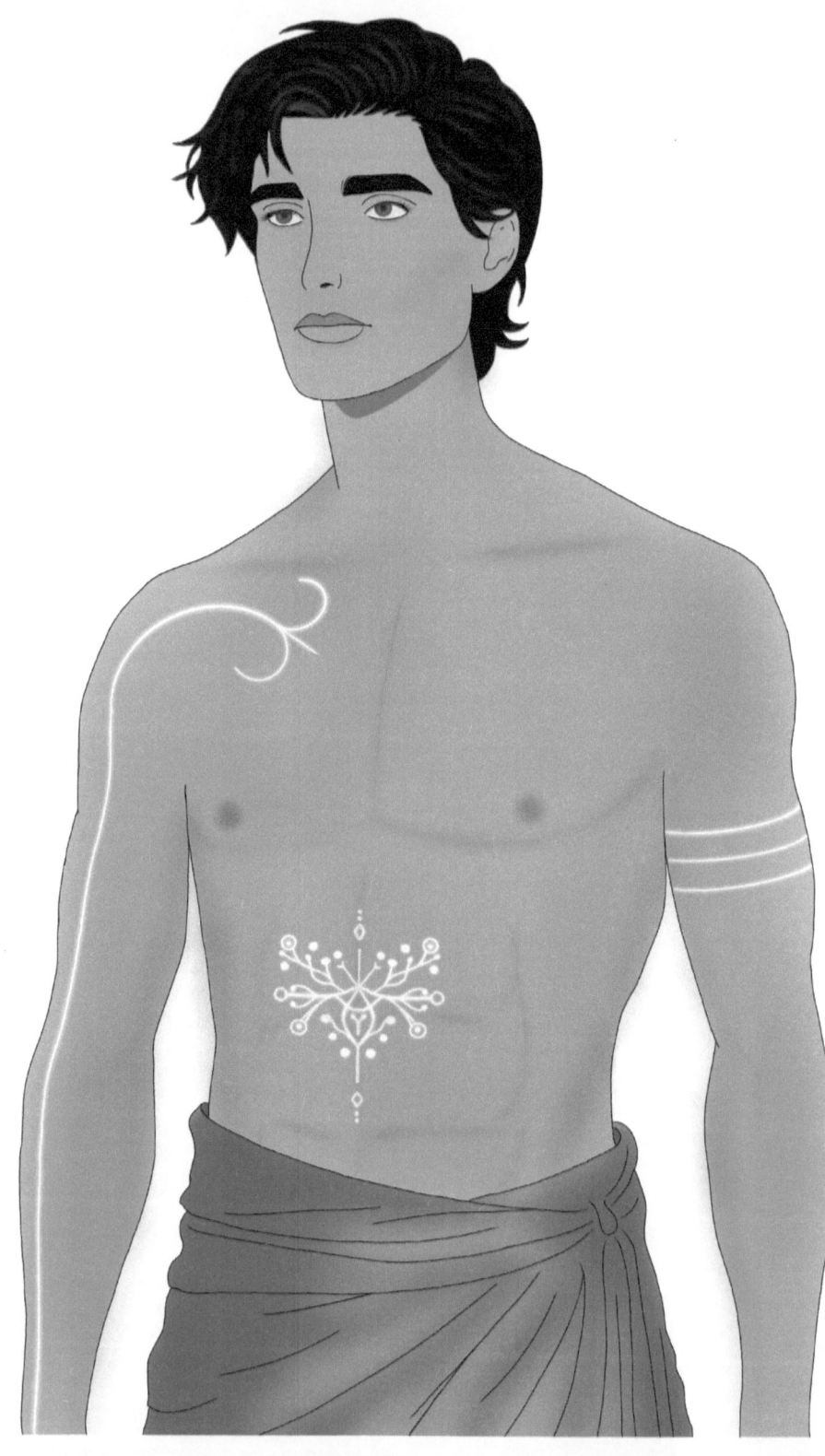

Chapter Seventeen
Caspian

The silence between Ariella and me feels charged as we walk through the castle halls. My muscles are still sore from our sparring session yesterday, but the physical discomfort pales compared to the storm in my mind. I glance at my wraith, her bright hair catching the morning light. She hasn't spoken much since her encounter with my mother, and I can't blame her.

The way my mother looked at her...there was recognition there, mixed with something else I couldn't quite place. And that comment about Valyria—Ariella's mother. I've never heard my mother mention her before, which only adds to the growing list of questions I have.

My jaw clenches as I think about the children being taken from their families. The peoples' anger haunts me. What could my father want with them? The guards won't tell me anything, and the castle staff avoid eye contact whenever I pass. Even Gavriel seems on edge, though he insists he knows nothing.

I should have seen this coming. The signs were there—the increased security, the whispers among the nobility, my father's growing paranoia. But I was too focused on other things...namely Ariella, but I cannot be blamed for caring for the woman.

My hand flexes at my side, remembering how she nearly released her forbidden essence yesterday. The raw vulnerability in her eyes before she ran. I've never seen her like that, and it terrifies me how much I want to see more. To understand every part of her.

But that will have to wait. My mother wouldn't request a private audience without reason. The fact that she's choosing now, after everything that's happened, is not a coincidence. My stomach turns as I consider what this could mean. Where do my true loyalties lie? With my family and the crown I'm meant to inherit? Or with the woman beside me who's shown me just how corrupt that crown has become?

And why does it matter so much to me? The king is the problem, not the queen or princess. I need to take care of him and do my best to leave my mother and sister out of it.

I steal another glance at Ariella, her face set in that carefully neutral expression she wears like armor. Her strength is so beautiful.

I pause outside my mother's study, turning to face Ariella. "Wait here."

She crosses her arms, leaning against the stone wall as her eyes form slits. "If there's even a hint that something's wrong, I'm breaking down that door."

"Didn't realize you cared so much about my wellbeing, angel." I smirk, unable to help myself.

Her eyes glisten dangerously. "I don't. But I need you to figure out what's happening with the Accord and your father. You're no use to me dead."

"Your concern is touching." I lean in to kiss her, but pull to the side at the last moment so my lips graze her cheek instead.

I do not miss her irritated expression before I enter my mother's study. The familiar scent of jasmine tea fills the air as I find her perched in casual elegance at her desk, hands folded in front of her.

"Mother." I bow my head before taking a seat across from her.

"My darling boy." Her voice is soft, but there's tension around her eyes. "I've been worried about you."

"I'm fine. Though I'm more concerned about what's happening here. Father's behavior is worrisome."

She releases a sigh from the depths of her soul, reaching to pour us both tea. There are lines on her face that weren't there just months ago; lines that surround her eyes and mouth, deepening when she frowns. She's just as stressed as me, and I've been a terrible son. Have I once asked how she's doing? "Yes. He's...changed. Grown more secretive. Even from me." I note the slight tremble in her hands as she sets down the pot. "He spends hours alone, won't tell anyone what he's doing. He's so temperamental that I'm afraid to even speak around him. This isn't the man I married."

I study her. My mother has always been politically savvy, choosing her words with precision. No matter the current events, she's always insisted as being a united family through everything.

The fact that she's openly criticizing the king means something is very wrong.

"The other day," she continues, voice dropping lower, "I saw him heading down to the tunnels beneath the castle. He was different when he returned. Almost feverish. I'm very worried about him, Caspian." My chest squeezes at the pain in her voice. She shouldn't have to worry this much, and while I won't reveal mine and Ariella's plans, I can at least try to alleviate some of her concern.

I nod, leaning forward to grab my tea. "I am looking into it. You can trust me to figure this out," I promise.

"Be careful, my love." She reaches across to clutch my hand for a moment before settling back. "Your father is not himself. I couldn't bear if anything happened to you."

"How is Vespera handling everything?" I ask, sipping the jasmine tea. The warmth helps ease some of the tension in my shoulders, and I relax back into the cushioned chair.

Mirroring my position, Mother's face softens at the mention of my sister. "She misses you. Though she's been keeping herself busy with her studies. That new tutor you recommended has been wonderful." Her smile is bright as she moves to sip from her cup. "She's already reading in three languages."

"*Three?* Last I checked, she could barely get through one without complaining." I chuckle, remembering how she used to hide her language books under her bed. The girl hates schooling and would much rather spend her days shopping her way through the kingdom. She is interested in fashion, and I believe she's begun to make some of her own clothing.

"Oh, you should see her now. She practically lives in her textbooks! Though..." Mother pauses, her lips turning down as a crease forms between her brows. "She asks about you every day. Wants to know when you'll be back for good. I think she's lonely without you here."

"I should visit her more." Guilt gnaws at my stomach. Between the competition, Ariella, and everything else that's arisen, I've neglected my little sister. "Maybe we could have dinner together soon? Just the three of us?"

"I would love that." Mother's smile reaches her eyes this time. "Though you'll have to suffer through her latest obsession; she's convinced she's going to train drakes now ever since she's learned the history of Invalle."

I nearly choke on my tea. "Drakes? Where did she get that idea?"

"Those stories you used to tell her about the griffin riders in the mountains. She found some mention in her texts that claim drakes are far friendlier than griffins, and now she's determined to be a rider just like in your fables." She shakes her head, laughing while a hand caresses the braid of her dark hair.

The mental image of my proper little sister chasing the beasts around the cliffs makes me laugh genuinely for the first time in days. I'm told the miners have a hard enough time securing their aid in relocating metals. While the drakes prefer solitude in their caves, they have been helpful to miners in recent centuries, accepting food offerings and inheriting newly forged caves after the metals are extracted. "That sounds like her. Remember when she tried to tame that fox that got into the garden?"

"Oh Angel, don't remind me. The groundskeeper still hasn't forgiven her for releasing all his chickens as 'bait'." We laugh together as she sets down her tea. Her scrutinizing gaze sweeps over my features before settling on my eyes, and I know she's about to reveal the real reason she wanted me here today.

Mother's expression shifts as she sucks in a breath before speaking. "Now, about the girl."

I tense, though try to keep my face neutral. I don't need to ask to know who she's speaking of. "What about her?"

"I must admit, I'm rather curious. The rumors say she's a very deadly and deranged woman, yet here she is, following my son around like a stray animal." Her tone isn't unkind, but there's an edge to it that makes my skin prickle.

"She doesn't follow me around," I counter, perhaps too quickly. "We're working together."

"Mm." Mother studies me over the rim of the cup she holds once more, almost as if she needs some way to occupy her hands. "And what are you working on that requires the Silver Wraith's particular skills?"

I choose my words with care. "We share similar concerns about recent events."

"I see." She pauses, something flickering in her eyes. "She looks so much like Valyria. The same silver hair, same fierce spirit.

Though Valyria was more gentle. Less," she pauses, waving her hand through the air, "hardened."

My curiosity peaks, and the question comes out before I can stop it. "You knew her mother?"

"We were close, once. Before." She pauses, pressing her lips together. "Tell me, does she have her mother's affinity for fauna essence as well?"

The question seems innocent enough, but there's a glimmer in mother's gaze that makes me wary. "Her records state just the flora strand from her living affinity." Curse my vague answers—she will catch the half-truths.

"Yes, I suppose that's true." She sighs, a sort of sadness crossing her features. "And you...how do you feel about her?"

I blink. "What do you mean?"

She smiles, giving me a look that says I know exactly what she means. Perhaps I do. "I am not ignorant to the ways of young people. I've seen how you look at each other. How she watches you as if her life depends on it." She purses her lips, considering. "I'm just curious. Whatever you feel must be strong enough to illicit such reactions toward her." I didn't realize she'd been paying so much attention to Ariella.

I shrug, idly running a hand through my hair. "I suppose you are correct, yes." I'm not sure why my body feels so uncomfortable.

"Has anything happened between you two?" The question catches me off guard and she sees the confusion, chuckling. "Not intimately. But, anything that has felt strange?"

Yes—too much. "No, nothing. Unless you'd consider her threatening my life at least once a day strange, that is." She sees right through my miserable attempt at deflecting. I know she does. She watches me for a moment, humming to herself before smiling once more.

"Just be careful with that one, Caspian. Her mother had good intentions too, in the beginning."

"What are you alluding to?"

"Nothing, darling." Another smile, though this one doesn't eclipse her eyes. "I simply worry. A mother's prerogative, you understand. Though I must admit, the way she watches you is curious."

Heat creeps up my neck. "Mother—"

"Oh, don't look so embarrassed, Caspian. I'm just making an observation." Her smile turns knowing. "Though perhaps we should discuss your rather interesting choice of training attire yesterday?"

I lurch to my feet, more than ready to leave. Without answering, I lean forward to kiss her cheek and say my goodbyes before exiting the study. Opening the door, I find Ariella and Gavriel in what appears to be a heated but whispered argument. My guard's face is red, flushed with blatant anger. I've never seen him this enraged before—well, aside from yesterday. He storms off before I can ask what's wrong.

"What was that about?" I ask Ariella.

She shrugs, dismissing the inquiry. "Nothing important. What did your mother say?"

"Let's talk somewhere more private." I lead her toward the back gardens. We need to discuss investigating the tunnels, but first I want to understand what has Gavriel so upset.

The sun beats against my neck as we walk behind the castle. The late morning heat is already making the air thick and un-comfortable—strange sensation when it should be chilled outside, regardless that I now know it's the balance's doing. I direct us to a secluded corner where stone benches rest beneath flowering vines, neither of us speaking the entire way. The sweet fragrance of blooming lavender and myrralyn settles my mind and eases the tension from my shoulders.

Ariella moves with that conditioned grace of hers, choosing to lean against a pillar rather than sit. Her eyes scan our surround-ings—a habit I've noticed she never breaks, even in supposedly safe spaces. It's moments like these I find it difficult to look away. When a pull in my chest implores me to close the distance between us.

"My guard seemed rather upset." I watch her reaction for an answer, regardless that I know her expression will not grant me one. Her jaw tightens almost imperceptibly.

"Gavriel has opinions about things that do not concern him." Her tone is clipped, warning me to drop it. But I can't. Not when his behavior has been so erratic as of late.

"He's never acted like this before." I step closer, close enough to catch the inviting warmth that always seems to cling to her skin. "What did he say to you?"

Her steady gaze meets mine. "The usual. He believes I'm a threat to you. I'm manipulating you against your father." A harsh laugh escapes her. "As if you needed any help seeing what kind of monster sits on that throne."

I run a hand through my hair, frustrated. "And what did you tell him?"

"That he should worry less about how many treats you'll give him later and more about keeping his head attached to his shoulders if he continues to question me. Fuck your demands. I'll drive my blade so deep in his heart that he'll feel it in the next life." Her fingers tap against her thigh, just above where she keeps one of her countless blades.

I sigh, reaching for her hand. She allows the touch, which still surprises me every time. "I love your murderous inclinations, I do, but he's just trying to protect me."

"I know." A brief vulnerability flashes in her eyes before she masks it, pushing from the stone to continue walking. "But he *will* understand that I'm not the enemy here, otherwise I've no qualms about becoming his."

The words hang between us, heavy with meaning. Because she's right—she's not the enemy, not truly. But admitting that means accepting everything else that comes with it. Including what we might have to do to my father. The thought of which is treason in itself, so maybe we're both the enemy.

I watch Ariella as we proceed through the gardens, her steps silent even on the gravel path. The weight of everything settles deeper into my being with each breath. Even the air feels dense, pressing down on me like a physical manifestation of my stress.

"We need to investigate those tunnels," I say, breaking our pleasant silence. "Something's happening down there and we need to know what before the week is up. Mother mentioned seeing Father emerge from them looking feverish."

Ariella's eyes narrow. "Your mother notices more than she lets on." Her tone carries a hint of suspicion, but I ignore it. The woman is suspicious about everything. "But yes, I agree. Though we need to be strategic about this; the king is not exactly leaving them lightly guarded anymore."

We reach the lake at the far end of the gardens, its usually peaceful surface reflecting an overcast sky. The water appears almost metallic today, reminding me of Ariella's hair. I lean against the old oak tree that's stood sentinel here for over a century, its thick trunk offering some privacy from prying eyes, though I haven't seen the normal abundance of faces mulling around today.

"What if we—" I start, but Ariella holds up a hand, silencing me. Her head tilts as she studies the lake's surface.

"What is that?" she murmurs, approaching the water's edge. I follow her gaze but see nothing unusual at first. Then I notice it—small droplets of water beginning to rise from the surface, and a sinking feeling drowns out all other thoughts. The drops hover like suspended tears before falling back down, creating ripples that spread across the lake's surface in circular patterns.

More water begins to rise, forming floating spheres that catch what little sunlight breaks through the clouds. It's beautiful in an unsettling way, like watching smoke curl into impossible shapes. The display reminds me of the stories my mother used to tell about the Aether realm, how sometimes strange things would occur and defy the normalcy we've come to know in this realm.

"By the Angel..." I breathe, unable to look away from the preternatural display.

"What in the Aether." Ariella's voice is subdued, her usual sharp edges dulled by what almost resembles concern. She trails off, her gaze fixed on a particularly large sphere of water rising to the height of the tree. Whatever force holds it falters, and the water crashes back into the lake with a resounding slap. I frown at the noise, turning to my companion as she bristles beside me.

I want to reach for her, to pull her close and shield her from whatever is coming. But I know better—she'd likely break my arm for trying. Still, the protective urge burns deep within me. I've watched her fight griffins, take down multiple attackers while poisoned, and face my father without flinching. Yet something about her expression now, as she observes the water go against nature itself, makes me want to gather her in my arms and never let go.

She pivots to face me, the usual hardness returning to her eyes, though there's more there too—determination maybe? Or fear? It's sometimes impossible to tell with her as she's seemed to have perfected her mask of emotions over the years. "I need to speak with Marek."

"I'll come with you," I offer, already knowing her answer.

She shakes her head, a hint of amusement crossing her features. "No. You have that meeting with your father, and I need to handle this alone." Her tone leaves no room for argument, though that's never stopped me before.

But the mention of the king sobers me. I would do just about anything to keep from going to this meeting—another discussion about *securing the kingdom's future* that is promised to be more justifications for stealing children from their families. My stomach turns at the thought. I don't know if I'll be able to hold in my raging thoughts, but I must try. Especially if Ariella will be away for a while. Who knows what my father will attempt to do to either of us. He seems hesitant to try anything when we're together, but he's right to fear the woman next to me, even if he doesn't know her secrets.

"Fine," I concede, though everything in me rebels against letting her go alone. "But promise me you'll be careful. Father's men are everywhere in the city now, and after what happened with the crowd earlier, I do not trust anyone around you." Hopefully, the people of Valoria still have enough sense to not provoke the Silver Wraith.

The lake's surface continues its unnatural display, and my hands itch at what it means. *We've already seen the effects through the unnatural weather phenomena.* Ariella stands at the water's edge, too close for my comfort, no doubt doing it deliberately just to get under my skin.

"I don't like this," I mutter, moving to stand beside her.

She hums in agreement, her eyes tracking another sphere of water as it rises. "As if we needed another fucking reminder of the damn balance."

"Just another thing my father's to blame for." The words taste bitter on my tongue as my fists clench at my sides.

"Precisely." Her voice carries that edge it gets when she's piecing something together. "Though this is more intense from the other signs we've seen. The other signs were more subtle, or what I'm thinking are signs, at least. This is"—She gestures to the floating water—"like the ground shaking."

I chew on my lip before stuffing both hands in my pockets. "And you think Marek will have information?"

"Yes." She finally tears her gaze from the lake to look at me. Her bright eyes study me, considering, before she continues. "I need to kill him, Caspian. This stops now."

My chest tightens at her words. She's right—we'd barely made it through the castle gates before witnessing his latest atrocity. The memory of those parents' screams lingers in my head, mixing with the sound of water droplets falling back to the lake's surface.

"I know." I step closer, lowering my voice, though we're alone. "But like you said, we need to be smart about this. There's far more than just royal sentries here. I've seen many direct from Frostwell, which cannot be a good sign." I pause and consider my words. "Actually, their bi-annual competition is supposed to begin tomo—"

"I don't fucking care." She cuts me off, but there's no real heat in her voice. "I will personally remove each of their heads if that's the kind of show Thalion wants before I send him to the Angel."

The admission shouldn't warm my chest the way it does. Angel help me, I was truly fucked up to feel pleased that she'd chosen to murder my father instead of me, and now I feel warm at her increasing threats? Foolish.

"I want to ask you something," I blurt before I lose my nerve. "The things my mother said about yours—"

"Not now." She glances around, though I know she'd have sensed if anyone was near. "Your *mother* is far too perceptive. I trust her not one hair more than I do your father."

I want to defend my mother, but we don't have time to sit and argue about trivial opinions.

"Fine. But we will discuss it later." Not a question, though surprising when she nods once, the movement sharp and decisive.

"After I speak with Marek." Her eyes drift back to the lake as she bites down on that fucking lip. "You should go. Your father will be waiting. And don't listen to a fucking thing he says, all the man seems to do is lie." She frowns as her tone shifts to something harder, more familiar.

I swallow around the growing thickness in my throat. "I know." And I do. The king sitting on that throne isn't my father anymore—hasn't been for a while, and I've ignored that fact far too long. "Will you come find me after you speak with Marek?"

She studies me for a moment, and I wonder if she can see how much I need her to say yes. Then, a single nod. "I'll find you."

The confirmation is nice, but I hear the silent promise in her tone: always.

The words drive heat through my veins, remembering all the times she's tracked me down. In the training room that first day, in my chambers after she was poisoned, when she trusted me with her entire life after the griffin attack...this little wraith has sought me out more than I think we both realized.

"Be careful," I mutter again, knowing she won't listen but needing to say it anyway. Why am I feeling so clingy? The thought of her leaving sours my stomach far more than it should.

A familiar smirk crosses her face. "You've clearly forgotten who I am, prince. The city was never safe." She closes the distance between us, her heat brushing against my skin. "Now it'll just be extra fun."

I groan. "Angel, don't talk like that right now. I have things to do, and unfortunately for both of us, you are not one of them." Her answering laugh is dark and promising.

It takes everything in me to turn and walk away, especially when I hear her mutter something about my ass under her breath. But I must focus. Whatever my father has planned for this meeting, I need to be prepared.

Still, I can't help looking back once more before I round the corner. She stands at the lake's edge again, silver hair catching the light as the water appears calm once more. She looks ethereal, dangerous, and beautiful in equal measure.

And entirely mine.

The thought should terrify me. Instead, it fills me with a fierce sort of pride. Let my father try to separate us. Let Gavriel question her motives. Let my mother warn me about her.

None of it matters. Because somehow, against every odd and probably against the Angel's wishes, the most feared woman in the kingdom has chosen me. And I'll be damned if I let anyone take her from me now.

Chapter Eighteen

Ariella

T he city streets are a disappointing kind of empty for this
time of day, as if everyone is too afraid to leave their homes.
Pity, I was hoping for a little entertainment.

Two women catch my eye as I pass through a main street and
they immediately spin to avoid me like death itself, though that's
nothing new. What is new are the closed shop signs hanging in
just about every window.

How did everything change so quickly?

My shoulders roll back as I push away the tingling under my
skin. I know what I'm capable of, but bringing down a king
requires more than just skill with blades. It requires patience,
which is something I am running out of after enduring it for
twenty years.

How uncharacteristic of me.

The familiar stone steps of the guild come into view, and I
force my breathing to settle. I don't feel guilty for leaving Caspian
behind while he meets with his father. And as much as I do not
trust that pathetic excuse of a king, I know he will not harm his
son.

But harm isn't always physical, and it's that thought that drives my feet faster.

I pause at the entrance, running my fingers over the worn handle. My father's journal presses against the pouch at my hip, its weight impossible to ignore—a constant reminder of everything I've lost and all still at stake. It's time I speak with Marek, though. It kills me to rely on others, but aside from Caspian, he is the one person alive who I can trust.

I'm not sure I would have even confided in Isaiah with this information.

The common area is empty save for one of the newer students sprawled across a chair, mouth hanging open as he snores softly. His hand dangles close to a blade, and I fight the urge to wake him with it pressed against his throat. Marek would not appreciate me terrorizing more of his students, but the idiot should learn to not leave himself so vulnerable.

Sighing, I walk with silent steps through the room, descending the stairs to where I know I'll find my mentor. Jaxon's voice drifts up from his briefing room, animated in that way he gets when explaining some new discovery.

"—the integration is seamless! The essence flows through these channels here, see?" His excited tone grows clearer as I approach. "It's unlike anything we've seen from Lumarna before."

I don't bother knocking before pushing the door open. Marek, Velora, and Jaxon huddle around something on the table, their heads snapping up at my entrance. Velora's eye twitches, and

Jaxon moves to shield whatever they're examining, but not before I catch a glimpse of gleaming metal and pulsing light.

"By the Angel, haven't you heard of knocking, Ariella?" Velora scolds, though there's no real heat in her voice.

I smirk. "No. But I have heard a blade to the heart does wonders for stress. Care to try?" I step closer to the stout woman, raising a brow as her cheeks heat. Before she can continue our game, my eyes catch on what appears to be some sort of holding device. It's small, no larger than my palm, with intricate channels carved into its surface. My brows crease at the essence flowing through them like liquid starlight. "What is that?"

Jaxon shifts, sliding a hand through his unkempt hair. "Just something from Auroria. A new type of essence amplifier, supposedly."

But it's not from Auroria—the craftsmanship is distinctly Lumarnan. I've spent enough time studying both cities' work to know the difference.

I pause, pursing my lips. The way the essence moves through it like blood in a vein...something clicks in my mind, a piece of a puzzle I didn't even know needed solving.

"Fuck," I breathe, my hand reaching out to touch it before I can stop myself. Jaxon snatches it away, but it's too late. I've seen enough.

The king's experiments. The children. The way essence seems to be bleeding from the realm itself—fuck's sake, it all connects. The realization crashes into me, my mind spinning with everything I was too distracted to not put together until now.

But the question that flashes through me is how I will rid of the king without knowing what he's done with his subjects? Perhaps he will use himself as a fail-safe—kill him, and the children die, too. Where would he be keeping them?

"I need to speak with you," I tell Marek, my voice leaving no room for argument. "Alone."

His resolute eyes study me for a long moment before he nods. "Velora, Jaxon, give us the room."

They gather their things, though Jaxon hesitates, reluctant to leave his precious device behind as he stumbles from the room. Once the door closes behind them, I pull my father's book from my pouch and toss it on the table between us, crossing my arms.

Marek's eyes widen—a nearly imperceptible indication of his surprise. In all the years I've known him, we've never spoken of my father. We've had a mutual understanding; an invisible line drawn between our boundaries that I'm about to cross.

"Where did you find this?" he questions, not reaching for it.

"My house." I note every detail of his reaction.

He curses under his breath, running a hand over his face. "You went back..." He trails off, meeting my eyes. "What else did you find?"

I tell him everything—about the Accord, the balance, the strange behavior of essence throughout the realm, Thalion's experiments. With each revelation, his expression grows darker.

"The Accord," he mutters when I finish. "It sounds familiar, but I can't place where I've heard of it."

I pace the length of the room, my mind racing. The man is old, but perhaps I was wrong about him holding information. I'd convinced myself he'd have something to share, considering he was around before even my parents were.

"You know nothing of it, then?"

He shakes his head, leaning a hand against the table. "I wish I did, Ari." His tone is haunting and genuine, as if it pains him to not have the answers I'm seeking.

There's one other place I've been considering. I'm less optimistic about finding anything there, but we still have a few days to figure this out.

"There's something else," I remark, stepping back to lean against a wall. "Do you remember Ally?"

His brow furrows. "The girl from Meridian? The one who—"

"Tried to kill me after she fucked Isaiah? Yes." I wave away the memory and ignore his string of curses, irritation simmering beneath the surface of my skin. "Thalion went *all* the way to Meridian to recruit her for the competition. Why? There are plenty of assassins here who would have jumped at the chance to take me down, especially for the promise of a crown."

Understanding dawns in his eyes. "You think there's something important in Meridian." Not a question. I swallow the smile that wants to appear at just how well Marek knows me.

"I think there are a lot of things the king doesn't want us to know." I halt mid-thought and whirl to face him fully. "And I think it's possible there's something worth seeking in Meridian. Perhaps he just chose the most gullible idiot he could find, but

Angel damn me if I'm not at least going to try searching there. This is too big to remain even the slightest ignorant before I kill him."

He dips his head, the movement deliberate. "How can I help you?"

The words cement the growing thickness in my throat, because he can't. Not anymore.

I don't answer, instead vowing that I will find him if he can help. The sadness in his expression pushes me out the door, and he thankfully doesn't press to hug me or whatever the fuck people do for such comfort.

My eyes find Jaxon's device once more before I leave Marek with the journal. I've read the fading pages so many times I've memorized every date and word, so it will be safer here than with me. I've no desire to give the king any other part of me. If he manages to raid my room, that is.

As I climb the stairs back to the common area, a familiar voice stops me in my tracks.

"Come to pay for your crimes, have you?" Isolde leans against the wall at the top of the stairs, her arms crossed over her chest. She's furious, which would normally excite me, but I've no time for her petty games today.

"Fuck's sake," I mutter to myself. "Move."

She laughs, the sound grating against my nerves. "Or what? You'll go tell your precious prince?"

My hand wraps around her throat before I can stop it, pressing her harder into the wall. A blade would create a beautiful mess, but I want to *feel* her pulse weaken as I squeeze the air from her body.

"I have never met anyone who wishes to die more than you do." I smile and curl my fingers inward. "I'm feeling charitable today, however, so I suppose I will grant your wish."

She tries to speak, her eyes bulging past their natural place. Her nails claw at my hand, tearing the skin and spilling hot blood over my steel grip. The pain is my pleasure, though—something she realizes too late as her body begins to panic. I could subtly weave my psionic strand to force her obedience, but her raw reaction is far more satisfying.

I hold still as she thrashes against me, the weight beneath my sternum slipping into a dark place. When have I ever given the impression that I welcome harassment? Why does the entire fucking realm continue to piss me off for their own amusement?

Perhaps I haven't made myself clear—my words mean nothing compared to actions, it seems. I've given far too many warnings. It's time I shut the fuck up and follow-through.

Isolde will be the perfect example to those who continue to question me. The bitch still doesn't know her place, so I'll craft her a new one. The Angel can figure out how to deal with her.

The thought makes me smile. The bliss I would feel to know the Angel put Ally and Isolde's souls next to each other, or whatever it does with them when we die.

I vaguely hear screaming as several people attempt to pull me away from the convulsing woman in front of me. It takes every bit of strength to hold myself in place before I decide to have a little fun.

I yank her from the wall, loosening my grip just enough to keep her awake longer. A rough cough rattles my hand as I drag her while I tug on my aero strand. At least I have one useful fucking strand that I can weave publicly. They want me away from her so badly?

Fine. I'll give them what they want.

Tossing her across the floor, to the center of the small crowd that has gathered in the common room, I wait for Isolde to catch her breath. She hacks up thick liquid, spitting it onto the pristine clean floors. Disgusting.

I feel Marek's presence storm up behind me, and I hold a hand above my shoulder without looking away from my charge. "Do not touch me, Marek, or you're next."

"You can't go around killing anyone you want to, Ariella. Leave her alone."

"Is that so? And what if I told you the prince hired me to kill her after she dared speak to him?" I look over my shoulder at my seething mentor. "Would it be acceptable, then? You should have kept a better leash on her because I'm done." His jaw tightens. He's clearly uncomfortable but maintains my gaze, his eyes matching the coldness seeping from mine.

"Leave her alone." He enunciates each word, pursing his lips before continuing. "Or you're out." Unfortunately for him, I don't fucking care.

A dark chuckle slips from me as I pivot on my heels to face him. I've the urge to look through each face here, but this moment is too important to remove my attention from Marek.

Isolde continues to cough behind me as I advance. My eyes watch the war in Marek's, and I cannot tell if he's upset with me, or upset with himself for training me as he did. Because he knows damn well there is *nothing* he, or anyone, in this building could do to stop me.

Angling my head, I lower my voice so he's the only one to hear my words. "Then I'm out." His eyes widen as I tug on my aero strand once more and send the essence down Isolde's throat. And because I'm a petty bitch, I raise a hand before curling my fingers inward as I drain the air from her lungs. I do not need my hands for such weaving, but I'm nothing if not dramatic when a point needs to be made.

The entire guild falls silent as Isolde's body convulses on the floor. The desperate clawing at her throat reminds me too much of my father's last moments, though I feel nothing but satisfaction. No one moves to help her. Not even Marek.

"You disappoint me," he whispers, his usually stern face softening for just a moment. "I thought you were better than this."

I laugh, the sound hollow even to my own ears. "Better than what, Marek? Better than the woman who has killed hundreds of people? Better than the reputation I've earned a thousand times over?" My voice rises with each word until I'm shouting. "Better than the woman who fell for the fucking son of the man who murdered her own father?"

His brows raise at that last admission, but I'm beyond caring. Burning rage courses through my veins, demanding retribution for every slight, every loss, every moment of pain.

"Or maybe," I continue, stepping closer until we're a hair from touching, "you thought I was better than the woman who is going to kill the king and watch his kingdom burn." I smile, but there's no warmth in it. "So sorry, Marek—I've always been exactly who I am. Perhaps you should have kept a tighter leash on *me*."

Behind me, Isolde's movements have slowed to weak twitches. I don't need to look to know she's moments from death. Good. Let them all see what happens when they push me too far.

"At least tell me why," Marek demands, his voice barely audible. "Why now? When there's so much else you need to do? Why bother with her?"

I consider ignoring him, but he deserves at least this much truth. "Because I'm tired of playing nice. I'm tired of pretending I give a fuck about any of these people or their pathetic lives." My hand gestures to the crowd surrounding us. "And I am so Angel-damned tired of everyone thinking they can challenge me without consequences."

Velora steps forward, her face pale but determined. "Ariella, we're your family—"

"Family?" The word is poison on my tongue. "As if you're any better than Isolde—where do you think she got her wretched personality from? If you speak to me one more time, Velora, you'll be joining her." I pause, letting my words sink in. "Because you want to know what happens to people who claim to be my family?

They die. So *please*, keep pushing me. I haven't tasted enough blood yet today."

The silence that follows is deafening as each student seems to shrink into themselves. My reputation has always preceded me, but now they're witnessing firsthand why I earned it.

A small whimper draws my attention back to Isolde. Her eyes are glassy, unfocused, but still holding onto that last thread of life. I could end it now, quick and clean...would that defeat the purpose of this lesson?

I want to be covered in her blood when I finally take her life, but I have things to do.

"Watch carefully," I announce to the room, my voice echoing in the stillness. "This is what happens when you forget who I am."

With a slight twist of my fingers, I completely block her air supply. Her body gives one final jerk before going still. Just like that, another life snuffed out. Another soul for the Angel to collect.

I focus on Marek once more, unsurprised to find disappointment etched in the deep lines of his face. "You've made your choice, then?"

"I made my choice twenty years ago." I spin and step over Isolde's body, striding toward the door. "Everything since then has just been preparation."

"For what?" he calls after me.

I walk through the threshold, not bothering to look back as I leave the building and ignore his question.

The walk back to the castle gives me time to process what just happened. I've always had a quick temper, but it's never something I will apologize for. Marek knows that, so the fact that he threatened disowning me is strange. I know I can still trust him, though, so my father's journal will remain there and he can come groveling whenever he's ready.

My feet carry me through the castle gates as my mind still churns with everything I've learned and have yet to do. Go to Meridian, kill the king, fix the Accord.

Simple.

"There you are." Caspian's voice breaks through my thoughts. He's striding toward me, his face tight and wary. "Where have you been? I've been looking everywhere. I thought you'd be back sooner and when I didn't find—" He halts, his eyes narrowing as he takes in my appearance. "Is that blood?"

I glance down at my hand, still bearing the stains from Isolde's desperate struggle. "Not mine." A petty lie, but I don't need the concern. I've already healed the wounds.

His jaw clenches as he lets out a deep sigh. "Ariella..." My heart skips at the way my name forms around his lips, but I ignore the fluttering and walk.

"Don't." I brush past him, turning left toward my room. I need to clean up and think before I leave. "I'm not in the mood for a lecture."

He follows, of course, and despite what I said, I inwardly smile that he knows I shouldn't be left alone right now. "What happened?"

"I killed someone who needed killing. Nothing new."

His hand catches my arm, spinning me to face him. The contact sends an unwanted spark through my body—one that almost burns.

"Talk to me," he pleads in a soft tone. "What's really going on?"

For a moment, I'm tempted. To let all of these disgusting feelings out and just allow myself five minutes to not be okay and seek solace in his arms.

But I don't.

"Just stressed, as usual," I say instead, watching his face. "Why?"

His expression darkens as his head shakes. "What did you figure out? Did Marek help?" I appreciate his change in topic, even if I do not wish to talk about Marek.

"No, but I did see something." I tug him with me so that we're out of the main part of the castle. "This device Jaxon had—it held essence inside, but it had these vein-like grooves that allowed the essence to flow naturally when it wasn't being used. But open the device, and the essence spills out." Saying it out loud only solidifies my assumption. "It's like it's..." I struggle to explain my whirling thoughts, but the prince understands.

"Bleeding," he finishes, his silver eyes meeting mine.

I nod several times. "Yes."

His forehead creases before something lights in his eyes. "You think that's what my father's been doing."

I nod again.

I can see the connections running through his head. It's oddly nice to have someone so in-sync with me. "By the Angel...he's actually stealing essence—it's not some metaphor. *That's* how the balance is off, because of the essence spilling from the veins of others while he attempts to take it for himself."

"Exactly. Which means we've no idea just how strong he is or what he's doing with all the essence."

"But why children? What makes them different?"

I've pondered this question since the moment I saw Jaxon's device. Are children better conduits? Perhaps their small bodies are ideal for storing or exchanging essence? That doesn't make sense, though. Their bodies are weak, and they have far less experience with essence than those twice their age, so it must be something else.

If I do not get the answers in Meridian, I'll slit the king's throat without them, and if there are consequences to the children he's taken, they can rest on my soul. It will be my burden to bear.

"I'm going to Meridian tonight," I blurt out in an attempt to thwart the gruesome images in my head.

"What? Why would you do that? My father made it very clear in the meeting that he will abide by the week he gave me, but no more. We haven't the time for such a trip."

"We have plenty—that's where Ally was from, and I don't believe in coincidences." I start walking again, realizing we've paused, my mind already planning the journey. "Your father went out of his way to recruit her specifically, and I want to know if there was a reason."

"I'm coming with you." My eyes roll, regardless that I was hoping he'd say that. I do not want to go without him.

But of course, I'm too fucking stubborn. "No, you're not." I spin to face him again, jabbing a finger into his chest. "You need to stay here and keep an eye on things." Miserable reasoning, but it's all I have to work with.

"And let you go alone?" he scoffs, crossing his arms. My eyes catch on the flexed muscle under his shirt, and I swallow around the forming lump in my throat. "Not happening."

"I work better alone, prince."

"Bullshit." His hand catches mine where it's still pressed against his chest. "We're stronger together and you know it. Stop pushing me away—I thought we were past this."

I yank my hand back, ignoring the hurt that flashes across his face.

"I'm not pushing you away." A lie. "I'm being practical. You're the prince; you cannot just leave. Again."

He studies me for a long moment, and I force myself to meet his gaze. Finally, he does something unexpected: he tosses his head back and laughs, the sound harsh. I bite my cheek to keep in the smile.

After several heartbeats, he stops and turns those glimmering eyes toward me. "Ariella." I raise an eyebrow. "You are an obstinate fucking woman. I swear you'd cut off your own arm just to make a point." My nose scrunches. Why would I do that? It would be impractical and a pain to heal. A couple fingers, though... "Let's go shower and pack our bags. We will grab dinner before we leave."

A disturbing warmth slides over my chest, and I keep silent as I walk to my room and close the door firmly behind me. Only then do I allow myself to slump against it, the events of the day catching up with my worn body.

The guild is lost to me now. It shouldn't hurt as much as it does, but I didn't lie. They were never my family, so I need to let it go.

After my shower, I begin packing what I'll need for Meridian. Weapons first—my usual blades plus a few extras. Then supplies. Enough for three days, though I doubt it will take that long. Always better to be prepared.

My hand pauses over the gilded egg next to my bed. I have the urge to bring it with me, but unless I plan on trading it, it will be of no use and a wasted effort.

A knock at the door interrupts my packing. "Come in, prince."

"It's not Caspian." Gavriel's voice comes through the wood, tense and angry. "We need to talk."

I consider ignoring him, but that would probably just make him more persistent. With a sigh, I open the door. "What?" My voice is emotionless, the complete opposite of the expression on his face.

He pushes past me into the room, his usual pleasantries notably absent. "I know what you did at the guild."

"News travels fast." But not that fast... "Come to congratulate me?" I close the door, leaning against it with forced casualness and a blank face.

"No." He runs a hand through his hair, looking nervous. Is that right? "I came to tell you that I will be joining you and Caspian in Meridian, but I want you to stay there when him and I leave."

That wasn't what I expected. "Excuse me?"

"Did you not hear what I said? I've been telling you to leave for fucking months, but you won't listen. And now, you're putting Caspian at horrible risk just because you wish to stay near him." His dark eyes meet mine, dead serious. "You're getting reckless, Ariella. Now it's gone so far that word of your senseless murder today has spread and the king has threatened his own son."

"It was anything but senseless," I state, though we both know that's not the point.

It's also false. What I did may have been a little too over the top for my usual taste, but I was feeling ridiculously on edge and she shoved me right off. That's on her.

"I don't care." He shortens the distance between us, his voice dropping. "I've watched you since the competition started." Creep. "You came here as an assassin, but something has changed. *You* changed. And now you're spiraling because you don't know how to handle it."

I laugh, but there's no humor in it. "Handle what? My burning desire to murder the king? That clearly hasn't changed."

"No. Your feelings for Caspian."

The words hit my stomach hard, flipping the organ several times, but I keep my face impassive. "I do not have feelings for the prince."

"Lie to yourself if you want." His arms cross and he appears pleased with himself. "I see the way you look at him, even when you think there's nothing but hate in your eyes. How your shoulders relax when you're near him. The way you step between him and any perceived threat."

"That's called protecting an asset," I snap. "He's useful to me alive."

"Is that what you tell yourself?" He shakes his head. "You're in love with him, Ariella. And it's only going to get him killed. This is no longer a game—his own father promised to have Caspian's head if he does not rid himself of you."

Simmering rage hangs in the air between us. I want to deny everything he just said, though he's right. But why the fuck does it matter if the king will be dead before he can even touch the prince?

"You don't know what you're talking about," I manage, my voice barely above a whisper.

"Don't I?" He moves to the door, pausing with his hand outstretched toward the handle. "Just think about what I said, wraith. He doesn't deserve to die for the likes of you."

The door closes behind him with a soft click, leaving me alone with thoughts I've been trying desperately to avoid. Every bit of fight has fled my body, a sensation I never wanted to experience again. It's too vulnerable.

You're in love with him. The mere possibility terrifies me more than anything the king could do.

Love is weakness. Love is vulnerability. Love is what got my parents killed, what got Isaiah killed. I can't afford to love anyone, least of all the son of the man I've sworn to destroy.

But Gavriel's words flit through my mind, impossible to ignore. Do I look at Caspian when I think no one's watching? The instinctive need to protect him is loud in my head, but that's my job. I suppose there's the way my heart races when he's near. How horrible I feel when he's not.

The way I would take the life of every single person in this realm just to save his.

"Fuck," I mutter, sliding down the bed to sit on the floor. When did everything get so complicated?

I need to focus. Fuck Gavriel. Caspian's fate doesn't change my plans to kill his father, and when the king is dead, the only threat left to the prince is me. I suck in a deep breath and center myself. Meridian first. Then the tunnels. Then the king. Then the Accord.

The rest...I'll deal with the rest later.

Rising, I return to my packing with renewed determination. Whatever I feel or don't feel for Caspian doesn't matter. What matters is stopping his father before he destroys everything.

Even if that means destroying myself in the process.

I finish gathering my supplies and change into fresh clothes before ensuring every weapon is perfectly positioned and easily accessible. The familiar routine helps clear any stress lingering under my skin.

This is who I am. This is what I do. Everything else is just distraction.

A glance out the window shows the sun beginning to set. If we leave now, we can make it to Meridian by morning. That gives us more than enough time to be back in the castle before the king follows through with his threat.

Chapter Nineteen
Ariella

The early morning air whips around us as we ride toward Meridian after traveling through the night, my thighs aching from hours in the saddle. I'd forgotten how much I despise horses, and I've never even traveled on one so far before. This is just pure torture. But Caspian insisted this would be faster, and for once, I didn't argue.

My eyes drift to a group of people on the open path we approach. There's a few walking across the bridge that passes over the river, and I immediately sense something off about them. Their movements are erratic, jerky, like puppets with tangled strings. One man stumbles past, his eyes unfocused and skin an unnatural shade of gray. He mutters to himself, words I can't quite catch, but the cadence is wrong—too fast and desperate.

"You see that?" Caspian's voice is low as he guides his horse closer to mine.

I nod, watching another group of travelers as I subtly tug on my psionic strand and feel around them. I wince at the wrongness of their essence. It feels empty somehow, and utterly abhorrent. But I don't need to think very hard to know what's going on. The consequences of the balance are getting worse.

The morning sun does nothing to warm the chill that settles in my bones. I'm unsure of why I didn't anticipate the imbalance affecting people, too. Essence exists in the land and elements first, but eventually flows into the people who weave it. The balance must be so off in this part of the realm that it's now spreading and attacking the essence in bodies.

Gavriel groans behind us for what must be the hundredth time. "Are we almost there? This saddle is trying to kill me." I'm so fucking close to flinging my blade at him—aside from Isolde, I don't believe I've ever despised someone so much. Especially as he still expects me to just remain in Meridian when we're done searching around. Fucking fool.

"Since when do you complain this much? Are you not a soldier?" Caspian asks, throwing a raised brow over his shoulder.

I ignore their banter as the first hints of salty air reach my nose. Meridian is the closest city to Valoria, and after more than twelve hours of riding, I expect us to be within the city limits soon. It's not long before the road curves, and the vast expanse of the Ebelan Ocean spreads before us, endless blue stretching to meet the horizon. My breath catches.

I've read about the oceans. Seen paintings. Heard vague descriptions from listening to random conversations in Valoria. But nothing prepared me for this.

Before I realize what I'm doing, I've dismounted and walked toward the top of the hill. The city of Meridian sprawls below, a web of white stone buildings that glint like pearls under the afternoon sun. Narrow streets weave between them, bustling with life even from this distance. Vibrant market canopies in shades of red, gold, and green create splashes of color, while thin spirals of smoke rise leisurely from chimneys.

Beyond the city, the Ebelan Ocean stretches out in shimmering shades of blue, so vast and endless it feels like it could swallow the horizon—possibly the whole damn realm. Short waves catch the sunlight, while a few distant ships appear as mere specks against the measureless expanse.

"First time seeing the ocean?" Caspian asks, appearing at my side.

"Is it that obvious?" I catch his eye before he focuses on the view before us.

He smiles but doesn't tease, and I find myself smiling back. I've spent my entire life absorbed in one goal: kill the king. I never paused my endless rage to consider what else might exist beyond the boundaries of Valoria. What other wonders I might have missed while plotting my revenge.

"I'll take the horses to the stables," he says after a moment. "Take your time." He gives me no opportunity to respond before guiding the horses just below the top of the hill, where the stables sit pristine and lonely.

I should protest—we have work to do. But I can't tear my eyes away from the endless blue. A few more minutes won't hurt.

The ocean stretches beyond the horizon, unbroken and alive, a restless mirror of the bright blue sky. My breath stalls at the sheer vastness of it. I catch the glint of a ship in the distance and cringe inwardly. I do not fear much, but after seeing the ocean myself,

I do not think I could travel through it—I'd be a constant mess, worrying that the water might swallow me whole.

The rhythmic crash of waves against the shore and docks carries up the hill, and my eyes slide shut as I allow the soft sounds to calm the pressure pushing against my chest wall.

It's overwhelming, this immensity, this idea of boundless freedom that I've never known. I thrive from having the answers and abiding by a routine, but I get the sense that it would be so freeing to just dive into the water and allow it to carry my body wherever it sees fit. It's only now that I realize that I *want* to let go. I need something—or someone—to take control of my body so that I may exist without the weight of everyone else's decisions for once in my fucking life.

I don't know if that revelation terrifies me, or if I'd truly be willing to relinquish control.

Scanning the city below, I watch the docks as they are a chaotic maze of wooden piers and shouting merchants. Even from here, the air is thick with the smell of fish, spices, and tar.

When Caspian returns, I follow him down the large hill and into the city proper. Everything hums with life, a mix of sun-bleached walls and dark brick buildings pressed close together. Fishing nets hang to dry, and the scent of saltwater blends with olive oil and spices. Boats painted in vibrant hues bob gently in the harbor, their masts swaying against the breeze. The streets are narrow and winding, buildings pressed close together with laundry strung between them. But unlike Valoria, where people scatter at the sight of my silver hair, the residents here merely stare.

Some whisper with wide eyes, but there's more curiosity than fear in their gazes.

"I think they like you," Caspian observes after leaning over to speak against my ear.

Something intense snakes down my spine, and I dampen my reaction, instead forcing a smirk as I snort. "Give it time."

My stomach growls, reminding me we haven't eaten since before leaving the castle. I didn't care to bring any food as the trip here is short, but I may be regretting it just a little now as I'm quite hungry. A nearby stall is selling some kind of fried fish that makes my mouth water, and my feet saunter over before I can stop them. I reach for a pouch of coins in my pack—still well-stocked from years of assignments and the competition winnings. I've never been one for luxuries, preferring to save my earnings for weapons and practical necessities.

"Three," I tell the vendor as I step up to the stall and drop coppers into his weathered palm. His eyes scrutinize the color of my hair, but he wisely doesn't comment.

I hand Caspian his cup before tossing the other one over my shoulder to a mumbling guard. So ungrateful.

I pinch a piece of fish, not caring to ask what it is before dropping it into my mouth. I moan from the flavor bursting over my taste buds, eliciting looks from more than just the prince. I wink at him, ignoring his chuckle before considering the city once more.

"Where do we start?" Gavriel asks around a mouthful of fish. He's still shifting frequently, looking more on edge with each passing hour. We're all exhausted, it seems.

They both turn to me with expectant gazes. I wipe grease from my fingers, considering. "The guild first. Ally claimed she was from there, so I want to find out what they know."

I scan the busy street, focusing on finding any sign of the guild. I'm told the one in Meridian is far more secretive than the one in Valoria, and I doubt locals know what building it is. We walk for a while as I search and Caspian attempts to recall anything he knows about the city's politics.

Something catches my eye. "It's that one," I mutter, gesturing to a narrow three-story structure wedged between what appears to be a dress shop and an armory. Interesting placement.

Dark green vines climb the brick facade, while weather-worn wooden signs swing above multiple shop entrances. The building looks unremarkable, which I suppose is the point. It is also quite small, which was unexpected—I assume there's hidden areas of the guild, likely underground, unless they have no room for training.

"How can you tell?" Caspian questions in a thoughtful tone, stepping closer until his arm brushes mine.

I roll my eyes. "The sigil." I point to a barely visible mark etched into the cornerstone—three crossed daggers. "Every guild has one, though it's never mentioned to outsiders."

We cross the street, and I am quite thankful for my appearance at the moment; the crowd is so thick, every person touches another, but they each have the sense to move from my path. Sometimes it's pleasing to be me.

The strong scent of fish and salt follows us as we enter the building through a plain wooden door.

The interior is insignificant, dimly lit and musty, with shelves of ordinary merchandise lining the walls. Why the secrecy? It doesn't make sense to me. A young woman sits behind a wooden counter, methodically polishing what appears to be a decorative blade. She doesn't look up.

"We're closed," she mutters, her tone dry and flat. I have a feeling they're always closed.

I smirk and straighten until my chest pushes out. "Even for fellow guild members?"

Her eyes snap to mine, widening as her jaw loosens. "The Silver Wraith," she whispers to herself, setting down the blade. Has she any regard for safety? "We heard you'd won the king's competition."

"I did." I take one step to lean against the counter, holding my face mere inches from hers. "I need to speak with your guildmaster."

She studies me for a long moment before her gaze shifts to Caspian and Gavriel, shock consuming her features once more. "You brought the prince?" she squeaks, acting as if I would ever care about bringing royalty into my world. "They stay here."

"No." The word comes out sharper than intended. "They stay with me."

The woman's lips thin, and she considers something before shaking her head. "The prince and a royal sentry? In our guild?" she scoffs. "I think not."

I feel Caspian tense beside me as his thigh settles against mine. Before he can speak, I lower my voice, dropping the friendly act. "This isn't a request. Take us to your guildmaster, or I introduce you to my blade before finding him myself." I let my hand drift down, her eyes following only to catch on my weapons. "Your choice." The threat is clear—I've no time for games today.

She mutters something under her breath but straightens, pushing against a door behind the counter. "Follow me. And tell your *friends* to keep their hands where I can see them."

I chuckle as we follow her through the door and down a dark, narrow staircase. "They're the least of your worries today." I consider killing her for being the most foolish person I've ever met—who the fuck gives their back to someone who's known for being a ruthless murderer?

The steps creak under our weight as we enter the basement. It's larger than I'd have guessed, with a stone hallway that leads to various rooms. We pass an open one where a few students practice with wooden daggers in one corner. They pause their sparring when they catch sight of us, whispering among themselves as soon as they think we cannot hear.

The woman leads us to another door, this one reinforced with steel. She knocks twice before opening it.

"Thaddeus, sir," she announces, "the Silver Wraith is requesting an audience with you." A large man swings the door open a moment later, which explains the lack of training and structure in this facility. A woman would never do such a piss-poor job of managing a guild—something Marek realized when he took over and brought in Velora as his second.

Thaddeus grunts and nods his head, inviting us to follow. The office is spacious but cluttered, with maps and documents covering every surface. Behind a massive desk, Thaddeus—who must be close to sixty, though his build suggests he hasn't lost much of his fighting capability—sits with a loud thump. His dark eyes sweep over us, their gaze like ice.

"Leave us, Marta," he commands. My eyes stay fixed on the man in front of me as his student steps out, closing the door behind her.

"Interesting company you keep, Silver Wraith," Thaddeus comments in a gravelly tone, leaning back in his chair. There's an intensity in the way his muscles rest, as if he expects to jump from his seat and defend himself at any moment. Smart. "To what do I owe this *honor*?"

I step forward and drop into the seat across from him, un-sheathing my blade to twirl it through my fingers. "Ally Dimir. She claimed to be a student from your guild."

His expression doesn't change, but something flickers in his eyes. "Never heard of her."

My answering laugh is quiet as I continue to stare at the guildmaster. "How would you like to find out just what I do to those that lie to me?" I lean against the edge of his desk, my blade not faltering once in my hold. "She was in the king's competition. Until I killed her. Ring any bells, yet?"

"Many competed in the king's trials. I can't be expected to remember them all." He shrugs, but his shoulders are too tense. "Now, if that's all—"

Quick as thought, I twist my blade so the hilt rests in my palm and slam it into his desk, embedding the steel deep in the wood between Thaddeus' splayed fingers. "You have one last chance to answer my fucking questions before your guild finds itself masterless." My voice is calm but harsh. I am exhausted from others' constant dismissal.

"Ariella." Caspian pauses as if he's about to continue, but I silence him by holding up my other hand.

"The king came here himself, did he not?" I press. "Specifically requested Ally be sent for his competition. What I want to know is why." I already have the answer, but I also need to know if there was more to Thalion's decision than choosing the most gullible woman he could find.

Now that I think of it, I don't believe Caspian knew of his secret betrothal to her.

Thaddeus' jaw clenches, his voice light as he insists, "Like I said, I don't know what you're talking about."

I was hoping he'd say that.

Before he can blink, I stand from my seat and twist my blade to shove it through his outstretched hand, securing it to his desk. The man makes a delightfully desperate noise, leaning forward to grab my blade. As he does, I unsheathe another and press it against the base of his throat where the adrenaline rushing into his system pounds against the skin of his neck. His eyes scream of betrayal—did he think I wouldn't follow through?

He will not make such a mistake again.

I lean in even closer, twisting the blade a bit. His teeth grind, the high-pitched sound something I wish to hear again. "You're lying again, Thaddeus. And my patience is wearing quite thin."

"You dare threaten me in my own guild, wraith?" He shifts to lean back as much as his hand will allow. "I could have you killed where you stand."

I bellow a laugh, the sound hollow and cold, though I will admit that was humorous. "Is that right?" I yank my blade free and press it to his cheek in one fluid motion. The seething man stills as he favors the wound I created. "We both know how that would end," I taunt, wiping my blade free of blood along the lines of his face.

"Marek will hear of this." His eyes dart to Caspian, who has moved to stand at the side of the desk, his posture guarded. "As will the king." The prince just smiles and shrugs.

"Good." I slap the blade against his cheek, directing the attention back to me. "Now talk."

He swallows hard, throat bobbing against my blade. "Fine. Yes, the king came here. Wanted one of our best girls for his competition. Said to keep it quiet."

"And you just agreed? No questions asked?"

"He paid well for my discretion." Thaddeus' lips curl. "Very well."

"What else?" When he hesitates, I press harder. "I know there's more, so let us not continue this exhausting back and forth. Because I will win every single time."

He grimaces, sucking in a breath. "He—he said to make it look like we'd sent three, the same as the other guilds, but only two were to actually compete." Interesting. I knew there was no chance Ally made it through those trials alone; she may have been an impressive fighter, but physical strength does not correlate to that of the mind.

"Why?" Caspian demands, speaking to Thaddeus for the first time since we entered.

"I don't know." Thaddeus meets my gaze, holding his good hand up in a placating gesture. "I swear it. He didn't explain, just paid and left."

I study him for a long moment before lowering my blade. He's telling the truth—or at least, what he believes to be the truth. Fuck. I was hoping we'd find *something* here. I exchange a look with Caspian, both of us in agreement: this is a dead end.

"If that's all you know," I say, sheathing my blade, "we'll take our leave."

"Wait." Thaddeus opens a drawer and pulls out a pen, a moment later handing me a folded piece of paper. "Ally's family. They still live here in Meridian. She only worked for me on a part-time basis, so she did not live here with the others. Perhaps they know something I do not."

I snatch the paper from him, memorizing the address before tucking it away and walking from the room.

We leave the guild in silence, emerging into the late afternoon sun. The streets are quieter now, most merchants packing up their wares for the day.

"Well, that was enlightening," Gavriel mutters.

I ignore him, spinning to Caspian. His eyes find mine and soften. "We should find Bastian. I'll bet the fool knows more about this than Ally's family, if the way he looked at her in Valoria before the ball was any indication."

"Agreed. My father visits here too often to ignore my cousin." Caspian stretches his neck and runs a hand through his hair. I nearly lose myself in the strands that shift with the warm breeze. "But not right now. We're all exhausted, and Bastian's estate is on the other side of the city. We should rest first."

As much as I hate to admit it, he's right. I'd sooner work myself to death before choosing to rest on my own. But my limbs feel heavy from the long ride, and my mind is sluggish from lack of sleep. So I nod once.

"Fine." I search the rows of buildings, spotting a sign down the way. "There's an inn toward the docks. Should be decent enough."

The inn turns out to be better than decent, with clean rooms and fresh linens. The innkeeper barely blinks at my hair or Caspian's fine clothes, just hands over two keys and points us toward the stairs before disappearing. What a strange city.

"Two rooms?" I raise an eyebrow at the prince.

He shrugs, a small smile playing at his lips. "Gav needs his beauty sleep. Wouldn't want to disturb him by all of us sharing just one."

I roll my eyes but snatch one of the keys from his hand and jog up the stairs. The room is simple but comfortable, with a large bed and a window overlooking the harbor. The sun is setting, painting the water in brilliant oranges and pinks. It's extraordinary.

It reminds me of the paintings I used to see in Valoria—the ones meant to romanticize far-off places I never cared to see. But this...this is *alive.* So different from any feeling a piece of art could invoke.

The smell of salt on the breeze, the gentle lap of waves against the docks, the atmosphere—it's not something a canvas could ever capture. For a moment, I let myself wonder if there's a world out there, past the horizon, where things are simpler. Where people live without wasting decades on a revenge they'll never get.

A knock at the door startles me, and I know it's Caspian before I open it—his essence has become as familiar to me as my own. Something I do not even need my psionic strand to feel.

"Thought you might be hungry," he says, holding up a bottle of wine and what smells like fresh bread.

I step aside to let him in, watching as he sets the items on a small table by the window. He moves with an easy grace that still catches me off guard sometimes.

"Where's your shadow?" I ask as I cross my arms, referring to Gavriel.

"Asleep already." He pours two glasses of wine. "Said something about never riding a horse again as long as he lives."

I accept the glass he offers, our fingers brushing. "He's been unusually quiet since we arrived."

Caspian pauses a moment to think about that, humming before he tears the bread in half, passing me a piece. "Try it. The baker said it's their specialty."

The bread is still warm, perfectly crusty on the outside and soft within. I close my eyes, savoring the taste. When I open them again, Caspian is watching me with an intensity that makes my skin tingle. It's almost discomforting—being perceived for more than just my hair. My reputation.

"What?" I breathe, suddenly self-conscious.

He gives a small shake of his head. "Nothing. Just...I like seeing you like this."

"Like what?"

"Relaxed. Real." He advances on me, setting down his wine. "You let your guard down sometimes, when we're alone. It's beautiful."

I should step back. Should remind him that whatever this is between us is just physical and can't last forever. Instead, I find myself drawing closer, unable to help the need to be attached to him.

"Caspian..." His name is a whisper on my lips before he's kissing me, gentle at first, then with increasing urgency.

I press against him, wine forgotten as my free hand finds its way into the prince's hair. He tastes like bread and berries and something uniquely him that I can never quite define.

"Stay," I breathe against his mouth before I can stop myself. "Tonight. Stay with me." He would have slept on the floor, ever the gentleman, but I no longer want him anywhere away from me during the night.

His answer is to kiss me harder, smiling into my mouth as he walks us backward until my legs hit the bed. We fall together, a tangle of limbs and half-removed clothing. I manage to set my wine down before shifting my entire focus to the man holding me as if I'm his savior.

Later, much later, we lie facing each other in the darkness. The moon displays the shadows across his face, highlighting the sharp angles of his jaw and cheekbones.

"What are you thinking about?" he asks, his voice low and soft as he traces patterns along my bare spine, causing me to shiver every few minutes. His touch feels so fucking nice.

I consider lying, but the more time I spend with him, the lower my desire is to do so. "Everything. Nothing." I sigh. "How complicated this all is. How I just want it to be over."

He tugs my naked body against his, pressing a kiss to my forehead. "We'll figure it out, angel." My ear rests above his heart, and my mind settles. It's so easy with him.

I want to believe him. Want to trust that there's a way through this labyrinth we've found ourselves in. But as I drift off to sleep in his arms, I can't shake the truth that we're running out of time.

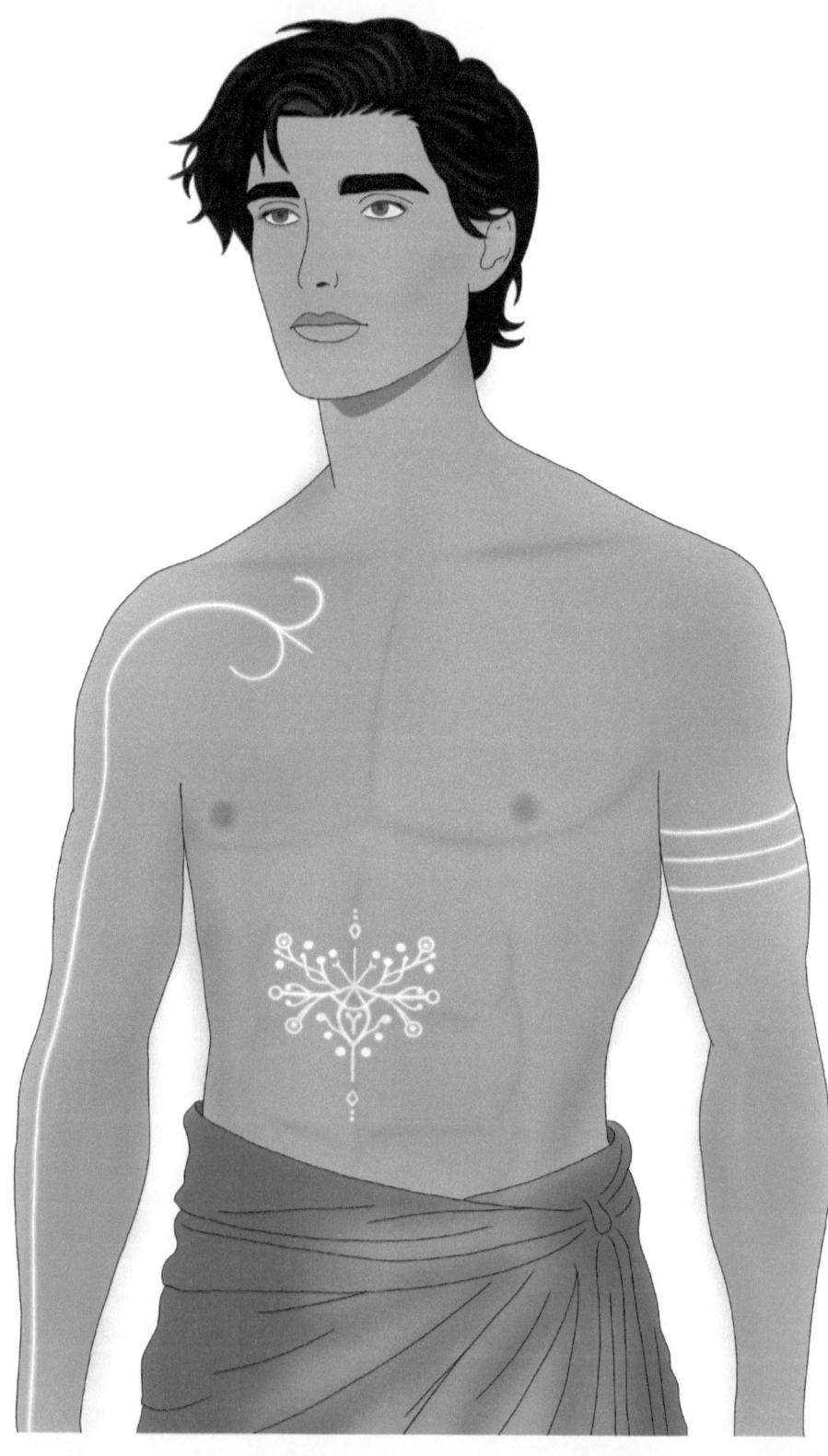

Chapter Twenty
Caspian

I don't bother hiding my irritation as we stride through Meridian's streets toward Bastian's estate. The sun is too bright for the morning atmosphere, and its heat relentlessly beats down on my exposed skin. The humid air clings to my lungs like a second layer, though I don't find myself hating it as usual.

Meridian always pulls me into a strange state of nostalgia. I spent years visiting this city with my father, shadowing his dealings with merchants and dockmasters who traded in goods and favors. I hated every minute of it back then—suffocating under his expectations while pretending not to notice the disguised threats behind each handshake.

Every few steps, my gaze drifts to Ariella, who walks with infuriating grace despite the heat. She isn't even sweating—I frown and focus on the quiet path ahead, drawing in steady breaths. Everything around us is peaceful, something I never experience when visiting Meridian.

"Are we certain this is necessary?" I mutter, mostly to myself. Gavriel grunts in agreement behind me. Bastian is a fucking bastard, and I want nothing more than to stay far away from my cousin. Especially after he put his odious hands on Ariella.

Though I was beyond enraged, the night ended as one of the best in my life. Not because Ariella allowed me to experience what it felt like to have her heat wrapped around me—fuck, the sounds she makes are the ones I wish to listen to as death takes me.

But it wasn't the sex. It was the connection...something that, to this day, I cannot explain. It was as if an ancient being settled in the depths of my chest—the same thing that now aches each time I'm near her and drains the life from me when she's away.

I've tried to understand it, piecing together fragments of old stories and rumors about things that tie people in ways no one can fully explain. Yet, even with all my digging, I'm no closer to an answer. What I do know is that it's not one-sided—I've seen it in the way she watches me when she thinks I'm not paying attention, felt it in her touch as if the same pull is unraveling her from the inside out.

"No one's forcing you to come," Ariella replies without looking back. "I'm sure there are plenty of noble ladies who'd love to entertain you both instead. Perhaps Jessenia is also visiting." She doesn't sound bothered, but the light tapping against her thigh tells me otherwise.

I smirk, sliding an arm around her shoulders, and to my surprise, she doesn't threaten me. Progress. "Jealous, angel?"

She scoffs but doesn't respond, which only serves to widen my smile. Even after everything, she still tries to maintain distance between us. As if we haven't shared more than just a bed these past weeks. I lean down and press a light kiss to her temple, my dick twitching when her full body shudders. The things she does to me.

The cobblestone streets gradually give way to wider, cleaner paths as we enter the noble district. Bastian's family estate rises before us—all white stone and ornate red and gold architecture, desperately trying to mirror the grandeur of the royal palace. I roll my eyes. My cousin never could resist showing off his wealth.

Two guards stand at attention by the main gates, their postures stiffening as we approach. One of them, a younger man with sandy hair, steps forward with his hand on his sword.

"State your business."

Before I can speak, Ariella moves past me. "Tell *Lord* Bastian his cousin is here." Her voice carries that deadly edge I've come to dream of—the one that makes most men's blood run cold.

Such is that with the sentry she directed her words to. He hesitates, eyes lingering on her silver hair. Recognition flashes across his face, followed quickly by fear. "I...the lord isn't accepting visitors today."

The sound of metal scraping leather permeates the tense space, Ariella flawlessly spinning a blade through her fingers while continuing to watch the guard. "My apologies, I must have misheard you." She takes another step forward, and the man flinches. "Because if you did just reject your prince in the name of some false, slimy lord, who's a mockery to the fucking throne, you and I will have quite the problem."

I should intervene, but watching her intimidate Bastian's men brings me more satisfaction than I care to admit. Establishing her as my guard was a damn great decision.

"My lady, please—" the guard starts, but Ariella throws her fist into his throat, rendering him choking and breathless. She saunters past them both, and neither makes a move to stop her. Smart men.

"Coming?" she calls over her shoulder. The woman is in a mood today, and I love every second of it.

I share an amused look with Gavriel before following, though his expression looks far less entertained, his jaw clenched tight enough I can see the muscle jumping. He's been on edge since we arrived in Meridian, though he refuses to tell me why, and has refrained from speaking often. All strange behavior; I'll wait until we're back in Valoria to address it.

The estate's main doors swing open before we reach them, revealing a harried-looking steward. "Prince Caspian," he greets with a hasty bow. "The king hadn't sent—we weren't expecting—"

"WHERE IS HE?" Bastian's voice booms from inside, followed by hurried footsteps. He appears in the doorway, his face deep red and scrunched so hard I'm sure it will remain that way for the rest of his years. "What in the Angel's name are you doing here? Get the fuck out, Caspian!" Always so dramatic.

"Is that any way to greet family?" I jeer, unable to keep the sickly sweet tone from my voice.

His eyes narrow before shifting to Ariella. Something complicated passes over his features—fear mixed with...desire? My hands clench at my sides as heat fills the space under my skin.

"Get them out," he snaps at his staff, before physically snapping in their direction. No one moves.

Ariella chuckles and takes one step. I swear the temperature drops several degrees. "Hello, Bastian." I curse at the carnality in her voice, biting my tongue hard to stop my hands from squeezing the life from my cousin. "We're here to talk, so invite us in, won't you?" The way he watches her is nauseating.

Until she allows her blade to catch in the light, and the color drains from his face.

"I don't invite psycho women into my house."

"No?" She moves closer, and he steps back. "That's unfortunate. You see, we traveled all this way just to see you, Bastian. Surely you can make an exception just this once?" Her free hands whips out to grab the collar of his red, button-down shirt. She holds him tight as her blade drags up his abdomen.

Fucking Angel. She's going to pay for touching him like this.

I swallow down the anger and watch with growing interest as Bastian's composure crumbles further. His eyes search for help, though not even his staff aid him as they remain back in the foyer.

"Inside," he manages after a minute, tossing some stiff gesture over his shoulder.

We follow him through marble halls decorated with expensive artwork and tapestries—each piece chosen to display his family's fortune and status. The whole place reeks of desperate nobility trying to prove their worth.

He leads us to his study, dismissing the staff with a sharp wave. Only once the doors are closed does he turn to face us, though his eyes keep darting to Ariella like he expects her to strike at any moment. If she doesn't, I might.

"What do you want to know?" he asks, shuffling behind his desk as if it might offer some protection.

"I'd like to discuss someone by the name of Ally Dimir."

His eyes widen. "What about Ally?"

"Everything," Ariella replies. "Starting with how you knew her."

Bastian laughs, but there's no humor in it. "Why don't you ask your friend Isaiah? Oh, wait..."

I move before thinking, but Ariella's hand on my chest stops me. Her touch burns through the fabric, grounding me.

"Careful, cousin," I warn, my voice low. "You're walking a dangerous line."

He sneers, but some of the false bravado leaves his shoulders. "She was my betrothed," he finally answers. "Before she left for the competition."

That wasn't what I expected. From the slight curl of Ariella's fingers that still rest on me, she's equally surprised.

"When?" she demands.

"Two years ago. We were to be married in the winter, but then..." he trails off, running a hand through his hair. He looks quite disheveled talking about Ally. "The king visited. Spoke with her privately. The next day she was gone, not even caring to say goodbye. I'd thought about joining her, but Thalion made it clear that I was to act as if I had never met her." He laughs, the sound empty. "He was pissed when I arrived in Valoria, but how could he expect me to just let go of the woman I was to marry? Then I saw the way she and Isaiah were together."

I clench my jaw as Bastian's words ripple through the stale air. His admission about Ally explains quite a bit, though my mind grapples with possibilities I hadn't considered before.

"So you pursued me out of spite?" Ariella asks, not even a spec of offense lacing her voice. "To get back at her?"

Bastian shifts in his chair, suddenly finding great interest in the papers scattered across his desk. What does he even work on—it's not as if he manages anything other than his own pockets. "Not entirely." His eyes flick to me before continuing. "The king suggested I...distract you."

White-hot rage courses through my veins. Of course my father had orchestrated that, too. How many other pieces has he moved without my knowledge? Against Ariella, no less?

"What else did *the king* tell you?" I demand, stepping further around his desk. "And think carefully before lying to us. You'd rather not know what Ariella did to the guildmaster for it just yesterday."

He swallows hard and looks between Ariella and me, conflict evident on his features. "I don't know much. He mentioned something about balance and power, but it made little sense. Said Ally would be what he needed to remove his problem so that he may restore our realm." He runs a hand through his disheveled hair. "This was at the ball, so I'd just thought the man was drunk and speaking in riddles."

"The Accord," Ariella states, voice flat. Not a question. "Did he mention it?" It seems we no longer require discretion or subtlety. I cross my arms and lean against the wall, watching my future queen interrogate my cousin.

And what a fucking sight it is.

Bastian's brow furrows. "The what?"

"Don't play stupid," I snap, impulsiveness overshadowing my calm. "The ancient agreement between realms. The one that's currently falling apart while my father conducts his twisted experiments."

He blinks, his forehead creasing. "Experiments?"

"Yes, experiments," Ariella cuts in, her patience eroding, if the tightness in her tone is any indication. "With essence. Ring any bells?"

Understanding dawns on his face. "That's what he meant..." he mutters, more to himself than us. "He kept going on about finding new ways to harness power, about making the kingdom stronger instead of being limited. I thought he was speaking metaphorically."

Gavriel shifts behind us, watching the entire interaction with wary eyes.

Bastian sits forward abruptly. "You know, now that I think about it, he'd visit every so often, asking strange questions about ancient texts on essence." His gaze darts to the elaborate tapestry behind his desk of the royal crest. "My family's library contains some of the oldest records in the realm, and he was always very interested in them, but insisted that they remained here."

I want to deny it. To say that my father hasn't been doing this for long—but that would be a complete lie. Valyria sacrificed herself for the king's decisions, and that was more than twenty years ago.

A sour heat fills my stomach—I should have noticed. Paid attention. Maybe I could have stopped it before we reached a point of no return.

"Show us," Ariella demands, backing from the desk as she gestures for my cousin to leave.

Bastian hesitates before standing with a resigned sigh. He walks from the room, and we follow him through winding corridors, descending deeper into the estate until we reach a circular room lined with what I assume are the very old texts my father utilized. The air here feels heavy, stiff. It's uncomfortable.

"Here," Bastian says, tugging a weathered book from one of the shelves. "This is the one that interested him most. I once read it to see what caught his attention, though I never thought more about it. There are details of old theories about essence manipulation—ways to combine different strands, to amplify raw power." He pauses. "And methods of extraction, if I'm remembering right."

Ariella snatches the book from him, her eyes scanning the pages at a rapid pace. "Fuck's sake," she breathes. "This is it. This is what he's doing." Her spoken thoughts confirm what I hoped wasn't true. But there's no denying it at this point.

I step just behind her, reading over her shoulder. Gavriel joins me, though remains a good distance away from Ariella. The text describes horrific experiments conducted centuries ago—attempts to forcibly remove essence from living beings and transfer it to others. Most subjects died in agony.

Fury builds in my chest. "I still don't understand what the children's role is in this. If these experiments are accurate, how would their small bodies be of any use compared to adults?" I can't think about that right now.

Gavriel grunts behind us, pacing to another shelf and back. "The guards at the tunnel entrance. They must have been protecting wherever he's conducting these tests. That much is obvious, though I do not believe they're aware of what's happening. Now that we know, it will not matter if we go through them to find Thalion."

I nod, my body more tired than it's been in years. Shifting on both feet, my mind races. "How long do we have?"

"Clearly not long." Ariella's fingers drum against her thigh. "We leave for Valoria tonight."

Bastian nods, eager to be rid of us, before herding our group upstairs. He doesn't escort us out, and I'm glad for it. The urge to punch his stupid fucking mouth remains strong.

The streets of Meridian seem different now, darker somehow despite the bright afternoon sun. Or perhaps it's just my perception that's changed, polluted by images and thoughts of what my father is capable of.

Ariella walks a foot ahead of me and Gavriel, lost in thought. She may be silent as a wraith, but I can practically hear her mind working through possibilities. Even distracted, she travels with lethal grace, drawing looks from citizens that she ignores as if she's oblivious to them. But I know the truth—she's aware of every soul in the vicinity and would have a blade in the throat of the first person that even *thought* about harming her.

I bite my cheek to dampen the smile, barely succeeding. She's fucking incredible.

We're halfway back to the inn when we encounter them; a group of people huddled around a wild-eyed man shouting from atop a crate.

"The end approaches!" His desperate cries raise the hairs along my arms. "The realms bleed into each other! Our essence fails us! Who among you hasn't felt the change?" The crowd murmurs, though I cannot tell if they agree with the sentiment or not.

The man continues. "The Angel abandoned us long ago. The coming is the price of our arrogance. The realms demand payment!"

Ariella halts, causing me to almost collide with her. Her head tilts as she listens to this nonsense. I am curious about where he found this information, though. After a few moments of the man repeating himself, she mutters something under her breath and stalks away.

The sounds of the crowd fade as we put distance between us, but the words linger in my mind. *The realms demand payment.*

It's nonsense—just the ravings of someone desperate to find meaning in the current predicament of our realm. Yet, something about it gnaws at the edges of my thoughts, as if some part of me recognizes a truth hidden within the madness. I can't shake the uneasiness within my gut, especially after hearing the same thing from Rael.

I want to ask Ariella, but her posture screams *leave me alone* as she practically jogs through the streets. I've learned when to give her space, even if every cell of my being wants to pull her close and promise we'll figure this out together.

"We should rest before heading back," Gavriel suggests as we near the city center. "It's a long ride, and we all need time to process today."

I expect Ariella to argue, but she glares at my guard, a dangerous glimmer shifting through her eyes. They stare at one another, seeming to have an unspoken argument, though of what this time, I'm unsure. They should really speak to someone about their issues—it's become far more irritating than amusing at this point.

Gavriel clears his throat, gesturing ahead. "We can rest at the inn near the marketplace. It will be quieter there."

I nod, though Ariella's already wandering away. My muscles ache from riding, but there's a tension thrumming through me that won't let me rest just yet. Too many questions plague my mind.

The streets of Meridian bustle with activity despite the heat. Vendors call out their wares while dock workers hurry past with crates and supplies. The salty breeze carries hints of fish and spices from nearby food stalls.

Ariella pauses, her attention caught by something in a shop window. I follow her gaze to an elegant dress displayed behind the glass. The deep orange fabric reminds me of a sunset over the Elysaran Mountains, flowing like water that has been frozen in time. Tiny crystals are woven throughout, catching the light in an intentional pattern. It's breathtaking—and unlike anything I'd expect to capture her interest.

She stares for several long moments before shaking her head and continuing down the street. I suppress the urge to offer to buy it for her. She'd slice off my dick just for suggesting it.

"Wraith!" a merchant calls out with notable excitement, waving from his stall. "You look troubled! I have exactly what you need—straight from Auroria's finest inventors!"

Ariella raises an eyebrow but approaches his table. The merchant grins, pulling out an odd cylindrical object that tapers at one end, made of soft, polished metal. It's about the length of my hand, with strange ridges and curves along its surface.

"What is it?" she asks, her curiosity evident as she picks it up.

"A revolutionary device that integrates with essence!" the merchant exclaims. "Simply channel your energy into it and—"

The object lurches to life in her hand, emitting a low humming as it vibrates intensely. Ariella's eyes widen and she grimaces, turning it over to examine it.

"What the fuck is this even supposed to do?" she demands, holding it away from her body. "It's just making noise."

I lean in to study it, equally baffled. "Perhaps it's meant to...mix liquid concoctions?" Even as I say it, I know that can't be right. The merchant's knowing smirk only deepens my confusion.

"You'll figure it out," he says with a wink. "Just remember to draw the essence back out when you're finished. And wash it thoroughly, of course."

Ariella tries to hand it back, but he waves her off. "Consider it a gift! The Silver Wraith herself, using my wares? Priceless advertising."

She scowls but stuffs the strange device into her pocket, clearly done with this interaction—as am I. "Whatever." As we leave, I catch a hint of a conversation between two women who are giggling over the same object Ariella was just given. Interesting.

We continue toward the docks, the crowds thinning as we near the water, though the atmosphere seems far more erratic. The ocean stretches before us, waves lapping at the wooden piers. The setting sun tints the water in brilliant golds and crimsons.

I watch Ariella as she consumes the view. The way her iridescent hair catches the light, how her sharp features soften in quiet contemplation. Even after everything, she still manages to steal my breath.

But something shifts in her expression—a hardening of her features that has my own senses heightening. "What is that?" Gavriel asks, also gazing at the water.

That's when I see it. What appears to be a wall emerging from the water, impossibly tall and rising by the second. "What in the Aether..." I breathe.

People begin to notice, pointing and shouting, their alarm creating chaos among others. The wall of water grows, almost blocking out the sun as it advances toward the shore with frightening speed.

"We need to move," I say, already calculating. "If we can get to higher ground, it may not reach us."

"No time," Ariella cuts in, her eyes still fixed on the approaching wave. "If we run, we die."

She turns to me then, and I know that look. The one that says she's about to do something very dangerous and potentially impossible. The one that makes my heart race with equal parts fear and awe.

"No," I say, even as I step closer to her. "I know what you're thinking, angel, but it's not worth it." This fearless fucking woman is preparing to expose her forbidden essence. I want to argue more, but not only do we have mere minutes until the wave reaches us, I'm certain that her choice is what will save her life. I could attempt to weave my aqua strand—I shake my head even as I think it. I've never trained in such a way and it would only serve to make me weaker.

"Do you trust me?" she demands as her breaths increase.

That may be the most stupid fucking thing to ever leave her mouth.

"Yes." I say the word without hesitation because it's true. Completely, irrevocably true.

Screams fill the air as people flee in panic. The wave towers over the city now, and Gavriel grabs my arm, but I shake him off as I shift to stand beside Ariella. Whatever she's planning will drain her of everything, and that only solidifies my decision to ground myself so that I may catch her when she falls.

Chapter Twenty-One

Ariella

"**B**y the Angel, we're fucked," Gavriel whispers, and for once in his pathetic life, I agree with him.

I've nothing to say as I cannot get my lips to move.

My feet root to the ground as I watch the wall of water rise, defying every law of nature. People scream and run, but my mind races through options as the prince stands next to me.

I cannot let him die.

I tug on my umbral strand without hesitation, ignoring the mere seconds left before we're hit, and pull shadows from deep within me. They pour from my skin as I weave a ward around us. Gavriel shifts uncomfortably, but remains quiet as the wave towers over our heads.

The water crashes into us with cataclysmic force, my fists clenching at my essence's inclination to dissipate amid the onslaught. I wince at the thunderous roar as we're buried beneath the raging ocean. My knees nearly buckle as I strain to hold the ward. We sink below the surface, murky water surrounding us on all sides while my barrier keeps us dry. My eyes flick up, peering through the essence to find that we're already feet under water. Something akin to pure terror settles in my gut when my hands begin trembling—I'm not sure how long I can hold this.

Sweat builds along my neck while I focus on maintaining the barrier. My shadows dance and swirl, creating a dome that should protect us. But fuck, I've never attempted something this intense before. I can feel my essence draining faster than it should.

"What the actual fuck?" Gavriel's voice breaks through my concentration. "You're using forbidden essence? How?"

I grit my teeth, unable to spare the energy to respond. My arms shake with effort as the pressure increases.

"You knew about this?" He turns to Caspian, who remains oddly calm. "How long have you known she possesses illegal strands?"

"Gavriel, this isn't the time—" Caspian starts, but his guard cuts him off.

"Not the time? She's breaking the highest law we have! She should be executed for this!" His voice rises with each word. "And you've been hiding it? What else are you hiding from me?"

"Will you shut the fuck up?" I scream, my focus slipping as rage courses through me. "I'm trying to save your ungrateful ass!"

The ward flickers as my control wavers. My chest heaves, and I swear I hear a bit of wheezing from my lungs. The brute continues to yell, and though I do everything in my power to ignore him, I snap.

"Gavriel, shut up!" The last of my words are immediately drowned as I lose my concentration and the ward slips from my grasp. It feels as though a stone building crashes into me, the pain of the water's impact momentarily blinding before I force my mind to focus.

The pressure in my chest builds as I'm tossed through the murky water. My body slams into something hard—likely debris from the destroyed buildings. The impact forces what little air I had left from my lungs.

I reach blindly ahead of me, my fingers catching on what feels like stone. My muscles strain as I pull myself along the surface, fighting against the current that wants nothing more than to drag me further into its depths.

Fuck water. Give me a dozen men with blades and a deep-rooted vendetta any day.

My lungs burn for air, but I force the panic down. Marek's voice rings in my head, reminding me that fear is what truly kills you. I need to keep my thoughts steady.

Which way is up?

I release my grip on the stone and let my body go slack for a moment. The current doesn't hesitate to pull me in one direction—that must be down. I kick hard in the opposite direction, my legs protesting the effort against the force of the water.

Light filters through the murk above me. Just a bit further...

My head breaks the surface and I gasp, drawing in desperate breaths between waves that try to force me back under. The city streets have become canals, water rushing between buildings that somehow still stand. Broken pieces of wood and stone bob past me as I tread water.

I need higher ground to spot Caspian—I can't see him any longer.

Several buildings ahead have exposed roofs rising above the flood. The closest looks to be about fifty feet away...I can make that swim if I time it between the surges. I wait for the next wave to pass before striking out toward it with measured strokes.

The current fights me the whole way, trying to sweep me past my target. My arms feel like lead by the time I reach the building's wall. I dig my fingers into the cracks between stones and haul myself up inch by painful inch until I can roll onto the relative safety of the roof, though I slip back and almost lose my grip.

Fuck, I need to start training in water. I'd no idea just how weak I was. It's an embarrassing struggle as I grind my teeth hard enough to break and finally pull my torso over the rooftop. My body hunches over and nearly convulses from coughing so hard. I chuckle to myself, glad I'm alone because fuck if I'd let the prince see me like this. I'd never hear the end—

The prince.

I'm on my feet not a heartbeat later, scouring the racing water for any sign of Caspian. Does he even know how to swim? He must...Royals learn shit like that. I think. My throat tightens the longer I go without seeing him; it feels like years, though I'm certain it's been just a few moments.

A familiar head of hair appears in my peripheral, and I've no time to bask in the relief I feel as I see Caspian's head accompanied by flailing arms. "You've got to be *kidding* me!" Of course the bastard can't swim. It's likely the current pulling him under, but I'm too angry to care who's at fault.

I pause. I fucking *hesitate* and watch with a horrific sinking feeling in my chest as the prince gets carried away.

I never hesitate.

Hesitation is the enemy of progress.

I shove Marek's stupid words down as I stand, my body immediately clearing from all emotion. I turn around and swallow the bile that rises when I see that the entire city appears as if it's a part of the ocean. It's a challenge to move my legs how I need, but I push until I'm sprinting across the roof toward Caspian—who is drowning.

Caspian is drowning.

Pure, unbridled fear shoots down my spine, allowing my body to move faster than it ever has before. I do not think twice before leaping over the roof's edge onto the next building. My eyes are a constant radar as they flit from my path to the prince and back. I force my legs to move even faster, and at one point I'm certain I feel something tear near my ankle, but fuck if that will stop me from getting to him.

I jump from roof to roof, gaining on Caspian quickly—*though not quick enough*, I think as a whimper escapes me when I notice his body floating with the water. I spot Gavriel clutching to the side of a building, struggling to hold on. His eyes widen when he sees me chasing after his prince, though he continues to grasp at the ledge of a window instead of going after the only one whose life matters here.

I'll deal with him later.

I'd deal with him now if the Angel allowed it; a life for a life. There would be no hesitation in my movements as I shoved his head under the invading ocean and forced the soul from his body, if it allowed me to save Caspian in time.

I need to hurry. Time slips away with every crashing wave, but I force my vision to clear and banish the thought of death. Not yet. Looking to my left, the prince is just behind me and not a moment later, I join him in the freezing water. I dive directly in front of his body, my own moving on pure instinct as I grab him and fight the current to get both of us to a roof.

It's the smallest relief when one appears that's partially in the water, making it easy for me to grab a piece of wood that sticks out from the rest. I will my fingers to fuse to it and completely ignore the nauseating pain from my nails being ripped off. My arm, wrapped under both of Caspian's over his chest, squeezes hard enough to drag him onto the roof. I wince when he drops from my hold, his head thumping against the wood, and I tell myself I'll apologize when he's breathing again.

I straddle his hips to hold him in place, lest the water rushing over the lower half of his body steal him from me again. Reaching deep inside, I just about tear my vital strand to pieces as I pull it forward to do my bidding. My hands rip the buttons from his shirt, exposing his pale chest. It's easy to ignore the unreasonable amount of blood seeping from the exposed skin my nails left behind, though I know it's going to fucking hurt when the adrenaline wears off. Leaning forward—

I pause.

I've never healed another person before; I do not know how to do it...

Nor do I have enough essence to even try.

"Shit!" I slap the prince's cheek several times. "Caspian. Caspian, please wake up—of course he won't, you stupid fucking idiot," I mutter to myself as hundreds of thoughts flit through my head every second.

How do they help someone who drowned? I've seen this done...I should know.

"You must force the water from their lungs and push air back in. Push, Macey!" As much as I hate Velora, the image of her scolding a young student for not getting her technique right just might be what saves my prince.

My hands send a wet crack through the thunderous atmosphere when they slap against Caspian's chest. I push and pull, push and pull, hoping that I'm doing it correctly. How many times do I do this before the air? I count to twenty before leaning down to pinch his nose and latch my mouth around his. Sucking in a deep breath, I blow the air from my lungs as hard as I can into his.

I lean back to scan his face before pressing my ear to his heart. Nothing.

"No, no, no, it was supposed to work. Fuck—please don't do this!" I scream at his un-moving chest as I struggle to control the trembling in my hands. My eyes drag up to glare through the blinding sun, a mockery of everything happening down here. But it's not the sun I want. No, my next words are for the Angel, so it better be listening. "If you take him from me," I snarl, my voice wavering with a rage that burns hotter than the freezing water around us, "there will be nothing left of me but vengeance. I will hunt you to the ends of both realms, and when I find you, I will tear your name from existence."

My fingers dig into Caspian's chest, trembling as I press harder, desperate for any flicker of life. Nothing. Still nothing. My heart clenches, but I refuse to stop. I won't stop.

"Your entire family, species, whatever the fuck you are," I spit through gritted teeth, glaring at the derisive sky above, "will cease to exist. I will kill them all, one by one, and use every ounce of essence you cursed me with to tear both realms apart—city by city, stone by stone—until there is nothing left but ashes."

The words pour from me like a dam breaking, a flood of fury and despair that drowns the sound of crashing waves. My vision blurs as I look back down at Caspian's still form. My prince. My tether to what little light remains in this wretched world.

"I will make you watch," I vow, my voice dropping to a venomous whisper. "All of it. And when you and I are the only things left alive...only then will I kill you. Slowly. Torturously. You will *beg* for forgiveness and wish you'd never created the realms in the first place."

My fists pound against his chest, the rhythm a desperate, unyielding plea. The edge of my voice breaks as I whisper, "*Please.*"

A large wave crashes over the roof, snapping me from my threat to the Angel. I cover Caspian's face—I don't need any more fucking water in his lungs—before making a fist with my good hand and punching his chest. I punch and punch, ignoring each rib I hear cracking as I use all my force to expel the liquid from him. If I had any essence left, I'd use my elemental affinity to drag the water out myself. But I don't have enough...I used most of the essence inside me to shield us from the initial crash of the ocean.

"Caspian, I swear on everything that I will fucking kill you if you die." New salty liquid slides over my lips, a more familiar taste than the water surrounding us. "*Please*, Caspian," I beg, each word cracking as my bottom lip trembles.

I've never been so fucking scared in my life.

Not even when my father was killed. Or when I walked into the guild for the first time.

My fist continues to pound against him—I refuse to let him go. He's mine, and I will not allow him leave me. "I can't do this again...I can't lose you, too." The longer he remains still, the more erratic my movements. "Don't you dare leave me, you foolish fucking asshole! I can't do this without you...*please*...I'll stop fighting whatever this is between us. I'll laugh at all your stupid jokes, and compliment you regularly, because I know how much your ego needs it. I'll even stop insulting Gavriel every day...well, the guy is a pompous idiot, you cannot expect me—" It's not until something wraps around my wrist do I realize I've been blindly punching the man underneath me, overtaken by my panic.

My eyes shoot open as Caspian rolls to the side as much as my thighs allow to cough, the sound deep but relieving. I slap his back hard on instinct to help, though I'm not sure it does anything;

the wet sounds coming from him are plentiful and horrific all the same. My surroundings are blacked out, as every bit of attention I have focuses on the prince. After an eternity, he falls to his back, panting as if he'd just ran through the entire city.

I suppose he did.

I'm frozen. I was so convinced that he was gone that my brain has yet to comprehend he's alive.

He winces with every breath, but I won't apologize for his injuries. Beautifully full, silver eyes peer up at me and drag over my body before meeting mine. Caspian attempts to smile, though it looks more like a grimace. "If I knew coming back to life was like this, I'd die more frequently," he whispers with a hoarse voice, a light chuckle shifting quickly to a deep cough. He watches me with tired features, waiting for a response I don't have.

Instead, a sob leaves me before I give in to the horrifying feelings I've ignored since my ward broke. My body is far from my control as it shakes with the force of my cries. Caspian's warming arms wrap around me, and I do not hesitate to do the same as I bury my face in his neck. He smells mostly of fish and salt, but there's still *him* under all of it. I focus on that and breathe him in, my heart slowing with each intake of his scent—he smells like home.

"Ari, it's okay," he says, grasping the back of my head before rocking slightly. "I'm here, angel—I've got you." His steady words soothe the part of my soul that was so close to dying along with him. "Did you think you could rid of me so easily? The Angel itself couldn't pry me away from you."

I lean back, pressing my forehead against his. "I thou—" I hiccup, willing my voice to sound even half as strong as his. How the fuck is he so calm right now? "I thought you—" Another sob breaks my sentence. I cannot say it out loud, lest I somehow speak such a fate into existence.

Strange is not a strong enough word to describe the emotions swirling through me. Mere months ago, I was planning on ripping the air from the prince's lungs so that I could shove his dead body in Thalion's face. And now I'm desperate to keep his air right where it is.

Maybe strange does explain it.

I sigh into his hold as he presses kisses all over my face, purposefully missing the one place I need his lips. He fists my sopping hair and pulls my head back just far enough to look between my eyes. "I am not going anywhere, Ariella. I'm here, and I'm yours." The declaration heats my frozen insides. I search his face, memorizing every hair, divot, and tired line. There is nothing I've ever needed more than to feel his mouth on mine—to feel the *life* swim between our bodies.

"Shut up." My voice strains as I reach to squeeze his cheeks together, pursing his lips. "You will kiss me. Then you will apologize for making me feel this way." Garbled noises barely make it through his mouth, so I release a little to allow him to speak once more.

"Apologize to you? As if I wasn't the one who just died," he exclaims. A playfulness flits through his eyes.

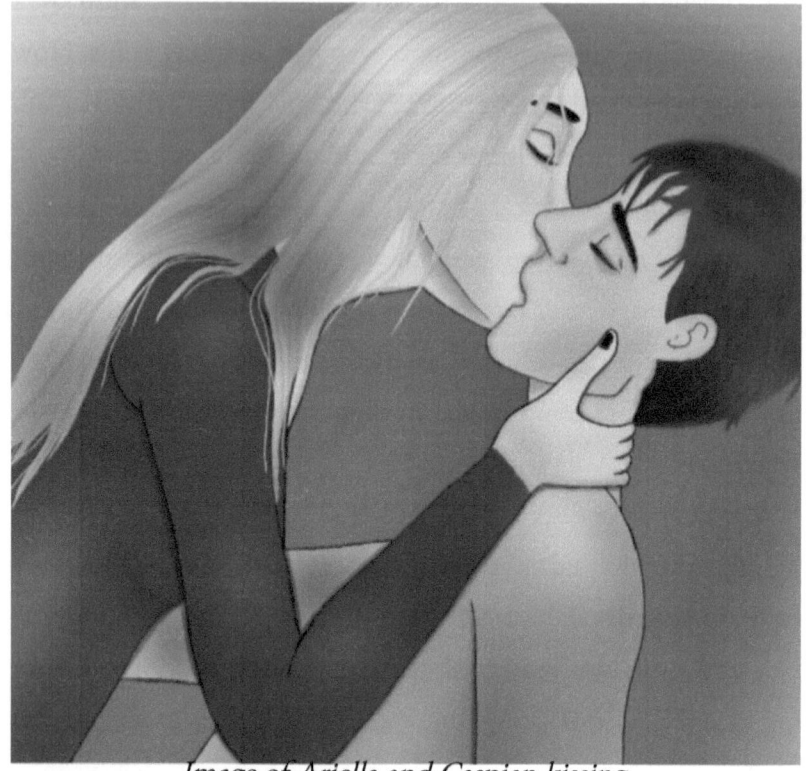

Image of Ariella and Caspian kissing.

"No, Caspian." I lean forward to capture his lips with mine. It's unbearable to resist any longer, but I find the strength to pull back when I'm breathless. My eyes remain closed as I speak against his mouth. "I want you to apologize for forcing yourself into my life. For making me feel things I never wanted to again, and carving a place for yourself in a heart that died twenty years ago when your father killed mine." Our lips entangle again, though it is the prince who pulls away this time. The cold of the water is nothing compared to the shivering he forces upon my body as his fingers trail up my spine.

"What else should I apologize for?" he whispers against my jaw, sweeping kiss after kiss down the side of my neck.

"For how crazy I feel whenever you're gone. And how much I miss your touch after you take it away." I'm sobbing into his hair, only now just realizing he's stopped kissing me, and instead is resting his ear over my heart. "I want you to apologize for how fucking badly I need you when I have done *everything* to reject this."

He pulls back, wincing, to study the mess I've made of my face. "You couldn't have avoided this any more than me. The only difference is I never fought it." Sweat beads along his forehead, and I gather the minuscule amount of essence that has replenished and tug on my vital strand. I have the sense that I suddenly know what to do to heal him, so I coax the essence to the tips of my fingers and place them against his waist. It takes a moment, but a familiar light seeps from under my skin and wraps around his torso, looking for anything that needs healing.

He sighs, only to groan when the crack of bones unbreaking sounds around us. I cannot hold it long enough to mend every part of his body, though I'm confident the worst of his injuries have been taken care of.

Has it been so easy all along?

Well, I wouldn't call this easy. I feel as if my very life is seeping from my soul. But I would do this for a hundred years if it kept him alive.

"Fuck." I wince as I sit back on the prince's thighs once more, breathing far too heavy to not be concerning. I've never used so much of my essence at one time—and I never want to again. I feel *horrible*. My muscles ache in ways I didn't realize were possible; my head is pounding, and if the sun gets any brighter, I may just rip it from the sky out of spite.

"Ari," Caspian says from somewhere far away. I want to protest. Shove him away so that I may rest for a while. But instead I listen to the nagging in my head telling me to open my eyes.

I have a feeling that the day is far from over. Wonderful.

I squint through a small opening in my lids, rearing back at how tilted the city around me looks. My eyes snap open to Caspian sitting up, his tight grip on my shoulder keeping me from falling over.

He just died. I need to be the strength in our duo until I get him to safety.

Water laps over my calves, and I frown. I'm on my feet in the next heartbeat, grabbing onto Caspian's offered hands and gently tugging him up with me. He attempts to hide a wince, ignoring my inquiring eyes as he inspects my body for injury.

"Are you okay?"

I breathe a humorous laugh, shaking my head. "No. But we can't think about that right now...we need to get out of here." The reality of our situation slams into me as I look around us.

Meridian, aside from the uppermost part of its hill, is completely under water. My body is too tired to swim as far as we'd need to reach the dry land, and there are no boats, or even useful pieces of debris, in sight.

I have to give it to the Angel. Not an hour ago was I commenting on the beauty of the ocean, only for it to retaliate. Impressive work—truly.

"I don't see Gavriel anywhere..." Caspian's voice trails off, a frown etched deep in his features. I scan the horizon with him, looking for the distinct red jacket amongst the other survivors standing on various roofs. "Wait—there!" He points to our right where a bit of bright crimson peeks through a group of people. I'm ready to toss aside thoughts of the guard when I realize that the small frame with long, blonde hair is certainly not Gavriel.

But that is his jacket—it's too distinct to be anything but.

The prince's shoulders slump as he concludes that same thing I did. "He must be with the group—there's no chance he would part with the royal uniform he's so proud of if it wasn't to give it to a child."

I scan the flooding city, my heart racing as I spot movement in the distance. The water level at our feet is lowering fast, but that's not what makes my blood run cold. Beyond the submerged buildings, a massive wall of water towers over everything, moving steadily toward us. Again.

"Fuck's sake...Caspian..." My voice catches. I've never felt so helpless. My essence is drained and my limbs feel like dense steel. Even if we could run, there's nowhere close enough to escape what's coming.

I look at my prince, still weak from drowning. His argent eyes meet mine, and I see the same realization there: we won't survive this wave.

I meant what I said before. I direct the thought toward the Angel. *If you let him die, I will tear everything apart. I do not care what it costs me. You better fucking do something.*

A piercing screech cuts through the air and my entire body goes rigid. I know that sound. It's impossible.

My head whips up as a massive white griffin circles overhead, its feathers gleaming despite the darkening clouds. Caspian stumbles back, but I grab his arm.

"Don't move," I whisper. "She's here to help."

"She?" My fingers tighten on his arm as the griffin's shadow moves over us, the sheer size of her wingspan enough to momentarily block out the sky. But the prince stares at me like I've lost my mind. Maybe I have.

If that's the cost of saving his life twice today, so be it.

The griffin lands on our roof with impossible grace, her intelligent blue eyes finding mine. She remembers me. I step closer, my breath catching at the sheer power radiating from her massive form. Every movement is deliberate, almost regal, and yet there's something undeniably wild about her—particularly her claws, which dredge up undesirable images of me dying after her attack.

The egg I took from her nest still rests in my room at the castle. Should I have brought it after all?

"We need to go," I state, not wasting time with pleasantries. If I remember correctly, she understood my words the last time we met. She lowers herself, and I do not hesitate to grab Caspian and practically throw him onto her back. He makes a strangled sound of protest, but I ignore it, climbing up behind him.

"Ariella, what—" We have no time for his worries, so I shove his back forward and cover him, rendering his voice silent. The griffin tilts her head back, letting out another sharp screech that reverberates through the air. It feels like a warning. One I don't intend to question.

The griffin launches into the air just as the massive wave crashes into the building we'd been standing on. The force of her wings pushes against us, forming a current strong enough to scatter the debris below. I wrap my arms tight around Caspian's waist as we soar over the devastation below. The mighty creature carries us to the highest point of the city—not struggling in the fucking slightest—where other survivors have gathered on dry ground.

The others scream and fall back, some slamming into the dirt in their haste to move out of the way. I spot Gavriel as he steps to the side, soaked with a feral look on his face. Despicable that he found himself safety before doing everything he could to save Caspian.

The griffin descends, gliding gracefully toward safety, her landing so light it seems impossible for a creature her size. The moment she ceases movement, I slide off and help steady Caspian. The griffin watches us with those piercing eyes, and I move closer to her.

"Thank you," I say softly, my words only for her. I dare to reach out, quite surprised when she allows me to brush my hand against her feathered neck. The softness is a strange contrast to the sheer strength she exudes. I wish we had more time. "Your egg is safe. I won't let anything happen to it."

She makes a low clicking sound in her throat and bows her head before spreading her wings. With one last look at me, she takes to the sky and disappears into the clouds.

"We need to find you a healer," I tell Caspian, supporting some of his weight as he sways. "And then we're going back to the castle." My voice hardens with resolve. "I'm done waiting. Your father dies today."

Chapter Twenty-Two

Ariella

The road ahead blurs with each heavy step my horse takes. We've been riding since dawn, after having rested for a while, and the sun now hangs low enough in the sky that shadows stretch across our path like eerie branches. My muscles ache from staying tense for so long; but I can't relax. Not after what happened in Meridian.

The sound of rushing water still echoes in my head. My screams. The helplessness as I watched Caspian being swept away while I did everything in my power to get to him. I squeeze my eyes shut, willing away the memories—a fool's battle. Those moments will haunt my dreams for the rest of my life, and likely even after the Angel takes me.

I glance at Caspian riding beside me. His eyes are distant, no doubt replaying the same scenes mine are. At least what he can remember. The way his shoulders slump tells me he's taking it harder than I am. Of course he is—he's the one that fucking died for several minutes. Then we left his people behind, deciding that our presence in Valoria is far more dire than helping the wounded in Meridian.

Gavriel rides ahead of us, his posture rigid. He's been quiet since we left, speaking only when necessary. Something about his behavior nags at me. The way he avoided meeting my eyes when we discussed the king's experiments. How he tensed when Bastian mentioned the trials.

He hasn't even spewed nonsense about my staying back in the trade city.

"We should rest the horses soon," Caspian asserts, breaking the heavy silence. "There's a clearing just ahead that would work."

I nod, though rest is the last thing I want. Every moment we delay is another moment the king continues ruining our chances to fix the Accord. But I do not think it's the horses that need to rest. I peer to my left for the millionth time since leaving the city, studying each piece of the prince. His skin is sallow and dull. His eyes are struggling to stay open, and I'm certain he keeps jerking every few minutes to not fall off his horse.

He will be riding with me the short distance back to Valoria.

The aforementioned clearing appears—a small break in the dense forest surrounding the road. As we dismount, I notice the slightest shake in Gavriel's hands as he ties his horse's reins.

"I'll get water," he mutters, grabbing the skins and heading toward the sound of a stream nearby.

Something in his tone makes me pause. Not even a hint of his usual hostility. I've heard that kind of forced casualness before—in targets who think me too dense to understand their attempt to placate and flee before I kill them.

"I'll help," I announce, ignoring Caspian's questioning look for now as I follow Gavriel deeper into the trees.

The guard's shoulders tense when he hears my footsteps, but he doesn't turn around. The stream gurgles, its sound masking our voices from the clearing. The prince doesn't need to be privy to this conversation.

"You're hiding something," I state in a flat tone. Not a question.

His hands still over the water skin as he crouches. "I don't know what you mean."

"Don't fucking lie to me." I keep my voice low but sharp. "You've been acting strange since Meridian. Why?"

He finally turns, and the guilt in his eyes confirms everything. "Ariella—"

"Answer me, or you'll find that I suddenly forget Caspian's wish for me not to shove my blade into your heart." The words taste like acid with the amount of venom laced in every syllable.

He contemplates the threat as rage burns through my veins, but I force it down. I need information more than I need revenge right now.

"Tell me," I demand. "You have one minute."

Gavriel runs a hand over his face, cursing under his breath. "I don't know how you do it—keep secrets from those you care about." He laughs, the sound dull, before straightening to face me. "Thalion approached me after the first trial. Said he needed my help to free Caspian from his obsession of you, to make sure certain competitors faced specific challenges." He tugs a chain from his breast pocket—it's a moment before I realize that he's holding some kind of locket.

My fingers itch to grab my blade. The fucking bastard helped the king, but I only manage two words. "The griffin."

His face crumples as if I'd spoken my thoughts aloud. "Of course I fucking helped him...why wouldn't I? I want you near Caspian even less than his father, so I was all too happy to follow him in to the design space and switch out your riddle and artifact before the other sentries distributed them." I inspect the gilded pendant he tosses at me as he continues. "But then I learned what the king is doing..." I turn the locket over in my fingers, its surface tarnished but etched with intricate, swirling patterns I do not recognize. I attempt to pry it open, but it doesn't budge.

I pin the guard with a dark look, something that feigns anger, though I'm surprisingly anything but. It was quite the brilliant feat on his part. "And now you feel disgusting for aiding someone who has been using children's bodies for his own gain?"

"I was protecting Caspian!" Gavriel snaps, his voice rising before he catches himself. "The king said you were a threat. That you'd destroy everything if left unchecked. And he's still right, though for the wrong reasons. You're the fucking Silver Wraith!" He throws an arm toward me as if I'm clueless about my identity. "*I saw* the way you two looked at each other, and I couldn't allow it to continue."

A twig snaps behind us. We both turn to find Caspian standing there, his face a mask of barely contained fury.

"What did you just say?" His voice drops to a lethal whisper. "How could you ever do such a thing?"

The words hang heavy in the air, suffocating in their weight. The color drains from Gavriel's face, his mouth opening and closing as he grapples for an explanation. But Caspian doesn't give him the chance.

"You helped him?" Caspian's voice is low and sharp, each word like a blade carving through the tension. "You helped *him*—and said nothing? Even after everything he's done since?"

"I—" Gavriel starts, his voice falters, but Caspian cuts him off, stepping forward with fists clenched at his sides. He looks murderous.

What an inconvenient time to become aroused.

"Do you have any idea what you've done?" Caspian's voice cracks, his composure unraveling as the skin along his face flushes. "How many lives have been destroyed because of him? Because of you? I trusted you, Gavriel. I knew you didn't like her, but this...disgraceful."

"I was trying to protect you," Gavriel insists, his tone growing more desperate with every syllable. He steps closer, but there's a flicker of hesitation in his movements, the way he flinches when Caspian's glare sharpens. "Everything I did—I did it for you."

"Bullshit," Caspian spits, his voice rising. His anger feels alive, thrumming through the space between them. I bite down on my cheek to ground my thoughts; now is not the time. "You didn't do it for me. You did it because you couldn't stand the idea of my attention on someone else. You wanted to keep me in line, just like my father."

Gavriel's face twists with a palpable distress, but there's a defensive edge to his posture now. "You don't understand. I saw what was happening to you. The way you looked at her—" He gestures toward me, his hand shaking. "You were losing yourself to her, Cas. I thought I was saving you."

"By *betraying* me?" My prince's laugh is sharp and humorless. He shakes his head, disbelief etched into every line of his face. "You don't save someone by stabbing them in the back."

"I didn't know what he was doing!" the guard yells, his frustration boiling over. "I didn't know about the experiments, or the people he would kill. Not until it was too late."

"And when you found out?" I interject, my voice cold and cutting. I step closer, just enough to remind Gavriel that I'm still here—and keep my prince from doing something he'll repent—my blade itching for an excuse to silence him. "What then, Gavriel? Did you run to Caspian? Did you try to stop Thalion? Or did you stay silent because it was easier than admitting you were wrong?"

He doesn't answer, his jaw tightening as he looks between me and Caspian. His silence is all the confirmation we need.

"Get out of my sight," Caspian commands, and the mix of fury and heartbreak in his tone catches my breath. He steps back once, as if the distance might somehow lessen the pain. "Go back to the castle. Request a new post. I don't care. But I never want to see you again."

"Caspian, please—" Gavriel's voice cracks, and for a moment, he looks more like a lost boy than the hardened soldier I've come to know.

"*Now!*" Caspian's shout echoes through the trees, and Gavriel flinches as if struck. His shoulders slump, his gaze falling to the ground as he nods. Without another word, he turns and trudges away, his steps heavy with the weight of his choices. The sound of hooves fades a few minutes later.

I examine Caspian. His breathing is ragged, his eyes fixed on where the guard disappeared. When he finally looks at me, the vulnerability there makes my chest ache. I don't do this—this comforting shit—but my arms just want to hold him against me forever.

"I trusted him, Ariella. More than anyone...and he—" He clears his throat before sucking a long breath through his nose. "It's hard to imagine trusting anyone now," he whispers more to himself than to me. "But you always feel like the exception."

Something warm and uncomfortable looms deep in my chest. I want to insist he not trust me either—that I'm just as capable of betrayal as anyone. But the words stick in my throat.

Instead, I step closer and touch his arm in what I think would be a consolatory gesture, but it only serves to make me cringe. "We need to move. Your father will not wait."

He nods, some of the steel returning to his spine. "You're right. But—" His hand grabs mine, lifting it to his lips so that he may press the gentlest of kisses to my skin. "Thank you. For stopping me from doing something I'd regret."

I pull him toward the horses, feeling itchy from the gratitude. When was the last time someone thanked me? "Let's go. We can make it back to the castle by nightfall if we ride hard."

After insisting the prince sit behind me the remaining journey, we mount up and push the horses as fast as we dare. The sun sinks lower, and the looming darkness feels like a warning.

The forest blurs past as our horses thunder down the path. With Caspian's arms secured around my waist, I can feel the uneven rhythm of his breathing against my shoulder. It's not long before he's asleep. The events in Meridian took more from him than he'll admit.

"Let's stop," I mutter when he rouses, slowing our pace. I do not want to stop, but I will for him.

"No," he protests. "We need to get back."

I roll my eyes, though he can't see it. "You're no good to anyone if you pass out and fall off this horse." His answering groan vibrates through my chest. "Besides, the horses need water. We didn't give them any before."

That gets his attention. Of course the damn prince would care more about the horses' wellbeing than his own. I guide us toward a small stream cutting through the dense trees, helping Caspian dismount when he sways.

"Sit," I command, pointing to a fallen log. He looks ready to argue but thinks better of it when I narrow my eyes. While he rests, I lead the horses to drink and check their legs for any signs of strain.

The fading sunlight filters through the canopy, something about the approaching darkness feeling like a warning. A tingling chill drifts down my spine as I notice how unnaturally quiet it is. No birds. No insects. Even the stream seems muted somehow.

I chew on my lip, remembering the way the ocean revolted against nature itself. The wave that was so close to claiming Caspian's life—

No. I refuse to stress over things of the past that did not happen.

"We should keep moving." I help him stand, chuckling when he waves me away. "Can you even ride, prince?"

"I'm fine." His stubborn tone would be more convincing if he wasn't leaning so heavily against me. I raise an eyebrow and he sighs. "Okay, maybe not entirely fine. But we cannot afford to delay."

"Then you're riding with me again." I mount first, pulling him up behind me before he can protest. His arms circle my waist once more, and I pretend not to notice how he presses his face into my hair. How his hands splay against the lines of my abdomen. How fucking warm his body feels wrapped around me like this.

As we continue toward Valoria, my mind wanders to Gavriel's confession. The locket he gave me feels heavy in my pocket. There's a familiarity to it that I can't place—if only I could get the old thing open.

"I can hear you thinking," Caspian mumbles against my neck, and I shift in my seat.

"Someone has to do the thinking around here." My attempt at levity falls flat. After a moment, I add, "Are you okay? About Gavriel?"

His arms tighten around me. "No. But I understand why he did it, even if his methods were wrong."

"That's very...mature of you." Not a lie. If he weren't Caspian's closest friend, his body would rotting be back in the clearing.

He chuckles. "Don't sound so surprised, angel. I'm capable of growth."

I hum in a teasing manner as we fall into silence again, the road winding through familiar territory. The closer we get to Valoria, the more tension builds in my shoulders. Our time is running out.

"We need a plan," I say, my mind whirring. "We can't just storm the castle."

"Why not? It's worked so well for us before." Despite his sardonic tone, I know he's right. Our previous confrontations with the king have only made things worse. Perhaps we wouldn't be on such a deadline—with Thalion's threat hanging over his son—if we were more careful. Well, if *I* was more careful.

"We need proof of what he's doing, and we need to find a way to stop him that won't throw the realm further out of balance. And we both know the tunnels are that proof."

Caspian shifts behind me, his thumb tracing absent patterns on my hip. "Then we venture into the tunnels," he says after a while, squeezing me harder.

My mind flits through ways I could subdue him—make him stay behind. The tunnels are creepy, but protecting him while focusing on my task will be rather difficult. It won't work, but I try anyway. "Maybe you should stay back as a distraction. If your father catches us—"

"He won't." The steel in his voice reminds me that he's not just the charming prince anymore. He's chosen his side in this fight, chosen me, and the weight of that choice is inarguably important to him.

I can practically feel him wrestling with everything, remaining quiet behind me. I find myself longing for his voice—the same one I'd almost lost just hours ago.

"Tell me what you're thinking," I demand with an awkward attempt at softness, frowning at myself because while I am perfect in most aspects of my life, conversation is not one of them.

He takes a shuddering breath, cuddling into me as if he cannot get close enough. I'm afraid to admit I feel the same. "I'm thinking about how everything I believed about my father was a lie. About how many people have suffered because of my choices. About how many more will suffer if we don't stop him."

I look over my shoulder, needing him to understand the truth of my next statement. "*None* of this is your fault, Caspian."

"Isn't it? I'm the crown prince. I should have known what was happening in my own fucking castle."

I guide our horses around a fallen branch before responding, having to lightly tug on the other one. "The king fooled everyone.

He's had years to perfect his deception. Even I didn't know anything, and I've been planning his death for decades."

"But you knew he was capable of evil. You saw it when he killed your father."

My hands tighten on the reins. "That was different. That was personal, and I did not care about his claim of treason."

"Then are my feelings not personal as well?"

I don't have an answer for that. I'd believe the same if I were in his position. Especially now, knowing that the Accord is involved. The balance of the realms isn't just some abstract concept that can be brushed off. It's the foundation of our realms, being torn apart piece by piece—so much so that it's now affecting the essence inside of people. That's a lot of burden to carry. Something squeezes in the center of my chest.

The sun is low on the horizon when we finally catch sight of Valoria. Even from this distance, I can see the changes...the city itself seems subdued, with fewer people in the streets than usual. The atmosphere is ominous. Foreboding.

"It feels worse here," Caspian whispers as we ride through the streets. "How can it be so much worse after just two days?"

I guide the horses toward the stables just inside the castle grounds, avoiding the main gates where we might be noticed by more people than I'd like.

"We will stop him," I answer, helping him dismount. His legs are more steady this time, though still tired and would be anything but helpful if we went exploring right now. "But first, you will eat and sleep. You're no good to anyone like this."

He starts to protest, but I pinch his lips, releasing when he smirks. "Fine. But only for a few hours. Then we will inspect the tunnels."

I nod with acquiescence, though I have no intention of letting him join me when I enter the tunnels tonight. I need to go alone.

We walk through the back halls of the castle, keeping from the largest crowds. These areas remind me of the treasury that Thalion so kindly invited me to, though the memory is fleeting as my focus shifts to the packs slung over my shoulder. I should take them to my room before heading out; there's still the matter of the strange device tucked inside one of them.

"Your room or mine?" Caspian asks when we reach our wing. I'm unsure of why the thought of this being *our* wing is troubling.

"Yours is closer." Fully functional again thanks to the staff, and less likely to be monitored, I don't add. The king is a cunning bastard.

Once inside his room, Caspian all but collapses onto his bed. I watch as he pulls off his boots and shirt with less strain than I expected, though there's still fatigue clinging to him. At least he showered before we left Meridian; he looks more rested than he did earlier, moving with ease as he replaces his clothing.

"You should eat something," I repeat my earlier demand, tossing one of the packs onto a chair in the corner.

"I will," he mutters, lying back for a moment before forcing himself to sit up again. He gestures toward the door. "I'll grab some food while you shower."

I nod as he exits, the faint sound of his footfalls echoing down the hall. My gaze lingers on the bag in the corner. I should unpack the damn thing, but exhaustion demands I leave it for later. The golden handles of Caspian's desk remind me of the griffin egg I have tucked away. And its mother. The sight of her is still vivid in my mind—how unapologetic and powerful she was. Perhaps that's why I like her so much, regardless that she attempted to murder me. Though I have a feeling she wouldn't dare do such a thing again, which raises the question: how the fuck did she know we were in trouble and where to find us? I'm riddled with the same confusion I was when she allowed me to live. Strange creature.

I push the thoughts aside and walk through my room to the shower, letting the scalding water soothe the tension in my shoulders. By the time I step out, wrapped in a towel, my mind is quieter, though the griffin still lingers somewhere in the background. I pause at the sight of Caspian sitting at my desk, a tray of food before him.

"I don't recall inviting you in." My tone is dry as I narrow my eyes at him.

He glances up with that infuriating smirk. "We both know you would've warded the door if you didn't want me here."

Damn him for being right. I move to my wardrobe, acutely aware of his eyes on me as I grab a large shirt. "How are you feeling?" I inquire, breaking away from the thoughts in my head. I unceremoniously drop my towel and tug the shirt over my head.

"Better." His voice is closer now. "Though I can't stop thinking about Gavriel." I pivot to find him just a few feet away, his face drawn. "When I saw you like that after the griffin attacked you, bleeding out..." He fidgets with his hands, casting his gaze downward. "And it was because of him? The person I'd trusted the most, who I thought was my friend? I knew he wasn't particularly fond of you, but I didn't think he would try to have you killed, Ariella. And by a fucking griffin, no less."

I take a step closer, unable to help myself. "You cannot blame yourself for his choices." When did I become such a wise, gentle being? My instincts tell me to revolt—to shove the prince from my room and demand that he stay away.

But I won't. I was not lying as I was screaming to his dead body that I would stop fighting this if he just came back to me.

The Angel could have asked me for anything in exchange for his life, and I would have granted it. There would not be *a single* person or city safe from me if that was the Angel's price.

So when the prince closes the distance between us, brushing the tips of his fingers up the exposed skin of my arm, I don't fight it. I sink into the increasing rhythm of my heart and allow the pressure in my abdomen to subsist.

His next words are nothing more than a whisper. "How are you not raging about what he did?"

"Because what Gavriel did is nothing compared to everything else done to me in my life." I shrug.

Pain flashes across his face. "I'm sorry. I wish—"

"Don't." I hold a finger to his mouth, suddenly needing to drown in those soft lips. "What's done is done."

He captures my hand, pressing a kiss to my palm that sends warmth coursing through the attached limb and up my neck. His other hand grips my waist, pulling me forward until I'm flush against the hard lines of his chest.

My breath catches as his lips find my neck, causing an intense fluttering to shoot straight down to my core. "Caspian..."

"Let me give us what we both need, angel," he murmurs against my skin, and I lose all sense. My hand latches around his throat before dragging his mouth to mine—something I cannot seem to get enough of.

Chapter Twenty-Three

Ariella

W arm hands grip my thighs as Caspian lifts me and stumbles over to the bed. Something digs into my backside, and I break our kiss to find the footboard just behind me. The prince smirks, adjusting his hold on me before I'm flipped around, my face shoved into the bedding. I protest, attempting to push up, but he tightens his grip in my hair until I'm grinding my teeth. I freeze when fingers brush up the back of my thigh and over my hips.

I'm entirely exposed, having donned nothing but a shirt—one that only reaches to my low back in this position.

Half my body is shaking with the need to fight back and force his submission, while the other half is curious about what he's planning.

"Something wrong, angel?" he taunts, his voice low. A knee-crumbling feeling of euphoria washes through my throat, down to my lower abdomen, and I swear I'm going to punish my traitorous body for loving this side of him.

I adjust my head to the left, sucking in lungfuls of air before speaking. "What exactly did you do to the prince? I wouldn't have expected such officious tendencies from you." A thumb presses into the base of my spine before dragging up, lifting my shirt along the way. It takes everything not to squirm.

Caspian leans over as his palm drags over the side of my breast, his lips next to my ear. "I suppose you won't make that mistake again," he whispers, and my pulse flutters in too many places. Standing once more, he releases my hair to grab both hips, and I no longer wish to move, despite my instincts. "I keep wondering when the day will come that I find you in a position in which you are not the most beautiful thing I have ever laid my eyes upon." I gasp as his foot kicks my legs open, baring me further. "Today is not that day."

There's a thump, and before I can move to check that he's okay, his tongue runs up my center, a long, torturous moan escaping me. His voice hums against my swollen skin. The footboard digs into my hips, though not even the Angel could pry me from this spot as the prince levels every thought in my head. He devours me so thoroughly, and it's divine.

But over too soon as he pulls away, nipping at the surrounding skin before standing. "I have a surprise for you, if you're open to it." I prop up on my elbows when I hear shuffling, finding Caspian digging through one of the packs we traveled with. His lip quirks as he finds what he's looking for, pulling out the odd device that the persistent man gave me in Meridian.

I blink. "That's the surprise?" A laugh falls from my lips, dying when the prince gives me a pointed look. "Your mouth is a far better surprise than whatever the fuck that is."

"As delighted as I am to hear how much you love my mouth, angel, you will not be confessing such things in a moment."

"And why is that?"

He smiles as his fingers twist over the device, the buzzing starting instantly. "The merchant may not have explained what this is, but I have a theory." My forehead creases—what the fuck? Has the man drank an entire bottle of cider?

I've no chance to respond as I'm shoved back down to the mattress with a gasp as Caspian drags the device over my backside. "What do you think you're doing?" I'm genuinely confused, but threats die in my throat a moment later when the device is pressed up against my center. An embarrassing noise leaves me as my body jolts away from the onslaught of sensation.

"You were saying?" I do not have the capacity to respond as I'm immediately thrown over the edge to a place only the Angel should know about. My vision wavers, and I struggle to be aware of the prince talking me through whatever the fuck is happening to my body. "That's it, darling. Sounds like I was right."

An eternity later, I shove my face into the bedding, using the lack of oxygen to slow my breathing. Only when I feel stable enough to speak do I address Caspian. "Are you trying to kill me? What in the Aether was that?" He hums before grabbing my legs to flip me over. I let him. I doubt I could even dare to stand at the moment.

"I am not privy to the name of the device, but I did hear a couple of women speak of it in Meridian." His pleased smirk falters at the incredulous expression on my face. "Did you not like it?"

I did—I'd have to be dead not to. "How could you trust random words from strangers? That thing could have burned me, or poisoned me, perhaps." His response is a breathy laugh, and my fingers curl into the bed to keep from choking him.

"Nothing you haven't experienced before, then." The prince's eyes look behind me before his palm lifts, two fingers pointed out, effectively weaving his kinetic strand to drag me to the center of the bed. He joins me a moment later, settling himself between my legs—ones I do not seem to command any longer. "I think you can give me another."

Caspian uses a hand to drag the vibrating device around the most sensitive parts of my skin while lifting the other to push my shirt back up, exposing my stomach and breasts. The motion introduces cool air to my already hardened nipples, burning them a bit. I bite my lip as he rolls the device over my clit before returning to the crease of my legs. I feel his smile just below my navel as he flattens his tongue and trails it up to the spot between my breasts. My fingers reach into his smooth hair and massage the back of his neck in time with each kiss he places toward my mouth.

I could lose myself in him for days and still want more. There is nothing in this realm that could compare to the feel of him against me.

His teeth grab onto my bottom lip before his breath consumes mine, our tongues working together languidly. The device shifts and my jaw drops as he slides two fingers inside me while circling the vibrations around my clit. This is the most exquisite torture. I can't discern whether I never want it to stop or never want to feel it again. It's too much and not enough at the same time.

Embarrassing noises fall from my throat as my prince's hand undulates, and I know I'm moments from a second orgasm. That shouldn't be physically possible, considering I just had one. But I'm proven mistaken when his teeth rake down my neck and I shatter. I curse my very existence as my thighs attempt to crush the man between them. By the time I relax beneath him, my body feels as though I've trained for weeks nonstop. But I can't. There's a flutter in my chest, a need to wrap my arms around him and hold us together until we die.

He chuckles against my mouth when he attempts to use the device again, and I reach my hand between us, snatch the brilliant thing, and fling it across the room. The fingers he's yet to remove pull from me with a purposeful slowness. I know before he does it that he'll demand I clean him off again.

Before he can speak, I grab his wrist and hold his gaze while I suck every drop of my arousal from his skin. His eyes watch every movement of my lips and tongue, darkening when I pull his fingers from my mouth with a pop. "I believe that was mine, angel." His voice is breathy and low, a muscle rippling low in my abdomen from the sound.

I hum and shove him back, rolling us until I'm straddling his legs. "As if I care—I'll take anything I want," I drawl, reaching for the buttons at the top of his pants in point. My hands are quick to flick them open before I lean forward, sliding one under the fabric to grab his cock.

Caspian reaches back for a pillow to rest his head on, both hands clasped behind his head as he smirks at me. "You may proceed," he states when I pause. "I just needed a better angle to watch *the* Silver Wraith willingly get on her knees for me." I press my lips together, struggling to hold back a laugh.

I may be smiling, but I am rather nervous. I've never used my mouth on a man before—what if I'm horrible at it? That *does* make me laugh. As if I'm horrible at anything.

Pulling him free, I run my thumb over his tip, fascinated that this thing somehow fits inside me. How much will I be able to take before I choke? I'm eager to find out. Bending down, I run my tongue from his base up until it swirls over the salty tip. I'm halted as Caspian tugs my hair up until my eyes meet his. His forehead creases and he studies me for a moment before speaking.

"Have you done this before?" Was it that fucking obvious? His lip quirks as a knowing look falls over his face. "I cannot imagine you freely sucking on another man's dick. I'm not sure I should allow your mouth near mine, honestly—what are the chances you'll bite it off?" He raises himself on an elbow, not releasing my hair, his eyes narrowing. "Answer me. Has another man's cock been in this mouth before?"

I should lie. Not give him this power over me.

No...he can take everything he wants from me. "No," I whisper, the word but a breath. His head drops back as he curses before looking to me once more.

"Words fail to express how fucking pleased I am that my cock will be the only one to ever slip past these perfect lips. And don't be nervous, angel...I'll talk you through it."

"Your confidence is truly unmatched."

He grins before nodding his chin toward me. "Open." I do. I allow him to push my head down, not once breaking our stare. That is until he presses against the back of my throat and I almost gag. He doesn't allow me to move, though. "You're okay—breathe through your nose and swallow." He sounds like a damn king right now, and I feel arousal dripping down me once again. But I do as he says, my eyes widening when the movements open me further; something Caspian notices as he shoves me down even more. I'm quite certain that his next obstacle will be physically impossible to pass, but I force myself to hold still, digging my fingers into his hip as a distraction.

"You are remarkable," he mutters as I get dizzier by the second from the inability to breathe. Finally, he releases me and I pull back a little, sucking in a lungful of sweet air. I melt internally as he pushes hair from my face with a gentleness that doesn't match his next words. "Now show me what you've learned." And fuck do I want to do just that.

With renewed desperation building inside me, I mimic the movement he'd experience while fucking me, bobbing my head up and down as I swirl my tongue over his velvety length. One of my hands shifts to the base of his cock, covering the part I cannot fit in my mouth. I revel under every moan and flex of his abdomen, not in the least bit worried about my reputation.

Me? Bending over to pleasure the Prince of Eldoria? I would have laughed at such a thought just months ago, knowing I'd never subject myself to be below anyone. Physically or metaphorically.

But now? I realize something—the same thing Caspian was wise enough to know the moment we met: we are equals.

Everything in my head screams that such a thing couldn't be true, but those are merely conditioned thoughts. Because the truth is me and the prince are one and the same, and I will happily lower myself at his feet if that's what he wishes. And not out of some perceived obligation. No, I *want* to. I want to be for him what he is for me and more.

So I hollow my cheeks and suck the very essence from his body. One of his hands finds my hair again as I move, and begins muttering out praise each time I do something he enjoys. Which apparently is everything.

"Fuck, Ari, just like that," Caspian groans, his cock twitching along my tongue. The rate of his breathing tells me he's close, so I pull in a deep breath before swallowing around his length, pleased when he curses as his cum fills my mouth. I drink in every bit of the warm liquid, questioning whether I enjoy the thickness of it, but continue to swallow it, anyway.

Once he goes lax under me, I pull him from my mouth and sit up. It's painful as I attempt to close my mouth and rub my jaw to aid the movement. Not a heartbeat later does my prince's hands grab my arms and tug so that my body lies flat over his. His presence is so comforting, I instantly sink into him, resting my ear over his heart. It pounds just as hard as mine.

"If I find out you lied to me about doing that before, there will be consequences." I burst out laughing, my head shaking with the bouncing of his chest as he joins me. "I'm being serious. That was too good to be your first time. I mean, I know you're basically an expert at everything, but I'm still not convinced."

"Basically? What am I not perfect at?" I lift my head to rest it against my hands and look into his luminescent eyes.

His lips purse for a brief second. "You want the truth?" I nod. What does he think he could say that I wouldn't want to hear? "You're shit at acknowledging your feelings. Not just for me, but everything." I look away, doing exactly what he just accused me of.

The thing is, I know I do not process my emotions well. But who would I be if I did? I'd be a mess. It shouldn't be possible for one person to feel so many things, and I'm certain that I'd kill myself if I allowed more than one emotion in at a time. Maybe it's possible, though. It was only a short time ago that I refused to concede to any thoughts that weren't of the king's head on a stake—and that's changed because of the man beneath me.

He's affected me far more than I thought. And perhaps that's not such a bad thing.

Later, I carefully extract myself from his sleeping form, cursing my weakness. I shouldn't have given in to him sleeping next to me. As I dress in the quiet dark, movement catches my eye. I spin, squealing when Caspian is leaning against the wall, arms crossed.

"Going somewhere?" His voice is deceptively casual while my heart has lost all function.

I didn't hear him move. He's learning too well, having come a long way since the day I caught him in the training room—perhaps I should cease helping him with that if this is how he's going to utilize his new skills.

I sigh, continuing to dress. There's no point in hiding what he already knows. "Wherever I please. Go back to sleep."

"Alone? I think the fuck not."

"I've been in the tunnels before, and I know the layout." Barely. "I pulled the blueprints out weeks ago," I mutter, though it's a complete lie. My hands adjust the blades along my person as I refuse to look at him. "I have several areas marked that could—"

"No."

I whirl on him, a blade appearing at the base of his throat. "This isn't up for debate."

He doesn't even flinch—cocky bastard. Why do I continue to threaten him with it... "Go ahead. We go in the tunnels together." He leans forward, forcing my weapon to nick his skin. "*That* isn't up for debate."

We glare at each other for several tense moments before I lower my blade while cursing his ancestors. "You're an insufferably stubborn prince."

"And you're an impossibly reckless assassin. Now, shall we?" He's lucky I do not wish to tie him to my bed—though that may not be the worst idea...

Getting to the tunnels proves simpler than expected. The royal guards are sparse, which only heightens my suspicion. We traverse staff passages until reaching the south entrance Gavriel mentioned a while ago.

I grab Caspian's arm before he can move forward, tight enough to bruise him, but that is a fleeting thought as the intensity of what we're about to do slams into me. "Listen to me. Stay silent, hold on to me at all times, and do *exactly* as I say without question. Understood?"

He nods without protest, which is somehow more unsettling than if he'd argued.

The tunnel entrance creaks softly as we descend into darkness. Though this is a different area than I was taken to for the first trial, memories of my last visit here flood back—the constant feeling of being watched, breath on my neck. I hate to admit it, but these tunnels fucking scared me and I did not want to come back here.

I weave my fingers through his—as if I'd ever risk losing him here—and quiet my breath.

We walk slow, hesitant, for a moment, and are maybe fifty feet in when I hear it—a raspy inhale that isn't ours. I shove Caspian against the wall, covering his mouth with my hand and his body with mine. Something moves in the darkness ahead, making wet, gurgling sounds that raise the hair on my arms. What the fuck? I press against Caspian until our foreheads touch as these tunnels are far too thin for my liking, and attempt to determine the creature's size from its movements. I'm unsure if using my essence will do more harm than good at the moment, so I rely on my conditioned senses.

Just over six feet tall based on the direction of sound, nearly reaching me at ear-level. It's heavy but unsteady gait suggests significant mass but poor coordination, as if it's just limping idly through the darkness. I do not believe it can detect us in any manner, as its stride and breathing hasn't changed. If I'm to guess, this is the same kind of being that harmed Caspian in the library, so it may have a weapon, but I do not believe it's any more dangerous than any baser instincts it still possesses.

My fingers hover over my thigh as I wait until the thing is nearly upon us before striking.

My blade finds its mark as I simultaneously tug on my luminal strand, filling the space with pale light. Caspian's sharp intake of breath reminds me he didn't know about that particular ability.

But any questions die on his lips as we see what I've struck down. I recognize him immediately—Obren, one of the quieter competitors from the trials. But he's wrong. His skin is mottled with bleached veins that spider across his flesh like lightning, all stemming from the center of his chest. *Like Jaxon's essence device*, I realize. The outer edges of his limbs appear burned, blackened and crumbling.

I reach for my psionic strand, sending out a pulse to gauge the now-dead creature. I gasp, the severe feedback nearly knocking me over.

"What is it?" Caspian whispers.

"Essence. So much essence." I steady myself against the wall. "This is definitely one of your father's experiments."

Caspian scoffs, regarding the light in my hand once more but not commenting.

We press on while I continue to weave my luminal strand, checking each room we come across. Nothing. Nothing. *Nothing.*

We turn corners that lead deeper into the tunnels, the walls closing in the further we go. There are no more creatures, no sounds, just...nothing. What am I missing?

The answer comes by accident as the lightest of drafts catches my attention—impossible this deep underground unless there's another passage. I lead us to a section that appears to be some kind of addition to the labyrinth. We step into the hallway and hairs rise along my arms and neck. This is the place we're looking for; I can feel the *wrongness* of it.

There is one door at the end, made of heavy steel and an over-sized latch. I hesitate for a moment, but I'm positive I can protect

Caspian if there's something beyond this point that attempts to kill us. Yanking the door open, I pause at the lab that greets us. My eyes scan the space, and fuck if it isn't something straight from a nightmare.

A viewing room overlooks what can only be described as a torture chamber. Notebooks filled with diminutive writing and meticulous observations are sprawled across a large desk. I pick one up, my stomach clenching at the detail.

The king describes how children possess far less essence than adults, and it is more malleable, making it easier to transfer and manipulate. After conducting experiments on the strongest of adults—the assassins from the competition—Thalion concluded that a body can only ingest a small amount of foreign essence at a time. Notes on the side mention how they cannot control how much essence leaves a person's body, so taking it from adults would end up being fatal to him.

But children...they have but trace amounts in their bodies, just enough to be safely consumed by the king in increments.

Their natural innocence makes them perfect vessels for harvest.

But where are they? The lab is empty save for one chair below. My stomach turns as I approach the window. The body strapped there is headless, but I'd recognize those clothes anywhere. They were next to me the day the competition began.

"Raine," I whisper. The third student from my guild. His rotting flesh rests motionless in the chair, and my lip curls at the gaping hole in his chest.

"We need to go," Caspian says, his tone urgent as he grabs my hand and reaches for the notebook. "We have enough—"

"Indeed, you do."

We both whirl to find the king flanked by Varrick and at least a dozen guards blocking the hall behind them. How were their movements devoid of any perceptible noise?

Blades are in my hands before my next heartbeat.

"Now, now," Thalion tuts, opening his arms as if he isn't the least bit afraid. "Let's be civil."

"Civil?" I spit as my body subtly shifts in front of the prince. "Like you were with those children? Or every single fucking contestant in your sham of a competition?"

His eyes flash with a dangerous threat. "I didn't experiment on your precious friend, now did I, wraith?" He chuckles to himself. "Well, that's not entirely true, but I did give his body back, did I not? Everything I do is for the good of this kingdom."

"You're insane," Caspian says, his voice shaking with the same rage simmering just under my skin.

"I'm pragmatic, *son*. Something you'll understand when you're king." His head shakes as he watches Caspian with ample disappointment. "It's a shame your loyalty to the throne—this family—is not a choice you will make on your own." The king sighs like he's been given an impossible task before nodding in our direction. "Take them."

Sentries file in, far more than a dozen, and I manage to slice the throats of three before I feel several pricks around my body. Immediately, my limbs grow heavy as my essence retreats, unreachable. The last thing I see is Caspian fighting to reach me before darkness claims my mind.

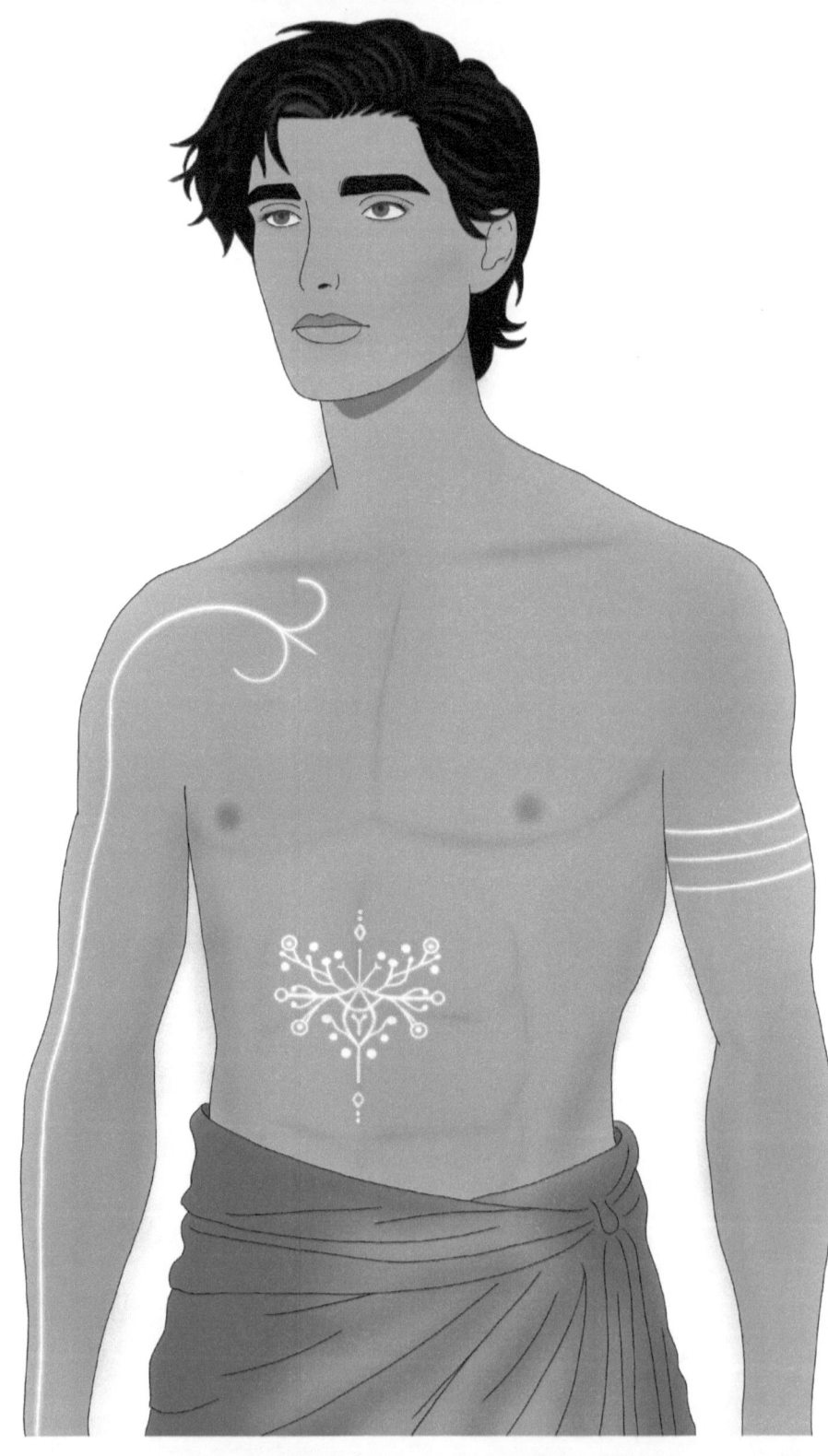

Chapter Twenty-Four

Caspian

A dull throbbing pulses through my head as consciousness creeps back. My tongue feels thick, coated with a metallic taste that makes me gag. I attempt to lift my hand, needing to rub my aching temples, but restraints bite into my wrists. The fog in my mind clears instantly as I jerk against the bindings.

"I wouldn't struggle too much. Those are reinforced with essence-infused steel." My father's voice drifts from somewhere to my left, but my vision is still catching up with my mind. "A fascinating discovery, really. When we learned to merge essence with metal, instead of just using it as a conduit, it opened up entirely new possibilities."

I will my racing heart to calm as my eyes adjust to the dim lighting of my bedroom. Father sits in a chair near the window, his posture relaxed as if we're having a casual conversation over breakfast. Moonlight catches on his crown, making him look eerie. He sits slouched, one hand draped casually over the armrest while the other twirls a crystal glass with something dark inside. It's unsettling—he never slouches, and the lack of his usual rigid formality would make my stomach churn if it wasn't doing so already.

I cannot believe this bastard is my father.

"Where is she?" My voice comes out hoarse, too quiet to sound confident. The last thing I remember is Ariella collapsing as guards surrounded us in that appalling laboratory.

He waves a hand, dismissing my concern. "The wraith is...being handled. But let's discuss what you saw down there, son." He leans forward, resting his elbows on his knees as his eyes hold mine with an evil look. The sharp angles of his broad cheekbones stand out as the dark strands of his hair contour both sides of his face. "I assume you have questions."

Heat burns through my veins. I do not want to give him the satisfaction of seeing me break, but against my better judgment, I snap. "Questions? You're experimenting on *children*. You murdered contestants in a competition *I* helped organize. You have single-handedly ruined the future of two fucking realms! What could justify *any* of this?" I clear my throat and try to gather any saliva I can, but it's of no use.

"Power, of course." He says it so simply, so unbothered, as if explaining basic arithmetic to a child. "Do you know how long our family has ruled Eldoria, Caspian? Centuries. And in all that time, we've been at the mercy of those born with stronger essence. Those who could theoretically overthrow us at any moment." His eyes gleam with a zealous aura that prickles at my skin and sets an unease I can't shake.

"So this is about control? Stealing essence from innocents to what—make yourself more powerful?" I tug against the restraints again, metal biting into my flesh. There's not a hint of weakness in these bindings, rendering my struggle useless. I'll only waste strength and energy if I continue.

"Not just control. Evolution." He stands and begins pacing, hands gesturing wildly. "Think about it, Caspian. What if we could choose who has what abilities? And how much? What if we could *ensure* the royal line maintains absolute authority through essence superiority?"

"You're insane," I breathe, but he continues as if I hadn't spoken. I stare at the dark ceiling of my room, unable to keep down the anxiety over Ariella's whereabouts. She's not dead—I would feel it. But I do not think she's okay, either. I need to get father to open these restraints.

"The adult subjects were too unstable. Their essence was too developed, too...resistant to transfer. But the young ones?" A genuine smile splits his face, and I feel nothing but rampant disgust at the movement. "Their essence is raw, malleable. Perfect for harvesting in small doses."

My stomach hurts—this shouldn't be happening. "And mother? Vespera? Do they know what you're doing?"

Something soft flickers across his features; the first crack in his composed facade. "Your mother, well she doesn't understand. None of them do. But they will, once we perfect the process." He moves to stand at the foot of my bed, crossing his arms. "Which brings me to an important choice you need to make."

A bitter laugh escapes me. "A choice? You've rather eliminated those, have you not?"

"No, son. Despite my anger, you still have options. It seems I have a soft spot for my heir." He grips the footboard, knuckles whitening before he continues in a venomous tone. "Will you persist in undermining everything I am building with that murderous whore? Or will you stand beside me—father and son—and help create the most powerful dynasty this realm has ever known?" He truly believes in what he's doing.

It's fucking nauseating.

For a moment, I consider playing along. Pretending to see his twisted logic, if only to buy time to figure out how to stop him. But then I remember Ariella's face when we found that laboratory. The horror in her eyes at what my father had written in his journals. The way she immediately moved to protect me, even knowing she was outnumbered.

"The balance is failing," I say instead. "The weather changes, gravity itself acting strange, plants withering before our eyes—can't you see what your experiments are doing to the realm?"

He blinks at me, head tilting. "Balance? What are you talking about?"

"The Accord, father! Your tampering with essence is destroying it." But even as I speak, I can see the words mean nothing to him. His eyes hold that same fervid gleam, focused solely on his grand vision of power.

"None of that matters," he dismisses, though I'm not sure he understands. His eyes didn't seem to recognize any of what I just said. "Once we perfect essence transfer, natural phenomena will be irrelevant. We'll have the power to reshape things how we see fit." Natural phenomena? He has no clue of what he's doing to the realms.

I study him—this man who raised me, who taught me about duty and honor and protecting our people. There's something wrong in his gaze now, something fractured in a way that I hadn't noticed before. His entire being is consumed by this single-minded ideology, blind to everything else crumbling around him.

"You're not well, father," I placate, managing to lower my voice just enough that I hope he will listen. "Something's happened to you. This isn't—"

"Disappointing," he cuts me off, straightening. "I had hoped you would see reason, but it seems the wraith's influence runs deeper than I thought." He strides toward the door, pausing with his hand on the handle. "No matter. You'll change your mind soon enough."

"What does that mean? Father?" But he's already gone, leaving me alone with the growing dread in my chest. "Thalion!" I scream, the effort useless.

Fuck!

I pull against the restraints again, my teeth grinding with the abysmal effort as metal scrapes my wrists raw. My essence feels strange. Muted. Whatever they injected us with must still be suppressing it, which is just my fucking luck. But through the dampening, there's—what is that? A humming energy I've never felt before. Or maybe I have, but not like this. It's familiar and strong, thrumming around one singular focus: Ariella.

I look to the window, eyeing the moon's long shadows across my floor, mind racing. Where is he keeping her? What did he mean about me changing my mind? And perhaps most disturbing—why didn't he know or care about the Accord when it's clearly linked to everything happening?

I think back to when I was young, before the ever-present guards and political maneuvering. My father would take me riding and teach me about our family's legacy of protecting the kingdom and its people. What happened to that man? When did he become this power-obsessed shell who sees nothing beyond his own ambitions?

The bindings cut deeper into my wrists as I twist them again, desperate for any give. Blood trickles down my hands, though I don't register the sting. My head spins with possibilities of where they could be keeping her, what they might be doing to her. Images of the lab flash through my thoughts...

I don't want to admit it—I can't—but there's no doubt where my father has her.

I growl, letting my head fall back against the headboard. What kind of prince am I, tied up in my own bedroom while Ariella faces Angel knows what? She'd berate me for such self-pity, telling me to focus on finding a solution instead of sulking.

My laugh cuts through the unnervingly silent room at the thought of her sharp tongue and calculating eyes. When she became my vitality instead of a mere comfort I sought, I'm not sure. But even now, thinking of her centers me.

My eyes fall closed as a memory surfaces of our journey back from the Verdantia Forest—how she'd started opening up about her fears, not of death or pain, but of failing. She wouldn't say more than that, but I know her. She thinks she failed Isaiah, just as I feel like I've failed the entire kingdom. She believes that her inability to save people from the impossible is a failure, so it's clear that everything happening has weighed heavily on her. Especially after Meridian.

I'd shared my own doubts then, about living up to a crown I wasn't certain I wanted anymore. She'd looked at me with those beautiful, discerning eyes and said, *"Then make it into something worth wanting."*

The sound of boots in the hallway makes me jolt up, wincing at the unintentional tug of my wrists. Two sets of steps, heavy and measured—sentries changing shifts. Father must have posted them outside my door. I strain my ears, trying to catch any snippet of conversation that might hint at Ariella's location, or my escape, though there's nothing but a maddening silence.

My eyes drift to the window again. The moon has shifted, far enough that I'm questioning things. How long have I been here? Hours? The essence-suppressing drug still muddles my strands and senses, making it difficult to gauge time. Though given that it is still dark out, Ariella and I have not been separated for very long. I flex my fingers, searching for even a hint of my aqua or kinetic strands, but there's nothing. Just that strange new humming energy that seems to pulse in time with my heartbeat.

"Come on," I mutter under my breath, closing my eyes to focus. The damn toxin has to let up at some point, but it's as if my entire well has been locked away in shackles stronger than the ones holding my body down. But the energy in my chest is calming. It feels...different from my normal essence. Warmer somehow, more alive. Like it's trying to reach for something—

Ariella would be laughing at me right now if she saw just how much I'm struggling. She probably has three different strands that could break these bindings in seconds, if she's not overcoming the same toxin I am. The thought of her ire almost makes me smile, despite everything.

She's taught me much about essence and combat, yet there's still a considerable amount I do not understand. The woman wove the fucking luminal strand in the tunnels...it took me a while to process her possession of each affinity, but now I'm certain she also has each strand. A fully universal weaver—unheard of. Except for the first weaver, who was said to have the same abilities.

Chapter Twenty-Five

Ariella

C old metal burns into my skin as I fight whatever the fuck
is in my body to stay awake. I ache everywhere, my head
and eyes pounding with each heartbeat. The sharp, chemical scent
of the lab fills my nostrils, and my stomach twists for an entirely
different reason. Groaning, my muscles protest as I shift to test
the restraints along my arms and ankles. Metal clinks against
metal—I'm in the Angel-damned chair. The same one that held
Raine's headless corpse.

"Finally awake, I see." Thalion's gravelly voice is so disgusting
and unwelcome that I consider spitting at his feet solely out of
spite, though I keep my face blank. "I must say, you look quite
lovely strapped down like that. I wonder how you would look
if I had you whipped like your father—perhaps then I could
appreciate you the way my joke of a son does."

My jaw clenches at the mention of my father. His wretched
words about Caspian. I want to inquire about the prince but
Thalion's attention is currently on me, which means he's leaving
his son alone. I'd like to keep it that way.

I force my mind clear, taking measured breaths. The bastard wants a reaction. He won't get one.

"Nothing to say, wraith? How disappointing." His footsteps circle behind me, and a familiar anxiety crawls just under the layers of my skin. It's disconcerting and uncomfortable as fuck. "You've been quite vocal about your opinions of me. Dare I say that I expected more fire."

I focus on assessing my body instead of his taunts. My essence is gone—unreachable. I recall being pricked before passing out, so I haven't been unconscious for long if the drug is still clouding the connection to my strands. But there's a faint presence of my essence deep in my chest, and I can feel it shifting its way through the suppression. Clearly Thalion isn't aware of just how powerful I am—surprising considering his obsession with sending spies to stalk and kill me.

If I'm being transparent with myself, I'm quite shocked that Gavriel appears to not have told him.

If I just keep him from injecting me again, I'm confident I can break from this chair and rip his fucking heart out before he can blink.

"You know, I've been watching you since the trials began." As if that's news to me. His voice draws closer, and suddenly my throat feels obstructed. "Such raw talent. Such potential. It would be a waste to just execute you." His fingers brush a slip of my hair, and I fight the urge to flinch away. "No, I have much grander plans."

I really, *really* do not want to know of these plans, because they're obviously not fucking dinner parties.

"Going to bore me to death instead?" The words slip out before I can stop them. Stupid, foolish idiot.

He chuckles, the sound devoid of warmth. "Still some fire after all." His hand grips my hair, yanking my head back so I'm forced to focus on his upside-down form. "You're going to help me build an empire, little wraith. Once I fill you with enough essence, you'll be the perfect weapon. The strongest warrior this realm has ever seen. A few of the others didn't survive the process—turned into pitiful, disgusting creatures after their injection. I thought they might serve some purpose, grow into something more, but alas, they're just as worthless as my son at this point. Truthfully, you did me a favor in killing them."

The things from the library and tunnel—they felt so wrong, and I can't help but wonder if there was any of *them* left in those abnormal heads, or if it was just the essence unable to escape? "Is that what happened to Raine?" I keep my voice steady despite the awkward angle, swallowing loudly. "How did that work out for you?"

His grip tightens to the point of pain as what I can only describe as a grimace falls over his features. "Raine was a learning experience. But I've refined the process since then. The young's essence, you see—it's more pure and malleable. The perfect foundation." He shoves my head away, though my scalp continues to sting. "But enough of that. It's time you be taught a lesson about remaining involved with my son. I thought your friend would be enough warning for you, but you've proven rather annoying and stubborn."

Loud footfalls approach from the corridor just as two sentries file in and stand before me. My heart pounds wildly in my ears, but I keep my face steady and breathe through it. Whatever they're about to do to me, I can endure. I have to.

The air is damp, thick with the metallic tang of blood and a sharp chemical that burns my throat. It clings to my skin like an additional layer, suffocating every pore. I shift against the ache in my ribs, my neck. Each breath tastes bitter, and the coppery slickness in my mouth only makes it worse. The place reeks of pain—the same kind I'm about to experience.

"Begin," Thalion commands, leaning against the far wall with an air of ease.

The first blow catches me across the face, snapping my head to the side. Blood fills my mouth as several teeth cut into my cheek. I move to spit it onto the floor, but the crimson doesn't even make it over my shoulder, earning another strike that blurs the fuck out of my vision.

They're methodical in their brutality. Precise hits that cause maximum pain without risking unconsciousness—at first. My ribs crack. Fingers break. Still, I don't scream. I won't give him that piece of me...the one thing I still have to myself.

Another hit lands against my temple, something much harder than knuckles, and the world tilts violently as colors bleed together in a curious medley. My limbs jerk hard at their prisons when one of the sentries punches the base of my sternum—cheap fucking shot. I can't help the sound that shoots from my throat while every ragged breath feels like fire scorching my lungs.

Sweat and blood drip from my face, burning my eyes as I'm unable to wipe any away. Thalion watches in silence, his expression unreadable, but I can feel his satisfaction humming through the air. He's a predator savoring his hunt.

"You're a fucking coward, Thalion," I grit through my teeth, my voice coarse and muted. "Do you often need to restrain women just to have them beat? How would your daughter feel if she saw you like this, hm?"

He chuckles, far too arrogant and unbothered by my bait. "What you think is no matter, Ariella—*you* are the one strapped to the chair, after all." I've no response, because it's the truth.

He continues to study me while his guards become more erratic in their torture, his gaze cold and detached, as if I'm nothing more than a mere moment of entertainment.

I bite down on the inside of my cheek, hard enough that a fresh wave of blood coats my tongue, focusing on the pain to ground myself.

You will *take this. If you break, he wins. If you break, his attention will shift to Caspian.*

The next strike is delivered in the center of my shattered ribs, but I'm too engrossed in being outside of my body to care about the sickening crunch that reverberates through the lab. I involuntarily lean forward to cough up a disturbing amount of blood, watching as it spatters against my legs and the floor like some grotesque painting. I whimper as a boot lands to my stomach, shoving my back against the chair once more.

"Pathetic," the king mutters, scraping his feet against the stone as he stops in front of me. "*This* is what my son chose to align himself with? You're weaker than I hoped—but it will have to do."

My throat sputters a laugh. "When I send you to meet the Angel, Thalion, you'd better find a good place to hide in the Aether." My lungs are ready to give out, but I'm not done yet. "Because the moment I arrive, your soul is mine."

My ears barely catch his hum before shadows descend on me once more. Time loses meaning in a haze of agony. My body feels distant, disconnected. The edges of my vision darken...

The lab fades away, and I'm standing in a meadow filled with silver flowers that glow iridescent in the different colors of the night sky. A mix of blues and purples swirl above, highlighting the red-tinged trees lining the clearing around—

"Ariella?" The voice is soft, achingly familiar.

Mom?

I whirl to find my mother standing before me, exactly as I remember—long silver hair, kind eyes, gentle smile.

"My brave girl." She reaches for me and I freeze, pain forgotten as her arms wrap around my form. She feels real. Solid.

This can't be a dream.

"How?" My voice breaks. "You're dead."

"Death is not the end, my love." Her hand strokes my hair like she used to so many years ago, and I realize my body is trembling when she begins swaying us in a calming gesture. "What's happening, Ariella? Why are you here?"

My head shakes as I pull away from her hold, checking my clothes to find them devoid of blood and tears. "Am I dead?"

"No," she insists, her hands twitching in my direction before she folds them in front of her. "But you must be close, so there are things you need to know before you go back." Go back?

Her silver hair cascades over her shoulders like liquid essence, a soft glow emanating from the strands. She's draped in a flowing gown that clings to her body as if it was made for her, highlighting every little detail. It somehow seems appropriate, though. Her eyes—sharp and unwavering—hold the same quiet strength I remember, though concern lingers in their depths. There's an aura about her that seems ethereal in nature, but not overwhelming or wrong.

The meadow hums faintly beneath my feet, the sensation subtle but rhythmic, like a heartbeat. Silver flowers shift around us, their petals almost luminous, though no breeze stirs the air. At the edge of the clearing, the trees loom tall and imposing, their branches curling inward as though they're watching—silent sentinels framing this impossible moment.

I take her in, memorizing the details—the faint crease in her brow, the way her lips press together, hesitant, as though she's weighing every word before she speaks. She looks...alive. More vivid and real than anything I've experienced outside of this place.

I can't stop staring at her. This is surreal—I must be dreaming. Hallucinating, at the very least. I believe her, as my body doesn't feel dead, but it's certainly been fucked up enough for this to happen.

"First," she starts, and my head snaps up to her tender eyes. She steps forward, grasping both of my hands in hers. I let her. "I am so incredibly proud of you, Ariella. You've grown into a beautiful, strong woman—I've wished each day that I could be there with you and watch you become exactly who you were meant to be."

I scoff. "A monster?" Something akin to what I think shame feels like burns in my chest for the first time in my life. "A killer? That's who I'm meant to be?"

Her gaze softens further, and she leans in, brushing a strand of hair from my face. "No, my love. Your strength, your skills—they are a reflection of the life you've endured, of the battles you've fought to survive. They were born from necessity, shaped by a realm that demanded them of you. But they are not who you are. You are *so much more* than the sum of what you've done to survive."

She tilts her chin down so that our gazes are level, cupping my face. "You are exactly who you need to be; how you were forced to get here does not make you less worthy of the woman you've become."

I—

I do not know what to say, let alone even *think.*

Her smile turns knowing, squeezing parts of my chest I never wanted to acknowledge again. "The realm needs you, Ariella. The Accord is dying—it is your duty to retrieve the artifacts and forge a new one before it's too late."

"How? I don't even know where to find the artifacts. Where do I even take them? The Aether?"

She nods once. "Trust your instincts. The artifacts are not pre-designated objects, but instead ones that hold strong sentiment to you alone. Their essence will leave a mark on your realm so unyielding that the Accord will be able to use them in binding both realms together." Her form starts to fade, her brows creasing as she realizes. "Only you can determine what they are from these words: what was stolen, yet always yours. What was broken, yet gave life once more. What was lost, yet grief still unites. Half binds all."

I blink, but she continues. "You're stronger than you know, Ariella. You must hurry." She's barely a flicker of light now—or is it me that's fading?

"Wait!" I reach for her, my hand grasping air with a desperation I cannot describe. "What happens if we fail? What—"

"Chaos," she whispers as everything goes black. "All will fall to chaos..."

I startle awake, lurching forward from the abhorrent smell being held under my nose. I gag, which forces more blood up, but I'm too dizzy to do more than let it drain itself from my mouth. My back slams into the chair as one of the guards shoves at my head—the foolish idiot is lucky I'm still strapped to this fucking thing.

I'd bet he wouldn't be so confident if I wasn't.

"Tomorrow, we begin," Thalion announces, his boots scraping against stone as he paces before me. "I am merciful, so you may rest for the night. After all, it wouldn't do to have you too damaged before we start."

My throat burns as I try to swallow around what must be swelling. My restraints make a mockery of me as I force myself to remain still, watching him through one good eye. The other pulsates uncomfortably, and I'm uncertain if it will still work if not healed soon.

The king smirks as he studies my battered form. "It really is quite fascinating how much pain you can endure. I am almost impressed. I look forward to seeing just how much essence you can handle before your mind fractures." His footsteps echo against the walls as he leaves, taking his sentries with him. Thank fuck.

I wait until their steps fade before allowing my head to fall back. Shit, everything hurts. My ribs protest with each breath, and I'm certain at least three are broken—though I know that's a generous estimate. Blood continues to seep from various wounds, but the flow is sluggish now. Given just how tired I feel, I'm guessing I lost more than I noticed.

Slowing my breaths to a more calm rhythm, my mother's words echo in my head. That wasn't a dream—it felt too real. Visceral. I'd left my body for Angel knows how long and was somehow taken to her. Where is she?

But the warmth of her embrace, the softness of her voice...I can still feel traces of her essence lingering on my skin. My working eye burns, but I blink the tears away. Now is not the time to reminisce on our memories or process whatever the fuck just happened.

Back to square one then, but with shifted objectives. Kill the king. Find the artifacts. Fix the Accord.

I'll think about my mother later. Right now, I need to get the fuck out of here. If that fraud of a king so much as touches Caspian, the realm will pay the price of my rage.

I direct my awareness past the injuries, looking for anything I can use. Essence pulses weakly under my skin, fighting through the drug that's still in my system. I focus inward, aiding it as I coax the essence to the surface. The connection is still foggy, making it feel like I'm wading through mud, but I can sense my strands responding. Their desperation to save us.

I grit my teeth against the pain and pull harder on my essence—I am stronger than anything that man could do to me. It senses my urgency and moves faster, pushing away the toxin. Leaving the essence to figure out the rest, I work on the metal restraints. They're tight, attached to the chair, but not impossible to break. I brace my ankles, using their cuffs as supports, before shifting all my focus, strength, and energy into my right arm. A small sound escapes my lips at the effort, but I can feel the slightest give to the metal. If I can just—there. A small crack appears along the cuff.

I can do this.

Time passes with agonizing slowness as I work at the restraint. My head pounds, vision swimming from the effort of fighting both my injuries and the suppression drug. But gradually, methodically, the metal weakens from my efforts.

The snap of the first restraint breaking is thunderous in the silent lab. I freeze, straining to catch any sign I've been heard. Nothing. I'm the only living body in here, thank the Angel.

My wrist is raw and bleeding, but I ignore it as I examine the other. The essence has reached a place that I am able to tug on it just a little, but enough that my umbral strand responds. The cuffs are sealed closed with not even a lock, which is just my fucking luck. It will take more effort to open them, but I've no other choice.

I guide the shadows into the restraints, forcing them to expand and destroy them from the inside. One by one, they crack and split until finally I'm free.

Standing proves to be a fucking challenge. My legs tremble with such force they threaten to give out with each step, but I manage to walk up the steps and make it to the cracked door, peering out into the dimly lit corridor.

A single guard stands watch, his back to me. Foolish amateur.

Chapter Twenty-Six
Ariella

I move from the lab in silence, irrespective of my injuries, years of conditioning guiding my body forward. My arm wraps around his throat before he registers my presence. He struggles as I flex my muscles, twisting his head until he goes limp. I lower his body quietly to the ground, despite my need to tear through something. Retrieving his blades, I sheathe two at my sides and grasp the hilt of the third, pointing the sharp end outward—I will not die from some avoidable injury by holding it incorrectly.

At least not until I find Caspian.

My feet guide me through several eerie tunnels before I pause, frowning. I don't know where they're keeping him, and yet...something pulls at my chest, urging me in the direction I know he is. I can feel the rightness of the pull. It makes no logical sense—but the feeling is insistent, impossible to ignore.

Calling to my vital strand, I heal the worst of my injuries, just enough to move and breathe properly. When that painful experience is done, I follow the humming under my sternum and run through the rest of the labyrinth. It's strange, but I've no need for light or touch as I move, seeming to know exactly where the turns are and how much further until I reach the main part of the castle.

The halls are empty as I enter from the west tunnels. No staff, no nobles, no guards. Either it's later than I thought, or something is very wrong.

I pause at the sound of hurried footsteps ahead. Gripping my blade tighter, I press against the wall and wait, forcing my breathing to slow. The steps grow closer, accompanied by hushed voices.

"—have to find her. The king will—"

"Shh!" the second voice hisses. "Do you want the whole castle to hear?"

Elowen and Jessenia round the corner, both freezing when they spot me. Elowen's eyes widen as she takes in my appearance, while Jessenia's hand flies to her mouth.

"By the Angel," Elowen breathes, rushing forward. I raise my blade on instinct, and she halts. "You need healing."

"I'm fine." My voice sounds like gravel, and I clear my throat. "What are you doing here?"

Jessenia steps closer, her usual shyness replaced with a hard edge. "Looking for you." She glances behind us. "Though I didn't believe we'd find you."

"Where's Caspian?" Elowen asks, and I notice the way her hands twitch, likely itching to heal me.

That pull in my chest tugs again. "The arena." They share a look I don't like. "What?"

"The king announced your execution to those attending the next phase of the Frostwell competition," Jessenia murmurs, her silky brunette hair falling over a shoulder.

Of fucking course he has.

I brace to move past them but make a quick decision. "Listen carefully," I command, straightening despite the protest of my muscles. "I need you both to do something, and you cannot fuck it up."

Elowen nods. "Anything."

"The king has taken children, experimented on them." Their faces pale. "I don't know if there are any still alive, but I need you to get them out if so. Find where he's keeping them and get them somewhere safe." I grab Elowen's arm when she makes to speak, pointing my blade at the center of the other woman's chest. She's still just as beautiful as when she was hanging from the prince's—*no, focus.* "If either of you get caught, I will kill you myself."

"How will we find them?" Jessenia questions, doing her best to avoid the weapon above her heart.

I shrug, releasing Elowen and stepping back. "There's an entrance to the underground tunnels through the south wing. Take it and follow the right path until you reach a fork. Go left, then take the second right. You'll find a door that leads to a lab—they are not in there, but I'm sure Thalion keeps notes on their whereabouts."

"What about the guards?"

"There won't be any. The king wants everyone to watch me die, remember?" I grin, my lips curling when even that hurts. "He's always been a dramatic bastard."

Jessenia's throat bobs, the movement soft. "And after we get them out?"

"Take them to Marek at the guild. Tell him—" I pause, considering my words. "Tell him I sent you and to wait for my return; he'll take it from there."

"*If* you return," Elowen mutters. My eyes snap to hers, and she lifts her chin. "At least let me heal you before you go."

I shake my head, allowing darkness to seep through my gaze. "No time. And I need you both focused on the children." I turn to leave but halt. "One more thing—if you see anything that resembles notes on his experiments, take those too, and bring them to Caspian's room." They do not need to find out that my doors are warded, and my prince cannot even be bothered to lock his. Foolish.

"Wait," Jessenia calls in that sweet voice as I start walking. "What if you don't come back?"

I peer over my shoulder. "Then tell Marek to get the children far away from here. The king *will* look for them." I meet their worried gazes. "But it's a waste of breath—I'm not dying today."

I don't wait for their response before continuing down the hall, that persistent tug growing stronger with each step.

Cool night air covers my face as I step outside, making me groan. The imposing arena looms just ahead, hair standing along my skin. My instincts scream at me to turn back—this is wrong, all wrong—but that pull in my chest only grows stronger. It's the reason I break into a run toward the unknown.

Why in the Aether would Caspian be in the arena? The bi-annual Frostwell competition is almost complete, but that has to be the last thing on mind after what happened in the tunnels. I cannot think of a valid reason for his presence there.

The tunnel entrance is unguarded and pitch black. More warning bells ring in my head. But I need to find him, so there is no hesitation in my steps as I rush into it, my breaths coming harder the closer I get to where I know he is.

Lights boom from every direction as I emerge into the arena proper. My feet halt when I spot him. Caspian stands alone—in the center—perfectly still, staring directly at me. Something about his posture sets my teeth on edge. His eyes, even from this distance, are void of any and all emotion. I'm used to seeing such an image in the mirror, but not from him...never him.

"Here she is!" Thalion's voice thunders through the arena. I jerk, cursing myself for becoming so focused on Caspian that I failed to notice the crowded audience. "The Silver Wraith, traitor to the crown. She has been sentenced to death for harboring forbidden essence. A treason that cannot be forgiven." So the bastard expected me to escape. "I bring this to you, my citizens, as an entertaining treat before we continue with the next phase of Frostwell events!"

The crowd erupts in a deafening roar, their cheers blending into a cacophony that embeds into my skull. The sound presses against my ears as if it's trying to burrow there for safety, making it nearly impossible to focus. My fingers twitch at my sides, the weight of so many eyes clawing at my resolve. Why are they here? Were they not just calling for his death?

I must still have a head injury, because it's only now that I realize this is a trap—he fucking knew I'd come for the prince.

I showed him my one weakness, solely because I didn't believe he'd be so heinous as to do anything that would harm his son.

I was wrong.

I'm unsure of what he's done with Caspian, but the prince is not himself and I need to save us both before Thalion continues with whatever he's planned.

I spin toward the tunnel, but the entrance has vanished, leaving behind smooth stone. The walls are extended past the threshold that would allow me to get us over them before Thalion could intervene. The king's laughter echoes off the walls as panic claws up my throat. I keep my expression void of any emotion.

Think. There has to be a way out.

But I do not see one.

And for once, I've no fucking clue what to do.

I whirl back to Caspian, reaching for my blade. The king wouldn't risk the death of his heir—I can use that. But as I approach, there's a shift in Caspian's eyes that stops me cold.

They're so empty. They lack all the warmth and intelligence I've come to know. His face is a mere husk, with features that are unnaturally still. This isn't my prince.

"Caspian?" I keep my voice low, searching his face for any sign of recognition. Nothing. "Caspian, look at me. Whatever he's done to you, fight it." Not even a flicker of a reaction appears, my heart sinking so low I could vomit.

"I'm afraid he can't hear you," Thalion calls down from his pretend throne, sick amusement clear in his voice. "My son has had a change of heart. He's decided he'd like to be the one to kill you himself."

I try to stop the trembling of my hands from his words, but I can't as pieces click into place. *Once I fill you with enough essence...* The king's earlier words, though sadistic, may be exactly what I need. He's controlling Caspian with essence.

But the only strand with that ability is psionic—why is there no one speaking about how Thalion is using the same fucking forbidden essence he's trying to kill me over? Pathetic. All of them.

"Kill her."

I've no time to register the king's command before I need to defend myself. Caspian moves faster than I've ever seen him move before, as his blade whistles through the air just a heartbeat after his father's words. My years of training save me as I jerk back. Even then, the edge catches my throat, opening a shallow cut that burns as blood drips from it.

I stumble back, one hand pressed to my neck as I tug on my vital strand—there's no point in hiding what the masses already know. The wound begins to close, but my essence is still weak. I'll need to preserve as much as I can.

"Caspian, please," I try again, dodging another strike. "This isn't you. Push him from your head—*fight him.*"

He doesn't even blink, instead marching forward with artificial precision. He swings fists and blades at me, each strike calculated and emotionless. Nothing like the passionate fighter I've trained.

I evade his attacks with relative ease, but I'm already exhausted and injured, leaving me vulnerable if we do this for much longer. My head spins as I dance against his relentless assault, while attempting to put distance between us.

What will he do to himself if he hurts me? *Kills* me?

My heart pounds violently against my chest as I search for a way to break through to him. Reaching for my psionic strand, I shove it toward Caspian, trying to force my way into his mind. But I hit a wall—one stronger than anything I've ever experienced. Thalion's essence is too severe, his hold too exhaustive and stable.

Why risk his heir like this? I could have Caspian's head within a moment, and Thalion knows it. I glance up, my thoughts stuttering when I find him watching us with undisguised glee. The bastard also knows I won't kill Caspian. He's using my own feelings against me.

And he's right...I will not do it. *I can't.*

But I will hurt him.

I spin and kick my foot out as he advances, wincing when bones crack in his leg at my contact. He grunts, still focused on me, though a bit slower as he limps. His blade slices into my arm, and I hiss from the pain. This isn't working. I can't keep fighting him—and why would I? There's no escape and no pathway into his mind. I will not leave here without the prince, so there is no justification for continuing this. My essence is nearly depleted from trying to heal and break his father's control anyway.

I've nothing left and I've failed. Failed to protect him, failed to stop Thalion. If I could just go back to—

Wait.

An idea forms—stupid and desperate and reckless, but what other choice do I have at this point?

I cease fighting. Drop my weapons, and leave myself vulnerable, willingly. Something I never thought I'd do. Caspian's next strike catches me across the ribs, reopening just healed wounds. I don't try to defend myself.

Blood pools at my feet as Caspian advances slower than before. His movements are predatory, even with a limp; not the graceful and confident man I've come to...care for. I want to cry, to scream at him until my voice gives out. But I remain still, allowing the sharp metal to slice into my skin again.

And again.

The audience's cheers fade to a dull roar as my focus narrows to the empty silver eyes before me. Eyes that once held such warmth when they looked at me. That crinkled at the corners when I said something particularly bratty. That blazed with desire and determination and something deeper. Something I was too afraid to accept.

"Fight back, wraith, or I'll have the prince make your death excruciating!" Thalion's voice booms through the arena. I ignore him, keeping my gaze locked on Caspian as his blade opens another wound. Interesting that he's yet to damage anything vital—it's as if he's holding back.

My prince is in there somewhere. I know it. I've felt the depth of his essence, witnessed the strength of his spirit, experienced just what it's like to be loved by him. No amount of the king's corruption could erase that.

Blood drips steadily from multiple cuts as the essence I'd gathered earlier protests, wanting to heal me, but I push it down. I need what little remains for what comes next—and I pray to the Angel I don't make a fucking fool of myself.

My legs tremble, begging to be released from the torture of holding me up, but I remain standing. Never taking my eyes from my prince. "Look at me," I whisper, though I'm not positive he can hear me. "Really look at me, Caspian."

For just a moment, I allow every one of my walls to drop. Let him see everything I've kept hidden, even after Meridian—my fear, my rage, my desperate need to save him. Most of all, I let him see how much I—

Fuck. How much he means to me.

His next strike falters. Just the tiniest hesitation, but it's enough to feed the glimmer of hope I'd long ago lost. I suck in a shaky breath, gathering what remains of my strength.

"Caspian...if this doesn't work, if it kills me, I'm sorry," I murmur as my lip trembles. "For everything. For pushing you away, for being too afraid to admit what you already knew." My voice cracks. "For not telling you what you deserved to know."

His blade hovers at my throat. Up close, there's the faintest flicker of recognition in the bright storm of his eyes. The barest hint of *him* fighting through his father's control.

It's now or never.

My essence pulses in weak protest under my skin as I reach for the last of it—for a strand I've only used once before, and the consequences of that almost killed me. But for him? I'd risk anything.

The crowd's bloodthirsty screams grow louder, demanding my death. Thalion's laughter echoes off the rugged walls. It's all too familiar. And none of it matters.

Only Caspian.

I close my eyes to the man whose blade wavers against my throat, allowing memories of him to wash over me. His stupid smirk when he thinks he's being clever. The way his hands feel tangled in my hair. The sensation of his lips pressed against mine. How he sees past my carefully constructed armor to the dark, broken pieces underneath, yet wants me anyway.

When I open them again, determination floods my every vein. I may be the most feared assassin in the realm, but right now I'm just a woman trying to save the man she loves.

And I will save him, even if it destroys me in the process.

I study his face one last time, savoring those beautiful silver eyes, committing it all to memory. Then I sink deep within myself, grasping my temporal strand with everything I have left, and hope my body's overuse of essence doesn't kill me before I see him again.

"I'm sorry," I breathe.

And then I run.

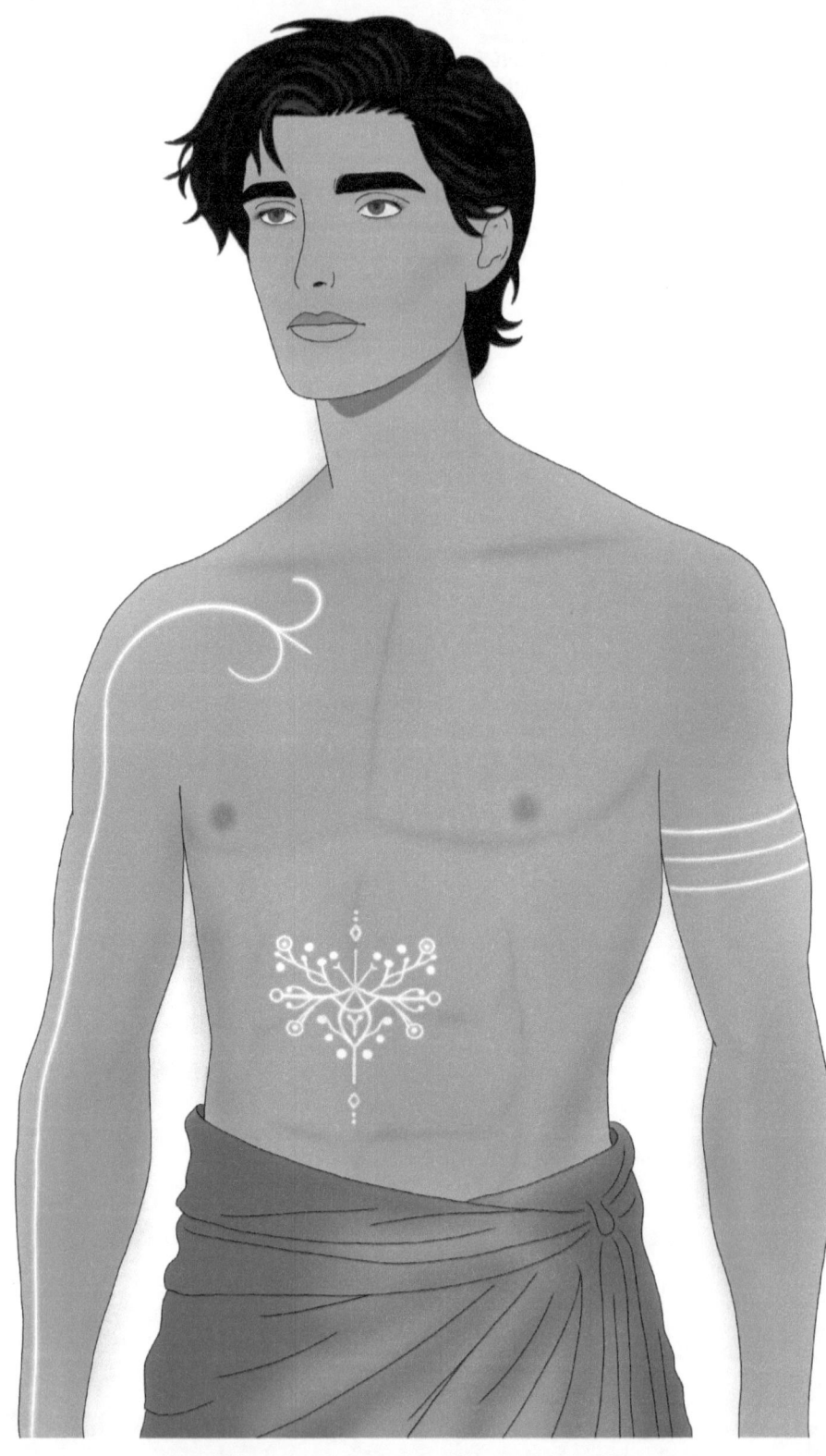

Chapter Twenty-Seven

Caspian

My screams bounce around inside my head, thrashing against invisible bonds that keep my consciousness trapped while my body moves against my will. Every muscle burns from fighting my father's control, but the essence flooding my system is too strong. All I can do is watch in mute horror as my blade slices into Ariella's skin again.

And again.

My father's essence twists inside me like poison, more insidious than anything I've ever felt. He didn't just steal too much of it—he learned how to manipulate it, forcing it into me in a way that lets him control my every move. It's as if his will has replaced my own, spreading through my body like a puppeteer tugging at invisible strings.

Stop. Please stop. But my arms don't listen. They continue their deadly motions, carving shallow wounds across her flesh while she simply...stands there. Taking it. The Silver Wraith, my feared angel, isn't even trying to defend herself.

I'm sick to my fucking stomach. This cannot be happening...

Fight back! I want to scream. *Kill me and run!* But my lips remain sealed, my voice and body locked away by my father's essence. I'm unable to do anything but stare through eyes I can't control as blood oozes from her wounds.

"Fight back, wraith, or I'll have the prince make your death excruciating!" My father's voice booms through the arena. The crowd's ferocious roars grow louder, but Ariella doesn't react. She keeps those piercing, viridescent eyes fixed on mine, searching for something.

For me.

I throw everything I have against my father's hold, desperate to break free. To drop the blade. To tell her I'm here. That I see her. That I'm so fucking sorry. But the essence binding me tightens its grip, sending waves of burning agony through my veins. The pain in my leg is *nothing* compared to the torture of my mind in this moment.

"Look at me," she whispers, her voice carrying despite the crowd's frenzy. "Really look at me, Caspian."

Something shifts in her eyes then—walls dropping away to reveal everything she usually keeps hidden. Fear. Rage. A bone-deep exhaustion. But underneath it all, more than that. My heart stutters at the sight, even through my father's control.

My next strike falters for just a heartbeat. Not much, but enough that I know she noticed. A tiny crack in my father's hold. Hope flares in my chest, giving me renewed strength to fight.

"Caspian..." Her voice cracks, and Angel help me, I've never heard her sound so broken—not even after my death. "If this doesn't work, if it kills me, I'm sorry. For everything. For pushing you away, for being too afraid to admit what you already knew." She draws a shaky breath. "For not telling you what you deserved to know."

My blade hovers along her throat as terror flickers through the haze. I can feel her pulse fluttering against the steel. So alive. So fragile. One wrong move and she's gone.

No. I rail against my father's essence with everything I have, and my arms begin trembling from the war. I will not be the weapon that ends her. I refuse.

The crowd's screams crescendo as the king laughs, the horrid sound resonating off each point of the arena walls. "Finish her, my son! Show everyone the price of treason against the crown!"

I want to vomit. Want to spin and drive this blade through his black heart instead. But my body remains frozen, pressed against the woman who means everything to me.

Ariella's eyes close briefly, and when they open again, there's a fierce determination burning in their depths. She studies my face like she's afraid she'll never see it again. Then her expression hardens, resolve flooding her eyes—a decision made.

"I'm sorry," she breathes.

Before I can process what's happening, she twists around and sprints toward the royal box where my father watches. For a moment, blessed relief floods me—she's fighting back. But then my legs give chase without my permission, the broken one seeming to pretend it's fully functional even through the pain. And though I still resist it, my father's stolen essence forces me to pursue against every bit of my will. I give everything to stopping my legs, but I cannot even determine the direction my eyes look. I'm fucking trapped in my own body.

I'll never forgive myself if I kill her.

The arena stretches vast before us as we run. Despite her injuries, despite whatever they did to suppress her essence, she's still impossibly fast. But my father's enhancements force me faster still, closing the distance between us with each stride.

She glances back once, her eyes meeting mine for just a heartbeat. There's so much emotion in them—most of all, a silent plea for understanding. I notice where she's leading us, and I truly begin panicking.

What the fuck is she doing? Is she going to kill herself so I don't have to? By the fucking Angel.

Then she slams herself into the arena wall and vanishes.

I stumble to a halt, my father's control momentarily shocked into stillness as we both try to process what just happened. There's no door there, no hidden passage that I know of.

She's gone.

"What trickery is this?" My father stands, leaning over the edge of the royal box to peer down at the arena floor. He scans the crowd, raising a hand at his guards before screaming orders. "Find her! She cannot—"

His words cut off in a wet gurgle as a blade erupts from his chest.

My attention snaps to the royal box just as my father's body pitches forward, tipping over the ornate railing. I watch him fall in slow motion, ignoring the prickling under my skin as my body becomes my own again. The blade protruding from his back glints in the afternoon sun as he descends, the external pieces of his royal jacket billowing around him like broken wings. He hits the ground with a sickening thud that sends vibrations through my bones.

My eyes flick up. Standing in the exact spot where he'd just been is Ariella, her silver hair whipping in the wind as she stares down at his crumpled form, her face unreadable. Relief floods through me at the conspicuous absence of my mother and sister. At least they were spared witnessing this.

I find myself walking toward my father's body, each step feeling both hollow and weighted. The crowd's screams—no longer cheerful in nature—fade to a dull roar in my ears as drop to my knees beside him. Blood pools beneath his chest, staining the sand a deep crimson.

It's almost picturesque, the way his blood matches the fabric he wears. It extends the color to the point that he appears to be flying, though he lies still on his side.

I rear back when his eyes flutter open and focus on me. "Son…" he wheezes, blood bubbling, leaking at the corners of his mouth. "Take me to Elowen…quickly. Before it becomes fatal." A wet laugh escapes him. It sounds agonizing—good. "The wraith couldn't even…properly hit my heart." His breaths rasp in a strange pattern, as if he's trying to breathe around the liquid filling his lung.

I glance up at Ariella, who is already watching me with knowing eyes. We both understand the truth of his words—if she'd wanted him dead instantly, that blade would have pierced his heart with precision. She deliberately missed, offering me this moment. This choice.

But the only choice I consider is how painful to make his last breaths.

"Why?" I ask my father, my voice but a whisper. "All of this...for what? Just to die from your own arrogance?"

"Everything I did..." he coughs out, more blood and snot spattering his chin, "was to make our kingdom stronger. To ensure *your* reign would be absolute." I huff a breath and watch his body struggle to survive.

This—my father dying—should bother me. It should scare me enough that I rush to find any healer that can save him. He's my father, for Angel's sake. The man who gave me life.

But now I sit here eager to take his, and all I feel is vindication.

I shake my head, disgusted by his words. "No. You tortured and murdered so many people. *Children*, Thalion. You betrayed everything a king should stand for." I shift to kneel, wrapping my hand around the hilt of the blade in his back. "And you tried to force me to kill the woman I love."

His eyes widen at the last of my words, but I don't give him time to respond. He deserves nothing more than his end. With one sharp twist, I drive the blade deeper to the right, angling it into his heart. His body jerks once before going still, cruel eyes glazing over as the last breath leaves him.

The silence that follows is deafening.

A soft thud before me announces Ariella's arrival. I look over my shoulder to find her standing a few feet away, her face tired and neutral as she studies me. Realizing I'm still holding the blade, I release the weapon and clench my jaw as I push to my aching feet.

"How did you?" I gesture at where she'd appeared in the royal box. I have a guess, but I want to hear her say it.

"Temporal strand," she confirms with a slight shrug, her mouth threatening to lift as she inspects every part of my body. "I'd always planned to use it when I killed him. I've dreamed of watching the bastard die over and over, both of us experiencing his last moments repeatedly until I got bored." Her lips twist into something between a smirk and a grimace. "Though I didn't think his death would feel so *disappointing*."

Temporal strand. I want to ask her how it works—how she shifts time, bending it to her will. Will halting it for a few minutes have a lasting impact on the realm? Does it matter?

I peer at my blood-stained hands, somehow understanding exactly what she means. Years of fear and hatred building to this moment, and now...nothing. Everything we went through because of him, everything we did to stop him, all comes down to a quick, mundane death.

"Are you okay?" I ask, remembering the numerous cuts and bruises marking her skin. The ones I put there.

She huffs a laugh, tilting her head. "Shouldn't I be asking you that? You're the one who just killed your father."

"I'll live." My voice comes out rougher than intended. "Though I wouldn't mind if you explained what just happened. How did you manipulate his control over me?"

"I didn't." She saunters closer, carefully stepping around the growing pool of blood as if she wouldn't be caught walking through it. "You did that yourself when you hesitated. It showed me there was still a part of you fighting." Her eyes soften, and I get the feeling she wants nothing more than to touch me—I feel the same. My fingers ache to hold her. "I just needed to give you something worth fighting harder for."

"By making me think you were going to die?" I probe, unable to keep the edge from my voice.

She shrugs again, but I catch the slight shaking in her hands. "It worked, didn't it?"

I shift on my feet—well, try to, but my bad leg barely holds me up—my body aching from the essence-enhanced fight. "You're fucking insane, you know that?" But there's no heat to my words. How can there be when she risked everything to save me from becoming my father's puppet? I know there was a point she'd accepted her death, but that did not dissolve her fight for me.

This woman. *This angel.* And every piece of her is all mine. I smile to myself—as if she could deny that truth now.

"So I've been told." Her eyes scan the arena, always assessing, as guards begin flooding in. "We should probably deal with them."

I turn to face the approaching sentries, many of whom look uncertain whether to attack or kneel. "Stand down," I command, pushing every ounce of royal authority into my voice. "Your king is dead. You no longer answer to him."

Most of the guards drop to one knee without question, but a few hesitate, glancing between me and Ariella. I raise a brow as one steps forward, his hand on his sword. "My prince, she must answer for her crimes. The king named her a traitor—"

"The king was wrong." I cut him off, my tone sharp. "He was a sick man. Anyone who moves against her moves against *me*. Is that understood?"

A tense moment passes before the remaining guards follow the rest and kneel. I dismiss them before turning back to Ariella, finding her watching me with an inquisitive, though unreadable, expression.

"What?" I ask.

"Nothing. Just—" She pauses, considering her words. "You're different when you embrace your authority. It's...not entirely unpleasant to witness."

I can't help the small smile that tugs at my lips. The chill from the last several hours is beginning to melt at her presence, something only she's capable of accomplishing. "Was that a compliment, angel?"

She rolls her eyes, but I catch the slight upward tilt of her mouth. "Don't let it go to your big fucking head." I enjoy this banter between us, and as much as I want to keep it going, to forget why the fuck we're here, her expression grows serious again. So I wait until she's ready to speak. "Now that your father so kindly announced my abilities to the entire realm, there's something I want to try. If you'll let me." She fusses with her hands, her fingers tapping together.

I raise an eyebrow. "You're asking permission?"

"Don't get used to it, prince." She steps closer, grabbing hold of my wrist to pull me toward the reappeared tunnel. How the king hid it is beyond me. I'd guess the terra strand, using the sand to create a wall in the opening, but it didn't feel like his essence was abiding by any of the normal laws. It felt raw and untamed. Plus, he didn't possess the terra strand.

The cool stone against my back provides little relief from my aching body as I slide down the tunnel wall. Ariella helps lower me to the ground, her touch more gentle than I've ever felt from her. I wince as my leg screams in protest at even that careful movement.

"Fuck," I mutter, leaning my head back. Though we're far enough in that no one can see us from the arena, enough light still filters through to illuminate her concerned features as she kneels beside me. "I'm pretty sure it's broken."

She nods, her eyes scanning my leg with an intensity that makes me wonder if she can see through to the bone itself. "I want to try something." Her voice is uncharacteristically hesitant. "I've never really attempted healing anyone else before—except for Meridian, but that was different."

I raise an eyebrow. "You've never healed anyone? With all the essence you have?"

"No need to sound so shocked," she mutters, though there's no real bite to her words. "Why would I have ever healed someone other than myself? I've watched other healers work plenty of times. I understand the theory—they need physical contact with whoever they're healing. The connection allows essence to flow between bodies." She pauses, chewing on that damn bottom lip. "I think. I'm just not certain if it matters where we touch, or if I might accidentally hurt you more."

"I don't care either way." And I mean it. After everything that's happened—after what my father made me do to her—I'd trust her with anything she asked for. Even if she does somehow make it worse, I know it won't be intentional.

She huffs but doesn't argue, instead reaching for my hands. Her fingers are soft and warm against my skin as she positions her palms above mine. "Close your eyes," she instructs in a soft voice. "I need to focus."

I do as she asks, though I can't resist peeking through my lashes to watch her when I'm sure she's no longer paying attention. Her face settles into deep concentration as her nose scrunches in the slightest, reminding me of how she looks when she's about to strike a killing blow. But her expression is softer now, almost vulnerable.

I feel the moment she begins drawing on her vital strand. Not because she's using it on me...no, deep inside I can *feel* her tugging on the strand. It's not a perplexing aspect of our relationship at this point. The surrounding air thickens with essence, making my skin tingle with its familiarity, as if in greeting. Through our joined hands, I sense her coaxing it toward her fingertips, silently urging it to bridge the gap between our bodies. There's a strange resistance at first, as if her essence is reluctant to leave her body for mine.

"Come on," she whispers, more to her essence than to me.

The connection snaps into place so suddenly that we both gasp, and I jolt forward from the force of it. It's unlike anything I've ever experienced, as if our essence shares one body. Her umbral strand was incredible, but they never sunk into my skin this deep—though I had a suspicion that they wanted to.

Every part of her essence flows through me, warm and devoted in a way that doesn't make sense. This isn't how it feels when other healers work on me. This feels right. Natural. Like her essence belongs inside me as much as my own does.

"Angel," I breathe, unable to form more coherent words.

She doesn't respond, but I sense the shift in intentions as her strand explores my body with purpose now, seeking out injuries. When it reaches my broken leg, the sensation intensifies. I grit my teeth against the strange pressure building in the bone, forcing myself to remain still against every instinct I have to pull away.

This is going to be painful.

"This will hurt," she warns, echoing my thoughts, a heartbeat before my leg explodes in agony.

I bite back a scream as the bone snaps back into place. Her essence wraps around the break, knitting the pieces back together with meticulous care. It's so strange, feeling it work as though it were my own—something I've also never experienced with other healers. Aside from a small prickle of heat at times, a healer's essence should not be felt in any capacity.

The pain slowly fades to a dull ache, then disappears all at once, sweet fucking relief settling in my tense muscles.

But she doesn't stop there—of course she doesn't. Her essence continues its journey through my body, detecting and healing injuries I hadn't even noticed. A cracked rib. Torn muscles in my shoulder. Countless bruises and small cuts. Each repair sends wave after wave of warmth through me until I feel more alive than I have in weeks.

Finally, the actual healing seems to stop, but her essence lingers. It swirls through me almost playfully, as if it's found a new home and refuses to leave. I admit that I don't want this connection to end, either.

Through our link, I notice Ariella's similar reluctance. Her essence hums with contentment, like it's discovered what it's been searching for. The hint of a smile curves her lips before reality seems to startle her, and she yanks her essence back so violently that she sways.

"Careful, angel," I assert, leaning to catch her shoulders as she starts to topple sideways. "Are you alright?"

Her eyes blink several times. "Fine. Did it work?"

"Yes, but..." I trail off, distracted by what I'm seeing. I tilt my head. Maybe it's a trick of the light filtering in from the arena, but her hair seems to be illuminated. She adjusts, but the glow doesn't change. No, it's not just reflecting the light—it's emitting a soft, silvery radiance. So similar to the brief moments after we've been intimate... "How did you do that?"

"Do what?"

"Your hair—it's glowing. I've never seen a healer's essence manifest visibly like that. Essence works inside the body, not out."

She shrugs, though I notice she won't quite meet my eyes. "No one else has silver hair or universal essence, either. It's probably just that I have more essence than most people."

I nod, though I'm not convinced. Everything in me screams to keep digging, that there's something more to it...but she's already pushing to her feet, ending the conversation.

"We should go," she breathes, holding out a hand in offering. I grasp it, though bear no weight on her as I stand. "Your father may be dead, but we have a lot of shit to deal with."

I hold her tighter, testing my healed leg. It feels perfect—better than before it was broken, even. "Thank you," I say in a soft tone. "Not just for healing me, but for everything you did back there." For saving me from becoming my father's puppet. For giving me the strength to break free. For trusting me enough to try healing me when you've never done it before. "And for being you."

She waves away the words with her hand, but I catch the softening in her eyes. "Don't get sentimental on me now, prince. We have work to do."

"I would never," I tease, and can't help but smile. Even after everything that's happened, she's still the same fierce, stubborn woman I fell for. "Lead the way, angel."

Her eyes roll as she chuckles, spinning to walk through the tunnel while she practically drags me close behind. As we walk, I find myself watching the way her hair catches the dim light. There's no trace now of that strange glow...

But I know what I saw.

Just like I know there was something different about the way her essence felt inside me. An instinct that went beyond simple healing. The memory of that connection makes me shiver, and I wonder if she feels it too—

Another thought slams to the forefront of my mind like a beacon of light. Is that related to what happened in my room when she bit me?

Even as I think it, I know it is.

I am desperate to know what it means, but she's right—we have more pressing concerns. The Accord is priority, and we're the only ones who know the truth about what's happening. Whatever this thing is between us, it will have to wait.

My chest aches.

Still, as we emerge from the tunnel into the late afternoon sun, I hope we'll have a chance to explore that connection again soon. I have a theory that we've only scratched the surface of what's possible when our essence combines.

Ariella pauses at the tunnel entrance, her eyes scanning the area. Most of the crowd has dispersed, though guards still mill about, unsure of what to do now that their king is dead. My father has already been removed from the arena, and I feel absolutely fucking nothing as the staff carry his covered body toward the castle.

Chapter Twenty-Eight

Ariella

"You need to eat something," Caspian insists as we make our way back toward the castle. My entire body aches, my vision has black spots in random places, and my feet tremble, but I ignore it all. I've no time for food—which is terribly depressing.

I tap a finger against my thigh as I consider everything that's happened the last few days. Caspian died. He came back after I threatened the Angel. I found a headless fellow guild member. Was tortured by Thalion's sentries—which reminds me that I need to find those two cowards. Then I followed some strange feeling to Caspian, finding him under his father's complete control. Used my temporal strand. And killed a fucking king with his son by my side after weaving my temporal strand.

The temporal strand isn't straightforward; though none of the strands in the ethereal affinity are. It's like trying to grab water with your bare hands—slippery, fleeting, and never quite what you expect. When I tug onto it, it's not just time bending around me; it's like I'm bending with it, shifting through moments that shouldn't be mine to hold. It's dangerous, unpredictable, and draining, but it worked. Somehow it worked. It gave me the edge I needed when everything hung by a thread and I thought I was going to lose him. Again.

I halt my movements as acidic realization floods through me: Thalion is dead. Twenty years of training, planning, raging, and he's finally dead.

And the most disturbing part is I hadn't considered any of this before...what happens after the king is dead. I've been so focused on Caspian and what we need to do now that it slipped my mind. Succeeding at the only thing I've ever wanted was overshadowed by my feelings for the prince.

I cannot tell if I'm disturbed by that truth or relieved.

And my parents? Their deaths were the catalyst for my plans, and I've just dismissed their long deserved justice without a second thought.

Do I feel guilty about it? I should, but no.

Would I do it again? Fail to drag out long-planned Thalion's death in their name, if given the chance? For Caspian? I absolutely fucking would.

"Ariella." I jolt at the prince's soft voice and touch as he drags his hands down my arm. "What are you thinking about?"

I purse my lips, narrowing my eyes before answering. "Are you sure you want to know?" He nods as both hands slide around my waist and hover low on my back.

He presses in, and I immediately step close enough that the heat of his body warms my cold thoughts. His eyes darken at my lips before I realize I'm biting one. Leaning to brush the lightest of kisses against my forehead, he whispers, "I *always* want to know what's going on in that beautifully violent head of yours." A giddiness flits around my abdomen as I smile, and—

Fuck, what is wrong with me? I'm positive that I've smiled more in the last two months than I have my entire life.

I relax into his arms—the one place I've ever felt truly safe. We remain silent for a few moments while I allow myself to be held by him. I must be quite injured, because I'm not in the slightest concerned about others seeing the Silver Wraith being held by their prince.

Perhaps I do enjoy cuddling, after all.

I shift when my legs tremble harder, bracing to walk back into the castle before I collapse, when a deep rumble vibrates through my bones, causing both of us to pause. The sensation grows until the ground beneath our feet quakes violently. Caspian adjusts his grip on my arms, steadying me as people around us scream and the castle groans.

"Fuck me," I breathe, watching as trees collapse and windows shatter. This is different from the shaking in the library. It's callous and erratic.

My mother's and Eris' warnings ring in my ears: *chaos.*

How? We've killed the one fucking with and hoarding essence—I want to believe that's why. That it's the king's harvested essence entering the environment once again that's causing this alarming shaking.

I cannot think that, after so much effort, Thalion's death would make the balance worse. I will not believe that eradicating that monster is going to ruin our chances of fixing the Accord.

I'm too fucking tired for this.

"Come on." I yank Caspian toward the castle entrance, dodging falling debris. His normally graceful movements are sluggish, as are mine, likely from the drugs and manipulation his father used to control us. The thought makes my blood boil.

Just as quick as it started, the shaking ceases without warning. I widen my eyes in an attempt to keep them open—I'll think about this more tomorrow. I've dealt with enough today.

We burst through the back entrance just as Gavriel emerges from a side hallway. His face is bruised, and he cradles his right arm against his chest. Something in my gut says he fought back when the king's men came for him.

Brave of him to show his face here after what he did. Foolish, but brave.

"Caspian, please—I just need to explain." Gavriel's voice cracks with desperation. I glance at Caspian, finding him slumped against the wall, eyes distant. Whatever his father did has fucked with his head more than I initially thought.

"He'll talk to you tomorrow," I snap, moving to guide Caspian away. Gavriel's hand clamps around my forearm, and I react on instinct.

I slam him into the wall, pressing a blade to his throat. "Fuck's sake, leave him alone, Gavriel. It's like you're in love with him or something."

The words leave my mouth before I process them, but the way Gavriel's face drains of color confirms what I'd suspected. His eyes dart to Caspian, who seems oblivious to our exchange as he leans his head forward, forehead scrunched tightly.

"If you ever touch me again," I breathe, leaning close, "I will personally ensure your body is never found. And trust me, that wouldn't be much effort on my part—no one would look very hard for the guard who betrayed his prince."

Gavriel's voice lowers to a sharp whisper, the brown of his irises darkening. "You don't understand anything. You never have. You're always so quick to judge—but only after you destroy everything."

"Destroy?" I hiss back, pressing my blade in. "You almost got him killed in Meridian. Or did you forget that part while you were busy swimming to higher ground while I saved his fucking life?"

His jaw tightens, widening the muscles that flex under my weapon. "I would die for him," he says, his voice trembling but steady.

"Great. Then do it quietly." Caspian shifts in my peripheral, and I peer at him before focusing on the man who betrayed him once more. "Because if you pull another stunt like this, I'll save you the effort."

We glare at each other, so close our chests rise and fall against each other. For a moment, I catch something in his eyes—a crack in his defiance. Something raw.

"I wasn't trying to hurt him," he whispers. "You don't have to believe me, but it's the truth."

I hesitate for the briefest heartbeat before shoving off him, sheathing the blade over my left thigh. The weight is comforting. "Your truth means nothing to me, Gavriel. Fix yourself before you try to fix him."

His eyes fall to the ground as he nods, swallowing hard before stepping aside. I return to Caspian, who's breathing heavily as sweat beads along his forehead.

"Up we go, prince." I wrap his arm over my shoulder and grab his waist to hoist him up. Despite his protests, his body sags against mine.

Behind us, I hear Gavriel whisper, almost too soft to catch. "I'd never let him fall."

I don't bother turning around, but the words stick in my head longer than I'd like to admit.

"I can walk," he mumbles, though his feet drag. "But it's unreasonably attractive that you can carry me."

I laugh before I can stop it, trying not to think about how natural it feels to support his weight. "Shut up before I drop you."

We reach his room, and I deposit him onto his bed as gently as possible. It's not a moment before he sinks into a deep sleep, and something in my chest tightens at how vulnerable he looks. Turning, my jaw clenches as I reach for my umbral strand and weave as strong of wards as I can manage across the door. And what a fucking effort it is—I need to train more.

"I'm going to shower," I announce to an unconscious prince when I'm done, needing space from the confusing mix of protectiveness and uncertainty swirling through me. He grunts in response, making me chuckle.

The hot water helps ease some tension from my muscles, but my mind races. I should leave—put distance between us and focus on finding the artifacts. But the thought of walking away while he's in this state makes me physically ill.

No, that's a lie. What makes me ill is the thought of being separated from him in any capacity. Even now, just a room apart, the pain and sluggishness I've been able to fend off are overtaking my body, and somehow I know the only way to rid myself of such ailments is to be near him.

Scoffing, I turn off the shower and dry myself. At some point, I've stopped making excuses to stay away from him and started hoping there were reasons for me to stay.

But I do not need any reason other than it's what I want.

When I emerge, he appears to be sleeping. I hesitate before slipping into one of his shirts, removing his outer layer of clothes, and crawling into bed beside him. I'm careful to keep distance between us, though it pains me to do so.

"Just until morning," I whisper to myself. "Then we figure out our next move."

Sleep claims me, my exhausted body finally giving in to rest. The last thing I register is the familiar warmth of my shadows curling protectively around us both, despite my lack of call for them.

Warmth caresses my face, stirring me from a peaceful sleep. My eyes flutter open to find Caspian studying me with a warm fondness, his gaze holding an unnerving amount of tenderness. I should move away—establish boundaries or some shit like that—but my body refuses to listen.

"You stayed." His voice is rough with sleep, yet somehow still manages to sound charming and pleased.

My eyes roll on their own. "Obviously."

"Obviously," he mocks with a smirk, trailing his fingers down my arm. "And wearing my shirt again...I'm beginning to think you like them, angel."

"They're comfortable." I try to sound dismissive, but it's a miserable attempt as his hand slides to my hip. Our bodies are so close, yet I do not feel the need to run from the intimacy. "How are you feeling?"

His features darken as his hand squeezes my hip. "Like my father invaded my mind and forced me to try killing you." He pauses, swallowing, a glimmer of panic flashing through his eyes. "I could see everything happening—*everything*, Ariella. But couldn't stop myself. I've never felt so fucking helpless."

"But you fought it." I prop myself up on an elbow, needing him to understand as I meet his eye level. "I saw you resisting him...that's why I knew my plan would work."

"Your plan to use your temporal strand?" His eyes narrow. "The one you conveniently failed to mention you possessed?"

I shrug, though heat creeps up my neck. "You failed to ask."

He laughs, the sound warming parts of me I didn't realize were cold. "You're an impossible woman." His hand slides up my side, fingers ghosting over my ribs. "What other strands are you hiding from me?"

"Wouldn't you like to know?" I attempt to roll away but he catches me, pulling me flush against his chest, and I lose a breath at the impact.

"I would, actually." Heat fans across my face as he hovers over me. "I want to know everything about you, Ariella."

The intensity in his eyes makes my heartbeat stutter—not the one in my chest. "That's a dangerous thing to want, prince."

A hum reverberates from him as he smiles. That fucking smile could melt even the coldest of souls. "I've never claimed to be particularly wise." He leans down, pressing his lips to mine with devastating gentleness.

Nerves prickle all over my body as I melt into the kiss, allowing myself this moment of vulnerability. His tongue slides along my bottom lip and I open for him, groaning when his head tilts to deepen the contact. One of his hands tangles in my hair, tugging with a tight grip while the other skims down my thigh, hitching my leg over his hip.

A knock at the door has me immediately rolling to reach for a blade. He chuckles, amused by my reaction—it wouldn't be so amusing if there were people here to kill him.

"Your Highness?" A staff member's muffled voice calls through the door. "The queen requests your presence immediately."

Caspian releases a heavy sigh before replying with a cold tone. "Tell her I'll be there shortly."

We listen as footsteps retreat before he turns back to me with a predatory grin. "Now, where were we?"

I press a hand to his chest when he moves to kiss me again, laughing when he nips my chin. "You should go. Your mother likely wishes to discuss what happened yesterday."

"Fuck." He drops his head to my shoulder, groaning as his arms encircle me—something I'm really starting to enjoy. "I hadn't even thought about that. The entire kingdom saw me kill my father."

"They also saw him admit to experimenting on people and controlling you with essence." I run my fingers through his hair, surprised by my desire to comfort him. "No one will blame you for what happened."

He lifts his head, searching my face. "Come with me." Not a question, though his voice is hesitant.

"To see your mother?" I bark out a laugh. "I don't think she'd appreciate that."

"I don't care what she *appreciates*." His jaw clenches. "I want you there, so you'll be there."

The authority in his voice has me nodding before I can think better of it—fuck me and my newly discovered perversity. "Fine. But I'm not changing."

His eyes darken as they rake over my body, lingering on my bare legs. "Good."

Chapter Twenty-Nine

Ariella

We dress—well, he dresses while I simply pull on a pair of shorts under his shirt. The walk to the queen's chambers is silent, both of us lost in our thoughts. The wary eyes of sentries glare at us as we pass, though none dare comment on my attire or presence. I assume the visible blades on my thighs are deterrent enough.

The queen's personal guard announces us before we enter her sitting room—who the fuck needs a *sitting* room attached to their bedroom? Royalty have such fatuous tastes.

She stands at a window, hands clasped behind her back as she stares out at the courtyard below. When she turns, her severe eyes home in on my state of undress.

"I asked to speak with my son alone." Her tone could freeze fire.

"You did," I agree as I direct a malicious smile toward her. "Yet here I am."

Caspian stiffens beside me as his mother's face hardens further. The queen moves with a practiced elegance that's sharp enough to cut flesh. Her gown, a deep indigo that shifts like water when she walks, is pressed and flawless—much like her demeanor. A streak of gray at her temple softens the severity of her dark waves, though it does nothing to dampen the animosity in her gaze. The full weight of her attention swallows me whole as she assesses whatever the fuck she seems to find interesting.

"I see," she mutters, just loud enough for me to hear. "Well, I suppose there's no point in requesting privacy now." She drifts from the window to sit in an ornate chair, gesturing for us to do the same on the couch across from her. "Though I must say, it's rather bold of you to parade around the castle half-dressed after killing my husband."

"Mother—" Caspian starts, but I cut him off with a laugh. I seem to do that a lot.

"Would you prefer I parade around *fully* undressed? I can slip your son's shirt off if it would make you more comfortable." I lean back, crossing my legs, not bothered in the slightest at the way she glares. Her ire fuels me—it's euphoric. "Though I doubt my attire is what truly bothers you, Your Majesty."

Her perfectly painted lips curve into a cold smile. "You're right. What bothers me is how easily you've manipulated my son into betraying his family."

"Manipulated?" Caspian stands abruptly. "As if she could coerce me into anything. Father was sick."

"Drunk on power, yes," she continues in a silky tone. "But the entire realm just watched you both murder him."

My chest tightens at Seraphina's words, but her features soften as she takes in Caspian's pained expression. "I don't blame you, my son. That man...he was not the one I married. The king I loved would never have harmed children or hurt his own son." In one graceful move, she rises to cup Caspian's face. "I feared for you and Vespera. His obsession with power consumed him entirely, and try as I might, I could not stop him."

I sit straighter, the weight of her words pressing on my chest. "And yet you don't seem surprised."

She turns her sharp gaze on me, her mouth twitching in what might be amusement—or warning. "I loved my husband once, wraith. But I stopped being surprised when his choices began tearing our family apart. If anything, you've spared us further destruction." Her voice softens, though her expression remains unreadable. "But don't mistake my relief for trust. You may have saved my son's life, but that doesn't mean I will allow you to destroy him in other ways."

Caspian's shoulders tense as he leans forward on his elbows. "Do not speak to her like that. I am sorry about father; I never wished for it to come to this, but you will not take those emotions out on Ariella."

She considers his words before stroking his cheek once, stepping back. Why does that bother me so much? "What's done is done. For now, I will remain queen until you are ready to take the throne." Her eyes slide to me for a mere heartbeat, and though there's still wariness in them, the open hostility has faded. "We must hold a ceremony for your father tomorrow to maintain appearances. Though I suspect no one in this room particularly cares for such formalities."

I bite back a smirk at her pointed look. At least she's honest about it.

Her attention flicks between the two of us, her gaze lingering on Caspian. "You may have stopped him, but the nobles will not forgive easily. They'll demand answers, and some will see you as weak for letting her"—she nods toward me—"influence your actions."

Caspian's jaw tightens, but I speak before he can entertain this argument his mother seems devoted to having. "If the court has any questions, they can bring them to me. I'd be happy to explain just how close they came to dying under their king's rule." My tone is saccharine, but the meaning is sharp. Seraphina's lips thin, though her eyes glimmer with approval.

"After the ceremony, Ariella and I have some matters to attend to," Caspian states, his tone carefully neutral.

Seraphina's smile drops, eyes narrowing. "What matters?"

"Just some loose ends that need tying up after Father." He shrugs, but there's tension in his shoulders that wasn't there before.

I find it curious that he doesn't mention the Accord to his mother. Perhaps he shares my instinct that the fewer people who know about it, the better. I wouldn't stop him if he chose to tell her, but I am pleased with his decision.

Seraphina hums and turns to leave, dismissing us. I can't resist asking, "Your Majesty, are you fond of Varrick?"

She pauses at the door, a knowing smirk curving her lips. "No." With that, she's gone, leaving me to wonder just how much the queen knows about what happens in her castle. And what a strange reaction to a threat on her chief advisor.

Almost makes me like her.

As she leaves, I glance at Caspian, my curiosity getting the better of me. "What's her deal with him?"

"Varrick?" He shrugs, expression hardening. "She tolerates him because she has to, but if she could replace him, she'd do it without hesitation. He was the king's choice, not hers."

"Interesting." My mind races with possibilities. "Well, perhaps I should replace him for her."

Caspian's smirk is faint but wicked. "Perhaps."

I jump up, suddenly full of energy, ready to change and deal with the late king's snake before he has a chance to flee. My eyes find Caspian, who remains seated, his face twisted in discomfort.

"What's wrong?" I ask, pausing in my rush to leave for our rooms.

He shakes his head, blinking several times. "I'm not sure. Something just feels...off under my skin. Heavy. I'm sure it's just lasting effects of whatever Thalion did."

That answer makes my skin crawl, especially after healing him, but I push the feeling aside for now. "I'll be back. I need to have a chat with Varrick."

Caspian springs up, a sudden hardness falling over his features. "*We* need to speak with Varrick."

I don't even bother arguing this time—I'm learning to pick my battles with this insufferable prince.

He grins as if I'd just spoken out loud. "Look at that. I'm finally winning you over."

"Keep teasing and I'll change my mind." But there's no heat in my words, and his answering laugh shoots warmth through my abdomen.

After I change, we venture to Varrick's office, and when Caspian raises a fist to knock, I roll my eyes and push right past him. Varrick flies out of his chair at our dramatic entrance, outrage clear on his features until he registers who has invaded his space. He attempts to compose himself, but I can practically smell his fear. It's delicious.

"Your Highness, I wasn't expecting—"

"Cut the shit," I snap, unsheathing a blade. "You know exactly why we're here. You were Thalion's right hand—there isn't a single chance in this realm that you weren't helping him."

His eyes dart between Caspian and me before hardening. "I was only following orders."

"Orders to help torture? To assist in essence manipulation experiments? To have your own prince controlled and nearly killed by his own father?" I advance as I point my blade toward him in silent accusation, enjoying how he backs away. Unlucky for him, there's nowhere to escape. "Tell me, did you get off on watching them suffer, or was that just a bonus to your cruelty?"

"Wait!" He holds up trembling hands, trying to placate a fucking assassin. As if I'll spare him if he gives me a good reason to.

Idiot. I step around the desk, and he doesn't attempt to evade my looming presence as Caspian remains on the other side, blocking the door. "I know things—things you'll need to know about the Accord!"

My blade halts an inch from his throat. "What could you possibly know about the Accord?"

"Don't kill me, and I'll tell you everything."

I growl—I don't have time for petty games. My arm draws back to strike, not wishing to listen to his sputtering any longer, but Varrick shouts, "Things about your mother!"

"What about my mother?" The hollow words leave my mouth before I can stop them. I haven't told Caspian of my meeting with her—or dream of her? I'm still unsure.

He shakes his head. "Not yours." His answer is so soft I barely hear it as his gaze slides to the prince.

Could he get any more pathetic? His foolish attempts to stay alive are just pissing me off more and I move to strike, but my blade hits an invisible wall. What the fuck? Looking down, my jaw slackens when I see shadows writhing around us—but they're not mine. I didn't even call to my umbral strand.

The bastard possesses the ethereal strand? Are you kidding me?

I'm proven mistaken a moment later as I study the advisor, who is just as shocked as I feel. I stiffen just as my stomach drops.

No fucking way.

Turning my head, a strange noise escapes me as I watch essence seep from the prince's skin.

These shadows belong to Caspian.

He doesn't seem to notice as he glares at Varrick. "What about my mother?"

"The queen, Your Highness...she knows more than she lets on. About everything." Varrick's eyes dart around like a cornered animal. "She has secrets that could aid your cause."

I've heard enough of his vague bullshit. My essence writhes under my skin, begging and pleading to be let out with Caspian's, but I ignore it. The knowledge that his shadows will not hurt me is an innate feeling, so I push through them and drive my blade into Varrick's heart, twisting it for good measure. His jaw drops as blood leaks from around the weapon, body crumpling to the floor unceremoniously.

I whirl on Caspian. "Care to explain what the fuck that was?" I sound far more angry than I have any right to be.

"What?" His brows furrow as if he has no idea that he's currently weaving the ethereal affinity.

I point to the shadows retreating into his skin. He jumps, eyes widening as he tries to shake them off and mutters a string of curses. Interesting.

"How are you doing that, Ariella?" He's less panicked, but still wary.

"I've not woven any essence in here. Those are not mine." The prince's head snaps up—he doesn't believe me, but as the shadows sink further into him, his head tilts in a way that suggests he's listening to something internal.

I know because I have the same essence. It generates from within and feels different from the others.

"I—I don't understand. I don't have the ethereal affinity. You're the only person I know who has it." He shoves both hands through his hair, breathing hard. "It must be remnants of whatever my father did—"

But I'm no longer listening. My attention is caught by the painting behind Varrick's desk—it's eerily familiar. The blueish-purple clouds that stretch endlessly, supporting trees with crimson branches and pale pink leaves.

"I've always been fascinated by that one," Caspian confesses, following my gaze. "Not sure who painted it, but they had quite the imagination. It's beautiful though, isn't it?"

"I've been there before," I whisper, my voice strange to my own ears. After Thalion had me beat, when I saw my mother.

My eyes widen as realization hits. "The Aether." That's where she was, where *we* were. It must be...there is no other explanation for this painting. This is no coincidence.

"The Aether?" Caspian questions, crossing his arms. "That's not possible. Texts say that no one alive can enter the Aether realm."

"Tell that to whoever painted this then," I gesture to the artwork. "Because this is exactly what I saw when—" I clear my throat, pivoting from the art. "In a dream I had the other night." I'm not ready to discuss that encounter—with his father or my mother—as I have yet to process it myself. "I think we have to *go* there to fix the Accord, Caspian."

He studies the painting more carefully now as his lips lean against a thumb. "Even if you're right, how would we get there?

The Aether realm is supposed to be sealed off from the living. And you are not killing yourself for this."

I huff a humorless laugh. "I don't know." The admittance hurts, frustration building in my chest. "But I know it's the truth." For once, I am not lying—not about this.

"Okay. I trust you." I didn't hear him step closer, but his hand finds mine, squeezing gently. "Maybe that's why Varrick was so desperate to tell us about my mother. Perhaps they're connected somehow. Thanks for killing him before we could get those answers, by the way."

I peer down at Varrick's body, now wishing I hadn't killed him quite so impulsively. It was irrational and unlike my usual calculating self. Whatever. "We need to find the artifacts and take them into the Aether realm ourselves." The rightness of that statement flows through me like it's the Angel approving my thoughts.

"We should start in the library," Caspian suggests. "I do not recall anything of the sort, but there might be something about crossing between realms in the texts."

I nod, already walking toward the door, but pause when I do not hear Caspian following. He's staring at the shadows still flickering across his skin. I am not keen to believe these are the product of his father's interference—my thoughts remain silent, though. He doesn't need to hear them right now.

I saunter back to him and run my hands along his arms, showing him there's nothing to be afraid of. His eyes drag up to mine. "We'll figure that out, too. But they protected you and I do not surmise they mean any harm, so for now they can wait. We need to focus on one impossible thing at a time."

He chuckles, and something flutters down my spine as his skin pebbles under my touch. "When did you become the voice of reason?"

I blink. "I cannot decide whether to be offended or not."

His smile is boyish as we leave Varrick's office. I peruse Caspian as we walk, his new essence occasionally reaching for mine like they recognize each other. Another mystery to add to our growing list. Although watching him try to process having the ethereal affinity is admittedly entertaining.

"Stop smirking at me," he grumbles.

"I'm not smirking." I am.

"You are. I can feel it."

I laugh, the weight of the past weeks lifting from me. "Feel it? What else can you feel, my prince?"

He pauses, whirling on me with an intensity that makes my breath catch—one I didn't expect. "Everything. Since my father did whatever he did, it's like my senses are heightened. Especially around you." His nose scrunches. "Even before yesterday, if I'm honest."

"What do you mean?"

"I'm not sure, but I think I can feel you sometimes. Earlier, when the—my—shadows appeared? It was because I felt your intent to kill Varrick, but I needed to hear what he was going to say. And they were the result of that impulse."

I hum as my mind processes this information, remembering how my own shadows have been acting strange around him for a while now. "That's not normal," I blurt, shifting on my feet. There's a mist in my chest that I can't seem to grasp. Something I'm missing, and it's right there, but it doesn't wish to be discovered yet. My thoughts shift to Rael's cryptic fucking words, and I sigh—why can't someone else do this?

"Nothing about you is normal, angel." He smirks, running a finger along my jaw. "Now come on, wraith, we have a library to raid." I want to be annoyed at the name, but instead a wave of heat drifts up the back of my neck.

As we continue toward the library, I can't shake the feeling that we're on the verge of discovering something massive. Something that will explain the million questions I desperately need an answer to.

I chuckle to myself—that thought was bizarre and overly dramatic.

Though, I can accept how much I like the sound of it.

"You're smirking again," Caspian teases, bumping my shoulder with his.

This time, I don't deny it.

Chapter Thirty
Ariella

I shift my weight, staring straight ahead while the queen recites some bullshit speech about Thalion's *devotion to the king-dom*. My lip curls—I should feel more satisfied that he's dead. That I succeeded in avenging my father. But all I can focus on is the strange pressure building in my chest and the way Caspian stands too still next to me.

The late morning sun beats down on the crowd gathered in the castle courtyard, though a chill slides over my skin. The weather has been erratic as of late—worse than usual. Even now, clouds gather and disperse rapidly overhead, as if they cannot decide whether to rain or not.

Something isn't right. There's been a prickling awareness at the back of my mind since the ceremony began, though I haven't figured out what is making me feel this way.

My lungs inhale to capacity, attempting to slow my heart and calm my racing thoughts. Salt. My nose scrunches as I take another breath. Not for this first time this week am I wondering how the fuck that's possible. We're nowhere near the coast, yet the distinct scent of ocean air drifts through the courtyard.

Seraphina's voice carries across the hushed gathering as she describes Thalion's *dedication to progress*. Progress. Is that what we're calling torture and murder now? The king and I may not be so different, but I've never hidden who I am—nor have I done such things for power. Sometimes for fun, though...depends on the assignment. My thoughts turn, and I struggle to refocus them. I've no wish to think about Marek, the guild, or my lack of communication with them.

Listening to the queen's forced words, my fingers twitch toward my blade, but I force them still. The queen may be full of shit, but she's not my target.

I have bigger problems.

My gaze slides to her as she continues speaking, studying her mannerisms more carefully now. After what Varrick said...I've no reason to trust the bastard, but there's something calculated in the way Seraphina holds herself. Too poised, too controlled. Some may excuse the mannerisms as appropriate for a queen, but I know better.

Because I wear the same masks.

Her eyes remain dry despite speaking of her dead husband. When she mentions how he *strived to strengthen the kingdom*, her fingers drum once against the podium—a tell, perhaps?

"You're staring," Caspian whispers, his breath warm against my ear. I don't look his direction, but my skin tingles at his proximity.

"Your mother is hiding something." The words are barely audible, meant only for him. We're standing to the side of the queen, where the crowd can drink us in at their leisure. I'm conscious of the dozens of people who whisper about the Silver Wraith and their prince. *What are they doing together? Has she threatened him? You mean to tell me she's his guard?*

His body stiffens, leaning just a hair closer. "What makes you say that?"

"Experience." I pause as the crowd murmurs in response to something Seraphina said. "People who have nothing to hide don't work so hard to appear innocent."

His chest expands with a deep breath as his fingers curl before he stops himself from whatever he wishes to do. "We can discuss this later." *Yes, master.*

I choke, running a hand over my lips to cover the cough. I'm going to tell myself that was sarcasm and forget about it.

Regardless of his thoughts, the nagging feeling about Seraphina won't leave me. I know when to trust my instincts—they've kept me alive this long. Still, we have more pressing concerns.

The artifacts. The Accord. Our realms falling into devastating mayhem.

That same word keeps echoing in my head: *chaos. Chaos. Chaos.* That's what awaits us if we fail. I'm not sure what that indicates, but the urgency in Eris' and my mother's voices told me everything I needed to know. We've little time left.

The pressure in my chest increases, making it difficult to breathe normally. My hands clench at my sides as I try to identify the sensation. It's like the air itself is growing heavier, pressing in from all sides.

"Do you feel that?" I mutter to Caspian, dragging my eyes away from the audience and toward him. He has a strained expression on his face, much like the one I'm wearing.

His silver eyes meet mine briefly before he mutters confirmation.

At least I'm not imagining it—though it does not reassure me that he knew exactly what I was asking about. The crowd shifts, restless, an unusual amount of people clearing their throats. Even Seraphina pauses in her speech, her gaze darting to the sky before she offers the people a wide smile and continues with practiced smoothness.

I scan our surroundings, noting escape routes out of habit. The courtyard is full—nobles, castle staff, and city residents all gathered to *commemorate* their king. The irony isn't lost on me. I'd pay a good fortune to know how many of them had privately celebrated when news of his death spread.

There's a shift in my peripheral, and I spot Gavriel lurking at the edge of the crowd. His dark eyes are fixed on Caspian with an intensity that has my jaw clenching. That's another problem we'll need to deal with eventually—it'd be much easier to just kill him and be done with it.

The weight in the air grows stronger, and I have to make a conscious effort to keep my breathing steady. Which is excruciatingly difficult, as it feels like what I imagine drowning to be. Something builds—in the atmosphere, in my chest, in my very essence. Like the calm before a devastating storm.

"We need to leave," I insist in a loud whisper, but Caspian shakes his head.

"We can't. Not until her speech is over."

A sound tears through the air, so piercing I swear my skull is a second from splitting open. My legs give out as I drop to my knees, hands clasped over my ears, but it does fucking nothing to block out the horrific noise. All around me, others do the same, their screams lost to the deafening shriek.

Through the agonizing uproar, I force my eyes open, immediately drawn to the scene above us. The sky...*fuck me.*

A jagged line splits the pale blue expanse, like a crack in glass. But instead of more sky behind it, there's...color? A void of swirling purples, pinks, and blues that seem to pulse with an otherworldly energy. My essence responds, surging toward it as if drawn by some primal force.

"Ariella!" Caspian's voice struggles to reach me through the tearing above. The sky is actually *tearing*—it's mimicking that of ripped fabric.

The prince's hand grips my arm, and I allow him to pull me to my feet despite my instinct to shove him away. The crushing pressure in my chest has become almost unbearable. I feel like my organs are going to explode before seeping through every orifice in my body.

People run in all directions, their panic a tangible thing in the air. Sentries try to maintain order, but they're just as affected as everyone else and are more stumbling around than they are helping. I watch a young noblewoman trip and fall, only to be trampled by those behind her. No one stops to help. I unsheathe a blade and push Caspian toward a wall, where I can watch each direction, lest someone use their hatred for the king and stab his son.

Someone like me.

The shrieking finally subsides, replaced by an eerie silence that feels wrong on a fundamental level. Like the realm itself is holding its breath. Or is that me?

"What the fuck is happening?" Caspian demands, his fingers digging into my arm. I almost laugh at the question—as if I have any idea what's going on.

But there's that word again. *Chaos.*

I suck in deep breaths, watching, horrified, as the sky expands and contracts, the colors beyond settling against the opening. The tear spreads—and I silently thank the Angel that there's no ear-bleeding sound with it—branching out like lightning frozen in time. "We start finding the artifacts *today*."

Seraphina's voice rings out, commanding everyone to remain calm. But her words cut off as the ground beneath us trembles. Not like before—this is different. The stones of the courtyard ripples like water, though they remain solid under our feet.

My essence writhes beneath my skin, desperate to break free—more so than I've ever felt before. I glance at Caspian and see darkness flickering around him too, though he doesn't seem to notice as he stares at the anomaly above.

"Let's get inside," I instruct, already moving as I grip his wrist strong enough to make him hiss, only squeezing harder in response. "Now."

He follows without argument or quip, which would be concerning under any other circumstance. We're halfway across the courtyard when the first scream starts. Not of fear—of agony.

I spin toward the sound and my blood runs cold. A woman near the castle gates clutches her chest, her back arched at an impossible angle. Light pours from her mouth and eyes, so bright it hurts to look at. When it fades, she collapses.

Dead.

Before anyone can react, it happens again. And again. Four more people dropping as their essence literally tears itself from their bodies. The kind of terror swimming through my veins should not exist.

But neither should this fucking mess we're in.

"Shit." I lace my fingers through Caspian's and run. We need to get somewhere safe, somewhere I can think and stare at him for any signs of his essence turning on him. The balance is completely shot.

We burst through the castle doors just as another crack appears overhead. This one is massive, stretching from horizon to horizon. Through it, I catch glimpses of...something. A forest, maybe? But the trees look wrong, their branches reaching down instead of up.

Oh, fuck. The Aether realm.

"That fucking bitch," I blurt, stopping so abruptly that Caspian runs into me. "She had to have known this would happen."

The woman didn't seem surprised by any of this, especially after knowing what Thalion did. Why didn't she warn anyone?

His face hardens almost defensively. "What are you talking about?" I gesture to everything falling apart around us. "No, that's ridiculous." He shakes his head, grasping who I'm speaking of. "She would've said something—she would not risk Vespera like that."

Another tremor cuts him off, this one strong enough to crack the castle walls. Pieces of stone rain down around us as we stumble toward the nearest alcove. I want to scream at the Angel to stop this, but I know it won't listen.

"We can argue about this later," I snap. "Right now we need to—"

Movement catches my eye and I shove Caspian behind me, harder than intended, unsheathing my second blade in one fluid motion. But it's just Gavriel, looking significantly worse than he did during the ceremony. Perhaps he'll grace us by exploding like the others. With my luck, he won't—but a girl can dream.

"What's happening?" he demands, his usual hatred of me forgotten in light of current events. He's worried.

Before either of us can answer, the air...shifts. Like reality itself is being pulled in different directions. My essence responds with a surge so forceful that I have to brace myself against the wall.

"Angel fuck," I gasp as foreign sensations assault me, pressing a hand against my sternum as if that will help keep my insides *in*. I can *feel* the realm breaking apart—feel the very fabric of existence straining against whatever holds it together.

Caspian's hand finds mine, and the contact sends a jolt through my system. His essence calls to mine, and the comfort I find in that connection should worry me, but I have bigger problems right now.

Like how to stop our realm from literally tearing itself apart.

A deafening crack echoes through the castle, and we all look up to where the ceiling is now splitting open. Through the gap, more of the strange forest peeks through. It looks closer now, more real somehow.

"We need to figure out what the artifacts are," I assert, my voice steady despite the fear clawing at my throat. "Then we need to find them and break into the Aether." A sentence I never thought I'd utter multiple times in a day.

"How exactly do you plan to do that?" Gavriel asks in his usual, brutish tone. "No one can just *walk* into the Aether realm."

I bare my teeth in what might generously be called a smile. "Watch me."

Chapter Thirty-One

Ariella

I shove Caspian into my room, slamming the door behind us as Gavriel flings it open again. I scowl, but wait for him to close it, my fingers flying through the motions of setting wards—I don't care who sees anymore. The king announced my abilities to everyone, anyway.

But then I remember the king is dead, and it would waste energy I don't have to weave wards right now.

"How are you so calm?" Caspian asks, running a hand through his disheveled hair. The usually pristine strands stick up at odd angles, and I hate how endearing it looks.

"Because panicking won't help anything." I stride to my wardrobe, yanking it open to grab my blade gifted from the Seer, lifting away the griffin egg I've kept hidden since the trials. I'm about to speak when the egg jerks in my hands, almost slipping through my fingers. What the fuck? I jump back, throwing the damn thing on my bed, watching as hairline cracks spider across its metallic surface.

"Ariella..." Caspian moves closer, his eyes wide. "Is that...moving?"

Another crack appears, this one deeper than the others. "It's hatching." The words come out barely above a whisper. I knew I had a feeling that keeping the egg safe was important. There was never any indication that something grew inside, but fuck me, it's hatching.

The mother knew. That's why she let me live—though why she would ever trust me with her child, I'm not sure. Definitely the worst decision she's ever made.

A small piece of shell falls away, revealing something dark underneath. My breath catches as more fragments break off, scattering across my bedding. Dropping to my knees at the edge, I watch with pure awe as a tiny beak pushes through, followed by a head covered in obsidian feathers that shimmer with hints of deep purple.

"By the Angel," Caspian breathes, shifting to stand beside me. His leg brushes mine as we watch the baby griffin struggle free of its shell.

It's nothing like its mother. Where she is pure white and sharp edges, this little one is darkness incarnate. Its feathers seem to absorb the surrounding light, creating an effect similar to my shadows. Bright violet eyes blink up at us as it shakes off the last bits of shell.

When my jaw dropped, I'm not sure, but this has to be the most incredible thing I've ever witnessed.

The baby chirps, the sound so innocent that my chest actually aches. It stumbles on unsteady legs, wings spreading for balance.

The wingspan is impressive even at this size—easily as wide as my outstretched arms would be.

"She's beautiful," I murmur, unable to stop myself from reaching toward her. A knowing deep inside tells me she's female. The griffin watches my hand approach, tilting her head in a way that reminds me so much of the mother. When my fingers connect with the soft feathers on her head, a jolt of...something...races through me.

Protection. Care. Trust.

Mine.

The overpowering feelings aren't my own, but they flood my system, anyway. The baby leans into my touch, making that sweet chirping sound again.

"I think she likes you," Caspian observes with a warm smile. He reaches out as well, but the griffin hisses and backs away, tumbling off the bed in her lack of coordination. I catch her before she can fall, and the large creature burrows against my chest.

I can't help but laugh. "Seems she inherited her mother's attitude."

He rolls his eyes but smiles once more. "I'll win my way into her good graces, eventually." His expression sobers as he studies the baby griffin. "What are we going to do with her? We can't take a baby griffin with us while we hunt for artifacts."

The griffin's head snaps up at that, her piercing eyes finding mine. Another wave of foreign emotions drifts through me—determination and...purpose? She pushes from my chest to sit straighter, wings extending to their full span.

Incredible.

"I don't think we have a choice," I respond, watching as she preens her feathers. "Besides, I will do whatever the fuck I want. And I say the griffin can go where she pleases."

The ground trembles again, but it's gentler this time, as if the realm's power is saying goodbye. Through my window, I can still see the massive crack in the sky, but the earlier chaos seems to have settled. I have a feeling this is not the last of the realms' tricks, though.

I glance down at the griffin. She fits in my arms like she was made to be held by them—probably just for the next hour if she will be anything close to her mother's size.

Her feathers shift in the light, appearing iridescent. She chirps and hops onto my shoulder, careful to keep her talons from piercing my skin—smart little thing already. The weight is substantial but not uncomfortable. Her wings brush against my hair as she settles into position, and I swear she looks proud of herself.

"You should take her outside where her kind belongs." My eyes roll at Gavriel's not-shocking choice of words. But the creature on my shoulder stiffens, clicking in the guard's direction.

"Can she understand what we're saying?" Caspian asks, his brows furrowed.

I shrug, though I'm certain she can. I cannot explain how I know such things about her. I just do.

He studies the griffin with new interest. "But how? She's just a baby."

The griffin makes an offended sound and snaps her beak out, nearing the prince's face. He jerks back, cursing, and I have to bite my lip to keep from laughing.

"She doesn't seem to appreciate your commentary, prince." I reach up to stroke her silky chest feathers, marveling at the hidden colors within. "Besides, we've seen stranger things these last few days. Honestly, this is the most natural thing to have happened in weeks."

As if to prove my point, the griffin spreads her wings and a soft golden light emanates from them. The glow travels down her body and into me, warming me from the inside out. My essence responds instantly, reaching for the connection like it's found something it's been missing.

"Oh, fuck," I gasp, steadying myself against the bedpost, fighting the dizziness. The sensation is overwhelming but not unpleasant—similar to how I felt when I healed Caspian, but still so different.

"What's wrong?" Caspian shifts to help me, but the griffin clicks again. He throws his hands up in a placating manner. "I'm not going to hurt her, you overprotective little beast."

The griffin considers him for a moment before chirping what sounds suspiciously like acceptance. I could laugh at how ridiculous this is. A griffin hatched in my room, attached herself to me, and somehow understands what we're saying, as if she wasn't just born into this realm. She hops from my shoulder to the bed, leaving me with an unexpected chill in her absence.

"I'm fine," I assure him, though I'm not sure that's true. I watch the griffin, who is now systematically shredding my blanket with those talons. "We need to name her." Where did that come from, and why do I care?

"We need to figure out how to get to the artifacts and then to the Aether realm," he counters. "Names can wait."

The griffin pauses her destruction to give him what can only be described as a withering look. Gavriel crosses his arms, widening his stance as he stays watching the interaction.

"I think she disagrees." I sit on the edge of the bed, careful not to disturb the mess of eggshell fragments. "Besides, we can't keep calling it 'her.' That seems rude."

Caspian sighs, dropping next to me as his arm slides around my waist. The griffin's wary eyes study him, but she doesn't protest, continuing her dominion over my bed. "Not sure when you began caring about being rude, but fine. Any ideas?"

I study our new companion. Her feathers remind me of the night sky—endless darkness scattered with hints of light. But there's no name that would fit her more than the one pounding into my head, as if the realm itself is demanding what she be called.

"Oranya." The griffin's head snaps up at my announcement, and I know I've chosen correctly.

"Oranya," Caspian repeats, testing the name. "I like it—it suits her." He reaches toward the griffin again, moving slower this time. Oranya watches his hand approach, not hissing or retreating again. When his fingers connect with her feathers, I feel a remnant of that earlier warmth.

Oranya chirps and pushes into his touch, deciding he's adequate for her attention, after all. The sight of them together does something strange to my insides that I refuse to examine too closely.

"Now that that's settled," I announce, pushing to my feet as I ignore Gavriel, "we need to figure out our next move. Everything seems stable for now, but that thing in the sky isn't going away." I gesture to the window, where the tear between realms cuts through the sky like jagged glass, shimmering with impossible colors. The air hums faintly, vibrating with a persistent energy that prickles against my skin. "And I very much doubt things will remain calm forever."

The griffin makes a sound that might be agreement, launching herself from the bed to land on my shoulder again. Her talons catch my hair, but she quickly adjusts her dangerous grip.

"We should gather supplies while we determine where to find the artifacts you need," Caspian states, his royal self showing through. "We don't know how long we'll be gone or what we'll face in the Aether realm. Nor do I have the first clue where to find what's needed for the new Accord."

I nod, already mentally cataloging each task. "Leave the artifacts to me. You can gather food, water, medical supplies—the basics. Though I'm not sure how much we can carry while still having the freedom to move as fast as we need to. I don't believe we'll be able to jump to the Aether, so we'll have to go south to Whisterra where the only known entrance is." I vaguely remember a tale my mother told me many years ago about a woman and her son who'd often visit the Aether. She'd said there was a ripple between realms that—I pause, considering. "Do you think Oranya needs anything specific?"

The griffin tugs at a strand of my hair and chirps. I get the distinct impression she's trying to tell me not to worry about her. I have a feeling I will, anyway.

"Right. Magical baby griffin probably doesn't need our help."

I run my fingers through Oranya's feathers, watching Gavriel shift uncomfortably near my door. His eyes dart between me and Caspian, his expression betraying the words he wants to say, but doesn't know how to voice after everything that's happened.

"Just fucking say it," I snap, done with his hesitation. The prince's arms cross as he regards Gavriel.

He clears his throat. "I know you won't believe me, but I am sorry. Not just to Caspian, but to you as well." His voice wavers on the last word. My eyes narrow. "I was...wrong about many things."

Caspian scoffs. "You went behind my back and tried to have her killed, even knowing what she means to me."

"I know." The guard's shoulders slump. "I thought I was protecting you, but I was just being selfish. I couldn't stand watching you fall for her when I—" He cuts himself off, but we all know what he meant to say. At least, I do. Caspian still hasn't figured out that his best friend wishes they could be more. Or perhaps he has and refuses to ruin their friendship by voicing the truth.

Oranya makes a low clicking sound that somehow manages to convey judgment. I stroke her head, the movement feeling a little too natural, as I consider the guard's words. "You're right. I don't believe you." Gavriel's face falls further. Good. "But I understand why you did it."

Both men look at me with surprise. "You do?" Gavriel asks.

"Love makes people do stupid fucking things." I ignore how Caspian's eyes snap to me at the word *love*. "Though if you ever try something like that again, I won't hesitate to slit your throat."

A knock at my door saves Gavriel from responding. Elowen enters without waiting for permission—poor decision making on her part—Jessenia close behind her. They both freeze at the sight of Oranya.

"Is that..." Jessenia starts, and I look over her form. She's foregone the dress from before in favor of tight-fitted pants and a burgundy jacket. The woman would be attractive in anything, it seems. She could wear one of the hideous royal uniforms, and I'd still find a way to appreciate her appearance.

"A griffin? Yes." I smirk as Oranya preens under their attention, not offering any other explanation. "What news do you have?"

Elowen tears her eyes from the little creature, her wavy hair jostled by the movement. "We found some of the children." Her voice hardens. "They were in cells beneath the eastern wing of the castle. Most were unconscious, though alive, thankfully."

"How many?" Caspian asks, his hands clenching into fists as he steps forward.

"Seventeen," Jessenia answers, refusing to look him in the eye, instead finding mine. Her loyalty for my previous threat would be sweeter if it weren't happening while the realms fall apart. "We took them to the guild." She glances at Elowen before swiping a tongue across her lips and continuing. "Marek was furious. It was quite frightening actually. But he said he'll personally ensure each child returns to their family."

"Good." I nod, pleased that the children will be cared for. Marek is a different issue I do not wish to think about. "What else?"

"The cells were..." Elowen pauses as her voice cracks, swallowing hard. Seeing that must have been rather difficult for her, considering her proclivity to heal anyone she can. "There were marks on the walls. Tallies. Some had been there for months."

My stomach sours. That fucking bastard of a king.

"We'll need to search the entire castle," Caspian mutters to Gavriel, who nods his head in quick succession. "There could be more we haven't found yet."

"Already started," Jessenia replies, looking between me and the griffin. She moves closer to examine Oranya, but Elowen steps between them.

"We shouldn't crowd the griffin," Elowen states, her tone leaving no room for argument. "They're dangerous creatures."

Jessenia's eyes narrow. "I think I can handle myself."

"Like you handled yourself in the tunnels?" The healer's voice drips with sarcasm. "If I hadn't been there, Jess, I swear to the Angel—"

"I had everything under control!"

"You nearly walked into a trap!"

"Ladies," I interrupt, fighting a smile. The tension between them is obvious, though I'm not so sure they realize that. "Perhaps we should focus on more pressing matters?"

They both flush and step away from each other. Oranya clicks again.

"What do we do now?" Jessenia asks as her hands wring together.

I exchange a heavy look with Caspian. "The prince and I need to leave Valoria." The ambiguity in my words is intentional. "There are things we must find."

"When do we leave?" Jessenia asks, not caring to question why. Strange woman.

"We?" I raise an eyebrow. "This isn't a group expedition."

"You can't go alone," Elowen protests, her arms crossing. "You'll need a healer."

"I can heal myself."

"And what about Caspian?"

I glance at him, remembering how it felt to connect our essence. "I can heal him, too."

Her eyes widen. "But—"

"No," I cut her off. "The fewer people involved, the better. Besides, someone needs to stay and help search for more children, among other things." I look pointedly between her and Jessenia. "Perhaps you two could work together on that?" Elowen's eyes narrow in my direction as if she sees right through my words, and I have to bite back another smile.

"Fine," she concedes. "But you'll send word if you need anything?"

I nod, though we all know I won't. Caspian moves to stand beside me when I force everyone out, his hand finding the small of my back. Gavriel lingers in the doorway, looking like he wants to say more, but eventually follows Elowen and Jessenia out to the crumbling walls of the castle. My prince's touch grounds me, reminding me that I'm not alone in this anymore. It's a strange feeling—one I'm not wholly comfortable with yet.

"We should rest," he murmurs as a hand brushes through my hair. "Tomorrow we can begin gathering supplies and planning our route."

Oranya bounds from my shoulder to the bed once more, already claiming it as her territory. She begins methodically arranging the blankets into what appears to be a nest, ignoring us.

"At least someone knows what they're doing," I mutter.

Caspian's answering laugh is comforting. "We'll figure it out." His arms slide around my waist, pulling me against his chest. "Together," he adds with force, and I chuckle. I may make light of it, but the truth is, I do not believe I could get through what's coming without him. Even if I wanted to, it wouldn't be possible.

I allow myself to lean into him, just for a heartbeat. Maybe several.

My eyes drift to the window, the crack in the sky seeming to pulse, as if responding to his words. Whatever we must handle next, I have a feeling our lives are about to become significantly more complicated.

But for now, I savor this moment of peace. We'll need to find the artifacts, figure out how to enter the Aether realm, and somehow restore balance before both realms collapse. Oh, and find Oranya's mother.

Easy. And terrifying.

Author Note

T hank you for reading Essence of the Throne! I cannot
tell you how honored I am that you've taken the time to
give this series a chance. If you enjoyed the next in Ariella and
Caspian's story, please consider leaving a rating/review. They are
so important to authors!

In this second installment to the Shadows of the Crown series,
we follow Ariella and Caspian as they face things they never
thought existed—things far out of their comfort zone. We watch
as they deal with secrets, death, betrayal, love, loyalty, and their
own inner emotions. They both grow in their own ways in
Essence of the Throne, but they also grow together. This may
have been a difficult part of their story for them, but there's so
much more they have to face and I cannot wait to see how they
handle it!

I want to thank my husband, sister, friends, and huskies for
being here with me through this process. It's nice to have people
that support me and my journey, and I love you all so much.

To my Beta Team, ARC Team, Street Team, and readers in my
Discord...THANK YOU. One thing I didn't realize about being
an author before I began writing Shadows of the Crown is it's

quite lonely. Creating worlds, characters, villains, adventures, and everything that comes along with writing fantasy is lonely. So it's impossible to describe just how much your support means to me. You may not realize the extent in which you help me, but just know that you do. So much.

Pronunciations

Characters:

Aether — a-thur

Amyst — a-mist

Ariella — are-ee-el-uh

Aris — air-iss

Bastian — bash-tin

Benson — been-sun

Caelum — kay-lumm

Caspian — cass-p-in

Desmond — dez-mund

Dysis — die-siss

Elara — ee-larr-uh

Eli

Elowen — ell-oh-when

Erendor — air-en-door

Eris — air-iss

Eva

Gavriel — gae-vree-ell

Isaiah — i-zay-uh

Isolde — uh-zowl-duh

Jaxon — jacks-un

Jessenia — jess-en-ee-uh

Julia

Khyla — kai-luh

Mabel — may-bull

Marek — mare-eck

Myst — mist

Noah

Oranya — or-on-yuh

Palmluvela — palm-loo-vay-luh

Rael — ray-ell

Raine

Seraphina — sare-uh-fee-nuh

Thalion — thail-ee-un

Valyria — vuh-lee-ree-uh

Varrick — vare-ick

Velora — vell-or-uh

Vespera — vess-pair-uh

Cities within Eldorian Kingdom:

Eldoria — ell-door-ee-uh

Frostwell

Grenport

Invalle — in-veil

Lumarna — loom-are-nuh

Meridian — merr-idd-ee-un

Valoria — vale-or-ee-uh

Cities outside Eldorian Kingdom:

Auroria — uh-roar-ee-uh

Ebonwood — eb-un-wood

Skydence — sky-deh-nce

Thalasire — thal-uh-sire

Vexail — vex-ale

Whisterra — whi-stare-uh

Other places:

Angel's Passage

Cindara Desert — seen-darr-uh

Ebelan Sea — eh-bell-an

Elysaran Mountains — ell-ee-sar-an

Meneau Sea — men-owe

Verdantia Forest — vare-dan-she-uh

Weaver's Torrent

Also By Dakota Monroe

About the Author

Dakota Monroe lives in a dark world and dreams of even darker fantasies. She has been a fantasy-obsessed reader since she was a child and now brings hers to life through her writing. As a neurodivergent woman, Dakota has always felt out of place with her thoughts and ideas; but books have been her savior, and a nonjudgmental place for her to escape the colorless world we call reality. She hopes her characters, and stories, provide an outlet for others, even if just for a little while.

www.ingramcontent.com/pod-product-compliance
Lightning Source LLC
Chambersburg PA
CBHW020645110726
47901CB00001B/63